Passing The American Charivari

A NOVEL

Sid Nasr

por mis hermanos

ISBN: 978-0-6151-4041-4

Book design by Sid Nasr

Photographs on front and back cover by Sid Nasr

www.lulu.com

Printed in the United States of America.

I wasn't scared; I was just somebody else, some stranger,
and my whole life was a haunted life, the life of a ghost.
I was half-way across America, at the dividing line
between the East of my youth and the West of my future,
and maybe that's why it happened right there and then,
that strange red, afternoon.

—Jack Kerouac, *On the Road*

Part One

I

And I hate that feeling of waking up before the rest of the world. You know when you peel yourself off the bed—sleep glue embedded in the cracks of your eyes and you have to deal? No one else is up. Nothing is going down. You look outside the window and everything is still because you're not *supposed* to be awake. Didn't all this have to do with the creation of the Sabbath or God resting on the seventh day? Conducting to business on a Saturday is a big no-no, is it not? It's just not done, but I've transgressed this cardinal rule through no fault of my own since I'm the one that answered the job ad in *The Hollywood Reporter*. I need a more permanent gig after the string of temping I've done for these staffing agencies which have pimped me around to various legal offices in L.A. where I've engaged in nothing more than menial file-clerk work. I feel like a readily available-to-be-stomped insect when I get sent out to these offices and meet with the Human Resources reps who give me the one-over and then escort me to the cubicle I'll be languishing in for the next couple of days, or weeks, or even months if I get lucky.

My ego is a fraction of its former self. My bitterness, I am certain, is clear to anyone within my line of sight. You would never be able to guess that a little over a year ago, I was swaggering through the halls of a large talent agency with the assured confidence of an agent trainee in demand—who was going places. But, put a pin on that. I'm now grappling with the fact that I'm one of those granted a reprieve from sleeping in on a Saturday and who has been summoned to break the night's fast early. I have to get out of bed in order to shower, put on my business attire, and then find the mindset necessary to interview. This motherfucker tells me the only day he is available to interview me is today at nine in the morning. Real nice. So, you know where I'm coming from. The sleep glue hurts like hell and every time I wipe it away new blotches instantly materialize.

Sometimes in the morning after a deep sleep, or alternatively, after a night where sleep is minimal due to some type of over-indulgence or other, I can experience a momentary loss of time. A mind gap. I splash cold water on my face and stare at myself in the mirror trying to piece together what has been lost. And when everything is O.K. and I realize it's just me in my apartment in Los Angeles at twenty-five years of age with a clean bill of health, I can safely start the new day. Last night, I did not go out so that I could be fresh for my job interview. I sank into a deep, deep sleep. But, it's the kind of haunting deep sleep with its trailer tease of dream that preys on your mind right up until your eyes open and then it disappears leaving you frustrated because you can no longer remember it. It seems like an eternity when the dream is with you and it's a cruel mental prank once the dream goes away just as silently as it came.

I only grasp flashes of my dream from last night. Inchoate, fleeting images and sensations. I can remember flying—physically. Yeah, that's it. I think harder and it becomes clearer to me. I dreamt my body was taken up high into the clouds and the wind swirled around me and held me aloft. I remember how I first took flight. I was out in a flat, green meadow with both arms outstretched at my sides and a blast of wind hit me from the front and took me up. I could see the curvature of the earth from my vantage point up in the sky and I did nothing but soar at the mercy of the gusts pushing me. Yet, the feeling that I can most assuredly remember from the dream is one of panic. I think that while I was flying through the sky the problem of landing *back* on earth popped up. Since it was the wind that propelled my flight, it would be the absence of wind that would bring me back to the ground. And how would I land? With a big, crushing thud? That worry was the last remnant of my dream before impact of my alarm's ring .

Standing here in front of my bathroom mirror, a mellow satisfaction comes over me as I recall the essence of my dream. But, lest you think the dream is a portent of things to come, I don't go for that analyzing of dreams bullshit. I think dreams are one hundred percent about truth and fantasy. I know that sounds like a paradox, but it's not. The mind dreams to get to where it needs to go and reorient itself from whatever nonsense it has to endure during the day. There are no hidden messages or latent insights to be gleaned from dreams. Instead, those messages and insights are *real* in dreams. They are actual manifestations of the very core of our being—so what if nobody else can see them or that they are not quantifiable. They are real nonetheless and should be accepted and appreciated—not analyzed and dwelled upon. The analysis and dwelling upon of dreams demonstrates denial and the disputing of their simple reflection of our true being. Dreams are like mirrors. You either dig what you see in them or you don't and then you look elsewhere to see whatever reflection you want.

However, I can't resist the temptation to ask why I had my dream. First, it's a recurring dream which started about two months ago, but who can tell? Dreams exist on a plane beyond human time. The dream always seems like it lasts thirty minutes, but I've read that most dreams are only a few seconds in duration. Second, flying? It's rather a disappointment of a dream. Too fairy-tale and too child-like while I'm very much into flesh and blood reality. But, as I've said, I refuse to fall into the trap of having to analyze why I dreamt the dream I had. Instead, I embrace it with open arms as a reflection of the kindling of a cartoonish desire within me. More importantly though, the remembrance of the dream resets my mind and I'm ready to deal with more serious things like landing a paying gig to make rent and to buy necessary shit.

I've gotten up around 7:30 which will allow me enough time to shower, shave, throw on the navy blue suit with conservative tie and to drive out to the 9 a.m. interview which is in Beverly Hills. I live in the eastern, non-touristy part of Hollywood. There is no direct route from here to Beverly Hills via freeway. Instead, I have to circumnavigate three different interlocking freeways to travel about eight or nine miles because I don't have the patience to take a more linear path through surface streets. I have to hop on the 101 East to the 110 South to the 10 West and exit on Robertson which I then climb north until I hit Wilshire. I continue west on Wilshire until I reach El Camino where I swing a right and find the office in the 200 block. The freeways are clear. Christ, it's liberating. I feel like I own them—like they're an extension of my own private driveway. I fly along practicing some of the voice exercises I learned in my acting class from college. Shit to open the larynx and to project and to enunciate. I even recite something from Shakespeare. Something my acting professor ingrained into my head. Complete with a terrible British accent, I blurt out:

> *To sit in solemn silence in a deep dank dock*
> *in a pestilential rainstorm with a life long*
> *lock awaiting the sensation of a short sharp*
> *shock from a cheap and chippy chipper on a*
> *big black block.*

I suddenly reflect on what I've said and realize that it is not the vibe I need right now. I also get the feeling that my acting professor lied when he told us this was an old Shakespeare quatrain. It sounds like an extra-long children's limerick about offing one's head. A little too cutesy and ominous if you feel me. But, at least my voice is solid and ready to go.

I pull up to the office on El Camino and park at a meter. The office is a ghost town. No one is in the lobby to sign me in or to direct me to the elevators. People sleep on Saturday mornings— what's this dude trying to pull? I find the elevators and go up to the fifth floor where again no one is around. I find the office suite and enter through a heavy wooden door. I walk into a waiting area where I take a seat and wait amongst the white walls and magazines. I pick up a copy of *Us* and flip through looking for pictures of skinny birds. Then, my soon-to-be-boss materializes out of the white walls and I force the magazine down and get up to shake hands. He has a limp handshake and even weaker smile. I can already tell this gig will be a disaster. He leads me to his office and takes a seat behind his black marbled desk. I sit down across from him while he pulls out my resume from a manila folder. He scans it briefly and then goes into a description of the job and its duties. I throw in "mmmhmms" and "certainlys" in the right places as he rambles on. He then stops as if he's just remembered the most crucial part of the interview and tells me:

> Look, if you're here to write the Great
> American Novel I'm not looking for you.

What the fuck is this? I am interviewing for a position as a legal assistant. I manage to force out a chuckle at his remark which catches me completely off-guard, but I can see from his expression that he is genuinely serious. I answer that I'm not interested in spending my time on the job pursuing other agendas which I think is the underlying point he is trying to make to me. Other cats before me have probably been caught using office time and supplies for either copying or printing up screenplays or friends' screenplays. This is L.A. where that kind of shit is the norm in many of these white walled offices.

He studies my response and then says, "Welcome aboard, I'll see you Monday morning at nine sharp." That's the entire interview. We shake hands and I exit his office and head towards the elevator. When I get back to the waiting area, however, I get the feeling that some things have been left unsaid, so I double back to his office but it's too late. The door is closed and I can hear him on the phone with somebody. I try to forget the feeling that something is amiss. I get back to my car and then it dawns on me—where am I supposed to park on Monday? Beverly Hills has zero parking and I see nothing for this office. There's probably some subterranean parking available, but I have no idea where that is. I can't believe the guy didn't tell me. I guess I'll have to park at a meter again when I arrive on Monday and then when I see him I can ask about the parking situation. I haven't even started and there's already stress.

There's no use for me to discuss what happens that Monday when I show up for my first day at work as a legal assistant. Instead, I'm going to fast forward to two months after my interview in which my soon-to-be-boss threw out those prophetic words, *"Look, if you're here to write the Great American Novel I'm not looking for you."* In short order, I call him an asshole to his face (completely justified), quit the job and plunge into the nether regions of joblessness. That's what goes down in a nutshell. But, the funny thing is, that way back when, the impetus for my move to L.A. was my plan to become a writer who would write: "The Great American Novel" (or at least something along those lines). My asshole boss in his paranoia and quest for the perfect yesman stumbled on to why I was in his office in the first place—procrastination. I had been putting off or simply forgetting what I had been wanting to do since leaving the bubble of college. I had to pay the bills in the meantime, so I went after gigs where I could do some mechanical work or paper pushing as was the case until I would undergo some epiphany which would trigger that need in me to create. That magic moment refused to come around even though I had moved across the country from New York to Los Angeles and away from the comfortable surroundings and familiar faces of my youth. And this should be briefly touched upon before I go any further—the surroundings I left behind.

I come from an extended family consisting of parents, grandparents, aunts, uncles, cousins, second and third cousins, cousins twice removed or whatever the fuck you call them. Everyone was involved in some way or other in rearing my generation even if the actual parents resented it or sought to avoid it, but were too polite to say anything and so never cut off the visitation rights of those extended family members they secretly badmouthed. There was always a lot of advice going around. Some of it solicited, most of it unsolicited. A bunch of over-achievers. Always comparing notes on who was doing what, who was attending where, and who was making how much. And it was a vicious cycle of meddling, passed from the older family members to their children and so on. I was the black sheep. I did a lot of drugs in college, played a lot of guitar and dissected *The End* deep into the night with captivated filles who like the poesy I composed to make the ordinary extraordinary. It wasn't rebellion either. I can honestly say that now as I stand back and look at those years. It was genetics. I had a recessive gene that gave me the propensity for performing the antics and embracing a worldview that could best be categorized as hippie-like. I liked the fashion and music of the Sixties. I was drawn to the ideas and consciousness of that era and I approached everything I did with an openness and willingness to indulge in my humanity and the humanity of others to the fullest extent. Ambition meant nothing to me. All I cared about was making the most of the here and now. The future would arrive on its own terms and I was not in a hurry to poke my head out of the present moment in order to somehow prepare for its arrival. There were others deep in the family's past who were like me. But, from the stories I heard about them they all, in short order, were summarily disowned, disinherited, and died tragically. Needless to say, I was never in high demand at family gatherings and my folks were always tight-lipped about what I was up to or what I *aspired* to do with my life. As far as they knew, I spent my time in college throwing a lot of frisbee and rolling spliffs as my mom discovered one Christmas break when while doing my laundry she found a pack of zig-zags absent-mindedly left in the backpocket of my jeans.

While various family and friends prepared for serious careers by taking pre-med, pre-law or engineering and computer science courses, I majored in philosophy. What an insane reaction that caused! I was much maligned for this choice both in and outside of school. I was bombarded by an endless stream of people asking me, "Philosophy? What the fuck are you gonna do with that?" This refrain rang incessantly in my ears when I slept, so I armed myself with a defense which I could immediately unleash when cornered for an explanation as to why I wasted my time on philosophy. It was about searching and I would rather spend time here within the sympathetic confines of college doing this searching than when I was released into the unforgiving world outside and locked into some career and then realizing that I really did not know who I was. The requirements of the philosophy major were also such that they encouraged the taking of lots of art history and literature and sociology courses since all these disciplines cross-pollinated with one another. Thus,

I could confidently tell people I was getting the most well-rounded liberal arts education imaginable which would directly translate into my success as a well-adjusted individual ready for the world. A solid answer, so I thought. And it bought me peace for a while—at least until graduation came. Yet, although I believed my defense of the study of philosophy had merit I have to admit that after taking thirteen or more philosophy classes and especially, after those endless, exacting hours spent parsing Kant's *Prolegomena to Any Future Metaphysics* and Wittgenstein's *Tractatus Logico-Philosophicus*, I didn't learn a fucking thing about the world, let alone myself. In the early part of my study, I was eager to think and write freely and take on the thought of Descartes, Berkeley and Butler, but when my first term paper was returned (of which I was so proud), I was panned and admonished by my T.A. thus:

> *You are in no position to be making the contentions that you make.*

I was shocked and any innocent belief I had concerning using the study of philosophy to actively search out the true nature of things vanished right there and then. In a final slap in the face, my T.A. took the time to handwrite above the paper's title the comment, "Evilly sarcastic." The title of the paper was *Sycophancy* which was in reference to the two hours long office hours session I had with the T.A. prior to writing the paper.

During the office hours meeting I had presented my interpretation of the readings and ideas we had covered in lecture. My T.A. proceeded to shoot down all my ideas and went into detail about how there were certain philosophical concepts and notions so undebatable that it was pointless to dispute them. The objective in studying philosophy was to know these concepts and notions so well that one could apply them to hypothetical contexts and illuminate the meaning of those contexts. I wrote the paper specifically highlighting the points he lectured me on during the office hours meeting and then he still burned me. I didn't understand why he thought the title I chose was a sarcastic potshot at him. I definitely didn't understand why it was evil. It was the truth. Student meets with his T.A. Student presents ideas. T.A. tells student he is misguided in his ideas. Student then writes paper presenting why his ideas are misguided. This was your garden variety kissing ass scenario and was an ancient code of conduct between student and teacher. I didn't understand why the T.A. thought the title was against this code of conduct and why the paper itself warranted a C+. It was a rude awakening for me in any event to the subjective ruthlessness present in academia.

I, of course, didn't give up the study of philosophy, but I never made any earnest attempt to truly question again. And that's what I lost—that *earnestness*—the general wonder to question. I started to just accept and accepted that even the pursuit of truth was tainted. I learned to expand my mind in other ways and hid out in the back of my philosophy classes plotting my next score or figuring out where I would be jamming that night. However, let me make it clear that I did not become some drop out. I continued actively studying other disciplines and especially excelled in the art and music history courses I took. All the literature courses I took were also cake for me. I read everything from Owen Wister's *The Virginian* to Henry James' *The Bostonians* to Toni Morrison's *Song of Solomon* to Maxine Hong Kingston's *Tripmaster Monkey*. But, the experience with my philosophy courses had definitely made me a cynic and I never shook free from the feeling that everything I was being told while in school was predictable and redundant and not designed to entertain fresh ideas.

When graduation day started become a reality and no longer some far off place in the sun, I had to think of my post college-plans fast. I was told to go into grad-school and further my study of philosophy. I scoffed at this and now had to explain my reasons for *not* studying philosophy to the same people who had four years earlier jumped on me relentlessly for my decision to select it as my major! There was no way I would ever dedicate the next four years of my life to pursuing a discipline so rooted within such strict orthodoxy that it consumed itself in its passivity. There was no room for growth—for outreach into greener pastures of thought. Philosophy, at least as I knew it in the West, was dead. Oh sure, few pockets of academia and religion still exist where intercourse in this art continues, but the pulse beats so faintly that any viability must be laughed at. I couldn't go on committing necrophilia and watching the world go by as it did while I would have the faux luxury to sit back and comment on why the world went by as it was so prone to do.

But, I must say that I did hold onto something from those four years of undergraduate study. It was a line from one of the British moralists. I can't remember exactly who it was—

maybe Hobbes or Hume or Cumberland or a
combination of them all—and maybe I've
embellished upon it so much through the years and
made something so comfortable out of it that I can
pass it off as my own. Nevertheless, I will assert
that it stems from one of those British moralists and
it is the supposition that "man is a slave to his
passions." The gist of this idea was that the
individual had to break free of her passions which
were ailments and hindrances that obstructed her
ability to produce and rely on her intellect in a clear,
unobfuscated manner. The reason I still remember
this line is that when I first heard it in my morning
lecture it zapped me out of the dazed doodling and
drooling that was methodically filling up the side of
my college-ruled notebook. I immediately sat up in
my chair and thought I was hearing things. But, no,
my ears weren't playing tricks on me. There was
my professor standing in front of the fifty of us and
elaborating upon this advocacy of breaking free
from our passions. Now, I can't recall how the term
"passions" was defined and it's not terribly
important anyways because I conceived of it as
reasonable people did: our thirsts, hungers and lusts.
In short, the intangible spark that makes us human
in the first place. Why was this a bad, obstructive
thing? It seemed to me that any serious push
humankind had made into the future had been
through the pursuit of one passion or another,
whether good or bad, whether lionized or abhorred.
That day in class, I could think of countless
examples of how unquenchable desires led to some
discovery, some knowledge or some invention
beyond the collective imagination of the day. It was
the individual whose unflagging allegiance to

whatever passion drove him or her who achieved remembrance in the world.

I wanted to raise my hand and partake in the discussion pointing out that I would gladly be a slave to my passions than be a master to my objective impulses. But, I didn't do any such thing. I held back and ate the time furious with myself. I thought it was better not to share such thoughts under such vulnerable circumstances and the lecture room was vulnerable because it buffeted a dialogue and banter between professor and student which was contrived and safe. It was generally accepted that anything based in empirical intellectual thought created a more suitable paradigm from which to examine the nature of things. The results of the application of this paradigm to whatever it was one was studying was called *truth* or the thing closest to the truth. Thus, the professor's interpretation of the supposition that "man is a slave to his passions" had to be correct in this setting. Our world no longer left any room for the unquantifiable or for faith. These notions did not lead to truth, but instead, led to false idols. That was where my thoughts were coming from that day—a paradigm based on my hunch that our false idols really were the truth. It was just nobody could bring himself or herself to admit this for fear that the last five hundred years of Western civilization would be made a mockery. I believed this back then but did not have the experience from which to explain this convincingly to the rest of the lecture hall. So, I did not raise my hand and chose not to remove all my doubt before such an undoubtedly hostile crowd.

I told myself there would be another time, another place for that doubt to articulate itself. Those moments of clarity are rare when you tap into some all-encompassing insight into existence in this world and you think you have everything figured out for just a flame of time. That day in lecture, I had one of those moments of clarity and was sure that the insight shed so much truth on the nature of life as we knew it that it would always stay with me. There would be no need to fear that the insight would ever disappear. I was wrong. As soon as the lecture finished that day and I packed up my notebooks and joined the rush for the door most of my thoughts had already seeped out of me. Though I tried and tried, I never pinned them down again.

What can I say but that I had no choice but to fill up the rest of college by taking road trips and partying with friends. With each passing year, any idealist notions I had about changing the world fell farther behind my thirst for maximizing the good times. When graduation came and went, I had nothing to show except an exquisite piece of vanilla white paper in which "Philosophia" was depicted in beautiful gothic calligraphy. I moved back with my parents and bided time—depressed and forlorn and betrayed by the fact that four years had come and gone and I was now spit out into a system which was nothing like those four years. Gone was the community of students and professors and all those hangers-on who dealt with one another across a delicious motley contingent of race, age, beliefs and class. Friends were moving on, going to grad-school or working in the City at prestigious Wall Street addresses. I was at the end of my emotional tether and became a hermit who did not want to deal with the pearls dished by family and friends. I was paid regular visits by those seeking to get me on the path to something respectable. What a cast of characters I had to endure! Telling me to do this, do that—get into this, get into that. There was no end to all the opportunities I could go after in their eyes. Problem was I didn't want to get too serious about my life. I felt there were still things about myself that needed to be addressed and brought up to speed. I told them I wanted to write. They cracked smiles and said that was a nice idea, but I had to concentrate on setting myself up first. Once I was set up—meaning I had a real job—I could do whatever I wanted.

I don't want to sound unappreciative about all the advice I received. There was a lot of love to go around in my family and the family who called or came to see me during that time had good intentions. But, love as expressed in my family was also the kind that easily crossed over into fear and loathing. You really loved someone when you felt that the person had wronged you and then you did not talk to him or her for ten years. Love was a double-edged sword. There were legends about family living in the same house even sharing the same room and not talking to one another for months or years at a time because of some slight that had occurred. So, listening to the advice so confidently dispensed by these characters was a real gas! As if they *knew* precisely the best passage in which I could navigate my life. It was all cookie-cutter hubris and it made me even more depressed. Going to college four and a half hours upstate had been too close in proximity to this bastion of familial emotional control, so after graduation I knew I would have to go away. I only lasted a couple of months back home.

I don't know what I expected to happen when I came to L.A. I didn't know a soul there and had never been one hundred percent on my own where I would be responsible for my own livelihood. I had naïve intentions of finding a little studio apartment and living off coffee and cigarettes all the while doing some writing. I never got close. Being alone gave me too much space, but I did use that to my advantage in the beginning by wandering around in the shadows observing and reinventing myself into whomever I wanted to be. Meeting low-lifes, dealers and derelicts and hanging out on the streets conversing about city politics and Maxine Waters and other shit that was going down at the time. But, I couldn't maintain this double-life of trying to make bread during the day in order to support myself and then consorting in the underbelly of Hollywood late at night hoping to gather material for a story. I just never had everything together and I never knew where I really was or where I was going and the plans I had to write dropped for the sake of my own sanity. I had to learn to put myself first and not get sucked into situations where I kept getting used or using others. I stopped believing that a moment of epiphany would come around and instead cleaned myself up and threw myself into the real world and corporate opportunities which I went after like a rabid dog. I stopped slogging through in and out of my life and became polished and focused. I took time out only to follow the Lakers and make occasional Sunday afternoon trips to Venice Beach so that I could remember how pathetic my life used to be: incense and natty hair, plenty of pot to go around conjoined with a lot of guitar playing. I made myself believe that this was to be it—that no great vision would suddenly hit me on the head and lead me towards some fantastic insight or truth that deserved to be written down and shared with others. I would now concentrate on amassing as much as I could and would enjoy only that self-aggrandizing pursuit. Everything else—happiness and stability—would fall into place eventually. But, this tact, with all its competition, setbacks, getting passed-over, political jockeying, has caught up with me as well. I'll soon get into the details of all that, but right now, quitting the legal assistant job embodies my failure to find a spot in the rat race.

I can't say that I'm alone in L.A. because I've managed to have a pseudo-relationship with some bird here, and I mean "pseudo" because if either one of us could really see one another as we truly are, then there would be no us. She is two years younger and was at first completely fooled by my ambition and drive to get ahead. Now, whenever I need to be reminded of that drive, I need look only to her because she tells me that she has patterned her ceaseless go-getter attitude after me! I laugh at this. But, yeah, when she met me I was fucking intense about becoming a talent agent and worked at one of the big talent agencies in town. My work ethic was beyond reproach. It must have turned her on and she keyed into my intensity. She had her own story which was so foreign from my own that when we first met I actually managed to get my mind off her hard, toned body and registered the fact that "Hey, this bird's story is farther out than any other I've heard in a long time." She is a stuntwoman. As a kid she was an amazing horseback rider and won all types of contests and because her dad was wealthy he funded her equestrian endeavors to the max. When she turned eighteen, she was a dead ringer—from the back— for a famous actress who just happened to be on a hit television show in which there was lots of horseback riding. One day she was spotted at one of the ubiquitous uber-malls in the Valley by this producer connected to the TV show and when she told him she was an expert horsewoman she was hired on the spot. She began doubling all the horseback riding scenes for the leading actress, who could not even get in the saddle without considerable whining and assistance. Then, she moved on to do other kinds of stunt work and developed a lean, tight body that just would not quit. The trick is that she has an average face which is fine by me, but she wants "the whole package" as she puts it and desperately wants to break out of the stunt world and into the world of on-camera principals. Join the club.

When I met her she was grieving the loss of her brother—another silver-spooned kid turning to adventure as he struggled with filling in the blanks of his life. This cat was a professional scuba driver. I guess that meant he was expertly skilled in the use of self-contained underwater breathing apparati. He dove all around the world and had some group which he formed to give scuba certification classes to others. He was twenty-eight years old when it happened. He was out by himself trolling for lobsters around the waters of Pismo Beach during October which was the beginning of lobster season. He had gone out early that day before other divers who were also looking to harvest good eating California spiny lobsters that mushroomed in population around the coast. The water was cold and a thick blanket of kelp covered the area where he was diving. He went down checking out rocks and reefs looking for lobsters, but when he tried to return to the surface he couldn't make it. He drowned just six feet from the surface. When he was found, his body was tangled in kelp and his scuba tank was still on his back and his air nozzle was out of his mouth.

The Coast Guard theorized that he must have been caught in the forest of kelp and had struggled vigorously to free himself, but in doing so only became more tangled, disoriented, and then drowned. But, he was no novice and no amount of theorizing could explain why he couldn't get to the surface. He was an expert diver and if he did become stuck he could have slipped off his scuba tank which was like a backpack and swum to the surface free of the tank. He also had thirty minutes of air left in the tank. When he struggled to free himself from the kelp he must have knocked the air nozzle out of his mouth, but he could have just put it back in and resumed his breathing. What the hell had happened? Did he think he had no air left? Or in his panic, did he simply forget to put his air nozzle back into his mouth? Kelp grows thick, but it's not impenetrable—not for someone used to the kelp beds that grew in the area. He should have found a way out, but he just couldn't get free. I still have images in my mind of his body floating in the dark water like a frozen marionette with those rope-like kelp vines bringing his arms up in different positions when the sea swelled.

She was crushed at the loss of her brother. She looked up to him and he was the glue that held the family together. Her parents divorced after his death and their mother—a professor of religious studies at Pepperdine had taken up with one of her male graduate students who was nineteen years her junior. Her father was the one who chose to remain in the family house in Chatsworth and her mother had moved into a condo in Malibu. She told me that if her brother was alive, the split would never have had happened. I only bring up her brother's story to suggest that she was drawn to me in the beginning like a younger sister is to her older, seemingly perfect brother. Somehow in the wake of her brother's death and parents' divorce, she thought I could make her safe and special again. I was going places at that time and could bullshit her with ease and talk about the world and all sorts of endless jive about the two of us finding one another at the right time. She bought it all. But, it was only a matter of time until I would become a liability to her. How we've switched roles! Absolutely amazing. I am now the meek, confused one looking to her for answers. When I quit the talent agency, she got me involved with temp agencies to tie me over while I pulled myself together. But, we're too far apart now and continuing down opposite directions. I know I've regressed and she, well, you could say she has decompressed into another Hollywood casualty. I don't know why I've gone about this bird. We've had some good times and it's not over between us yet, but I can admit that in the final analysis when everything is said and done I never truly advanced beyond looking at her solely as a regular source for sex. The other shit was just that—shit.

 I now go back to the beginning where I said my initial impetus in coming to L.A. was that I was actively seeking a moment of epiphany to come around and trigger that need in me to create. I was hoping for an epiphany like the one that grazed me that day in my philosophy class when suddenly my mind was so utterly tuned into the truths behind our lives. But, alas, the "real world" caught up with me and I chucked all plans I had to write. Now, I'm in a quarter-life crisis where any ideals I had coming out of college are long gone. It's been three and a half years. Three and a half years of post-college blues and reinventing myself and then dealing with large doses of the real world. Fantastic. You'll be amazed at the stagnation that occurs in the social and cultural circles of the individual during such time. After cyclical temping gigs, I've grown impatient and that impatience manifests itself in delusion and desperation. I try to suppress this delusion and desperation by going after a more permanent job and so I take the legal assistant job thinking that maybe I can return to life as a normal tax-paying citizen. But, my delusion and desperation cannot be restrained and when the right time comes, I call my boss an asshole and lose my job after only two months. True, my boss was simply an asshole, but I know the bottom line is that I'm not cut out for a nine to five life. So, what am I supposed to do? The only person who should be on my side, but who is not, is my girlfriend whose "get ahead at all costs" 'tude I've spawned through my own example when I tried living by that credo. But, again call it genetics. My true predisposition for a life outside the mainstream is again resurrecting itself and things are getting interesting.

I regroup. It is January 1999 and a week has passed since I quit life as a legal assistant in Beverly Hills. For a second, I think about calling all the temp agencies which have my resume and asking them to start pimping me out once again. No. I can't go down that road again right now. I need change. Thoughts which I had hithertofore banished from my head as "irresponsible" start budding again. Moving to San Miguel de Allende, a quaint colonial expatriate town a couple hours to the north of Mexico City and tending to a friend's stepdad's bookstore is most appetizing. I chicken out though. I barely know the guy and although he and I hit it off when we met and he invited me down once, I don't want to be a burden or mooch coming to Mexico when it's suddenly convenient and passing time with my friend's stepdad. Rationalization sets in. You know, I just can't really up and leave everything for an extended period of time. I still have responsibilities and obligations here that I can't ignore for more than a couple of weeks. I do nevertheless want to go somewhere. I've been stuck in L.A. so long that I accept the brown air and low or high-speed car chases as typical hallmarks of each day. A week away will suffice. Just enough time to become a stranger again in a strange city and lose myself for a bit. That's all.

      I brainstorm. It is winter and I'm not in the mood to go some place where I have to freeze my ass off. The lack of a white Christmas is one nicety of L.A. that I'm not willing to give up. So, where to? I flip through a calendar and stop in the month of February where I notice that Ash Wednesday falls on February 17. Aha! Mardi Gras in New Orleans just might do. I'm off.

II

I find myself on the corner of Bourbon and Toulouse hanging off a lightpost, clutching a mojo ball I bought in one hand and a daiquiri in the other, all the while clamoring for some bird to show her tits—the quid pro quo being a circular piece of string containing bright shiny balls. Ah, wilderness!

"Hey, man!!! You're not gonna get anywhere with that bullshit!!" Somebody from below yells at me.

I don't pay any attention. As it is, I am out of my mind and letting the good times roll. Everyone is yelling at everyone anyway so it all blends into one curiously melodic strain of "aaaaaaaaaarrgghhhhhhhhahhhhyyyyyyyyyya". That's all I hear. I conned two younger cousins of mine into joining me here in New Orleans when I promised them that they would see more breasts in two days than they would in the rest of their lives, but they have already left and gone back to their lives. However, I'm still having the time of my life partying like crazy and all but erasing the last two months of misery. But, the next thing I know, this prick is climbing the lightpost which I myself am barely clinging on to and there's no way both of us will be able to hang on at the same time. No holds—too slippery. He stops about halfway up to where I am and tugs on my pant leg. I want to kick him off.

"You know they usually Vaseline these things down?" He says as he continues to climb up until he finally reaches me.

What a dickhead. I'm up here first. Why is he starting something? I have to adjust my hands to

maintain my hold and his hands grab hold of the
pole near my waist. Now, face-to-face it looks like
we're getting it on. I'm about to drop off because
obviously this cat is crazy. But, I do a double-take
as his face becomes clear in my mind. Even in my
fucked up befuddlement, I know who this is. One
of my best friends from college. The one who
forced me one night to pull *Dark Side of the Moon*
out of my stereo and threw on *Bitches Brew* by
Miles Davis instead. It completely blew my mind.
A friend who I have seen once after graduation.
"Land Morales??!!" I ask trying to believe my
eyes.
A wickedly familiar half-grin flashes.

Yeah, this cat's name is Land. I remember
during freshman orientation when we first met what
my reaction to his name was like. He lived on my
dorm floor and during the proverbial "Please
introduce yourself and where you're from" sit down
meeting with the Residential Advisor, he said his
name was Land and that he was from Buttfuck,
Pennsylvania. Everyone broke into laughter, but I
was thinking to myself, *What did he say his name
was? Lando?? As in Calrissean?* So, I asked him,
"What is your name again?" He said, "Land" and
spelled it out "L—A—N—D" for me. Then, I
impulsively pointed at the ground and said, "You
mean like the *land*?" I could tell he was annoyed by
my question and didn't appreciate my gesturing to
the floor that was covered by a tattered and frayed
off-yellow carpet. But, he nodded at me and then
added that he had hippies for parents—the standard
cover for those with nouns for names. Of course, I
had never met anyone *named* Land, but more to the

point, little did I know that I had never met anyone like Land before either.

Maybe because of the inconsiderate manner in which I first spoke to him, Land and I did not become fast friends. We did not share any classes during that first semester and I would only see him in passing through the dorm halls. Then, one day someone told me that Land had called his American Studies professor an "imperialist scum" after a heated in-class discussion. The professor answered Land by saying that such a name-calling was an "oversimplification." This incident quickly became gossip of the highest order and because I had a fledgling streak of the anti-authoritarian in me, I was intrigued by Land. The cat was crazy or he had guts—I just knew that I would have to find out for myself. Brief chats between us when we bumped into one another in the dining area turned into hours long discourses on everything from the vagrancy of pop culture to the potency of sensimilla versus indica. We were both drawn to similar books and ideas and even spoke alike. He learned things from me, but it was crystal that I learned far more from him. Land had a knack for walking into any room and turning whatever contents were inside upside down with a couple of smirks and a litany of witticisms and disarming flattery. He reminded me of a Mercutio-like character except with equal substance and brains to go along with the flair and swordplay. When he was on, if you were lucky to know him and were able to plug into his mindset, it could be magical. And as an eighteen year old who was coming into his own, teaming with Land made me feel invincible. There was nothing that we couldn't do together. We were Rubin and Hoffman, Laurel and Hardy, Batman and Robin, and Sitting

Bull and Crazy Horse all rolled up into one. As we became upperclassmen, the first cracks of our own individualities started to clash, but nothing serious, because at that time we had already spent a couple of years creating memories and one flashback to those memories could squash any tension before it ever took root.

Now, here we are in N'Awlins in the middle of a vast orgy of colors, odors and flesh. Three and half years out of school and having seen each other once in the interim. He had come out to L.A. to see me about four months after graduation, and I will never forget his parting words to me as we said adios. I asked him what he planned on doing— working for his dad's tractor company for some down time or moving to NYC and getting involved in some activist organizations there or joining the Peace Corps for a couple of years. Land was in a boat similar to me. He majored in American Studies, which even I scratched my head at. American Studies seemed to me to be just a nice catchall term for your generic four years of college. It was not a standard liberal arts discipline, but apparently there was a department called American Studies on our campus with a couple of floating professors and enough interested students to require its funding at our university. Anyway, Land looked at me when I asked him about what his plans were and said:

I'm going to look for a community.

That was it and he drove onto the Christopher Columbus transcontinental highway and was gone. He gave me no explanation, but the way in which he so matter of factly answered me suggested that he thought I would understand what he meant. But, I had no idea what he was talking about. *Going to look for a community?* His words dogged me for a couple of months afterwards. In the beginning, I was just lazy about staying in touch with him, but when I drifted into the brave new world of working full time and setting goals for myself, I intentionally tried to forget Land. That is the truth.

"What killed me was that she hung out with this circle of women from work. You know the type—early 40s, sagging, divorced and complaining about the lack of good men. They got together once a week after work. Went out for drinks at a happy hour somewhere. They called themselves *Les Bitches*. When she and I would talk, it was always under the auspices of what *Les Bitches* had told her to say or do. A real drag."

Land and I have gone over to the Café DuMonde. A twenty-four hour canopy of face time and great café au laits. I am inhaling one beignet after another trying to pacify my munchies. We haven't seen each other for over three years and already Land is laying a lot on me. Apparently, after I said adios to him in L.A., he married this bird he had found while staying in Las Vegas. In not atypical Land style, they had gotten drunk, fucked, met the next day and decided to get married. But, you know what? It worked out for nearly eight months. They both had jobs. She worked as a secretary in a law firm specializing in gaming law and he somehow managed to open a small shop selling silkscreen T-shirts he would design and print. She then woke up one day and said she no longer loved him, filed for divorce that same day and the marital part of their relationship was over. One problem. Neither of them could afford to strike out on their own so they opted to stay together until they could work things out financially. Land had had enough of this arrangement after a month.

"So, how about you?? Still in Hollywood with visions of that house in the hills?" Land asks me.

"Uh, yeah. You know how it is, just trying to make some good bread and stay in the game."

"Mmmmhmmm. Right on."

Land had crashed at my apartment when he came out to L.A. It was in a shitty area of Hollywood, but was decked out in black leather sofas with matching dining and coffee tables and had a big king-sized bed with custom-built dressers also made of black leather. It just so happened that a couple of Colombian coke-runners had skipped out of town one day, leaving behind all their shit. The Colombians didn't bother to notify the landlord that they were leaving. So, the landlord who was satisfied with the Colombians' security deposit still being in his possession offered to throw in all their furniture into the unfurnished apartment I was going to rent. I accepted this proposition which added about $80 to the rent, but it was well worth it. I even nabbed the Colombians' 5-CD Sanyo Hi-Fi which still had CDs in the CD player. There were two CDs by the Hermanos Zuleta, one by Vicente Fernandez and one called *Campesino Parrandero*. I started listening to all the CDs and I got hooked, especially on "Cente" Fernandez. Man, that cat can sing!

I was apprehensive during the first couple of months in the apartment. After all, I had managed to score the spoils of a once profiting drug enterprise for myself. I didn't know whether the

Colombians would pop up one day and leave me in a puddle of blood as payback for taking over all their shit. It was indeed a contrast to live amongst such swanky indulgence whilst in one of the poorest sections of Hollywood. It was the same area where Dashiell Hammett lived in the early Thirties and tapped into the old noir vibe in order to create black and white characters for Humphrey Bogart. That time had long since vanished. Hollywood was a shell of its former grandeur. Broken pavement and cheesy neon tourist traps littered the street. Closed theaters and boarded up stores. Crack pushers, unemployed actors, Scientologists, Mexicans, El Salvadoreans, Guatemalans, Armenians, Russians, Thai, and Koreans all side-by-side. Cars emblazoned with slogans blaring everything from *"Jesus Es El Dio, Lea la Biblia"* to *"Jesuscristo es el mismo ayer, hoy y por siempre"*. This is what I dug though and could not bring myself to leave. Admittedly, I typically spent my days working in the clean and immaculate environs of Beverly Hills and Century City where I was far removed from Hollywood. Yet, when I could, I would scurry around Hollywood on foot and eat at a pupuseria for lunch and then go to the Armenian grocer up the street to buy fresh pastries he would prepare. At night, there were gloriously seedy pockets. I lived across from a bar, whose owners would only turn on select portions of the lights of their sign so that it would read "HE STUD" on certain nights. I once read in the L.A. Weekly "Best of L.A." edition that it was a favorite watering hole for gay black vaqueros. Suffice it to say, I never went in, but I didn't hold it against Hollywood either.

Land stayed with me for four days. It was a whirlwind of driving here, there and drinking here, there. I drove him around in my beige, beat up '84 Buick Skylark, which croaked on the corner of Sunset and Western one night. A sleazy intersection, but it was incredibly peaceful that night. As we waited for Triple A, we saw the last patron of the porn theater across the street exit and then the theater's pink bubbling lights shut off. The owners came out and tenderly pulled the black iron gates around the doors of the theater as if hugging their child goodnight. We saw the USA Today newspaper guy hop out of his truck and stuff the newspaper stand, then hop back in his truck and drive off. Land remarked that there was a crazy Christmas morning feeling in watching the nation's newspaper being delivered—like we had the opportunity to get inside info on today's news before the rest of L.A.

Triple A never came. We had to walk back to my apartment and passed "HE STUD" and all its ten-gallon hat wearing patrons. The next day we went back for my car, but of course it was gone. I had to coax the Lebanese Armenian gas station owner into telling me if he knew anything about the '84 Buick Skylark left near his establishment early that morning. He at first pretended not to hear me, but when I got in his face and asked him again about my car, he pulled out the business card of one "Bakajian Towing Co." No doubt a friend or relative of his. Land and I took a cab over there and I had to go into a real junkyard in the middle of Hollywood, complete with a gnarling Rottweiler as resident junkyard dog in order to identify my car and then sign papers for its release. You just couldn't survive in L.A. without a car and when the Rottweiler was put on a leash and restrained, I went into the junkyard and found my car lifeless. I tried turning the ignition, but nothing happened. The thought of permanently losing my car terrified me. I sat in the driver's seat petrified and silently prayed that when I would try the ignition again some divine spark would bring my car back to life. But, nothing happened and my car officially died in Bakajian's junkyard on that afternoon with Land bearing witness.

Land didn't understand why I was so upset. He was used to an existence *sans* automobiles. I freaked at the death of my car because I knew how helpless I would be from that point forward. I needed my car more than it needed me and I couldn't understand why it chose to leave me high and dry after all the time we had spent together. I ended up selling my car for scrap for $101 and Land and I rented a car for the remainder of his stay with me. As I adjusted to driving the rental car, Land continued to bemoan L.A.'s lack of public transportation. His complaining got on my nerves even though he was absolutely right. Nevertheless, I put forth some arguments. "We have buses—a great bus system here," I told him. I even had him ride the Metro subway that connected downtown to the corner of Wilshire and Western at the time. "What a trip!" Land had said as we took our seats on the Red Line. The seats were brand spanking new with no graffiti or scratchiti on the walls or windows and no need to purchase tickets! There was an automated ticket dispenser and people stood in line to get tickets. But, there were no turnstiles and no conductor came by to collect tickets either. In my brazenness, I had taken to riding the rails on the house. And why not? They needed some kind of positive P.R. in order to bamboozle Angelenos into parting with their beloved cars and taking the

Metro—underground—amidst promises by City Councilmen that it was "earthquake proof." But, the Metro is much ado about nothing. It doesn't go anywhere and it doesn't connect Hollywood to the Westside which are the two points where the bulk of people travel between anyway. If you work in downtown, then, O.K., it makes life a bit easier. But, for the rest of us, we don't even know L.A. has a subway. Land thought the Metro ride I took him on was "cute" and a lot like the Disneyland monorail. I convinced him of nothing.

While in college I had gone up to Buttfuck, Pennyslvania a couple of times to see Land and his parents. One drive occurred two weeks before Thanksgiving and the start of deer hunting season. It seemed the deer were on advance notice of this and so had embarked on a mass suicide as was evidenced by their numerous carcasses strewn like life-size detached hood ornaments alongside Highway 81. It wasn't clean eithcr. There were pools of blood, guts and gore everywhere for miles on end. I thought to myself who the poor souls were who would have to spend their Thanksgiving clearing the mess.

When I first met Land's parents I was startled by how completely physically dissimilar they were to each other. Land's mom was a third generation Rumanian Orthodox Catholic born and raised in Philadelphia. She had a round, fat, pink face and wore her brown hair tight in a small bun. She was only around 5'2 in height and on the chunky side. Land's dad was red and striking. A mestizo of Mexican and Zuni descent, who was brought up in New Mexico. He was wiry and tall with a pointed nose and jet black hair. He had grown up on the rez and got out through sheer panic of the thought of turning into his father, who was an old school Zuni who had gotten his Mexican wife to learn the Zuni language and culture and wanted his kids fully brought up Zuni. Land's dad was very intelligent and into music. He got a scholarship to Oberlin College in which he enrolled and met Land's mom. It was the late Sixties then, so the two of them tuned in, turned on and dropped out— neither of them got their degrees. Instead, they moved out to rural Pennsylvania where Land's dad began working as a ranch hand on a farm and Land's mom worked at the local state trooper's office. Eventually, the two of them got married and scrapped together enough bread to buy a little farm of their own. Land's dad then started a tractor company that did quite well for a spell during the Eighties.

Land was their only child. His dad, Land told me, was so overjoyed at the birth of a son that he performed an old Zuni dance when Land was born. Hah. Sounded to me like even though Land's dad had tried to hard to get out of the rez, he couldn't get the rez out of him. This dance was supposed to protect Land's spirit from earthly evils once Land had left the safety of the womb and came into being. A bit of a stretch for me, especially since it appeared that Land's dad had abandoned any Zuni trappings long ago. He kept his hair closely cropped underneath an omnipresent dirty, blue baseball cap emblazoned with the Jim Beam logo. He didn't dig my shoulder length hair or my habit of saying "man" in every other sentence. He would say, "Land, can't your friend here ever complete a sentence without saying *man*?" This coming from a guy who met his wife during a sit down protest against "the man."

My attention is focused on this queen dressed like George Washington who is standing on a table serenading everyone at Café DuMonde to his strains of *Proud Mary*. It is a scream. Then this queen turns to me since I am only a couple of tables away and motions me to join him atop the table. Land cracks up and the birds at the table next to ours pass the more ornate and fancy kind of beads to me which means that these are mine if I will oblige and join this queen for an encore. "You gotta do it, man!! Check out those beads! That's some serious currency. God only knows what doors you can open with those!" Land eggs me on.

I catch his drift. During Mardi Gras time, a curious thing happens. Almost like a tribalistic regression. People barter. Paper money becomes just that—*paper*. It has no value. It's just green paper with old white faces on it. What carries weight and gets you things are beads and the bigger, longer, shinier, and more bulbous the beads the greater the cachet value you have to throw around. Beads for going to the head of the line, beads for getting a nicer table, beads for tits, beads for blow(s), and beads for being able to use a port-a-let instead of having to sneak between parked cars in order to take care of your business. Greed then leads me atop of the table with the queen and we link arms and sing the final bars of *Proud Mary*. It's exhilarating. For a few moments all of Café DuMonde is riveted by George Washington and I belting out lyrics about working for the man every night and day. I wish I can bottle the scene and refer back to it whenever I start taking my life too seriously. Anyway, the dude is cool. Doesn't grab my ass or anything.

"Right on!! You just had your fifteen minutes. How did it feel?!?" Land screams at me as I return back to my seat.

I laugh. Land and I always tried to one-up each other when it came to who could make the bigger ass out of one's self. I don't know how this practice started or why. But, as long as we had known each other, we forged a bond based on seeing the other in the most stripped, most ludicrous of situations. I guess it made us feel more alive, since living was what we both had craved.
"Just another one for the books, old sport." I say in a British accent. "Now, let's go get some gumbo. I know this unbelievable Cajun dive in *Le Vieux Carre*. It's up on Iberville."
"Well, tally-ho then! Back into the Quarter, I believe?" Land counters.
"Follow me, man."

I vaguely know my way around New Orleans. I've been lucky enough to visit through the years, albeit most of that time has been spent in various altered states of consciousness, so I've probably been everywhere in the Quarter though I don't remember and possibly don't want to. It's all about choosing a different adventure each time you come here. Choosing a different jazz club to dig. Choosing a different restaurant to sample their gumbo. What a place—the Crescent City. Where whole genres of style and music were invented. It has this magical vibe. Always brings a big, sloppy smile to my face. When you set foot inside the city limits you embark on a sensual journey through sight and sound. Throw in its occupation by six different peoples at six distinct periods, the vodou and bayous and gators and the fact that anything's game for an etouffé—there's nowhere in the U.S.

like it. I absolutely adore this city. It makes me dream.

　　　　We walk along Decatur and towards Iberville. Sounds of sax hit us as we cut across Jackson Square. By chance we stumble across a little streetway called "Pirate's Alley" and find ourselves in front of a residence where a plaque states Faulkner lived and wrote *Soldiers' Pay* here. I don't know why, but this prods me into going into a story about a friend I had who had lived and worked in New Orleans for close to a year. He came to work at the corporate headquarters for a retail company so he could be groomed into a manager for the company's Charlotte office. This cat was smart and more important clean. He started out living in the suburbs—a place called Metarie— famous for its one hundred acre plus cemetery which consisted of mesmerizing tombs built six feet above ground, since the French had found out that interring loved ones in this area proved horrifying once it rained and the already below sea-level land became inundated and corpses floated though the center of town. You can imagine the ghoulish scenarios: You're out for a late night stroll after the flooding has subsided and suddenly you come upon Uncle Joe propped up against a tree and then it dawns on you—Uncle Joe had been put to rest three months earlier! These kinds of scenes must have given rise to the tales of zombies popping up around New Orleans.

"So, I keep tabs on this cat. Every other week I hear what he's up to and it's pretty much business as usual. Then, one day he says he's quit work, moved into the Quarter and is living with a couple of strippers from Big Daddy's. You know that place on Bourbon where the fishnet stocking covered legs of a female mannequin swing out of a window?" I ask Land, who nods.

"Anyway, he's now dealing coke in specially tagged ziplocked bags which enables anyone using the coke to know that it came from him. It's really a small town here, man. The motherfucker was a helluva entrepreneur and his finance degree definitely came in handy."

"I can imagine," Land says.

"Get this. So, each bag of coke bears special tags. He didn't give out his name when dealing. He was known by the tagged bags. If the coke was of really good quality, everyone who saw his yellow or red tagged ziplocked bags would know that the good shit was coming from my friend. It was like his calling card. But, the flip side was that if the coke was bad or cut with some other shit, everyone would also know that it came from him. Something ultimately went down and he split."

"Where's he at now?"

"He lives with his mom in Tampa. But, what a ride he had while it lasted."

"Made some good money too, I bet."

"Mmmmhmmm. He made some good bread. I think he's now looking into grad school."

We find the place. There are about twenty people standing in line outside of it. I don't want to wait. I hate waiting for food. After all, for the entire Nineties, I have been basically weaned on a steady diet of KFC, MickeyDs, Burger King, In-N-Out (unfortunately only to be found in the West) and the crème de la crème, Taco Bell. Those taco supremes are top to the notch! It makes my mouth water just thinking about those things. Someone once told me that additives or some shit was added into the food in order to hook the public. Sort of like Big Tobacco spiking up the nicotine in their cigarettes with that secret ingredient Mike Wallace exposed some years back. When a Taco Bell opened up in Buttfuck, Land told me that there was a mile long of cars waiting for drive-thru.

"No worries. Just flash those beads you just got from your performance with George." Land instructs me.

I dangle my newly earned beads in front of the maitre'd's face. They are nice looking beads. The kind Dutch settlers could have bought a hundred Manhattans with. Big white balls with purple, gold and green harlequins interspersed throughout. More important, they are long and fall to my knees. Top notch beads alright.

"Sorry, that doesn't work here. You'll have to go to the end of the line."

"Come on, man. Do you have any idea what this cat did to get those things?" Land asks.

"Sir, we are at our maximum capacity right now. There is a line, so please wait like everyone else. I'm sure your friend's efforts in obtaining the beads will not go unappreciated during the rest of your time here." He then breaks off. "Johnson, party of four?"

He looks at the front of the line and the Johnson party gathers up and walks by Land and I as if divinely anointed. One of them even smirks at Land as the maitre'd waves him inside.

"What about hitting up another place?" Land asks.

"No. The gumbo here is amazing. It's like they take whatever they can get their hands on in the bayou. Chop it up. But, not into small chunks. No. I'm talking big chunks with hunks of tooth, claw and nail still visible. Pile it all into a stew of okra and rice and you got some serious gumbo."

"You're making me salivate."

"Wait—the trick to their gumbo is they keep it pure. Pure, in the sense, that real gumbo must first start with an ample helping of lard. That's the secret. No lard and you don't have gumbo. Some of these other restaurants don't use lard, they use filé powder or something. That's for pussies."

"Alright, man! We'll stay here. Only you could get so dramatic about a bowl of soup! Let's hang around and try to hook up with some people and get in with them."

We size up those in line. Each donning various beads around their wild-eyed, starry faces. When you come to New Orleans—Mardi Gras time or not—it's best to check your ego at the door and gel into the throng of characters that surround you. It's easy to assume a new identity and here in this line, Land and I can see whom we can count on to sweep into our maelstrom of well-placed giddiness and tag-team irrepressibility. A group of three girls, probably not more than eighteen and in over their heads. Their eyes are glazed and their sentences stagger with thick Long Island accents, and most importantly, they are the third group in line. Slim pickings for Land and I. We move in and begin the show, but in typical Fat Tuesday fashion it is the beads that do most of the work.

"How did you get those!" One of the girls blurts out as Land and I come closer.

"Do you really want to know?" I respond.

"He probably bought them," another of the girls answers.

Land and I laugh.

"You girls come down from the Island?" Land asks.

"Yeah, Massapequa." The same girl says.

"A different world here, isn't it?" Land goes on.

"Are you two from the City?" The third girl asks.

"We went to school in upstate New York. Graduated a few years back and we decided to meet up this year for Mardi Gras. What about you all?" I lay the groundwork.

"Oh, we're students at Adelphi. It's our first time down here. It's insane!"

"At least, you all have come to the right restaurant. This place is a local favorite. Great food." Land says.

"Yeah? We just came upon it by accident!" The first girl gets back in the conversation.

"We actually called up ahead to make reservations. But, I guess there was some kind of mix up," I say.

"Is that what you were talking to that guy about?"

"Yeah, he didn't have our names down."

"Well, you can join us if you want." The other two girls nod in unison.

I look at Land. He smiles back. Green light.

"Sure, if that's O.K. We really appreciate it." Land says.

"Why don't you take this as a small token of our appreciation." I take off my beads and put them around the neck of the first girl. She seems to be the leader of the group, so it's only appropriate that she gets the beads. I feel like a head of state conferring a high honor upon a deserving citizen. She lights up. The other two girls mutter something about being left out. Land and I quickly take our places in line and exchange pleasantries with the girls and the classic jive about life in NYC as compared to New Orleans.

After fifteen minutes or so, the maitre'd motions us into the restaurant. Inside, it is a scene whose kinetic frenzy smacks me in the face. People in all types of masks, costumes and feather boas. Elton John's *Crocodile Rock* blares from the ceiling and people are dancing on tables while others are devouring crawfish like it is going out of season. Just pinching the tail and sucking the head so fast— throwing endoskeletons on the floor. We follow the maitre'd deep into this calamity and to his credit the maitre'd tries his best to provide for our safe passage—picking routes that steer clear from the gastronomical and maniacal minefields. He leads us to our table and then disappears. As we take off our jackets and get ready to take a seat we realize that there are five of us, but the table has only four seats.

"Looks like one of us will be sitting on someone's lap!" Land jokes.

But, before we even have a chance to figure out what to do, one of the girls, and I can see this coming, suddenly keels over a chair and vomits onto the floor. No one even blinks. The frenzied madness that engulfs us make this display of reverse peristalsis inconsequential. Who cares? Just part of the territory, but her two friends are concerned, especially when their friend continues dry heaving and her face turns green. They help her stand up.

"You should take her outside for some air," Land says.

"Yeah. Do you need some help?" I ask. I wink at Land. A little chivalry always helps.

"No. That's O.K. We'll be back."

"We'll hold onto your seats." Land yells back as the girls drag their friend farther away from us and closer to the exit.

"This happens a lot. Uh, thanks for the beads…"
The girls' shouting dissipates as they pour onto the street.

"Happy Mardi Gras!!" Land puts in a final farewell. We know it's sayonora to those birds, but they served us well.

I am starving. The beignets have not cut it and I have been pretty wasted since ten in the morning. It is now a quarter after one in the afternoon on Mardi Gras Day. I had extracted myself off the banks of the Mississippi around 7:30 this morning (having passed out on a bench there the night before) and then taken a stronghold position on St. Charles, so I could have a prime vantage point from where I could watch Zulu and Rex roll by. These two are the final big parades and cap off the two week carnival season. Zulu is one of the oldest parades and was first begun by blacks who were excluded from the other white krewes or social clubs that set up their own themed parades and balls during Mardi Gras. Even in 1999, remnants of Mardi Gras' segregated past is present as Zulu's parade route differs from all other parades, which basically start at the Superdome, flow past Lee Circle along St. Charles through the Financial District and dump into Canal Street. When Zulu had entered Canal it did not simply run north to south, but rather kept going north on Canal passing the St. Louis Cemetery No.1 and going through the ghetto. Throwing out parasols, spears, beads and coconuts to those who the other parades bypassed in favor of the hooligan masses glutting Canal. I was even hit by a wayward spear launched off a Zulu float today. It left a gash on the top of my head. When it bounced off my head, the people around me behaved like a pack of hyenas as they shrieked and thrashed their way to the spear that had left me stunned and bloodied. I had no idea what had happened. Like the sky opened and singled me out for retribution. Blood trickled on to my forehead and no one stopped to ask if I was O.K. I had to scramble to find something clean to place on the gash. I did a makeshift first-aid job on my head by using Domino's pizza napkins as gauze. Rex was scheduled right after Zulu and there was no way back to my hotel since all the roads were blocked. I was stuck on Canal with one hand on my head holding the gauze in place as I watched Rex roll by. When Rex finished and the roads were opened, I went back to my motel room and examined the gash in the mirror. Not bad—a minor cut. I didn't have time to waste by bleeding. I cleaned myself up and combed my hair, put on new clothes and went back to the chaotic roar of the Quarter where Land then found me dangling off a lightpost.

"So, what should I go with? The brown jambalaya, blackened alligator or crawfish etouffé?"
Land has his face buried in the menu as he asks me this. You can't blame him. Nowhere else has such a selection of eye-catching foods and saying their names is like magical anticipation dancing on your tongue.
"You gotta start with a bowl of the seafood gumbo. It's got oysters, crab, crawfish, and etcetera. And you know what's distinct about it?"
"What?"
"It tastes dirty."
"That sounds appetizing, bra."

"No, that's a good thing. Genuine. Like swamp water! Then, I'm gonna have the brown jambalaya and a bottle of Abita beer to wash it all down."

"I'll go with that too."

Land yells for the waiter to come over. You have to yell. There's no other way of getting the waiter's attention with all the shit swirling around. "We're ready to order. We'll have two bowls of gumbo and two brown jambalayas. A couple of Abitas as well. Gracias." Land says and the waiter turns to go.

"Wait!" I yell at the waiter.

"Yes?"

"Throw in an order of your beer-battered gator bits."

"Sure thing."

The waiter turns away into the abyss.

"Had to tack on the gator?" Land asks me.

"Yeah, bra. I want to splurge."

I take a look around the restaurant. I see people engrossed in the act of eating. I can't wait until the food comes out.

"So, where did you say you were staying again?" Land asks.

"The Days Inn out on Lafayette. I came down with two of my cousins. They went back last night."

"They couldn't stay for the *fin-de-siécle* Fat Tuesday?"

"Job obligations, man. I'm free at this point. I quit work last month and decided to head down here à la Fonda and Hopper. Except, I'm not sure which one I am."

"You still subscribing to that hippie bullshit?" Land says as the waiter returns with a bunch of rolls and the gator bits. I go after a roll fast. Butter one up and shovel into my mouth. I barely catch Land's remark.

"What did you say?"

"I said I can't believe you are still in that hackey-sack playing mentality you had back in school. Times change, I thought you had evolved with them."

I know Land is fucking with me, but I can't resist fueling the conversation.

"Whooaa, Land! We both had that mentality. Who had me strumming my git while they tried rapping *Howl* over it?"

"Yeah, yeah. *I saw the best minds of my generation destroyed by madness...*" Land trails off. "I don't remember those lines anymore. But, it was a bunch of self-promoting nonsense, wasn't it?? Don't get me wrong, I still dig Ginsberg's contributions. I never went much for his faggie stuff like that thing he would play."

"You mean that squeezebox?"

"Whatever. The guy writes some unbelievable shit then he goes on William F. Buckley's show playing a squeezebox while trying to sing. That was the kind of shit that made Kerouac cringe."

I gobble the gator bits and push the plate towards Land so that he can indulge as well.

"Thanks," he says as he grabs a couple and sucks them down. "You know when Cassady, Ginsberg and the Merry Pranksters journeyed all the way to Kerouac's mom's house in St. Petersburg, Florida to see Kerouac, Jack refused to come out. He left those cats high and dry at the gate of his mom's house. That was a very symbolic move on Kerouac's part. As if he was effectively turning his back on the entire Sixties."

I had heard this jazz before. One night, Land had explained to me the whole evolution of the counterculture movement in America. It all stemmed from the Beats and their voice Kerouac. Sure Cassady was the muse, but it was Kerouac who was able to distill all the unchoreographed and spontaneous sojourns of the Beats into legend. This legend, which itself sprang from the culture and music of Black America—namely jazz and free verse musical stylings—could have only evolved under Eisenhower's post-war military industrial complex. Land contended that San Francisco's predisposition for the flower children came about as a result of the Beat presence in the city which opened various doors of perception from the ordinary into the subversive. The rock music that grew out of their presence was originally characterized by free-verse like jams and the Grateful Dead—basically a jug band gone wild— was at the fore of this new type of musical consciousness providing the amorphous backdrop for Ken Kesey's acid parties. However, Haight/Ashbury, Leary and Richard Alpert-cum-Ram Dass and the whole hippie trip about flower power and shit like that were actually a *perversion* of the Beat philosophy according to Land.

"*Fuck* Tom Wolfe," Land emphatically had stated to me years ago. "That guy got it all wrong in *Electric Cool-Aid Acid Test*. Kesey and the Merry Pranksters represented the ecumenical *On the Road*. And that's why Kerouac didn't answer the door that day. He couldn't stand to be the forefather of an androgynous and pacifist movement that had absolutely nothing to do with the righteous machismo or vagabond theosophy that he so believed in. They—hippies—were a thin guise, an embarrassing pretext for changing the world."

"And fuck Tom Wolfe. The guy isn't a writer, he's a chronicler. There's a big difference. Writers are about art, movement—not chronology or journalism. Plus, writers don't dress up all in white and prance around as if holier than thou."
Ah, the old Land surfaces.
"Land, don't play if off like I'm the one who is still clinging on to the old days. Your passionate dislike of Tom Wolfe comes from how dearly you believe in what the Beats represented and how the counterculture fucked that up."
"Don't simplify it, man. I know you were once a hippie sympathizer, but even you could never be like them. You were too literate. You just dug the music and tye-dye of that time."
"You've still got me pegged—er—how were those gator bits?"
"Not bad—tasty."
"Pretty healthy meat," I say as I reach for another roll.
"You still trying to write?" Land asks.
"*Trying* being the operative word."
"Yeah, I hear you," Land pauses for a second.
"You know, man, that writers write from experience. Problem is, the American experience nowadays doesn't offer much. It's routine. So, these cats writing now—it's about clichés and fantasy and possible movie deals. There's nothing of consequence. Nothing you read lasts. Let me guess, bra, your writing has been in a big rut."
I don't like lying, but I don't feel like cluing Land in on my complete abandonment of writing.

"There's nothing to tap into. You know? I don't have time to pursue anything which would be meaningful or insightful anyways. I can't get off the ground with anything that moves. I don't want to write a fuckin' novel about lawyers saving the day or virulent bacteria spreading!!"

"Forget it, man. I don't wanna bum you out or thwart your desire to write, but I know you—what you want to write can't be written as long as you're meshed into our society. Very few people here still have access to the type of experience and insight into the human condition which you probably want to write about. I remember some of the shit you wrote in college. It was all over our heads, but shit, it was chock full of promise!"

There is a brief silence. I'm a bit depressed at Land's remarks but quietly assent. He stops talking too, maybe thinking to himself that he was overly discouraging.

"What was that term you used to describe your writing?"

"What?"

"Come on, man. You remember that creative writing class we were in? The prof—what was his name…"

"Weingrad."

"You remember. He asked you to explain your writing style that one day when we all had our writing reviewed by the class. You made up some term!!"

"I didn't make anything up, man. I said it was *modal verse*."

"Modal verse? What the fuck is that! You really bullshitted Weingrad good that day! I think he bought it."

"Land, that was no snowjob. I got the idea indirectly from you."

"From me?"

"Yeah."

"Hey, I'll take credit if you want me to, bra. But, I have no idea what I did."

"Miles—you introduced me to his music—*Bitches Brew*."

"Miles Davis? Ahhh, I see where you are going. Like modal jazz. That's what you tied you're writing to. Weingrad had no idea what you were talking about."

"Just improvising upon sketches or a series of sketches rather than a predetermined narrative structure—that's what I meant by modal verse, man."

Land thinks about it for a second.

"You know, bra, I dig you creative leap from jazz to writing, but it can't be done. With Miles—come on, man. That's genius. Moreover, music is a different medium and with each note a lasting artistic imprint is made. It's not the same with words."

"Sure it is."

"C'mon, man. You think that when a phrase or sentence is put together—each word carries an artistic imprint upon the same level of consciousness as a musical note?"

"I don't see a difference. Whether you listen to a single note from a stereo or read a single sentence upon the page—the mental imprint is the same."

"I think there's a difference between the mental image you get from hearing musical art than what you get from reading the written word—it's a deeper, more primal thing. More visceral."

"I disagree."

"Well, think about it like this. Early man first *heard* the world he was in way, way before he could ever articulate it into some written form of communication. I guess what I'm saying is that it was the sensations of sight, sound and touch which obviously formed the template of our initial understanding of the world around us. So, when we hear music today that auditory sensation has a deeper resonance within us because it goes back to our more primal core."

I think about this. It makes sense to me to a certain degree, but I'm just a big believer in the power of the written word.

"That sounds nice," I start. "But, the fact is here we are now as sentient beings who when we close our eyes or dream we have thoughts constantly floating around. And these thoughts are not without form. They are linked to sentences, phrases, and words. So, I think language is the big key to the expression of what our sensations depend on in order to actualize themselves."

"You're losing me, bra." Land shakes his head and takes a big swig of his Abita. "I will say though, that modal verse, that's a ballsy concept. But, I think you're pushing it with all the rest."

"So what?"

We then hit another awkward silence. I must say that I am surprised that my old passionate feelings about writing are still intact. I have not spoken like this about writing in a long time. Now, I've run out of what to say. Thankfully, we are quickly saved from this lull when the waiter brings out our gumbo. An easy transition.

"Bon appetit, Land," I say.

We slurp and suck. The only way to have good gumbo. I have crab claws one second, shrimp the next, then oyster and other unidentified floating objects. The brown jambalaya comes out afterwards. Zesty brown rice with shrimp and andoubille sausage interspersed in between.

As I gorge myself, I begin to sober up and it is then that I realize how much Land has changed. He seems physically aged like he is in his late thirties. Something about the way his brown eyes now droop and seem burned out. He is still slim with an indented, cleft chin framed against a high cheekboned face. He is a complete physical mishmash of his mom's fat, flat face and his dad's pronounced nose and high forehead. Tough to describe really. But, he was there and when you first met him you couldn't help but think where the hell he was from.

"Do you remember what you told me when you left L.A.?" I casually remark.

"Uh-uh. No." Land stops to wipe his mouth. "I'll see you when I see you?" He asks.

"No, man. You said you were gonna look for a community."

Land's face becomes serious. His eyes avert mine and he concentrates on his jambalaya.

"Listen, I got hitched in Vegas. That quest never panned out."

"But, you said you were married only for eight months. What have you been doing for the last two years?"

Land studies me before responding.

"Probably the same shit as you."

"Working like a dog?? I doubt that, man."

"Oh, sure I worked. But, also did a little traveling here and there. You know…"

But, the jig is up. Land knows I know when he is bullshitting and his rambling is going nowhere. He decides to come clean.

"I didn't find anything," he says with disgust.

"What do you mean?"

"Just what I said."

"You didn't find a community?"

"Yeah. I've come to the conclusion that there is no such thing as a community in America. It no longer exists."

"No longer exists? What do you call this?" And I motion around the frenzied restaurant and all the people milling around, interfacing, and doing shit.

"This? I call this running a business. I'm talking about a real community…it's extinct. Just a dead social practice or used symbolically as a weapon by some. I don't want to say anything else about this, Tal. I know you didn't come out to Mardi Gras to randomly bump into me and then have me bum you out."

But, I am fascinated by Land's words. And what an earnest conclusion: *There is no such thing as a community in America.* Who sets out in search of this? Kerouac? That cat's only contact with a community in America was having a scoop of vanilla ice cream and a slice of apple pie in every state between New York and California. Purely in search of the self, not a community. Did Land do some kind of field research? How the fuck could you come to such a conclusion that the American community was extinct and then have the balls to tell someone about your findings. They'd think you were out of your mind.

"Just explain what you didn't find," I ask.

"Check out this food." Land points toward our empty gumbo bowls and our nearly empty plates of

jambalaya. "It's authentic not gimmicky. It's got real flavor and you can taste the *history* in it. You know what I'm talking about?"
"Of course."
"You know this shit is a symbol of somebody's survival—whether the slaves or the Cajuns or the Creoles or the Indians or all of them together. When you go out and get inside America, and I don't care if it's the big city or some little town in the Midwest, there's no more authenticity—it's all mediocre—fast food and sound bites. There's nothing lasting or rooted in any type of history. People come and go, make and lose money and somewhere in between the concept of community has ceased to have any viability. It's not the civic center or these town hall meetings that they air on C-SPAN. Those are fly-by-night, convenience store versions of community force-fed to us every once in a while to make us think we're part of some larger social fabric."
Jesus H. Christ, I think to myself. I've opened a real Pandora's box here. But, I still listen intently.
"Like the television—you know, Springer and now these money-crazed game shows and so called reality-based shows on primetime. That's the American community—broken and fickle—aimless and creating a generation of *amorality*."
Heavy shit. I'm a blank. I spoon up some more rice and desperately rack my brain for some rejoinder. But, nothing. Land, however, is not done.
"Let me expand on some things," he says polishing off the plate. "When I'm talking about community I'm referring to the concept of community that you and I and the average American has. Community is about having some social infrastructure in place

which instills ethics, democratic principles, family values and all that shit. It's a composite of citizens coming together to solve problems and maintain order. Right?"

"Sure. That's what I would say it is."

"O.K. What I've found is that the concept of community is really an empty shell. There's nothing there. It's become a rhetorical device that enables certain segments of the population to reinforce themselves and remove those who they deem as being outsiders. That's why I said that the idea of community is like a weapon some people wield over others—to keep them in check."

"I don't understand," I say innocently. But, of course, I understand. I'm having flashbacks to ghosts of campus rallies past. I've just repressed thinking about this type of shit for so long now.

"It's like this. I've seen things over the last couple of years and because I'm not tied down to any job or place I've had time to really ponder the way things are set up to interact in America. I've just pieced things together. Things that I would never otherwise be able to put together if I was plugged into some job or something. You have these cats in America who call the shots—whether you see them or not. They get to define community in terms of some arbitrary social history or personal memory they have of America. Those of us that can't share in this view of history or memory are labeled as outsiders. Then these cats—I'll call them the insiders—perpetuate these histories and memories so much so that they've become sacrosanct components of American life. These insiders go around championing *it takes a village* slogans and the need for all Americans to get along with the community, and then when some conflict arises, these insiders identify the cause of conflict, label it as something destructive and anti-American and marginalize it to the outside of what they call the American community."

Land takes a second to eat some more jambalaya and then with rice still in his mouth continues, "So, what you have is one group creating their own myth of what the American community is and then using this myth to weed out outside elements."

"Whew, man. That's—" I try to get a few words in, but can't.

"—yeah. That's what I found. Community in the way you and I would think of it is dead, but for some people it is a lightning rod that wards off religious, social and political pluralism that has arisen in America. It's the last buffer between keeping the *have* with the *haves* and away from the *have-nots*."

I am speechless. I make a feeble attempt at spooning up some more of the jambalaya but my plate is clean. A few rice fragments remain which are impossible to round up with a spoon. I have to say something.

"But, uh, what did you do for those two years? Stay in Vegas? What kind of insight could you possibly have gotten there?"

Not a bad filler question I think to myself.

"No, I didn't stay there. I bailed. I first drove through the desert into New Mexico. I actually went out to the old rez where part of my dad's family still lives." Land tilts his head sideways as if dealing with some haunting images.

"What was that like?" I ask.

"Man…that was like…like going to the fourth world. You know what I'm saying? Like going beyond what we think of as the third world and

entering something else. Something riddled
with…with heaviness."

"Heaviness?"

"I mean you can feel the weight of your existence
there. It preys on you. You wouldn't believe how
these cats live. Everyone thinks Natives live well—
rolling in casino money. That's just not the case,
bra. There's something like four hundred and forty-
four federally recognized tribes. And that obviously
doesn't include those Indians or fool's gold Indians
who are around but don't qualify because they don't
meet the government's criteria for qualifying as an
Indian. I saw conditions that you just couldn't
believe. Thirteen people sharing a cramped trailer
with no heat and one toilet. You had these rusted
generators providing electricity, lights. Yeah, some
of the tribe had it better and had TVs and houselike
structures, but still it was like entering a place
completely removed from the American dream."

"More like the American nightmare, huh?"

"That's the funny thing. On the rez, in the middle
of all the downtroddeness, I felt a closeness, a
warmness. There was a community there. There
still was some tradition, some genuineness holding
these people together and enabling them to survive.
But, it's wavering—unsure how to continue."

"Shit, man." That's all I muster up.

Land looks away from me and stares at the floor.
"I don't know how my dad ever left the rez. He
never talks about it."

I don't respond thinking that it's better to let Land
collect his thoughts and continue when he's ready.
I catch the eye of our waiter and motion him to
bring our check.

"After that I went out to this place in Silver Cliff, Colorado where I camped out on a preserve for wolves."

"Get the fuck outta here!" I say.

"Seriously. This place I found out about while in school. You go to this preserve for wolves and you help put up boundary fences for them and drag road-killed elk and pronghorn for them to eat."

"What?? The wolves can't hunt for themselves?"

"Yeah. They're all wolves that the preserve adopts. They come from people who abused them or couldn't take care of them any longer. So, they've lost the ability to hunt or never learned in the first place. That education a wolf gets from the pack in learning how to hunt is irreplaceable."

"What did they call you, *Running with the wolves*, or something?!"

"Haha. Yeah, something like that. But, seriously, if you never learn to hunt from your pack, you just ain't never gonna learn how to hunt. It's lost forever."

Land polishes off his plate.

"Can you imagine the horrible irony there?" Land asks me.

"With the wolves you mean?"

"Uh-huh. Can you imagine a wolf who can't hunt? I mean, it's fuckin' horrible. That's how I got to camp among them for a couple of weeks. The preserve welcomes volunteers with open arms to help provide for the wolves. What an experience, man."

"I'm sure it was."

"I would be boiling up water for my Ramen on this little propane stove I had and when one of the packs would suddenly come into the area, I would go completely still. The world just stilled around me and sometimes the wolves would howl and sometimes they wouldn't. It didn't matter. Just their presence made me feel small. I felt like I was in their service. Weird, man."

I absorb Land's words and can't help but smile. His vivid description of things is always so catching.

"I'll tell you, bra, something else—going back to what I was saying about the state of community in America. I found a pocket of something close to a community when I went up to Yosemite to do a little climbing. I drove out there after I left Colorado. Those were some good times just being able to pick up and cruise from one place to another with a minimum of fuss."

"Yeah," I just blurt out on instinct.

"Anyways, at the time, I was driving the same Jeep Cherokee that I came to see you in L.A. with. I had all my gear in there. When I arrived in Yosemite, I was too exhausted to get out of my Jeep since I had basically driven from Colorado to there in just under eighteen hours nonstop. I was dead tired so I basically lived out of the back of my Jeep for three days. I had everything I needed there and only came out to use the bathroom or to shower. I lived off cliff bars and cans of fruit syrup until I regained my strength. Then one night while I was chilling in the back of the Jeep, these guys knock on my door asking me why I was holed up in my car for so long. They thought maybe I was hurt or tripping hard on acid. When I explained my story, they invited me to their campsite which happens to be Camp 4—a legendary rendezvous site for rock climbers around the world. I went and hung out with them. Ate red meat that we cooked over big, open fires. Passed around the bong, they played guitar and we all sang some songs and swapped

climbing stories. It was such a thrill to go from living out of my Jeep and into this warm glow of happy faces and humanity. That was real, man."
"I bet...," I quietly murmur as a twinge of regret sweeps across me. But, I quickly shirk it off.
"As close to a community as I got. I think it was because everyone was on the same wavelength. There was no distinction. We were all out there to enjoy this most beautiful of places and to dig the nature of the place. There were no expectations to be had from one another. It was fantastic. And I had the best sleep of my life the next day when a group of us crashed under El Cap—the largest freestanding slab of granite in the world. I fell asleep counting more shooting stars than I could keep up with."
"Didn't you give me a call when you were out there?"
"Uhhh, yeah. I think so. I asked you to come up and you fed me a lame excuse. You missed out, bra. I ended up scaling a big wall. It was a climb that took more than one day to complete because the rock was so massive. I slept in this used port-a-ledge I had bought in a climbing shop in Berkeley. I spent three nights sleeping in this thing, pinned to granite, suspended in the air at varying heights off the ground. It took fourteen pitches to complete. A motherfucker. But, what a feeling, man, when I scaled that sucker."
"Wholly shit," I shake my head in disbelief. "I can't imagine what that must have been like. Sleeping on a port-a-ledge? Your sense of space must get fucked up."
"Hahahaha. You ain't just whistling dixie! Space as you normally know it...ceases to exist. You are climbing these vast rocks which shoot into an

entirely new conception of space. One that throws
any laws of physics out the door. You got a roof
that blocks your route and you have to extend your
body out into that space and scale it. It's sketchy.
You escape from any normalcy that you have ever
known in your life. And that's why I've given up
climbing, man."
"What?! After a story like this, you're telling me
you've quit?!"
"It's too escapist. You always want to push farther
out on the edge. Farther out into space. It fucks
your head when at night you lie on your port-a-
ledge which is about two and a half feet wide and
about five and a half feet long and *this* becomes the
only medium between you and oblivion."

Land has always climbed (at least until his
revelation to me that's he quit now). One summer
before our junior year, he suckered me into going
on a belay climb with him which left me with a near
death experience. A belay is basically a two person
pulley system where one guy leads up with a rope
while the other guy provides slack or is "off-belay"
or then braces the lead guy by going "on-belay" and
stopping more rope from being released. Land gave
me a crash course in this system at seven in the
morning while we were at the base of a jumbo-sized
rock that was in some national park in upstate New
York. Land started going up a crack system in the
rock, then went on-belay while I climbed up behind
him. Little did I know there was a roof blocking my
route. This roof loomed over my head and I
couldn't get around it. I had no technique. I tried to
smear myself over it. No dice. I then made a lunge
at a handhold and slipped but since Land had gone
off-belay I took a free fall of about ten feet but

which felt more like *one hundred feet*. I freaked out as I dangled above the ground like a puppet in Land's hands. Land, that bastard, was laughing his ass off and that was the only time I can say that I seriously was pissed at him and chewed him out for not being more vigilant with a novice climber like me.

"After Yosemite, I really just trekked around the country as my basic aim was going back east to Pennsylvania to see my folks. I drove through Reno then went out in the boonies as I passed Elko, Nevada. Nothing there, man. Cruised through Denver and went southeast to Kansas City. Headed up the Mississippi to Chicago—have some friends there—then went through Cleveland, Buffalo and came back to Buttfuck. I hung out with the folks for a couple of months and then went to the City. I stayed in Hoboken with Chazz. Remember him?"

"Sure, yeah. What's he up to?"

"The guy lives right around the corner from where Sinatra was born. He works at a consulting job. I think with Goldman Sachs. He used to live in Manhattan with Jeremy."

"Did Jer go to work for Goldman Sachs right after graduation as well?"

"No. He took an offer to trade for Lehman Bros. Pulled in 250 Gs in his first year."

"Jesus."

"Right. But, the fucker became an asshole. Chazz had enough after the first year and split to Hoboken. He told me that Jer wouldn't even have the decency to keep a six-pack in the fridge for when friends would come over. What kind of asshole doesn't even provide some brews for his friends when they come over?"

"Yeah, that's not right."

"It's criminal, man. Especially when the guy's getting a quarter mil a year."

More success stories it seems. Not what I really want to hear, but I let on that I'm happy that our former cohorts have now gone ahead to enjoy such profitable careers. I've lost touch with most of them so it's all new information to me. But, Jer was always a fuckin' miser even before pulling in the quarter mil. The cat always held back which during the communal days of college was a big no-no. None of us really worked at the time. My part-time gig at the bookstore was for some extra beer money and that's where it ended. Fashion was kept to a bare minimum. Some solid black boots, a pair of Levi's and a big trench coat. That's all you needed, and when you went out to eat or drink it was usually with a big group where everyone chipped in for a round or a pitcher or another order of wings or another pie. No big deal. But, to be out of that world and into another one after only three years where you're now pulling in a quarter of a million dollars is too incredible for me to fathom. What the fuck would I possibly do with that? Insane. I can't comprehend it at all. Keep some sixers in the fridge at least when you have your friends coming over. That's common decency and courtesy. Fuck. That lucky motherfucker! He's on easy street. But, still what do you *do*? Or what are you *supposed to* do with that kind of cash? Put it away somewhere, buy everything you want or lavish it upon women who live for such lavishment. Jer—now Jeremy H. Mills soon to be millionaire.

"And get this, man," Land continues. "At the rate he's going, he'll be able to retire by twenty-nine." Great. Before jealousy completely destroys me, I manage to think of another mutual friend. A friend who I hope to God is also fucking up his life, so I'm not alone.

"Hey, whatever happened to Jeeves?" I ask Land, thinking that Land probably has kept in contact with Jeeves as well.

"Second year at Wharton."

"Where?"

"Business school at Penn."

"Good for him," I cringe.

This cat was famous for sucking down a two-liter bottle filled with urine after losing a bet. He never puked.

"Yup. Good for him." Land says.

A lot of our friends from college had good heads on their shoulders. If they didn't they would have never been accepted in the first place. But, how could they all be so confidently pursuing such big dollar sign careers in only three and a half years? What meeting did I miss out on? Like I explained, I studied philosophy and the other courses I took were in one way or another about art, history and books. And I passed on grad school. What did that leave me with? Just my own personal desire to make something out of myself. I dropped the writing dream for the more pragmatic one of becoming a talent agent. Why? I could *see* myself doing it. I was good at putting things together be they deals or words or people. I liked the glamour of the business as well. But, my personality just wasn't cut out for the long period of supplication one had to endure in order to climb up the ranks. I cashed in my chips and now here I am.

III

We split the bill which is incredibly
reasonable given the delights we have just
vacuumed down. The food hits the spot big time
and warms and lifts up my spirits. The restaurant is
still in the throes of chaos so Land and I carefully
make our way to the exit. We stumble back into the
Quarter which is roaring.

"Where did you say you were staying again?" I ask
Land.

"Didn't I tell you?"

I shake my head no.

"I'm crashing at Genny's pad."

"Who? You talking about Gen with a G?"

"Yeah, man. She lives in N'Awlins."

"What is she doing down here?" I ask incredulous
at the idea that another classmate who I hadn't seen
since graduation could possibly be here too.

"She went to law school at Tulane. Graduated last
year and went back to New York to take the Bar last
July. She got the results back this November.
Didn't pass, bra. But, she sees it as a blessing and
since she loved living here so much, she moved
back and got lucky with a decent apartment on
Dauphine. It's just around the corner from here."

Oh, shit. I hadn't seen much of Gen during
the final two years of school. But, I saw enough of
her to fuck her one stony night during our freshman
year. It was before Land really even knew her. A
bunch of us went up to Syracuse to see Dylan in
concert. When we got back, I busted out my git and
played some songs. It was a good time. As we
entered into the wee hours of that morning, most of
the group had slipped away. But, there was Gen

sitting Indian-style on the floor in front of me with those ga-ga, blue-green eyes of hers. I knew I was in. I put my guitar down. My voice was hoarse and she said that I sang well. I acted humbly about my guitar playing and singing and said it took a lot out of me to play for that long but it was worth it to share good tunes with friends. That sealed it.

The one thing I remembered clearly about that night was that I was so aware of the notion of how women love the *idea* of being in love. When Gen and I were just laying on my bed with our hands on each others' faces and not saying a word to one another, she finally opened her mouth and said, "*I love you.*" My only reply was a terse, "*Yeah.*" I know that's a pathetic scene, but the reason why I couldn't even respond properly to her was because I was grinning ear-to-ear inside at the fact that I had gotten laid and so I had momentarily lost my command of basic English. I was reduced to the Neanderthal. But, it dawned on me later that she didn't know the first thing about me except through whatever image she had created in her mind as to who I was or what I represented. And there she was telling me that she loved me! We were incredibly stoned both during the concert and afterwards and I don't remember if she had done a hit of X that night, but even if she had, her words to me were still about loving the idea of being in love. What she wanted to really say that night was "I *love* love," but it came out "I love you" because that was what she was socialized to say. I'm sure she does not even remember uttering those words to me, but she did, and my macho reaction probably made her nauseous when she thought of what she had done the next day.

Anyway, we had one shared time and the next time I saw her, she and Land had become good friends. I had no idea how they met since Gen lived in a dorm on the other side of campus and I never introduced them, but it happened. I never told Land about Gen and I and didn't plan to. She was just a bird who now had a friend in common with me, and that's how I treated her—as a friend of Land's. She never appealed to the sober me and our night together had slipped into the far recesses of both our memories. I know she went on to major in Women's Studies and was active on political issues on campus. She loved the Kennedys. Land told me she was so distraught after Jackie O.'s death that she had holed up in her apartment and blew off all her courses for a week. I even told Land to express my condolences to her. I also once saw her sitting under an elm tree on the main quad of campus reading a book entitled, *The Fitzgeralds and The Kennedys*. She was so imbued in the book that she never saw me coming until I was standing directly over her and blocking her sunlight. The book was enormous. She waved it in front of me and showed me the incredible binding of the book that was responsible for holding over nine hundred pages together. I asked if she was reading it in connection with a class and she replied that it was just for personal reading. Another time, I saw her face on the front page of the school paper and underneath it was a Kennedy-esque caption attributed to her that stated, "We need to demystify feminism." She had chaired a big symposium that semester on "The New Feminine Mystique." I actually tried to go because I was curious to see Gen's transformation from stoned groupie to a Steinem-esque leader. The problem was that the event started at 9:30 in the

morning on a Saturday in February. Stupid. When I
first got up and looked outside, I was relieved to see
that it was sunny out. However, once I turned on
my radio and the local radio station mentioned that
the high for that day was *zero* degrees, I thought
better of going and retreated back into bed. Land
would fill me in on the symposium later.

"You should come by and say hi," Land says.
"Uh, yeah. I haven't seen or talked to her since
graduation. Lead the way."
        We walk up Iberville and hang a right on
Dauphine. Gen's apartment is just past Dumaine.
It is in the heart of the Quarter! How did that freaky
bird land this dig? We walk up to the second floor
and Land uses a key to let us in.
"Did Gen come out with you today?" I ask Land.
"Yeah. But, we got separated in the madness. We
were supposed to meet back here at around four
o'clock anyway."
"Well, it's only around 3:30 now." Maybe she's
not back yet, I hope.
        I close the door behind me and take in Gen's
place. There are lots of candles and black and white
photos of relationships on the walls. A coffee table
with issues of Cosmo, High Times, and Life. A shit
load of CDs are laid out on the shelves in the back
wall of her living room. As is my practice, I check
out the selection of music she has stocked. It tells
me a lot about the person. I scan everything from
Sara McLaughlin to the Buena Vista Social Club to
The Platters. A nice variety of tunes. I look for
some Bob Dylan CDs just as some kind of
connection to myself.

"Land? Are you back?"

Gen enters from her bedroom which is tucked behind the kitchen area.

"I just got in. You're never gonna believe what lowlife I found loitering around the Quarter!!"

I come into view.

"Gen!! How the hell are you!!" I try to act as excited as possible.

"Tal?!?!" Gen says and her eyes open wide. "What are you doing here??!!"

We don't hug hard. There's an unmistakable *j'e ne sais qua* about running into someone in whom you were once inside—years later—when you least expect it. It's as if you have to disavow any carnal knowledge and meet like it's for the first time. But, the past is right there and still simmering—at least in my mind. You have no choice but to act gallantly in order to snuff it out.

"Hey stranger. I came down for a respite from my unproductive life out in L.A. Just digging the scene here, the food, all the crazy cats running around. Land says you couldn't bare to leave this town behind." I ramble.

"Yeah, well, the legal career in the City didn't work out."

"Sorry to hear that," I say.

"No, it's all right. Things happen for a reason. I loved it here during law school and could see myself doing things I was really interested in if I'd come back."

"So, what are you doing now? Stripping?" So much for being a gentleman.

Gen shoots me a mock look of shock. I smile back. But, she knows that in this town my kidding is more than half serious.

"No, you ass. I work as an assistant to the curator of the New Orleans Vodou Heritage Museum."

"You're joking!"

"No, I'm not."

I try to register this. Gen, who loved the Kennedys and loved politics and went to law school works in a vodou museum?

"You went fr-fr-from law-yerrr to-to a-a-a vooooo-dou apprentice?" I sound like an idiot as I trip over my words.

"I do research, help set up new exhibits, give talks at schools and lead small tour groups. This town was borne out of the practice vodou by the slaves. People are curious about it, Tal! It lures all types of people here and we do a lot of business by selling dolls, spells, amulets, talismans, mink penises, gator feet—the usual."

I look to Land to see if Gen is playing me. He nods his head in acknowledgment of the truth of what Gen has said.

"Alright. O.K." I say as I take a seat on the couch in the living room area. "Let me get this straight. Could any of us ever have imagined this? You, me and Land—once three promising Ivy League grads. Fast forward three and a half years. Now, one cat moves from dead end job to dead end job and is unemployed as of this moment. The other cat climbs rocks, lives among wolves, goes to the rez and now, he, uh—what do you do now Land?"

"I dig ditches."

"I believe it. And Gen flunks the Bar and now helps put together exhibits and sells animal parts in New Orleans. Great. So, this is something that you really wanted to do, huh?"

"The road is long, Tal. There's no rhyme or reason

to it, bra. Either deal with the curves and hazards or pull over and kill the engine, man." Land tells me.

"Don't get me wrong, Land. I think it's funny. It's a sort of freedom, isn't it? Us three and our situations?"

"Well, man—" Land starts off, but Gen cuts him off fast.

"—so, Tal, who did you come down here with?" A nice change of subject.

"I was with a couple of cousins. They went back last night, but I had to stay for tonight's culmination. I'm staying at a motel on Lafayette. Land found me on Bourbon." I take a second to think about my day so far. "What a small world," I wonder aloud.

"Yeah, that it is. There's nothing like coincidence, huh?" And Land looks at me and then Gen. "I'm gonna use the little boy's room," he says as he walks away. This leaves Gen and I alone and she hits me with this look that smacks of awkwardness. I gotta dwell in the silence. I think fast for something to say.

"When, uh, when did Land arrive?" I ask.

"Ummmm, about a couple of days ago. He, uh, he took a train down from New York."

I don't pay attention to Gen's hesitation in answering the question. It has been a long time since we have talked to one another.

"A train? That must have taken a couple of days."

"A couple."

"Have you two seen a lot of each other since graduation?"

"Mmmm. Not really. We talked on the phone a bunch. But, I didn't see him until this summer when I was studying for the Bar in the City. Even then I saw him only a couple of times because I was too busy studying."

"It must have been hard."

"What??"

"—studying for the Bar."

"Yes."

"What did you do afterwards?"

"Ummm, after the Bar which was in late in July, I took a job working as a junior attorney in the DA's office in Brooklyn."

"What was Land up to? Causing trouble as usual?"

"No. Be nice."

"Gen, you know I'm only kidding!"

"Sure. Land—he, uh, bounced around from Chazz's place in Hoboken to his parent's place in Pennsylvania. He then got a job in the City."

"Oh, yeah?? Doing what?"

"Uh, I think it was in some public relations company. Anyway, when I found out I didn't pass, Land was the first person that I told since we were in contact and he was working close by in the City."

"Must have been a tough time."

"I was pretty depressed. But, Land helped convince me to move back here and I just did it."

"When did you come back?"

"Middle of December. Land kept saying Mardi Gras fell on February 16 this year and he promised to visit me then."

"Well, you certainly scored a nice dig here. Smack in the Quarter! Must make some good bread at the museum."

The toilet flushes and Land comes back in the room.

"How's this lovefest going?!?!"

I freeze. It dawns on me that I probably never told Land about Gen and I. Not that he would care. But, it would be odd that as close as he and I were I never made some type of comment about it.

"So, I hear you masterminded Gen's move back to N'Awlins." I try to draw Land into the conversation.

Land flashes a glance at Gen.

"You know—after the Bar results came in—you guided me back here." Gen explains.

"Oh, yeah. Yeah, I was telling her to take time off. Go back to a place she dug and not force herself into restudying for the Bar so soon. And now look, here the three of us are with Mardi Gras raging around us!"

Random shit like this sometimes just happens. It is strange that the three of us are here now at this time in our lives—each of us with our own unique baggage. But, I cannot partake in this coincidence for much longer as this day's exploits have finally caught up and beat me. I am about to pass out. I ask Gen if I can crash for a bit somewhere in her place. She says of course and tells me to crash in her bedroom. I thank her and tell them to wake me up if I don't get up voluntarily in a few hours. I make a beeline for the bedroom, kick off my shoes and take off my shirt and watch and flop on the bed. Gen's alarm clock reads 4:17 p.m. My lids are heavy and I can feel a deep sleep taking control of my body. Outside the bedroom, I can hear Gen and Land speaking in hushed tones, but my mind fades out on beads and breasts and I am gone.

This city, arched in the form of a crescent upon the banks of the Mississippi, exudes history. By sleeping in the Quarter, one melds into that history. It's as if I'm cradled in the bosom of the city which heaves in syncopation with the manic activity of Mardi Gras. I sleep hard and long and have scenes in my mind of being masked and riding on a giant dragon float. I throw out beads and doubloons on those below me. I see two drop-dead gorgeous women, one sitting on the others' shoulders, both with their tops off. I rush to throw them beads only to find that everyone else on my float also pushes their way to join me and our float gets so heavy on the side that I am standing on, that the entire float tips over throwing us onto the street and hysteria erupts. I then jump out of Gen's bed. I'm O.K. Some instinct in me suddenly snapped me awake. I look at the clock which reads 10:03 p.m. Panic. Two hours left in Mardi Gras and I race to put on my shoes, shirt and watch. I stomp out of the bedroom and into the living room and rub the sleep glue out of my eyes. The room is lit with dozens of candles and Land and Gen are on the couch watching TV.

"Hey, why didn't you guys wake me up?"

"We came in around eight, but you were out, man. We went out and got a bite to eat. There's some red beans and rice for you in the fridge," Land says.

"I'm cool. Thanks. I guess I really crashed out."

"We could hear your snoring," Gen says.

"Sorry about that."

Gen and Land still have their eyes fixated on the TV screen. I am curious to see what they are so interested in watching, so I go over and take a chair near the couch they are sitting on and figure out what they are watching. It is *Last Tango in Paris*. And then get this, the scene that I have walked in on is where the Brando character asks the French bird to cut two of her fingernails and to then sodomize him with the newly clipped digits. Yeah. Don't bother asking what this means.

"I still can't believe she kills him," I mutter aloud. Land suddenly turns to me with disbelief in his eyes.

"You fucker!! We haven't seen this before. You just ruined it for us!" He doesn't shout at me, but he is angry.

"Relax, Land. This film is full of climaxes. Don't lose the forest for the trees. Just keep following the dialogue. You'll be fine. I haven't ruined anything," I explain myself.

Land waves me off and returns back to the film. Gen is silent and buried in the film. We watch in silence for about ten more minutes, but I can't sit still. It's pushing 10:30 p.m. As exciting as it is to run into Land, and even to see Gen after so long, I haven't come all this way to New Orleans only to *miss* the orgiastic climax of Mardi Gras.

"Look's like I better get my ass streetside. There's less than two hours of Mardi Gras left. You guys going out??" I ask while I get up and dramatically stretch my arms out.

"Shit!! I completely forgot. Let me grab some brews and a jacket," Land says. He gets up and heads to Gen's room.

"You coming Gen??" I ask.

"Yeah," She stops the film and gets up without another word.

She goes to her room just as Land is coming out and the two make eye contact in a way which I can tell means something more. Land goes to the fridge and grabs some beer. He comes back into the TV area and hands me a bottle. I thank him and soon Gen comes out with a coat and we leave her apartment and are outside on Dauphine. We can hear the wail of the frenzy of Bourbon which spills all over the Quarter. Land gives a beer to Gen and she takes a couple of big swigs. As we turn onto Dumaine and near Bourbon, a massive sea of humanity appears. Swells of bodies pushing upon other bodies packed ten to fifteen bodies deep. There is no more Rue Bourbon. Instead, it has become one large river of flesh. The sheer amount of persons per square inch is mind-boggling. Land, Gen and I are quickly in the thick of it and we hear a group of cute Southern birds saying, "Y'all— We're gonna get molested in here!" I look at Land and laugh at this and he winks at me. Gen isn't as happy about our predicament. We can't take more than three steps in any direction because bodies are braced against other bodies and the bodies only move when a sudden wave of bodies manages to push all the bodies in one direction and then you can flow along with this push. I glance around and see all these birds trying to protect themselves from being groped by lassoing one hand around their breasts and another behind their asses in a feeble attempt to ward off would-be opportunists. It's as if Gen can read my mind because soon she is yelling over all the voices around us mumbling something about *chikans*.

"What the hell did you say?!?" I ask her.

"I said this is chikan heaven!!" She tells me again.

"What is a cheekan?!?" I ask her again.

"In Japan—they call gropers *chikans*. Women now have to ride in same sex only subway trains because there was such a big problem with chikans groping them during the morning and rush hour commutes."

"Leave it to Gen to introduce the concept of chikans while we try to enjoy Mardi Gras!" Land says.

Gen laughs. I try to push my way down Bourbon, but have nowhere to go. I turn back around to face Land and Gen.

"I'd like to pull some chikan tactics on that bird over there," I motion toward this tight-jean wearing blonde that I can only see from behind.

"Well, you'd love Japan. They have places for guys like you. The sex clubs there have gone so far as to build replicas of subways cars and a guy pays like 30 yen to grope a woman who is dressed up in business attire so it's as if the guy is doing it in public."

"Are you serious??" I ask.

"Yeah, I did this paper years ago on sexual subordination of women in Japan. Talked about chikans—hentai animation—"

"—Alright, go Tal!!" Land pushes me ahead. He is right to do so, a big hole just opened behind me and bodies behind Land are thrusting him forward. If I don't move ahead, I will be trampled on. So, I make a quick move with Gen and Land following right behind me. We get about ten feet before we hit a stonewall of people—mostly male—whose faces are fixed at the balcony above us and the quid pro quo of beads for breasts is in full effect. I temporarily pry my eyes from the flimsy nineteenth century balconies positioned all around and above us and look back at Gen.

"I gotta admit you always have something new."

"What do you mean??"

"Chikans?? That's great—what a concept!! You actually wrote a paper on it!!"

My words come out patronizingly although I definitely did not intend them to. I genuinely dig the new info. It's interesting shit.

"Tal—one of the biggest selling books in Japan in the last five years was a book called *Confessions of a Chikan*. It was, basically, one chikan's testimony of years of groping unknowing, helpless Japanese women."

"That's great—," I yell. Land cracks up. Gen punches me on the shoulder. "—I don't mean the groping is great—just the fact some guy actually took time to document his obsession and then people found it interesting. It tells a lot about the society!"

This is too much. Land takes the lead now—as if to demonstrate that Gen and I have dropped the ball on our plans to have fun. It gives me a chance to just follow Land and not worry about being the person trying to find the holes in the bodies. I look up again at the balconies. These cats and birds with beads dangling from their necks and fingers and shouting out at those of below asking us to do this and that in order to score these beads. I then look at a bunch of purple-haired and black leather clad kids propped up on one another against a wall. They are ogling the bodies not out of sexual interest, but instead are looking for those weak in the herd so that they can target them for a quick pick-pocketing. These kids, I feel for them. I read an article in the Times-Picayune the other day about these kids and how the city of New Orleans was trying to get them all out of the Quarter before Mardi Gras got into full gear. The article called them "gutterpunks"—teenage vagabonds from all over the U.S. who congregated in New Orleans for each Mardi Gras because of the opportunity to get easy money, food, etc. These kids look they are now planning a hostile take over in retaliation for the deportation of their friends who the Crescent

City police have already rounded up and bussed out of the city limits. Land keeps pushing ahead. A bunch of guys get in between Gen and Land and they ask Gen to show her tits. Gen refuses and pushes ahead. I shake my head. She has nice C cups. This is Mardi Gras and the beads she were offered were of top quality. I think she is lame for not obliging. As she walks ahead of me, I get to check out her body. It's not bad, but she just doesn't know how to dress and that earth mother shit just doesn't do it for me anymore. Gen then comes to a stand still and I almost plow into her from behind. She puts her hands over her eyes and points to Land. I look over. There's Land. Birds on the balcony above have somehow singled him out and he has now dropped his pants and with penis in hand he wiggles his goods to the delight of the birds above. Some phat beads drop out of the sky and Land quickly dons them. His eyes are luminous in triumph. He screams at me because he has one-upped me for all the ages. I don't see any way of possibly topping him. I'm not gonna drop trou and copy him—that's a loser move. He has trumped me this time round. I slam down the rest of my beer in acknowledgment of his feat. Pandemonium.

Through empty cups, puke, piss, beads, and more plastic, we continue the push down Bourbon. We go past huge religious placards held up by the gutsiest men that I have ever seen. The placards tell us we are in Sodom and these guys wield megaphones through which they preach the words of the gospel to us. What dedication!! They are insane! Sure enough, one cat in our already punched ticket-to-hell crowd gets everyone to join in a chant of "Fuck the preachers" and the religious zealots are drowned out by voices coming from all around and above them. It's a lost battle. The megaphones are dwarfed by the enormity of the chanting. Land, Gen and I continue passing through the madness. We've all become adept at this point in looking for those sudden holes that appear when a mass of bodies shifts in unison to one side or the other. The bodies are so tightly woven with one another that it is suffocating. I wonder what would happen if no holes ever opened up. It would be like those soccer games in Europe—we'd all get crushed and die. Thankfully, holes continue to appear and when a big one opens, Land makes a violent lunge and Gen and I follow quickly on his heels. When we emerge on the other side we come out directly in front of these three cats with flower pots on their heads. In these pots, cannabis grows and on their shirtless torsos the words "Pot Heads" are scrawled in black magic marker. The experience is like making contact with extraterrestrials who are interacting with the blob of revelers as if on an advanced level of consciousness. They look at us as if we are peons. We have all been drinking non-stop and the beer that Land brought for us is finished. We pile into a daquiri stand and order three foot and a half plastic tubes of imaginatively named rum and fruit juice combinations. We get blasted and again become one with the mob. Midnight falls.

Out of the blue, a large squadron of New Orleans' finest complete with squad cars, street sweepers, and tank-like vehicles claim the western end of Bourbon and begin pushing east. Cups and beads get crushed and a disembodied voice tells everyone:

Mardi Gras is now over. Please evacuate the street.

Once people realize what is going on, the sea of humanity miraculously parts and we all scramble for footholds along the sparse sidewalk space of Bourbon. People throw beads on the squad cars and yell out obscenities at the cops or pretend to cheer them on. Gen, Land, and I are squished along the wall of a souvenir shop and this huge street sweeper creeps by us—spraying all the shit it chews up onto the sides of the streets. What killjoys I think to myself. Do they really have to make such a concerted effort to *clean* at the exact moment Mardi Gras day ends??

While I grapple with this, I don't notice Land moving away from Gen and I. He then makes a break. I don't believe what I'm seeing. The crazy motherfucker runs into middle of the street and stands in front of the street sweeper. He puts his right hand out signaling the vehicle to stop. The scene reminds of me that ballsy Chinese cat who stood in front of that People's Republic army tank in Tiananmen Square. But, this sweeper has no where to swerve and doesn't show any signs of stopping. Some unexplainable force then sends a jolt through my body, and the next thing I know, I am running out to the street and tackling Land out of the sweeper's path. The adrenaline pumping through me is so hard and fast that I think my heart is going to rip out of my rib cage. I don't have a chance to pick myself up or say anything because ten cops have stormed down over Land and I. "What kind of stunt are you trying to pull?" One of the cops yells at us.

"Are you two boys stupid?" Another cop tells at us.

I am too shell-shocked to respond. I look over to Land hoping he has an answer. But, he mumbles some bullshit about trying to cap off the last Mardi Gras of the Twentieth Century with eleven o'clock news memorability.

"You are lucky that the parish jail is full tonight, otherwise you'd both be arrested and spend your Mardi Gras there. Wouldn't that be a nice capper for your night?"

No response. The officer then tells me to watch Land and to keep him out of anymore trouble. I say whatever the officer wants to hear. I am amazed and relieved that we are not cuffed and hauled off in some paddywagon to jail. It really is a miracle that we are getting off so lightly.

When the cops have left and are out of earshot, I grab Land and yell at him, "What the fuck were you thinking!!"

Land doesn't answer me. He points toward Gen who is still standing on the other side of Bourbon and wears a blank stare. She can't cross while the police are still mowing through.

"Hey, man. What was that bullshit you just pulled??" I ask him again.

Land thinks for a moment and then responds.

"I don't know. I just wanted to see what would happen."

"I don't dig that shit. Trying to cause a scene just for the sake of causing a scene?"

"Yeah?"

"Yeah. What the fuck is that about? There's no substance there, man."

"There's more to it than that, bra—"

Some asshole gets in between Land and I.

"That was awesome, man. I got it all on my digital camera!! I'm gonna post it online on this website…" And he recites some unintelligible web address.

"Right on!" Land says. "Hey, Tal you got that website address?"

"Fuck off, man."

The cat with the camera looks confused, but he shakes it off.

"Hey, what the hell made you do it?" He asks Land.

"I wanted to send a message. No one tells us when to break up our party, man!!" Land tells him.

"Yeah, man!! Well, take care. Don't forget to check out my site!!" The asshole waves goodbye to Land and I and walks back to his friends.

I get to my feet and look over to Gen who is now as white as a ghost. Land smiles at Gen and gives her a thumbs-up sign as he gets to his feet. I don't say anything to Land. Instead, I try to calm down and relax. I wonder what would have happened if I had not tackled Land out of the way. I am sure the driver of the sweeper would have stopped, but there was no way of telling. It looked to me that Land was playing chicken and he wouldn't have flinched unless I had thrown him out of the way. That's how stupidly stubborn he could be.

A few minutes later, the last police group finally passes through and Gen can cross over.

"Land? Are you crazy?? Were you trying to get yourself killed??"

Gen physically pushes Land for an explanation.

"Easy, Gen. Come on now. You know me. I don't do things without having a good reason."

"What's the reason?!?" Gen snaps back.

Land steps back onto Bourbon, which is slowly emptying out.

"Simple, Gen. It was a reminder."

"A reminder of what!!" Gen yells at Land.

"A reminder that I still call the shots. I caused myself to go out there. I need to remind myself from time to time that I don't have to go through the motions like others. I can actively change whatever present external forces are being foisted on me."

This is the first time where I really feel that Land's thinking is askew. No question I embrace his carpe diem philosophy just as much as he does or least I used to, but willingly causing yourself to break from a social pressure in order to remind yourself of your own free will is nonsense.

"I hear your need to do your own shit. But, why risk your life by intentionally doing something you know is dangerous? You know what I mean. If you want to remind yourself that you are so in control of your life, why exert that control in a situation when you could get killed!" I tell Land.

"Addicted, bra. I'm addicted to that rush of being able to suddenly make a choice that matters big time—which severs me from the sad normalcy of just going through the motions. You know what I'm saying??"

"Not really, man."

"Sure you do, Tal. How did you feel when you ran out there and threw me out of the way??"

"I, uh, I felt like I was on fire."

"That's what I'm talking about, you—"

"—no, Land. It wasn't a positive feeling though. It sucked a lot of life out of me. I almost went into shock."

"That's cause you're not used to the rush like I am. I know how to handle that rush and I need that rush every once in a while to keep me honest. My biggest nightmare is being utterly absorbed into keeping banker's hours and having my life choreographed by something that I can't see or don't even realize is controlling me."

A little too out there for me and from looking at Gen's face she seems a bit lost too—or at least preoccupied by something else. Land starts walking back onto Bourbon while Gen and I stand still on the sidewalk trying to understand Land's antics. Mardi Gras is officially over and a few pockets of people are still hanging around Bourbon carrying on with the festivities. But, you can feel the energy being sucked out of the Quarter. It is seeping away in gradual increments, but the loss of energy is very palatable and sad.

"Why are you two so bummed?" Land asks Gen and I.

Neither Gen nor I respond. I feel strung out.

"Let's get this show on the road!! It's not even one in the morning yet!!" Land breaks into a tap dance routine to enliven our spirits.

I let out a chuckle.

"There you go, Tal!! There you go!!" He says as if I have reinforced him in some way.

"Dude, I'm not on the level. Just kinda feel sapped of any energy," I say.

"We don't have to stay on Bourbon. Let's go sit down somewhere and chill." Land studies our body language which is drooped and withdrawn. "Gen, what about that jazz club you were telling me about?"

Gen pretends not to hear.

"Gen??" Land says.

"The Absinthe," Gen says dejectedly.

"Yeah. Can't we check it out? Tal, what do you say, man?"

I am mindful of Gen and where she is coming from right now. She is not happy with Land. I don't want to force the issue of going out, if it means Gen has to then cut out and go home alone while Land and I go out. I say something non-committal.

"Is it nearby?? I don't think I have the energy to walk out to the Marigny for instance if it is located there. I still have to walk back to my motel which is on the other side of town."

"Gen??" Land asks.

"It's actually up on Rampart—a few blocks up from where we are now."

"Is there a cover??" I ask. Now, trying to find a way out.

"No cover—I think." Gen says.

I guess Gen wants to go, otherwise, she could have been put an end to things very easily.

"Alright!! Let's go," Land cheers.

We walk towards The Absinthe. Land is in control and Gen and I have no choice but to follow. Land goes on and on about absinthe being an illegal liquor in the U.S., but apparently, it is still a legal drink in Spain and Portugal and other parts of Europe. Gen and I mindlessly listen to Land's ramblings. We both understand Land is just trying to keep this night going and is hoping to get our minds off his stunt on Bourbon.

We reach The Absinthe in about fifteen minutes. It is a black-bricked dive, so you know it's gotta be good and it is. From the moment we walk in, this old woman is singing in that sad, vibrato of the old blues singers. We take a seat at a small round table and as I take off my jacket, the lyrics blow me away with their rawness and tell-it-like-it-is honesty. She's singing:

*The judge says listen Bessie tell me why you
killed your man.
I said judge you ain't no woman and you
can't understand.
You can send me up the river or send me to
that mean old jail.
I killed my man and I don't need no bail.*

"Gen, good call!! What a place! I really dig it," I
say as I come back to life.
"They always sing this song here. It's an old Bessie
Smith tune. It must be eighty years old, I think."
Gen says.
"Bessie Smith! Wow! This is like history coming to
life for me," I say.
"Yeah?" Gen asks.
"Yeah. I remember reading about how before there
was Billie Holiday, Sarah Vaughn, Carmen McRae
or Ella Fitzgerald, there were these two fat blues
singers that paved the way—Ma Rainey and Bessie
Smith."
"Whoa! I know Ma and Bessie ruled the day, but
don't forget the men—like Blind Willie Johnson,
Big Bill Broonzy and Robert Johnson. They were
the true origins of the blues and really paved the
way," Land replies.
"Here he goes, Gen!" I cut in.
"C'mon, Tal. Let's give props where due. It's just
that the male singers were marginalized and
emasculated. I think the black female blues or jazz
singer was an easier sell than the black male was.
The white promoters knew this. So, the male
bluesmen, they got short shrift." Land explains.
"You've been brushing up on this shit?" I ask
Land.

"I've picked it up here and there. You got to really *know* your history, man. But, this joint does rock, doesn't it!!" Land answers.

"There are lots of places like this in New Orleans. This was Louis Armstrong's birthplace," Gen says.

"Yeah. But old Satchmo got the fuck out of this country. He bailed out to Ghana—went into exile and died there à la W.E.B., dig?? Can you imagine how disgusted that cat must have been with all the racist shit he had to endure in order to just play trumpet and share his music with us?? I once saw this picture where a bunch of Ghanians were carrying Satchmo on a throne when he had just arrived there. The cat was all smiles!!" Land exclaims.

"He was always all smiles, Land," I say.

"That was just calculated P.R. on his part, bra. *Don't truss it*, like Public Enemy says."

"Can we enjoy the music, please?" Gen pleads. She seems on edge or nervous about something. Maybe she's getting it on with Land and I'm spoiling things. Who knows? I drop it.

We dig the music until 2:30 in the morning. We exit onto Rampart and I have the long walk back to my motel to worry about. I say goodnight and Land invites me to crash at Gen's. I decline. "My flight's not until eight at night tomorrow. We'll hang until then—if you're free." I tell them.

"Right on. When you check out, head over to Gen's. Cool?"

"O.K., man. See you then."

I say goodnight to Land and Gen and turn away to begin my trek back to my motel on Lafayette. It's a bitch of a walk. I walk fast. I pass Tulane Medical Center which is lit up in brilliant hues of red which come from the spinning lights of all the ambulances transporting the bodies of those in need of stomach pumping. I can hear the clinking of the beads of others who are also making the trip back to their lodgings. It all seems like a hejira of demented clowns spilling out of the Quarter and back to their regular lives. What a long, completely unpredicted day! I think of sleep and bumping into Land and Gen and the insanity of Bourbon and Land and I think of sleep again.

IV

 Check out is eleven in the morning. Tough to pull off, but I don't need to be charged an extra $140 special Mardi Gras rate for a normally $35 room. I shit, shower and shave, pack my bag and go down to the lobby to check out. I walk back to Gen's apartment with my bags. I figure the walk will help the alcohol in my system clear up even faster. Plus, I don't want to fork over $30 for a cab ride. It's close to noon when I get to Gen's.
"Anybody in??"
I've already knocked and no one has answered. I turn the doorknob and I'm not surprised to find it open. They probably left it unlocked for me and must be around the corner grabbing some food. The smell of incense and candle wax is all around. I put my bag down and turn on the TV. Something catches my attention on the mantle. I get up to take a closer look. It's some kind of antelope horn with a hole in the narrow end of the horn. I pick it up and examine it.
"It's a shofar."
I almost drop the thing while turning around. Gen and Land have returned.
"Pretty cool. What is it??" I ask Gen.
"It's called a *shofar*. It's a ram's horn. My grandfather gave it to me. You gotta blow it. The ancient Hebrews used to sound it before entering battle."
"Can I try it??" I ask.
"Sure. It might be dusty though."
I wipe off some of the dust and then blow. A fuzzy squawk comes out. Unbearable.
"A helluva call to arms, eh, Tal?" Land laughs.

I put the shofar back on the mantle.

"Where were you two?"

"I had to return the video by noon today," Gen says.

"Did you dig the film?" I ask.

"Tough to stay with. It's gonna take a while," she answers.

"What about you Land?"

"A piece of shit. A bunch of babbling. What the fuck was that line?? Oh, yeah. *Fuck the anarchists* or some bullshit like that as he's giving it to her up the ass."

"All righty—well, kids, what do we have in store for today?" I say as I abruptly switch gears into a new topic.

"You ever been to a plantation?"

"No, Gen. And I don't go for that *Gone with the Wind* romantic trip you'll probably lay on me." I curtly respond.

"Heheheh! Always so quick to judge, man. No worries. What about a trip out to the bayous?" Land asks us.

"Can we stay here in the city?" I plead.

"Of course, Tal, old buddy," Land replies.

"O.K., then. What about going to the cemeteries? I've been meaning to meander through St. Louis Cemetery No.1 and checking out Marie Laveau's tomb," I say.

"Also, Homer Adolphus Plessy is there." Gen says.

"Who?" Land and I both say.

"Plessy—the famous octaroon plaintiff in the Supreme Court case *Plessy v. Ferguson*."

"Never heard of it—have you, Land?"

"Yeah—the one where they came to the brilliant idea that people could be *separate but equal*?" Land answers.

"That's the baby!" Gen exclaims.

"So, he's at St. Louis Cemetery No.1 as well?" I ask.

Gen nods.

"Well, what are we waiting for? Let's go." I say with glee.

"A lot of people get mugged there. It's dangerous." Gen tells me.

"Gen, Gen!! It ain't dangerous when you got Land Morales and me at your back! Have you forgotten what a fearsome duo we make!"

"Funny, I don't remember you two as striking terror in the hearts of men."

"Well, then, here's your chance to see us in action—right, Land?"

But, Land doesn't seem enthused about going to St. Louis Cemetery No.1 either. He gives me a flat smile and throws out his own idea.

"I'm wild about getting a chance to see that vodou museum you work at, Gen. Tal, what do you think about us checking it out?"

"Uh, I'd love to see it—" I put on a happy face, but am deeply disappointed in Land not backing up my idea to go to St. Louis Cemetery No.1. "Are you sure the museum is open today, Gen?"

"It is, even though I have the day off. I can give you a tour through it. We're gonna have to take a street car there since it's close to Audobon Park."

"Cool," I say.

"Does *Desire* still run?" Land asks.

"I'm not sure. I've never been on it before. It may have been shut down—so, do you wanna go?" Gen asks.

"Yeah."

We leave the Quarter and head towards the corner of Canal and Carondelet where we wait for the St. Charles streetcar. When it pops up we jump on and pay the $1.25 fare which goes a long way. The streetcar heads south on Canal and then swings a right on St. Charles. We head west, passing under business route 90, past Martin Luther King Jr. Ave, past Jackson Ave, past the big homes of the Garden District and past Louisiana, Napoleon and Jefferson Avenues. I stare out the window and remember reading that the Garden District was created as a result of the newly arrived Americans who were not accepted by the French colonists who lived in the Quarter. The mass influx of these Americans occurred after Napoleon sold Louisiana to the U.S. All these Yanks came in and the French who had already been there for years didn't dig them and did not let them move into the Quarter. So, what did the Yanks do? Make their own version of the Quarter—except bigger, more elaborate and more exclusive. And now today, it's the Quarter which welcomes everyone with open arms while the Garden District remains quiet, aloof and untouchable.

We finally get to Audobon Park and drop off on a street called Natatorium. We walk a block up the street and there it is, The New Orleans Vodou Heritage Museum. Gen leads us in and she greets the lady who accepts donations at the entrance. Land and I are welcomed in and are immediately struck by a "Pe"—an altar with lithographs of Catholic saints and bottles and jars said to contain ancestral "gwo-bon-anjs," which literally means "big-good-angels." These are spirits of people which derive from Bondye, the Godhead. There's a lot of other shit too, like bells, crosses, baby dolls, books, a potted plant, coins and even Mardi Gras-esque beads. On even closer inspection of the altar,

I can see pennies, chicken feet, mummified snakes and gator hides draped around the bottles and jars that form the heart of the Pe. There's a small gift store to the left of the altar where I see gris-gris bags, ju ju beads, vodou stick dolls and mojo balls for sale. It's funny to me that I had by chance bought a seventy-five cent mojo ball earlier in the week while rummaging through a store called Marie Laveau's in the Quarter. I last remember clutching it while on the lightpost where Land had found me. I have no idea where it is now.

"Wow. I don't know what this means. But, just looking at this altar freaks me out, man." Land whispers to me. I concentrate on reading the factoid card placed on the wall near the altar.

"What you have to realize is that vodou is a mix of West African religion and Roman Catholicism. Most of the *lwas* or vodou deities are identified with Catholic saints," Gen begins.

"Give us some examples," Land says.

"O.K. There's Ezili which is the water goddess of love in vodou which is identified with the Virgin Mary. The god Damballah, which comes from Benin's python god, has been identified as St. Patrick—you know because of that story of the triumph of St. Patrick who beat a drum and drove out the snakes of Ireland. And then Legba, who is the guardian of destiny and holds the key to the doors of the underworld, he is identified with St. Peter."

"You know your shit, Gen. This is all new stuff for me. I feel like a school kid on a field trip. Carry on," Land says.

Gen takes us through the museum and she does know her shit. She even talks about the role of vodou in facilitating Haiti's independence from

Napoleon's France in 1804. Unbelievable story. How do a ragtag bunch of maroons take out *seventeen thousand* battle-tested French troops? The French have guns and ammo on their side and the maroons have zero—except their religion which freaks out the French so much so that they hightail it back to Paris in no time. Land and I pick up all kinds of crazy shit from Gen. Like the word "boa" which in English refers to pythons comes from the vodou term of the same name for Legba's penis. It's a symbolic shaft, identified with the central pole in the "peristil," which is a roofed structure supported by four poles where ceremonies take place. The central pole or "potomitan" functions as the major avenue to the sacred world and Legba controls the order in which the "lwas" appear in the possessed bodies of *Vodousiant* (the faithful) when they summon Legba to the peristil. Powerful stuff. We learn about zombies and zombification too, but it's not in the malarcky vein of *Night of the Living Dead*.

"Basically, a zombi is a soulless body. A person whose soul has been removed, whose body has been buried and raised again," Gen explains to us. "But, here is the interesting part. Other people then use the body—the zombi—for specific kinds of slave labor, like tending to garden plots, working in households or building houses."

"So, that's what a zombi really is?" Land asks.

"Yes. It's a soulless body who goes around doing the usual mundane tasks of life for somebody else and doesn't even realize it because—"

"—because he's already dead." I jump in.

"No—it's got nothing to do with death—it's about the soul. You gotta understand that while in Western religions death is viewed as a *period*, in

African religious thought, death is part of a continuing journey for the being. With a zombi, the soul has been removed and there is no death. The fact the soul has been removed is why the zombi is not in control of any of his actions and does the bidding of whoever controls him."

"Oh," I say.

"That's a helluva a way of looking at it," Land adds.

Gen continues with the tour and Land and I eagerly follow. Our heads swim in this fantastic, new history. Land and I just keep on digging the info Gen kicks our way. When we finish the tour, nearly two hours later, we thank Gen so much so that she blushes. We do go overboard in our laudatory remarks, but so what, she taught a couple of know-it-all schmucks a lot in only a couple of hours. We decide to grab some lunch. It's close to three in the afternoon. Only five hours until my plane jets.

We hop back on the St. Charles streetcar and head to the Quarter. We get off on Canal and on one of the side streets we find a restaurant called the Half-Shell. Good no-nonsense food and we enjoy the eats there. Land disappears for a few minutes after he finishes his food. He tells us that he wants to check out the bookstore across the street. Gen and I still have food on our plates and we tell him we'll stay at the table until he returns.

Gen looks good today. She definitely got dolled up and is wearing clinging clothes that accent her body in the right places. We each busy ourselves eating quietly.

"Soooo, Tal, any women in your life these days?" Gen asks me.

I have a mouthful of food and wait until swallowing before answering.

"Yeah. I've been seeing this bird on and off over the last year."

"Bird??"

I know Gen hates the word. But, I pay no attention.

"What can I say? L.A. is such a bizarre place. She's a stuntwoman."

"Stuntwoman? Good for her."

"Yeah, well, you should hear some of the shit I have to sit though when we're together. I'm sick of hanging around these birds who refer to themselves as actress-slash-model-slash-dancers."

"What does she tell you that's so vexing?"

"Just some of the shit, I mean—well, listen to this for example." I first shove some bread into my mouth and suck it down. "One night she comes over and I see that she has bits of brown paint or something on her hands and behind her ears. She's really fair-skinned. So, I ask her what's going on with the brown flakes on her body. I can tell she's stressed and she gives me this *look*."

"What *look* is that?"

"You know the look, Gen." And although I know Gen wants to get into a conversation about the significance of "the look" and what I read into it, I continue with the rest of the story with enough exaggerated animation to throw her mind off the deeper significance of what I interpret as "the look." "She tells me she was in the shower for the last hour scrubbing herself with turpentine because her hands, legs and face were painted brown for the last eight hours because of a scene she had to shoot." I shake my head in disgust of what I'm about to get into.

"Why are you shaking your head?" Gen asks as she tries to anticipate where I'm going.

"Gen, do you know what this is called?"

"What is what called?"

"The painting of a stuntperson or other body double for a scene that's gonna be filmed. Do you know the *industry* term for this?"

"I have no idea."

"A *paint down*!! That's what they call it. Crazy, huh?"

"Are you kidding??"

"No. Just hear me." And I take another spoon of food and swallow before continuing. "So, she's complaining because this is the third paint down she has had to do in as many days and it's a big drag to get all the shit off."

"Why do they need to paint down people?"

"Yeah, I ask her the same thing." I finish off my plate at this point. "She looks at me as if I'm an idiot..." I dab at the corners of my mouth with a napkin as I get ready to explain the intricacies of why paint downs are needed. "It's because there is such a lack of minority stunt people—Native American, Asian, Mexican or Black—that when a lead character is a minority and needs to be doubled for a stunt, they bring on whites or caucasians—whatever they call them—and have to paint them down in order to match the skin shade of the minority character they are doubling for."

"That is so weird."

I nod my head in agreement and take a drink of water.

"But, I guess a lot of those types of things must occur. I mean, not many minorities are involved as leads in the first place, right?" Gen asks me.

"Uh, right. It's actually illegal—these paint downs. It's against the union or something. But, all these producers still do it. Anyway, can you imagine having to relate to that kind of twisted experience day in and day out? I can only take so much of her at a time. Then, I gotta bail. She has no clue I'm out here. She's out on location in Montana, I think."

"I can see where you're coming from."

"Here's another one. Another night, we're just strolling down the sidewalk after dinner and are getting ready to cross the street. On the wall to our left, somebody had sprayed in bright, pink spray paint: *Gary Oldman is God*. She thinks this is some divine sign to her—"

Gen explodes in laughter.

"I'm serious!" But, I start laughing too.

"I'm sorry!!" Gen says as she tries to compose herself. "I don't mean to laugh!"

"She says he's her favorite actor and she's always dreamed of being in a movie with him and this is some kind of good omen. I tell her it's just some moron who's getting his jollies graffiting this shit. This ain't like the *Clapton is God* phenomenon. I mean that cat would get big with one group, break it all up, then comeback with another group and do it all over again. That was like being God—such creative prowess!! But, here my girlfriend is just latching onto some random graffiti and putting stock into it!"

"That is sooo funny!"

"The latest, Gen, is that she wants to now join the Church of Scientology to advance her career. That's a whole other can of worms I can get into, but forget about it."

I take a moment to pull myself away from my griping. I take another gulp of water and then decide to square up and ask Gen a question that has dogged me.

"What about you and Land?"

"What about me and Land?" Gen answers in a puzzled tone.

"Is that just a friendship or is it something more?"

"Come on, Tal. You know Land and I are just good friends. He's like having a crazy brother!"

"Hmmm. Interesting."

"What??"

"I've just never subscribed to that man and woman friendship jazz. A cat is only friends with a bird when he doesn't find her physically attractive."

"Get out. There are plenty of guy-girl friendships between attractive, straight and single people. And don't call us *birds*. I hate that pseudo-hipster crap you and Land like to dabble in so much."

I roll my eyes.

"In every one of those quote unquote friendships, there is one party secretly lusting after the other. They're shams—friendship is just a pretext. A means to an end," I reply.

"Tal, do you really believe that?"

"Of course. It's the truth—straight up."

"Well, you're wrong. Land and I are just good friends."

I smirk.

"I have returned!"

Gen and I both turn toward Land who has returned into the restaurant holding a blue plastic bag in his left hand.

"What did you buy?" I ask.

"Some maps." Land answers.

"Yeah?? Of where?"

"Mexico, Tejas."

"Really? Planning a trip?" I follow up.

"Possibly," Land glances at Gen. Then, he suddenly springs back to me, "Oh shit, Tal!"

"Yeah, man?"

"Your flight is getting close!"

I check the time. It has flown by.

"Better start heading back to Gen's, so I can get my bags." I say.

We all get up to leave. It's pushing 5 p.m. By the time we can back to Gen's, it's 5:30. The airport is about twenty-five minutes away on a good day and I should check in at least an hour before my departure time. That leaves only one final hour in New Orleans. I tell them I want to go to this Italian deli on Decatur to grab a muffuleta for the flight and also have a final cup of coffee and an order of beignets at Café DuMonde. Land says he will give me a lift to the airport.

Goodbyes are always bittersweet. But, saying goodbye to New Orleans is the worst. No other place replicates the magic. Sure, you can't copy NYC's kinetic madness, but it's just a concrete jungle. There's no mystery there. The mystery of New Orleans is what makes it so unique and so everlasting in your mind. I have no antidote to the symptoms of withdrawal that last for weeks after I leave New Orleans. It's horrible. I say goodbye to Gen and lie about wanting to stay in touch. Land throws my bags in the back of his Cherokee and we head out on I-10 and toward the airport.

The drive is quiet for the most part. I gaze at the dirty green flatness that surrounds me. Old warehouses and factories line both sides of the highway and when I turn around in my seat to take a last look, I see New Orleans shrinking. I turn back around and see Land merge toward the airport on ramp. I feel the dread of returning to the banality that awaits me in L.A. and I try to keep the bad feelings at bay by focusing on the good times of the last few days. Suddenly, Land pulls the car off to the side of the road.

"The fuck you doing, man? Taking back roads?" I ask bewildered by Land's action. Land puts the car in park.

"Relax…we're only about two miles from the airport." Land reaches into his pocket to grab a Camel light and lights it, pulling his driver side window down and leaning his left elbow out the door.

"You mind telling me what you're doing, Land?" Land rubs his chin takes a deep breath and begins.

"You ever ask yourself why the siesta did not get exported to the U.S." He asks me.

I flatline.

"Come again?" I ask bewildered.

"In this great industrial and technological trajectory of the U.S., why is it that the concept of the siesta got wiped out? And I don't necessarily mean the literal siesta like they have in Spain. More like just the notion that a man reaps what he sows by being able to step away from the sowing at his leisure. You catch my drift?"

"Not really. Hey, man—Land—I can give you my email address. You should write this shit down and email it to me. I'll be able to parse it then."

"Tal, can you just give me a couple of minutes, bra?"

"O.K.," I reluctantly say.

"There's no notion in American society that encourages a siesta ethic. And I mean the encouraging of spending quality time at rest. Idleness when done in the context of nourishing the soul is not a bad thing. The old Jeffersonian yeoman farmer would work hard for four months getting the harvest ready and then would take off four months in the winter reaping what he'd sown. There was a needed balance. One didn't have to break his back with worry and stress in the hopes of getting something more. He had what he had to have and that was enough."

Land pauses, takes a big drag and exhales out the window.

"There's no room for artistry in this place anymore. Creative minds either die or get lucky. There's nothing in between. You should understand what I mean."

I don't want to understand, so I throw in some bullshit to make it appear as if I'm responding to what he's saying.

"What about the Renaissance—the Enlightenment?? Artistry was at the fore. It drove the ideas that have pretty much made America what it is today," I phone this in.

"That will never happen again. In today's world, art has no place. It's been supplanted by instant gratification—by Starbucks and corporate artifice. That's what has survived. That's the legacy of what historians call the Enlightenment. It's the legacy of America. What a paradox!!" Land starts laughing.

"What??"

"Can you believe it, Tal? This paradox of the survival of the fittest which in socioeconomics has been the instantization of everything. Food, communication, sex. Anything. Every single thing that makes us human in the first place. The paradox is that the *mediocre* is the fittest. That's what has outlasted artistry in America."

"Land, why are you telling me this right now? What's really on your mind, man??"

"I'm trying to give you a backdrop for what I'm about to say."

Land sizes me up to see if I am ready for whatever it is he is about to lay on me.

"I told you about the fact that I found no community in America. It's just emptiness and I see it sucking people into this mindless choreographed existence. Go to work, pay your bills and die. It scared the hell outta me that I would have to be a part of that. I want to maximize my experience in this world. Expose myself to as much of it as possible. But, fuck I can't even get off the ground. I did stupid shit, like getting married. But, that t-shirt gig I started was a great time. It was something of mine which I was sharing with whoever looked at my designs. It didn't last though."

"Hey, it's not the end of the world, man. It was a great experience for you. To have your own business."

"Business?? Come on, man. It was a little stand off the Strip. I'm mired in my school loans and have not gotten any offers for jobs I dig. Instead, I get offers for jobs I can't stand. And then I realized that the thing that makes an economic system like ours work is to maintain control over people and make them do jobs they *hate*. I got desperate, man."

"When? After leaving Vegas?"

"Later—the second summer outta school. I tried to buckle down and still get myself into something.

Did some serious job hunting. I moved in with
Chazz—thought he'd be a good influence."
"What happened?"
"I got worse. I remember one morning getting up
and trying to pretend that I would hit the pavement
with resume in tow. I looked in the mirror—my
hair was graying!!"
"It happens, bra."
"I was getting no phone calls, no interviews. I just
got out of bed that morning and then took a *three
hour shower*, man." Land shakes his head.
"Three hours!! Come on."
Land nods and then in a soft, serious voice says,
"You know why??"
I shake my head no.
"Because that way I wouldn't be able to hear the
phone *not* ringing. Do you understand?"
I don't blink.
"I was seriously fucked in the head, Tal."
"I'm sorry, man." I don't know what else to say.
Silence ensues. I steal a glance at my watch being
careful Land doesn't see. I still have some time.
Land takes a couple of more drags until he finishes
his cigarette. He flicks the butt out the window and
stares straight ahead. I get ready to say something,
but he beats me to it.
"Tal, I'm on the lam, man."
I reel. I utterly forget what I was about to say. I stop
and take a second to register what he has just said.
"What?"
"I'm, I'm on the lam," Land says. This time he
faces me when he says it.
"Don't fuck around, man."
Land says nothing, which tells me he is serious.
"Please don't bullshit me after all this. That's not
cool. My flight's gonna leave."

Land breathes out heavily and runs both his hands back through his hair.

"I robbed a fuckin' bank. It was something I was moved to do, bra. The opportunity was there and the time was right. I was, I was…tired."

He looks at me for my response, but he gets nothing. I have a million thoughts flying through my mind. Flashbacks of other Land bombshells. But, nothing like this.

"Tal, man. Say something. I know it sounds like I fucked up."

"This time—this time you've really fucked up, man. That's it. I don't have anything else to say…" I try to cut off my words, but then something in me breaks and I go off on Land.

"You elitist fuck! Let me get this straight…you end up robbing a bank. With the hope that what?? You get to self-realize your need for a siesta or some bullshit like that?? The fuck, you shoulda just moved back with your folks until your mind settled down."

"Don't give me that shit, man. *Elitist fuck*??!! Where do you get off calling me that? I'm a goddamn humanist. I believe in that irreplaceable spark of humanity in all people. That's why I'm drawn to people from all walks of life."

"Land, shut up. You robbed a bank?"

"Yeah."

"Out of all the obvious things. Incredible. What—with a gun too?? I just can't believe this shit."

"It was this bank in Pennsylvania. I've known about it for years. I even had a friend who had worked as a teller there years ago. I planned it all out. No worries. I, uh, I did use a small glock—something I bought in the City. But, it had no bullets. You know I can't stand fuckin' guns, man."

"Oh, really?" I sarcastically answer.

"Cut me some slack, bra. There…there was only about nine people in the bank when I went. It was close to closing. I had them all get on the ground and sing the *Star-Spangled Banner* in unison. Hahaha!!"

"Yeah, man, real funny." I give Land a look of contempt. I can't believe he's trying to make light of the situation he is in.

"It was a crazy scene. No one knew the words after halfway through the song!! It was kinda funny in a twisted way. These cats sprawled on the ground, being held up at a bank and stumbling through the national anthem!"

Land starts laughing hysterically. It scares me. I'm shocked by his quick change in emotion. Just five minutes ago he was telling me about the terrible funk he was in and now he's laughing like everything's all roses. I can't believe it.

"I had the teller stuff whatever cash she had available and grab anything in the nearest vault to her. I was outta there within five minutes. A rush, man. I thought I was gonna pass out."

"Shit," I manage to say. "God, what the fuck are you gonna do?"

"I got some plans."

"Some plans? Land, this is serious."

"I know, I know. I've got things figured out though—you know me."

"Yeah, that's what I'm worried about."

"Well, don't worry, bra. Things are under control. I just wanted to let you in. After all, you and I have been through some times." Land starts the engine, but doesn't pull back onto the road, yet. He lets the car run.

"Not like this, Land. We just clowned around in college—nothing like this, man."

"Right."

"You really did it, huh?" I ask Land again.

"Yeah."

"I-I-I'm stunned, man."

Land switches on his turn indicator and looks out his window waiting for cars to pass.

I try to ground myself. O.K. Land tells me has robbed a bank. He justifies this in his own metaphysical nonsense which sounds compelling to the unsuspecting. This leads me to ask a final question.

"Does, uh, does Gen know??"

Land doesn't immediately answer. He waits until a van passes and he gets back on the road to the airport. I think maybe he hasn't heard me.

"Land??"

"Tal, Gen was in on it."

Part Two

I

Like some stoner Nick Carroway, I had observed Land's antics in college. Most times I would join in and partake in the lunacy. I egged him on and he would run with it, but I knew I couldn't keep up with his furious drive in pushing things to the extreme. Watching Land in action was like the rest of The Doors watching Jim Morrison spiral out of control. You go along with the ride at first and then you think about stepping in and doing something, but it's pointless. There's nothing you can do. At the end of the day Land would get his way and do whatever it was he wanted to do and he could justify whatever it was that he planned to do in ways that most people bought and the results of his action would be either ingenius or disastrous. There was no in between. The reasons for all his actions made sense or seemed grounded in a deeper mode of thought.

Part of the reason why I didn't put more of an effort into maintaining contact with Land after school was that I knew I was particularly susceptible to getting sucked into his laissez-faire approach to life, and the other reason was that I *did* want to take part in the game. Land would never change, I knew that. He was what he was, and he fervently believed in achieving some alternate lifestyle which emphasized the ideals he pushed on me and others. I more or less pretended to want the same things when deep down I really wanted to try my own hand in procuring a portion of the American dream and then consorting with all the material decadence that would come with that.

After Land came out to see me in L.A., he did call and leave messages for me many times, but I never called back. I wanted to distance myself from Land and that past life of mine that he represented. Becoming utterly self-absorbed and selfish has been my M.O. the last three and a half years. I can't deny it. What a fucked up transformation it has been. But, it's about survival and it's been a conscious self-absorption in that I am aware that I am cutting myself from things and people which no longer serve me. And I mean "serve me" in the sense that these things and people no longer give some kind of edge or angle or insight which I'm gonna need to propel myself farther into whatever scene I want to get into. Land has become obsolete. The time we shared had become old—a bygone era. I know only three and a half years have passed, but shit is hyped-up in our fickle society. The here and now is replaced by the already-here future in a nanosecond, and so, yes, the passing of three and a half years feels like an eternity.

I couldn't call Land back when he left those messages. I would play them sometimes over and over again. These weren't short messages saying, "Hey, man, I'm at so-and-so and thought I'd give you a buzz." They were carefully crafted lines letting me know that he was living life at another level. At a level, which he knew I once had desired but had since run away from. I even tape-recorded a couple of the messages and listened to them late at night in the dark when everything was quiet and I could envision Land's passing through America looking for a community. I knew he had been married/divorced, had gone to run with the wolves in Silver Cliff, Colorado and I knew he went to the rez and lived there for awhile and the tastes that the experience left with him. I couldn't call him back and talk to him and then *lie* about my own situation. That was too painful. I still cared for him as a best friend, but one who was a potent distraction. I weaned myself off him little by little until Land stopped the calls. He never once left a message saying, "Where the hell are you?" or "Why the fuck don't you call back?" He knew I was turning my back on him. Land was no fool. So, he went back East and I know now that despite all his fantastic meanderings for a community the answer he had found was too horrible for him to face so he ran away from things too.

I don't know what I felt when I listened to his messages. Jealousy probably. That he could do these things and the zest and gusto with which he could still live his life, while I rotted away in a game where the rules were so gray that it was more about chance and sucking dick than actual hard work. My existence had become so trite, so ordinary, but I motivated myself with visions of what I would be able to reap in the future. The dues I was putting in surely would pay me back in spades. I constantly reassured myself. I thought I could be a major player and things started out promising. I started with an entry level position in a large talent agency making only $300 a week for stuffing envelopes and faxing documents to key players in the business. There was this whole philosophy that this was the way you had to start— in the mailroom. By printing up address labels and putting the correct titles for these people like "Senior V.P. Business Affairs," you would learn the infrastructure of the business. Land soon became an abstract reminder of my fall from grace. I was the quintessential sell-out. Even cut my hair and stopped smoking buds to boot. I didn't want to hear about Land and his adventures and all his good times. Yet, I could never bring myself to erase those messages of his that I had recorded. Though I stopped listening to them, I held onto them as if I expected some kind of second coming of Land. I needed to be ready.

So, I did a four month stint in the mailroom of this talent agency. I was fast and polished and was promoted to the Commercials Department for another four month stint. I kissed as much ass as was possible and soon became an assistant to this veteran agent. The guy was a social blob, but I played ball hoping for the recognition that would allow me to get selected as a junior agent who would work with him. I got this fucker coffee, called him "sir", picked up his kids from school— all for naught. I got passed over. I stayed a couple of more months keeping hope alive. Then, he called me by the wrong name—twice—in one day and that was it. I had enough. Adios. I quit. Nothing more than temp jobs after that. All I cared about was making next month's rent and being able to make up upbeat stories to friends and family who would call from New York to check up on me.

I remember that I fell into an all-time low after I left the talent agency. My girlfriend buoyed me to the best of her abilities, but when you start feeling like a drifter, it's extremely scary. And the amount of bad thoughts that start swirling through your mind and which keep you up during the night and prey upon you during the day when you're trying to make a change in your life make you *hate*. They color your perception of the immediate reality around you with horrible Rothko-esque burning black swaths. You're forced to hyper-analyze everything around you in order understand why you now drift and are connected to nothing. It is still an existence though and you have to go on making yourself believe that things will change. Your mind then looks for signs of good fortune and will mistake the mundane for an augur of something bigger that lays in wait for you just around the corner. I pressed on with the taking of temp jobs and my girlfriend filled in the black times though our roles had now switched and she was the one planning the next steps in my life. I had no choice but to succumb to her control.

She doesn't know anything of my past as a Nineties incarnation of a Sixties radical and knows nothing about Land. I don't think I've ever mentioned Land to her. She only knows me as a fast talker who is full of promise, but who is just down on his luck right now. Things will certainly turn around for me and I will get back on my feet, make a lot of money, and she can then use me as necessary for her own career or emotional ends. That's gotta be how she looks at our situation. Otherwise, why stick it out with me? I'm going nowhere while her star is starting to rise. I don't get it. This is clearly not love. L.A. is no place for fairy-tales. I think it empowers her to see me in my state. She can advise me, nurture and take care of me while at the same time working and getting ahead herself. If she had any idea of what I was like in college, I think she would be ashamed of herself for falling for someone so raffish. You looked like what? You read what? You did what? You were involved in what? With all these realizations, she would disappear from my life in a flash.

II

  Needless to say, I am dangerously close to
missing my flight. I tell Land to get to the airport
pronto and that we can really talk about things later
after I mull it over. He and Gen on the lam. What
does he want to me to do about it? We get to the
airport and I tell Land that I am leaving on
American. Land drops me off at the American
entrance, but I know I am too late. Still, I go
through the motions and grab my bags and rush to
the ticket counter where of course I am told the gate
has already closed and the plane is on the runway.
Next flight is at eight tomorrow morning. I fume
until the count of ten, and then turn back to the car.
"Missed the flight, huh?" Land asks as I approach.
"Yeah, man."
"Is there another one you can get on tonight?"
"Not until tomorrow morning."
Land hangs his head and seems genuinely sorry.
Then, that gleam in his eyes returns.
"Tal, I'm real sorry about this. But, listen you
might as well come back with me. Stay at Gen's
and I'll bring you back tomorrow for the flight."
I rock back and forth on my boots. This is classic.
"Land, you know what's gonna happen if I come
back with you?? There's no way we'll make it back
to my flight in the morning. Let me think about this
for a second." I take a moment to study Land and
the situation I'm in.
"What are you thinking?" Land asks.
"To be honest, man. I really have no obligations
back in L.A. I've paid rent through the end of
February. So, I waste my return ticket. A one way
ticket back to L.A. shouldn't be that bad now that

Mardi Gras season is over, right?"

"Oh, yeah, Not a problem. You can find a cheap ticket. Why don't you stay for a couple days, man. It should be an interesting time."

"Yeah, right. Really interesting, man."

"Hey, I know it looks bad, but I'm keeping a happy face on all this. Get in!!"

Land's smiling face. I can't believe it still works on me. I know I shouldn't get in the car, but I don't see any other options. The cat is smiling and check out the mess he is in! I don't want to carry his baggage as well, because despite his beaming those bags are definitely there and they are heavy. I throw my bags back in the back seat and get in the car. An odd feeling comes over me like this is what was supposed to happen all along. Where is a friendship after three and a half years of living in different worlds? I will soon find out.

Land floors it back to the Quarter. As it comes into view, an uneasiness now grips me about re-entering New Orleans. I have already said my goodbyes, so it feels like I've worn out my welcome here. I don't want to mooch off the Big Easy. This can definitely ruin the magic.

As we climb the stairs up to Gen's, I think about her part in all this. She's in on it? Must have bought Land's bullshit about how great it would be. The rush. All that jazz. Here goes.

"Gen? We're back," Land announces as we enter her apartment.

Gen is on the phone and the TV is tuned to CNN. She says good-bye to whoever is on the phone and puts on a fake smile when she sees that I'm still in town.

"He missed his flight," Land explains.

"Oh, that's too bad."

"Yeah, well, we had some delays on the way," I say as I glance toward Land hoping he will fill in Gen on what has transpired.

"When's the next one, Tal?" Gen asks.

"Eight o'clock tomorrow morning."

"Well, you're more than welcome to stay here for the night. You better leave around 6:30 tomorrow though to make sure you catch your flight."

"Uh, yeah. Thanks." I say.

Things get quiet. I'm still waiting for Land to clue in Gen so this charade can stop. But, he's headed to the fridge to grab something. He returns and hands out an Abita beer to each of us.

"Hey, here's to us. Cheers," Land says.

We touch bottles and each take a big swallow.

"Gen, Tal might hang around for a couple of days and take a flight later in the week. Is that cool?"

Gen does not know what to say and she searches Land for an explanation.

"Of course..." She starts.

I take another swallow and wait.

"Tal, you can stay for however long you like—but, uh, Land—don't you want to—"

"—Gen, he knows."

I keep pounding the beer now hoping for a quick buzz to make this situation less tense. Gen's face registers a whole spectrum of emotion. Her blue-green eyes flash a baffled-angry-betrayed-ashamed-pissed off look all at once.

"It's O.K. He might be able to help us," Land says and he goes over and puts an arm around Gen, pulling her close. But, Gen pulls away and walks stoically into her bedroom and closes the door without a word.

"Land, maybe I should stay at a motel. This is getting too serious for me, man. And how the hell can I help you? What do I know about any of this??"

Land takes a big gulp of the Abita.

"First off, you're not going to any motel. Gen's upset now but she'll calm down. I had promised that I would not tell anyone about it. But, don't worry I'll explain this to her. What we need from you is just to pool our resources. You're gonna help give us a fresh, outside perspective of the facts as they stand. See, Gen and I, our thinking is clouded right now because of the paranoia and, uh, fear that we got trailed here."

He takes another gulp.

"You're gonna be useful to us as someone we can trust and who can provide a steady outlook in all this. You dig??"

"Uh, I hear you, man. But, you gotta get Gen to be cool with this as well. I don't want to fuck things up for you or blow your cover."

"Sure, man."

"I'll help out in any way I can, but Land..." I stop to make sure Land is listening. "I don't want to be part of your further plans. Just gonna try and give you some options if I see any. That's it, bro."

"Cool. That's all I'm asking for."

Land finishes his beer and puts it on the coffee table. He then walks away and my first thought is that he is going to get another Abita. But, he moves to Gen's bedroom and knocks. He goes inside and closes the door behind him. I sit on the couch and watch CNN. Some story about another lone, mid-forties white guy who takes a gun and opens fire on unsuspecting co-workers. He kills seven people, wounds twelve others and the

CNN correspondent presses a bystander for more facts. Land reappears after about twenty minutes or two commercial breaks in the CNN coverage.

"Everything's cool, bra. She just has to deal with the reality we're in. I explained things to her and she's not angry that you know."

"Good. I feel a little more comfortable now."

Land takes a seat next to me and faces the TV.

"I feel guilty for getting her involved in the first place. She really didn't have the stomach to go through with it."

I want to blurt out "No shit!" but hold back.

"Look, Land. I don't want to know anything about what you guys did. Let's just concentrate on where you are at now and what you and Gen want to do."

I look at Land who motions me with his eyes to look behind me. I see that Gen is walking into the room. I think she's been crying a little but she puts on a brave face in front of me.

"Hi," she says.

"Hey, Gen, it's cool. I want you to know that you can trust me in all this," I try to be as reassuring as possible.

Gen smiles, but I can tell by her body language that she feels deeply betrayed by Land. She sits on a chair to my left and positions herself so that her left shoulder faces Land and I.

"Gen, Tal doesn't want to hear anything about the robbery itself. Let's just discuss our options at this point. O.K.?"

Gen chuckles. The kind of nervous chuckle where you know you're fucked no matter what.

"Sure. O.K. I, uh, I drove down here after the incident," Gen explains. She does not make eye contact with either Land or I and stares at the TV.

"Ummm, I think, Tal, we need to backtrack here.
We have to fill in some of the facts. O.K.?" Land
says and he looks at both Gen and I before
continuing, but Gen still does not look back at
Land.
"This thing took place just after New Year's so it's
been over a month. Gen came to New Orleans—
what? A week later?"
"Yeah. I drove down in my car. I sold it right away
when I got here. An Accord—always in demand."
Land looks worried by Gen's automaton response.
"Right, right. We used her car as the getaway,"
Land says as he tries to meet Gen's eyes to see
what's going on. When Gen doesn't face him, he
turns back to me and says, "Tal, man, we used her
car as the getaway! Far out, eh!"
I'm in disbelief at Land's braggadocio and I think to
myself Gen must be cringing inside. But, I force
out a smile at Land and sit through his histrionics.
"So, Gen came down here and I went to New York
after the robbing gig and joined her here two weeks
ago. The important thing is that no one saw her car.
The bank is on a corner at the end of one of the
major streets in the town. It gets dark there in
January around 3:30 p.m., man. It's crazy. We
went in close to closing, so it's pitch black and the
street lighting sucks. No one could possibly see us
bail."
"If you say so, Land," Gen grumbles.
Land laughs.
"I know so," he says. "Anyway, we drive straight
to New York to cool out. Then, Gen came down to
New Orleans with half the cash. I kept the other
half. Pretty equitable, huh, bra??!!"
"Um, yeah. I don't think though I'd brag about it
too much though," I say.

"Come on, man. It's all right. What's done is in the past, now let's look toward the future. It's been a month. If they have any idea who did it, I just don't see how they can find us here in New Orleans."

"They can find us anywhere, Land." And Gen looks back at Land this time as if to hammer her concern home.

"Well, maybe they're just waiting for the madness of Mardi Gras to stop before making a move. So, now it might be key for us to take off to another place with the loot, which really isn't a whole lot. It's only around—"

I jump in.

"No, Land!! I don't want to know how much the take was! O.K., man? The less I know the better for me."

"Alright, alright, man. You gotta rep to protect. I see what you mean. But, I gotta say this…I still can't believe you cut your hair!!"

"Can we please stick with your situation? It's a tad bit more critical."

"O.K., so we should make a move—maybe tomorrow? Get on the road and leave town for a while. See what happens?"

Land rubs his chin as his thoughts roll.

"Maybe even have one of Gen's friends keep an eye on her place to let us know if anyone comes around asking questions?" He says.

"Where are you planning on going?" I ask.

"Monterrey. In Mexico. I have family there on my dad's side who would love to have me come down and stay with them. Gen would be welcomed too. We could hang there for a while. Lay low. They even have internet access there, man! We could probably find a website that would allow us to keep tabs on the local news surrounding the robbery. Gen, what do you think?"

"I, umm, I think, we're gonna fuck this up."

"What's with the pessimism? You gotta push on through this. Don't get down on me now."

"Don't feed me that shit, Land. Just last night you almost fucked everything up by running in the middle of the street like a crazy person and having a squad of cops come down on you. What if they didn't let you go?? Did you ever stop to once think about our situation during all that? I just can't believe that you did such a stupid move without thinking about our situation."

"Good. Now, we're getting somewhere. Let's deal with our feelings. I'm gonna go and grab a couple of oyster po-boys from that place around the corner. You guys want any?"

"Uh, sure. I-I-I'll take one," I stammer, completely taken aback by Land's strange non sequitur in responding to Gen's plea with shellfish sandwiches.

"Gen?" Land asks.

"What??"

"Can I get you something??"

Gen shrugs.

"You sure you don't want anything?" Land again asks.

"Are you serious?" Gen says.

"As a heart attack, babe. You want anything?"

"How about some peace of mind?"

"I'm working on that, doll. In the meantime, I'll pick up one for you as well. Be right back." And Land goes after our dinner.

I try to get ready for what is sure to come next.

"Do you think he's losing it?" Gen asks.

"Who? Land? He's always been on the edge. That's who he is."

"What did you think of his behavior last night? All that shit he said. He's got this whole wonderful sounding philosophy—I, uh, I bought it, Tal."

"What do you mean?"

Gen tunes out. I look at her and can tell she's in her own world.

"Gen?"

"Uh, yeah?"

"Why—I mean, why did you go along with Land's idea?"

"Ohhh," Gen exhales and her head drops into her hands. Her long auburn hair falls in front of her face. "It's not his fault. I knew what I was doing." She sits up and with her right hand pulls her hair back away from her face.

"What was going on?" I ask.

"He came to me just after I found out I didn't pass the Bar. I was crushed. I had landed a great job in the DA's office. I was about to examine witnesses, Tal."

"That's a big deal, huh?"

"For me it was like realizing a dream I had worked so hard for..." Gen wipes away a few tears from her eyes. I want to go over and comfort her, but I can't budge from the couch. It's as if some tractor beam has pinned me down and won't let me get up. Gen composes herself and continues.

"When I found out that I didn't pass, they had to let me go. They didn't give me another chance because there was so much work there and they were in immediate need of someone licensed."

"Assholes," I say softly.

"It was horrible. I had been there for four months. Four months! I built professional relationships and garnered some equity in that job. I lost it all—

everything—in one weekend. Can you imagine how devastating that is??"

I say no. Even though I went through a similar harrowing experience at the talent agency. But, right now it's best to go along with her pain and let her steer.

"I was depressed and reeling. I put so much work in this past summer in studying for this stupid test. I have no idea what I could have done differently. I just moped around and one day Land called and cheered me up in his usual crazy way. The pain didn't go away though. I missed New Orleans and Land told me I should go back there and regroup. I liked the idea, but just couldn't afford moving again and my law school loan's first payment was due in mid-December."

"Your folks could have helped, no?"

"I didn't want to get them involved, Tal. It's always such a whole package deal with them. I just couldn't reach out to them," Gen again wipes away tears.

"What happened then?"

"Then, Land talks about having a fool-proof plan to rob a bank. I laughed. You know I thought it was just another one of his jests. But, he got more and more serious about it and then asked me to help him. It was crazy—I needed to do something crazy—to just seize something and feel in control of my life...I, uh, I had to say yes."

"I don't blame you, Gen."

"You don't?"

"Come on. You were in a tough place and Land offered a deliverance. I probably would have gone for it too. God knows, I've followed Land into some crazy shit." I shake my head.

"Do you think he's serious about going to Mexico?" Gen asks.

"Probably. He bought maps yesterday, didn't he?"

"That's not what I mean, Tal. Obviously, if he's got family there, then that's a viable option for us to go there. But, I'm beginning to think Land is really after something else. Going to Mexico is just a ploy for us to grab onto. He's up to something else."

"I've never known Land to screw over his friends. He's looking out for you Gen."

"I don't mean that he wants to mislead me and then leave with all the money. He has other plans—like he's on some crusade, but we just see him as Land as usual. That's what he wants to project to us. I have to watch him closely from now on."

The first thought going through my mind is that Gen has become paranoid. Luckily, before I say something that may upset her, I hear footsteps coming up the stairs. I go to the door and open it and Land rushes in with bags of sweet smelling food.

"Let's chow all," Land blares.

We divide up the goods. I grab an oyster poor-boy, splash some Tabasco on it and grab another Abita from the fridge. No one talks for what seems like ten minutes. Each of us is too preoccupied with succulent food and drink. And everything is relaxed between us. When we finish, Land brings out a map of Mexico which includes Louisiana, most of Texas and the southern parts of New Mexico, Arizona and California.

"Getting to Monterrey is no sweat. It will only take two days. We first take I-10 all the way to Houston. That only takes about five to six hours, I think. The next day, we hop on Highway 59 which goes all the way to the border at Laredo. From Laredo to

Monterrey—it's about three hundred miles. No
worries."

"What about the conditions of the roads there?"
Gen asks.

"The roads are paved and fast. We can get there.
Don't worry about it. My dad's cousin and his
family are there. I'll let them know we're coming."

"Uh, what about me, man? What do you want me
to do? Stay here and watch Gen's place for a
couple of days until shit settles down?" I ask.

"Gen, what do you think?" Land puts her on the
spot.

"Can't he come with us?"

"Hey, I can't go to Mexico. I don't want to tag
along on this one. I got some things to take care of
back in L.A."

"Tal, why don't you, uh, come as far as Houston??
From there you can catch a plane to L.A.," Land
says.

Here we go. Land is weaving his web and I'm
already ensnared and won't be able to get unstuck.

"I do have a friend who lives in Houston. But, it's
short notice."

"Give him a call," Land says.

"Yeah. I can try. Maybe he'll be around and I can
crash at his place until I find a flight back."

I feel like Land's jedi-mind tricks are controlling
my answers.

"Yeah, Tal. That sounds good. Come with us to
Houston. We can talk a lot on the way and then
we'll go our separate ways."

"Do you really want to take off tomorrow, Land?"
Gen asks.

"Yeah. I think it would be best to make our move
in the morning."

So, I'm in. I agree to hitch a ride with Gen and Land to Houston and I call my friend to let him now I'll be in town tomorrow night. He says it's cool for me to crash with him for however long I like. It's been awhile since we've seen one another anyway. He himself is in between jobs, so he'll be around and waiting for me. I still have time to enjoy myself before getting back to L.A., so, yeah, I might as well bum around Houston for a couple of days. Everything's a go.

We have a couple more rounds of beer. I pick up Gen's piece of shit guitar and play some songs we dug from college. The classics—*Peaceful Easy Feeling, Rosemary, Like a Rolling Stone, Wild Horses, Brown-Eyed Girl*, et al. It's funny how despite my not playing these tunes for so long, my fingers magically remember where to move. We wrap it up close to midnight and plan on leaving the house by 10:30 in the morning. Land sleeps in Gen's bed with Gen. I get the couch and Gen gives me a blanket and a large overstuffed goosefeather pillow. As soon as my heads hits it, the lights go out.

III

The next morning I'm stirred awake by the faint tinkling of ivories coming from Gen's neighbor's room. Someone is learning to play a song on the piano. Whoever it is plays in a very stilted and tentative manner at first—stopping and then repeating the same few notes. I can just barely make out the voice of the piano teacher instructing the person as he or she practices. The song is familiar to me and when whoever playing it gets it right and lets it flow, I see past images from my life dance by. It's amazing. Not images like fully fleshed out whole scenes from life, but rather, those particular innocent instinctive times from my life where I really felt *being*. That's what this music releases in me. My eyes shut on the simple, deliberate cadence of the song.

"Schumann."

I open my eyes and see that Land has come into the room and is seated on the chair across from me. His head is titled toward the wall from where the music is coming.

"Definitely. It's Robert Schumann's *Kinderscenes – Scenes from Childhood*," he explains.

"Get out of here!" I say as I get up from the couch. "You know this?"

"Sure. This particular song is called *Von Fremden Landern und Menschen*."

"In English, man."

"*About Strange Lands and People.*"

Land knows all kinds of shit about everything. A real renaissance cat. He took courses in German, Classical Literature, Opera, Art History,

Rhetoric, Cybernetics—the whole gamut. Back in school, he was always unstoppable when it came to pure knowledge about the world and mankind's contribution or detraction from it. Simply amazed everybody, myself included, and I was no shrinking violet either. I had liberally dosed in the humanities as well. But, Land was also a *doer* and he actively, deliberately applied the liberal arts most of us just passively absorbed into his own ad hoc scheme of life. It is obvious that three and a half years later, he still has his touch.

"Amazing, Land. You've retained your knack for knowing the unknowable! I love this song. I've never known what it's called and really I thought—I thought this was a song that I had imagined myself. From time to time, I hear it by chance and it stays with me for a while, but then it just fades and I don't remember it anymore until the next time it pops up."

"It's a nice melody, isn't it? Like sprinkling fairy dust on the listener."

"Haha. Yeah. I can't believe that the name is what? *About Strange Lands and People?*"

"Right, but it's from a larger work called *Scenes from Childhood.*"

"How apropos. Perfect title, man. That's exactly what I go through whenever I hear this song. Just hearing the notes transports me to a lighter place. Into childlike wonderment. That's fuckin' wild that the name of the song fits like that. It's—"

"—perfection. That's the power of artistry. When you get it right it resonates to the core of your being. That's what you experience when you hear the song, Tal. It's a perfect stilling of the world around you and all your senses are heightened. You tap into something deep, man."

I hang on Land's words. I have never had someone explain this to me in such a glowing way. I tell Land he is right and I get a little insight into what he means by the lack of *artistry* in the world. "There is this story about Proust—Marcel—if you don't know which Proust I'm referring to. I think there was another Proust—a chemist?," Land starts off.
"Yeah, man. I know which one you're talking about. I read some of his stuff," I say, a little annoyed by Land's patronizing tone to me.

An aside though is required. I know *of* Marcel Proust. I know him as being a revered French writer who wrote an epic and I had heard about his dueling. Someone once told me a story about how Proust was seriously ill when a book of his was initially published. First off, he self-published this book and was in debt. Then, while he's on his sick bed, the critics' reviews come in. One critic bags on his writing and Proust challenges the guy to a duel to the death although he was still prostrate on his bed and hadn't stepped out of it in weeks. Based on all his writings that followed, Proust surely must have won.

"One day Proust is clearing out his study and as he is throwing shit away and dusting off other shit to keep, he comes across an old handkerchief that he can't quite place in his mind. He stops to examine it and then takes a big whiff—smelling it." Land mimes the act with an imaginary handkerchief and inhales deeply through his nose. "Just from the smell of this old handkerchief, he remembers a lost time and it triggers a marathon composition. The cat writes several thousand pages nonstop, man!! The result is *À la Recherche de Temps Perdu. Remembrance of Things Past.*"

"Yeah, sure. I've read some of it like I said. A truly monumental piece of work."

"All because this smell transported him into this perfect state of being where he was able to write effortlessly and have his writings resonate for nearly a century later."

Land stops to collect his thoughts.

"The *Proustian* moment, Tal. That's what you just experienced."

"I didn't realize there was a name for the experience."

"So, now you know. Count yourself among the lucky few that actually has been able to be conscious of the moment. Most people simply ignore or don't realize the moment that has gripped them and opened something inside them that has been so locked up until it's too late and then they try and try to recapture that moment but it never comes back around."

"Yeah, yeah. But, I can't hold on to the emotions and ideas it released in me. You know?"

"I know. That's the hard part. But, you gotta be mindful of what you felt and remember where it is inside so that you *can* use it some day. Just don't waste it."

Gen walks into the room and sees Land and I intently listening to the music coming from her neighbor's place.

"Every Thursday—piano lessons." Gen points to the wall where the music comes from.

"Usually, I'm off to work before it starts. Which reminds me, Land, I can take only a week off from work—if we really are going to Monterrey. Is this for real?"

It's funny to me that Gen is worried about her job obligations given her situation. I bite my lip though. "It sure is and you better call your boss at the museum and tell him that you're gonna be gone more than a week. I mean, they need you don't they? How many assistants are as knowledgeable as you? Your boss will accommodate you. Tell him that you need a week off initially, O.K.? Have a friend keep an eye on your place while we're gone. I think you can come back after a week anyway. I just don't think we got trailed here. Everything's cool."

"Easy, Land. These cops are always slow. It takes a while to piece shit together. Ask, Gen she worked in the DA's office," I say.

"It depends on the case. I think with the bank, the Feds have to get involved—a jurisdictional issue. But, uh, what do I know? The only serious case I had had to do with a woman who brought charges in order to get her face back."

"What??" Land and I both ask.

"It was a medical malpractice and because it involved criminal negligence the DA's office was involved. This maniac oral surgeon was going around masquerading as a dermatologist and plastic surgeon. He had no license and performed a facelift for this woman and ended up butchering her face. It left big scars. The woman's forehead is so discolored that she has to wear her hair in bangs from now on. So, she wanted her face back as she put it and this guy was facing charges that woulda sent him to jail. Of course, I don't know how the case ended. I was let go before it went to the jury."

"That's tough," I say.

- 134 -

Dead air follows.

"O.K., kids, no more wallowing in the past. Time to move on. Dig? Let's get this show on the road!" Land chirps as if on cue to cut through the silence. "Let's get outta here. We gotta get back in business!"

We break. Land gets his gear together and I'm already packed. Gen calls her boss and gets the O.K. to take a week off. She then puts together a suitcase in record time and drags it into the living room.

"Let's put the money in one bag. O.K., Gen?" Land asks.

"Yeah, O.K."

The cash is put into a black duffel bag that Land swings over his shoulder and Gen and I each pick up our bags and follow Land out the door. I want to guess to how much money is in the bag in terms of how hard Land has to struggle in carrying the bag down to the steps and to the car. But, I cast my thoughts elsewhere. This is not about the bank robbery which in all honesty I could care less about. I'm with people with whom I share a past and I want to stay within this old familiar circle for a little longer. Gen exits her apartment last and locks the door. She says that she will call a friend when we are on the road and tell her to watch over the place. We load up the car, which Land tells me he just bought used and dirt cheap two weeks ago. He has to mention that the proceeds to buy the car came from the take. We then pile into the car with Land behind the wheel and Gen and I both sitting in the front passenger seat. We drive a couple of blocks through the Quarter to Gen's friend's place where Gen drops off her key and a little note in a secret spot for her friend to find. She gets back into the car and we head out to the interstate. I say good-bye to New Orleans for the second time in as many days.

We drive past Lake Pontchartrain, which Land points out has the longest causeway in the world. It's huge. Thirty-three miles long and spans the swampy lake from the north to the south. We head west toward Baton Rouge, capital of Louisiana.

"Isn't it ironic that so many cities and towns here have these eloquent French names in the middle of redneck territory? As soon as you leave New Orleans, it's like get ready to duck and watch out for lynch mobs," Land says as he drives within the speed limit, unlit cigarette dangling from his mouth. "Ah, come on, guys, what's with the glum faces?" He asks.

Gen and I say nothing. We each look straight ahead through the windshield. Land senses we are both tired and that any conversation will have to wait for a while. He shuts up and drives. Gen is sitting in between Land and I. We pass waffle houses and rest areas and Shoney's restaurants and get to Baton Rouge in close to an hour. As we drive past Baton Rouge, we really get into the South. The South that, as Land alluded, can make you nervous and vigilant. And sure enough, at one point, two semis, each with the Confederate flag strapped over their massive hoods drive us off the road. These trucks come barreling down on us from behind and pass one after the other at a distance so close to us that the gusts coming off them blows us off the road. Land has to grapple with the steering wheel in order to regain control of the car, and when he does he pulls over until the trucks are well out of sight.

"I guess those are the welcome wagons." Land says.

"Jesus," I say and for the first time I long for the *friendly* confines of L.A.

"And what's with the fuckin' flags? Don't they realize that they lost the war? It's like these Deadheads that are still moping around lost. Jerry's dead, man. Come on, get a life!"

"Uh, I think it represents more than just the Confederacy, Land. It's a whole ethic of *don't tread on me* mentality that got perverted into secession." I don't really know what I'm trying to say, but this is what comes out.

"Like all that shit about Texas—the Lone Star State? What the fuck is that all about? It's like the only thing we value as Americans is being able to sustain ourselves as islands. Well, islands always cry, and this country is on the verge of bawling, bra."

"Explain that Land," Gen asks.

"The signs are everywhere, Gen. This place, much like the Romans did with Rome, is eating itself alive. We're a bunch of obese, unsatisfied people. Sensory deprived, using television and now the internet as a surrogate for true experience. That's where we're headed—a purely vicarious existence. You pull out one more pillar and it will all collapse. You dig, Gen?"

"One more pillar of what?" Gen says.

"Like that shit you told us about the *peristil* in Vodou. What was it again? The place where ceremonies take place?"

"Right."

"And it's basically a roofed structure supported by four beams. The central one being the pathway between the sacred and the profane world. Am I right?"

"Yes. I'm impressed that you got all that."

"Give me some credit will you, Gen?" Land turns to smile to Gen, but Gen doesn't smile back.

"Anyway, in the West's, especially America's, push for everything being bigger, faster and better—the central pole has been knocked down and things are beginning to crumble. It's like I was telling Tal earlier today, the moments of artistry in human existence are beginning to disappear. There are fewer Proustian moments in people's lives that spark new, creative ideas. Nothing of any lasting resonance thrives anymore nor is encouraged. I'm dead on, Gen."

"I think that if you have a chance to grab hold of a legitimate stake in the American dream, then you should take it. It still exists you know. That's why people still flock here. To start new lives and so what if there are no more Proustian moments in our lives. We have a great chance to attain a good standard of living, get public education for our kids, live out a high quality life."

Land starts to laugh. I crack a smile and then quickly pull it back. Gen slaps Land's arm.

"Don't laugh! You must be a realist in this world which goes on at a pace beyond our control, Land. I know most people nowadays are disconnected from themselves and others, but you gotta let it go for your own sake. You do what you can do within the construct of our society—get educated, get a good job, raise a family. America still lets this get done at a lesser cost compared to the rest of the world. The opportunities are still available here."

"Then why did you decide to do what you did with me, Gen? You coulda just licked your wounds after the Bar. Taken another job in the meanwhile, right? Restudy and give it the old college try one more time?"

Gen gets quiet. No one speaks and I want to make a joke or something to diffuse the situation. But, Gen gathers herself and answers.

"I can't deny that I find your views on things tantalizing, Land. I saw a way out of my situation and I grabbed it. I, ummm, I have no excuse. I wanted to change my situation by grabbing the opportunity you gave me."

"Ahhh, opportunity," Land says. "And how did that make you feel, Gen?"

"It felt...it was fantastic. I felt the system had screwed me and I really had no choice. Payback, I guess."

"Right on, Gen. That's all I'm talking about. You chose to change your situation and so you take some money. That's it. In a cosmic sense—just a drop in the bucket. No one's gonna miss it. We did them a favor by taking it off their hands and we'll put it to good use, eh?"

A master, Land is. The cat plays with words and entrances the listener. He's hard to shake off and Gen and I are putty in his hands at this point. At least, I'm only going as far as Houston.

We drive past Lafayette and stop for a break at a town called Jennings which is right off the interstate. Land pumps gas and then we go into a diner for lunch. We each keep it simple ordering turkey sandwiches and sides of cole slaw. Land lights a Camel light.

"You wanna a cig, man?"

"Yeah. What a thrill to smoke in public! You know that nowhere in L.A. can you legally smoke in a public place?" I say.

"Get the fuck out of here!" Land exclaims.

"What about bars or clubs?" Gen asks.

"Not even in bars or clubs. People do still light up, but you're not supposed to smoke in any public place. Can you believe that?"

"Crazy. I can understand not smoking on airplanes, but if I'm going to a bar to get smashed and smoke a few cigs, then by golly I'm gonna do that. That's why the tavern was invented in the first place." Land takes a drag. I follow suit. "It seems Cali has all kinds of these laws, huh, Tal?"

"Yeah."

"Like mandatory seatbelts and helmets too, right?"

"Mmmhmm."

"Look, if I choose not to put on my seatbelt, it's that simple, I've made a choice not to put it on. It's my car, my body, my life. I don't need some politician telling me what's good for me," Land sets out his position as usual.

"I hear you," I say.

We get back in the car and drive in silence for an hour or more. It's that after lunch crash. We all just wilt and I see why the siesta was created. But, Land keeps going and takes us past little towns like Crowley and Rayne. We finally get to the casino town of Lake Charles which you can tell gambling-starved Texans must populate on the weekends. An hour later we enter Texas and are greeted by a sign that says, "Welcome to the Lone Star State." Land has a laugh at this and I hope this doesn't lead to more butting of heads between Land and Gen.

We have to get off at a town called
Beaumont so Gen can go to the bathroom. I get out
of the car, stretch, and notice Land studying the
map.
"You're not gonna believe this. We're about
seventy miles south of Jasper."
"Where?" I ask.
"Jasper, Texas. Remember that story about how
those three white boys dragged that black guy
behind their pick up truck until the guy got
dismembered? It happened a couple years back."
I think for a second and then something registers.
"Oh, shit, yeah. I remember. I had such a visceral
reaction to that. Turned my stomach," I curl my
lips with disgust. "Is that where we are? Stay close
to the car, man."
"Can you imagine? The same country responsible
for Coca-Cola and Disneyland hangs blacks from
trees and drags them behind cars."
"At least two of them got the death penalty," Gen
says as she walks back towards us.
"What about the third guy?" I ask.
"He got life—I think it was shown at the trial that it
wasn't his idea and he was just in the car when it
happened."
"What's that??" Land says as he gets into the car
and turns the engine on.
"Those three white guys. They recently got
sentenced..." Gen gets in and I get in behind her
and close the door.
"—Is that some kind of retribution? Gimme a
break. That kid Emmett Till whistled at a white
chick and they fuckin hung him from a tree and then
dumped his body in the bayou...or was that the
Freedom Riders? I still have those images from
Eyes on the Prize in my mind where the FBI was

throwing nets and poking at the swamp floor with poles trying to find bodies. It happened so often, I can't keep the stories straight."

"Times haven't really changed," I say.

"No, not at all. It's a lot worse," Land says and he slams on the gas pedal as if to emphasize his point. Thankfully, we're out of Beaumont.

Back on the road and in the homestretch to Houston. It takes another hour and a half. When we arrive in the city, it's close to eight at night. I call my friend and get directions to his house. On the way there I jot down my phone number and email address on a matchbook I had picked up from the diner in Jennings and hand it to Gen.

"Keep in touch you two and let me know how things go. If you need to come to L.A. don't hesitate to contact me."

"Yeah, right. You never can see the handwriting on the wall can you, Tal?" Land says. I feel like he's challenging me.

"Excuse me?"

"Where do you have to go?"

"Uh, my buddy's place," I answer confused by Land's question.

"No, man. Where do you *need* to go?" Land asks again.

"You're losing me, man," I say.

"No where. You have no where to go, bra."

"Sure, I do. I gotta go back to, uh, back to L.A., man."

"There's nothing waiting for you back in L.A. except emptiness and a couple more years of plowing through the system before you totally burn out."

"What?!" For some reason when I say this I look to Gen for some answers. But, Gen is just a pair of dull eyes and she is no help at all.

"Why fight it, Tal? Just come with us to Monterrey. It was destined to happen this way."

"But...," I try to speak and look at Land who is cool and continues to drive through Houston.

I have always been a big Beatles fan— primarily of their latter years when Lennon really stretched his lyrical legs and put together songs like *A Day in the Life, Don't Let Me Down, Revolution,* and *Across the Universe.* The songs in his solo years were even more complex and raw—just listen to *God.* It's unbelievable testimonial honesty. Yet, the lyrics running through my mind on and off over the past three and a half years are from the B-side of *Abbey Road,* which besides Lennon's *Come Together* is basically a long McCartney *idée fixe.* There's a verse in one of the songs which goes:

> *Out of college money spent*
> *got no future paid no rent*
> *all the money's gone no where to go.*

There's another verse right after this, but I've never been able to make out exactly what McCartney is saying. Then the lyrics become:

> *But, ohhhhh, that magic feeling, no*
> *where to go.*

He was right on the money with that one.

I'm feeling this loony vibe where paradoxically I can *afford* to do this. I really have no where to go. Like I said before I made plans to come out to New Orleans, I did have obligations and responsibilities in L.A which I could be away from for *no more* than a couple of weeks. Well, I've only been gone for four days! Another few days away will mean nothing. Fuck it. I gotta go along with this ride. I know it. Bumping into Land in the Quarter wasn't just a coincidence. It was one of those things you could feel in your bones and made sense no matter how hard you tried to resist. It was *the* Proustian moment. I'm completely sold on this notion. Magic.

I tell Land to pull over at the nearest gas station. Gen looks at me waiting for my answer. But, I don't say anything yet. I get out of the car and walk towards a pay phone.

"Man, check out how low gas prices are here!" Land yells as I walk away from the car. I call my friend and tell him I've changed my plans and will take a rain check. Land fills the tank while Gen buys some gum, cigarettes and beef jerky. I walk back towards the car.

"So, what's it going to be, bra?" Land asks.

I see Gen also walking back to the car holding a little plastic bag containing the rations for our trip.

"Land, I'm down with your plans. You're right, I gotta come along!" I say.

"Alright, man!" And Land walks around to give me a hug. I then turn and hug Gen too. I feel jazzed up and sing out loud, "*One sweet dream came true today!*"

Gen looks at Land and they both laugh at my outburst. Good times.

We all get back in the car. Smiles all around. Land is one big happy face.

"Let's get to Mexico!!" He says and he puts the car into gear and we head south to Laredo.

Out on Route 59, there's pretty much only desert and black, black darkness. With the high beams on, you can see occasional armadillo shells squashed along the road. One lane goes northeast and one lane goes southwest. It's getting close to 10 p.m. and we decide that's enough driving for today. The next mildly inhabited place is where we are going to find some lodging. We hit the junction between interstate 37 and Route 59—about seventy-five miles northwest of Corpus Christi. In a town called George West, we find a motor inn to crash at. The stars twinkle like crazy above us as we grab our bags. Land picks up the duffel bag with the cash and we pay for two rooms for the night. The rooms are side by side and Land and Gen take one room while I take the other. My room is the generic motel room: a hard bed with two pillows complete with a TV that gets exactly thirteen channels. I hop in the shower for a quick wash. The faucets only make the water hot and hotter. It kills me. I'm this close to getting a serious scalding and suffering first-degree burns. I get out and towel off being careful that I don't come into close contact with anything but the bed. Ever since I watched a *Primetime* news special on all the filth that remains in motel/hotel rooms even after a thorough cleaning, I've tried to watch out about where I place my hands while in the room. After getting dressed, I go over to Land's and Gen's room and knock on the door.
"Come in," Land says.
I walk in. Land is on the mattress watching the local news—probably being broadcast from

Corpus Christi. He's rolling a j with that look of seriousness that only seasoned pot smokers have. Gen is in the bathroom showering. I take a seat in a small chair off to the side and the sight of Land sitting on the bed cross-legged and rolling a j gives me major déjà vu. I try to remember where I've seen this image before and instead I get a little dazed and for a second forget where I am and the situation I've volunteered myself into.

"You O.K., man?" Land asks.

"Uhh, yeah. Just trying to remember where I've seen this scene before. I just had some major déjà vu."

"Mmmhmm. Probably a flashback from those heady days of college."

Land finishes rolling the j and holds it up, waving it at me proudly.

"Look at the size of this j, man!" He brags. "Please do the honors." And he reaches down from the bed and tries to hand me the j.

"No, thanks. I've retired from partaking."

Land's face drops. He has utter disbelief written all over. He thinks I'm putting him on.

"Whaddya mean, *no thanks*? What is that you're giving me?"

"Hey, man, I'm done with smoking up. I just don't appreciate it anymore."

"I can't believe I'm hearing this. I can't believe I'm hearing this. Hey, Gen, get over here!!" He yells for Gen, but she is still in the shower and can't hear him.

"Now, don't overreact, Land. It's not a big deal."

"*You don't appreciate it anymore*? Is that what you just said?"

"Yup."

"Oh, this is good! This is good!" Land bounces up and down on the mattress like a little kid. "You my dear, dear friend, you are the same cat who for two months went around campus proselytizing the powers of LSD after you dropped a tab one night! You kept on saying, *Oh, if only the world leaders would indulge in a massive dose at one time and then conference, a lot of petty rivalries could be resolved and wars could be a thing of the past!*"

I bust out laughing.

"Oh, so you remember that shit, huh?"

I don't answer. I just grin back at Land because I know there is more.

"What are we doing here? Just having a j amongst old friends. That's all. That's what it is for in the first place, man. A purely communal indulgence. To hang out and bond with friends. Is that what you don't *appreciate* any more? Too busy thinking about the future, huh?"

"Partly, man." I manage to say something in my defense.

Gen finally comes out of the bathroom.

"Gen, check this out. Tal, won't blow trees with us! This the same cat who used to grow plants in his closet during subfreezing winters and now he passes on sharing a j with us."

"If he doesn't want to Land he doesn't want to. It's his prerogative," Gen says.

"This is one for the fuckin' annals. I never thought I would see this day. I mean, you used to teach everyone about...what was that called? Uh, uh, hydrophon—"

"Hydroponics," I say laughing some more.

"Yeah! You were like the bloody civil engineer of pot growing in arctic climates. Now, you don't partake?? When you pass on buds, you officially sell out. I'm gonna consummate this anyway."

Land lights the j and takes a mammoth hit just to spite me. He exhales and the sweet, warm glow of cannabis permeates through the room. I still think it should be legalized, but for me the experience of smoking has ceased to have the transcendental effect it used to have when I was in college. Everything flew happily around me back in those days. Now, I have found that smoking makes me paranoid and my senses are blunted and I can't afford that when I need to be as polished as possible in this cutthroat, rat race cult of capitalism which controls the real world. It has never been about escapism for me. But, seeing Land so triumphant because he is smoking a j and I am not, makes me wonder what he is getting out of it now. It has to be safe harbor for him. One that takes him out of the ugliness around him and puts him back into the place where communion with satisfaction is easy and cheap. That's not how it used to be. Land was filled with desire and yearning in school and smoked to enhance his perceptions and ideals not to escape.

Land and Gen take turns taking hits. All the while, Land flips through the TV with the remote. "Land, what is this place called again? George West?" I ask.
"Yup. We're in George West, Texas. Along way from the City, huh, Gen?"
"Yup." Gen answers.
"He must have been some oil tycoon who got a town named after him," Land says.
"Who?" Gen asks.
Land laughs.

"George West," he responds.

"Oh," Gen sighs. I can tell she is already stoned.

"Is anyone hungry?" Land asks.

"Getting the munchies already?" I say.

"No. It's just that we never grabbed dinner. We last ate at that diner way back when."

"I'm not hungry," I say.

"Gen, what about you?" Land asks her.

Gen is baked now and has melted into the mattress.

"Uhh, what?" She asks.

"Are you hungry?' Land again says.

"No. Just tired. Think I'm gonna close my eyes for a little while."

"O.K.," Land says and he makes a funny face as he looks back at me. Gen draws back the bed sheets and slides underneath. She turns to the side and her still wet hair covers her face as she shuts her eyes. "Forget dinner tonight, huh, Land? It's late and I don't think George West has a Taco Bell."

Land is mesmerized by the sounds coming from the TV and barely manages to acknowledge my assessment of the dinner situation. He has found a public broadcast station and an orchestra is performing some classical song. The song is beautiful and I tune in as well.

"Listen to that, man. It's just one instrument. An oboe. Holding on to a single, unwavering note. Absolutely beautiful. Listen…," Land whispers to me as he closes his eyes.

It is sublime and simple, yet tragic and fleeting. One instrument, one note which drops into another note and then sits there before escalating to another. I look at Land and a single tear falls out his right eye and hangs on the inlet by the bridge of his nose before he wipes it away. I am a little embarrassed to say anything so I sit silently trying to ignore what I have just witnessed. The music finishes and the audience claps. The scene then cuts to a man and a woman sitting in chairs and asking for our support. A 1-800 number appears at the bottom of the screen and then fast shots of volunteers answering ringing phones are shown.

"I'm gonna be a member of these PBS stations now that I have some cash to donate," Land says. "Public broadcasting is all that's good on TV."

"You think?" I ask.

"Oh, yeah, yeah. The other day, I saw a piece with Henry Louis 'Skip' Gates, Jr. He was in Ethiopia. The cat goes all the way to northernmost Ethiopia to a town called Axum. There's this whole lore in Ethiopia about how the ark of the covenant is in the country. They have parades where they create replicas of the ark and they carry them above their heads as they retell the story of the ark's arrival in Ethiopia."

Land stops to take to another hit of the j which at this point is reduced to a roach.

"Uhh, anyway. Here's the point of the story. Gates goes to this town where the ark is said to be kept. It's called St. Mary's church and it's a little place surrounded by a high, iron fence. There's a couple of clerical guards there, but the only person who *actually* sees the ark and takes care of it is this old priest who doesn't give a fuck who you are or who you represent—you still can't see the ark or even be allowed to enter the gates of the church. This priest is one of a long line of priests who have taken care of the ark after Solomon's son, I forget the dude's name, brought the ark to Axum."

Another deep hit.

"The priest, uh…," Land coughs. "When this priest dies, he chooses his successor with his dying breath, man. That's deep."

"What did Gates do?" I ask genuinely interested in the story.

"He was definitely frustrated and being a professor, he was after proof of the ark being in the church. I think Gates got a good glimpse into what faith is all about though."

"He must have been pissed that he did not get to go inside," I say.

"He was and he did ask one of the guards why no one was ever allowed to see the ark, since if it was really there this would be so meaningful to mankind. The guard said some shit to the effect of: *This is our faith. We believe in it and that's it. We don't need to ask for more. We don't ask for proof and we don't ask to see proof.*"

Land takes a last hit. He seems wise to me, sitting there on the bed, digging classical music and then making the transition into discussing the ark being in Ethiopia. The way he connects things is astounding. Like a soulful sage. He goes on.

"The significance of not being able to see the ark really speaks to what human faith is all about. It ain't easy. Especially, when we live in a world where everything is about results and the bottom line. There is something greater than us out there."

"Are you telling me you now believe in a god, Land?"

"I'm not talking about believing in an all-powerful god, man. Shit, I need a roach clip." Land scrutinizes what's left of the j.

"I think that j is spent, Land."

"There's always one more hit left and that last one is where the THC is the strongest. That much I've learned my friend."

But not tonight. Land's efforts to squeeze the last remaining hit out of the j prove unfruitful. He looks silly at one point as he tries inhaling so hard that his cheeks completely disappear, and loud sucking noises result. He finally gives up and throws the j into the trash next to the TV. Gen has completely passed out and Land reminds me to keep my voice down.

"So, you were saying…," I start off.

"Ummm, about what?"

"The ark. Faith…"

"Oh, oh, yeah. I still don't buy that jive about one all-powerful god who created us in his image. What I meant with the story of Gates' desire to see the ark was that it's impossible for people brought up in a society like America to have real faith. For the Ethiopians it's easy. It's embedded in their culture and they've had to survive civil war and famine with their faith still intact. So, they don't go around questioning why it is only that some old priest gets to see the ark and no one else. They believe the ark is there and that belief gets passed on and so forth until it becomes faith. There's no parallel in Western countries because there faith has been pinned down under the scrutiny of science."

He breaks off and starts flipping through the TV which he now mutes.

"I think it was Francis Bacon who said man must break down nature and force her to reveal her secrets, right, Tal?"

"I dunno. I think so."

"Yeah, it was. Well, that's what we did. We broke nature down and in the process not only fucked shit up environmentally but also spiritually."

"How do you mean?"

"What time is it?" Land instead asks.

"Close to one," I say looking at my watch.

"Fuck. Where has the time gone? Let me get back to what I was saying. You look at homo sapiens and you see that each race when it was starting out believed in these great cosmologies and mythologies explaining from whence man had sprung. Haha! You like that one! *Whence!*"

"Nice choice in words, man," I say understanding that now Land is a gooey-eyed stony mess who is being sidetracked by his own word selection.

"So, the myth was the tool which early man used to bring balance between himself and the environment surrounding him. And with the advent of religion, the myth became more organized—eventually becoming faith. But, things went wrong because religion became politicized and the rise of science exposed a lot of the fallacies in religiosocial views. That's where you had all the shit with Galileo and the Catholic Church."

"Right." I assent.

"Now, in the Twentieth Century, where more technological and industrial progress has occurred than in all the history of man before it, we got a technocracy. Faith is a fossil. So, it was real refreshing to see that the myth in the way I've described it—or faith—still existed in Ethiopia. That was the import of my musings."

"So, you see myth and faith as sister concepts?"

"Oh, yeah. Very close. I think the myth becomes faith when a larger pool of people accept it as being true."

"Hmmm. Interesting way to say it."

"Nah, bra, these are just things I think about from time to time. You were the philosophy major, remember?"

"Yeah, right. You had to remind me that I learned absolutely nothing from that. I think I got more out of your soliloquy tonight than from four years of philosophy lectures."

"That's nice, Tal."

I'm not sure if it is the second-hand smoke or the sight of seeing Land wipe a tear off his face or the words he has just laid on me, but I'm overwhelmed with a barrage of emotions. Elation. Sadness. Fear. I feel curiously emboldened though. Like I have been privy to some great insight that may serve me somewhere down the line. I collect myself and then tell Land that I'm tired and that I'm going to crash. Land seems to understand my sudden wish to cut things short and to retreat to my room. He himself is about to pass out as well. He mouths goodnight to me and I slip out of the room quietly.

George West, Texas?? I just came in last Saturday night on an American Airlines flight from LAX to New Orleans to partake in Mardi Gras. It is now Thursday night or should I say early Friday morning and I've joined up with Land and Gen who are both on the lam and headed to Monterrey, Mexico. I am having trouble sleeping and remember that I once read that the average American falls asleep in nine minutes. I must neither be average nor American because the clock near my bed now reads 2:07 a.m. and I've been in bed since 1:30 and I'm still not close to falling asleep. My mind is preoccupied with this ride.

I think back to what Gen told me in New Orleans about Land not really wanting to go to Mexico. That it was really a front for some other ulterior motive or a "crusade" as she called it. Land seems serious to me about going to Mexico, after all, we're only one hundred and fifteen miles from the border. But, I can't get over his idiotic behavior out on Bourbon either. Bolting in front of an oncoming street sweeper? His excuse for tempting fate like that still troubles me and I resort to turning on the TV in order to keep myself from analyzing this.

Late, late night TV with its infomercial insanity and plethora of B-movies provides a welcome diversion. I listen to one inspirational speaker talk about how Walt Disney was turned down by four hundred banks before procuring his first loan to finance his vision of Mickey Mouse. Then there's Prozac. The godsend, anti-depressant drug which saves relationships and makes people happy. I remember a line from Henry Rollins' *Boxed Life* where he quotes Jim Morrison saying, "*Hold on to your depression*" because it provides balance. Prozac must then really fuck everything up because it imposes an unnatural balance on the user. I switch to another channel and see a movie which I recognize as *Orca*. It's a scene where an erstwhile whale hunter played by Richard Harris is following a killer whale—whose family Harris' character had slaughtered—out into the Arctic. Harris is lying down on the floor of his boat listening to the sonar calls of this killer whale with which he is now locked in mortal combat. A female marine biologist (played by the then-still sexy Charlotte Rampling) has come along with Harris and is also listening to the whale's calls. She asks

Harris what the whale's calls mean, that is, what the whale is telling him. Harris, who is in a melancholy daze at this point in the film, translates the whale's call for her. He says the whale is his "drunken driver" or something like that who is luring Harris out to the cold sea to meet his fate. Though this scene is meant to be poignant, I find it funny and can't stop laughing. I really think it's hilarious.

I've seen this film dozens of times. It's meant to be a sad tale of the savagery of man, but this scene suddenly contorts into a comedy now! It's clear to me as I now watch the scene that Harris' character is simply bullshitting heavily in order to impress this bird! That's it. Just another cat and bird story, no deeper meaning. I laugh and the laughing tires me out. I turn off the TV and feel ready for sleep. As I fade out, I think of Land as alternatively the priest in St. Mary's church in Axum and as the killer whale driving Richard Harris into glacial waters. I can't see what insight Land possesses so confidently into life in this world or whether he will ever be able to pass this knowledge to someone else with his dying breath. I also don't know what Land means half the time and have no idea where our journey is actually headed. If only Charlotte Rampling were here to help.

IV

"Time to get up, man," I hear Land say as he knocks on my door. I roll to my side and read the alarm clock through foggy eyes. It's 10:17 a.m. I slowly get to my feet and take a second to gather myself. Land again knocks.

"Yeah, man, I'm awake!" I tell him. I get to the door and open it.

"Morning. Grab a shower and meet in the lobby in half an hour," Land orders.

"What's the rush?" I ask.

"Nothing. We just want to check out and find a place to have breakfast. Dig?"

"O.K. See you then."

I close the door and walk to the shower. I try to be as careful as I can when I get inside this time. I don't need to get scalded again. But, it just doesn't happen. The water coming from the showerhead can't be tamed in any way and I'm too groggy to come up with any creative body positioning in order to wash myself without getting burned. Instead, I end up washing my face and head in the sink. I do a quick brush of my teeth and throw on some jeans and a white t-shirt. I pack my bags and glance around the room one last time making sure I haven't left anything behind. I then head for the lobby.

Gen and Land are already there waiting for me. I say hello and Land tells me to place my room key in a drop box. We all head to the car, load it up and get back on 59. Gen seems very refreshed and more in tune with Land today. She's looking at the map intently as Land drives.

"The next place coming up, where we'll probably find some place to eat is Freer. About forty miles away," Gen tells us.

"That's fine. Freer it is. Cool with you Tal?"

"Sounds good," I say.

Land reaches for a tape cassette as he drives. I see his right hand fumbling through a bunch of tapes nestled under the tape deck.

"Need some help?" Gen asks.

"Nah, I found it." Land says. He then pops the cassette into the tape deck and soon the lost words of early Leonard Cohen come out hand in hand with his pre-gravelly, nicotine stained voice.

"Nice, Land," I say. Gen agrees with the musical selection as well and she lights up as she listens to the music.

I haven't heard this song in years. It's called *So Long, Marianne* and was sort of an anthem for Land and I. At the end of any meaningful, collaborative thing that we did together whether it was a big bash, or some coup we had pulled on campus, somehow this song would find its way into our stereo. It was the ultimate flashback song for us, and as you may have guessed it played constantly during our senior year when Land and I lived in this great duplex in the heart of our college town. Gen got hooked on it as well because she hung out in our living room a lot during that last year and so was incessantly exposed to it. The three of us each zone into the lyrics and we get ready to explode when the chorus rolls around. It's simple with a cyclical ring to it:

*So long, Marianne, it's time that we began
to laugh and cry and cry and laugh about it
all again.*

We each sing the chorus loud and way off key each
time it's time to sing it. For three minutes we block
everything out of our lives and revel in the
memories the song brings back. It has the strange
effect of making me feel optimistic about where our
journey is headed.
"You know he's now up in the mountains in your
neck of the woods, man." Land says to me.
"Serious? I've been wondering what happened to
him."
"Yeah. I think it's called Mt. Baldy. He's there on
a permanent retreat practicing Zen Buddhism under
the tutelage of some fabled Buddhist monk!"
"No, really?" Gen asks.
"I read about in, uh, I think it was *Rolling Stone*.
He's become a disciple of some sort and shuns the
materialism of his former life. It's true."
"Wow. Like Cat Stevens becoming Yusuf Islam.
Same kind of sudden turnaround, you know?" Gen
says.
"But, I don't buy it. You don't pen shit like
Moonshadow in the case of Cat Stevens and *One of
Us Cannot Be Wrong*—which by the way is coming
up next on this tape—and then become an ascetic.
Ascetics don't share, and art—whether sung,
painted, written, performed or played—is
fundamentally about sharing. These two cats—they
still want to share. Trust me."
"Interesting take on things as usual, Land," Gen
says and she looks at me and I smile back.

The deceptively monotone delivery of the lyrics to *One of Us Cannot Be Wrong* starts playing in the car now. Again, it's been such a long time since I've heard Cohen's songs. I know I have this album in my collection, but it is probably buried somewhere in my apartment in Hollywood. I think this song was recorded in the Sixties when Cohen first broke onto the scene. I always picture something different when I hear this song. I also have heard this song sung by Cohen on another album which he recorded in the late Eighties and I remember that the song took on a completely new complexion of meaning because of Cohen's age-riddled voice.

The verse that comes in three quarters of the way through the song is this:

> *I heard of a saint who had loved you, so I studied all night in his school*
> *He taught that the duty of lovers is to tarnish the golden rule*
> *And just when I was sure that his teachings were pure he went and drowned himself in the pool*
> *His body is gone, but back here on the lawn his spirit continues to drool.*

"What do you think of when you hear that verse?" Land asks us.

"It has to be an allusion to Jesus Christ," Gen says.

"Hmmm. I guess I can see that. What about you, bra?" Land asks me.

"Jay Gatsby, I think. I just imagine this cat who had worked so hard to get everything and now's he's floating in the water face down. Consumed by all that he created. Arms outstretched and body bloated."

"Interesting shit, Tal."

"Thanks, man." I start to laugh. "But, don't take it so seriously, Land."

Land laughs too.

"Well, what about you, Land. What do you think of?" Gen asks.

"Hmmm. You know, I'm just taking a straight-line view of the lyrics. I see Brian Jones of the Stones dead in his English manor's backyard pool. Didn't he go out that way?"

"Yeah, I think so," I answer.

"Yeah. That's what I see. Sorry, there's no deeper imagery there. But, other times, when I listen to the lines, I don't think of an individual person. I just think of a faceless corpse of hypocrisy. That's what the lyrics are really about anyway—being told things which are supposed to be the truth and then finding out it was all con. A con designed to control others and keep them suppliant."

"I knew it was more than Brian Jones!" I exclaim.

"Me too!" Gen shouts.

"You guys know me too well. But, I am serious. Right now, I just see Brian Jones wrapped in the latest Sixties fashion and being fished out of his pool by the bobbies."

About fifteen minutes later, we arrive in Freer, Texas. We pull up at a small family restaurant. We are all starving and ready to chow on the local cuisine. A hostess takes us to a table and hands us each a menu. It's like Denny's without the $1.99 Grand Slam Breakfast. A waitress comes over and we eagerly give her our orders. Gen then brings out a map and again seems to be intently analyzing something.

"What's up, Gen?" I ask.

"Nothing. Just checking out how much longer we have to the border."

"We're probably only eighty miles away," Land says.

"A little less. About sixty-six miles to the Rio Grande." Gen says.

"Oh, yeah? At long last I get to see where the word *wetback* was coined!" Land screams.

Gen and I laugh out loud too. We all have the sense that we're going to make it. We're going to pull this shit off! We're definitely at ease and start to crack jokes about the Texan drawls we hear coming from the tables around us. The food comes out and it is as good as gold. I have French toast and two eggs sunny side up. Gen dittos this and Land takes a steak and egg medley. Good fresh orange juice and strong coffee offer nice bookends to our meal. We eat in silence for about ten minutes. Only the clang of silverware with our plates accompanies our eating. Land finishes first and motions the waitress over for a refill of coffee. I look over at him as he drinks his newly refilled coffee, puts it down, and then surveys the restaurant. He is triumphant at this very moment. He smiles at me and nods as if to tell me he really appreciates me being here with him and Gen.

"How is the French toast?" Land asks us.

"Real good," I say. "What do you think, Gen?"

"Good, I didn't realize I was soooo hungry."

"Coffee isn't bad either," Land says and he holds his cup to us as he takes another sip.

"Gen, you want a refill?" Land asks.

"Nooo. Coffee runs right through me. If I have another cup we will be stopping at every rest area from here to Laredo!"

"I hear that. You know, I think I'm gonna take a celebratory piss myself!" Land almost shouts this! When he gets up to leave the table, other people in the restaurant are staring at him in disbelief.

"Sorry folks for that outburst. It's just so good to be back in Freer!" Land tells the unblinking patrons looking at him, and he then saunters off to the restroom.

I shake my head in a mix of admiration and embarrassment. I look over at Gen who is laughing hysterically.

"He's quite a character isn't he?" I say to her.

"Yes he is," Gen says. Then, she quietly whispers, "I'm beginning to think that I'm in love with him."

I freeze with coffee cup mid-air to my lips. I get it together though and finish bringing the cup to my lips where I take a light sip.

"Mmmm…," I have to clear my throat before beginning. "I take it you're serious and not fucking with me?"

"Yes."

"And he doesn't know about this?"

"I'm not sure if I know about this."

"You gotta know, Gen. This isn't a time for you to be pussyfooting around your feelings."

"Uh, yeah. I know. It's just that he's so hard to read, but we've gotten so close because of all this—and that's what makes me uncertain about my feelings. I don't know how much of what I'm feeling is because of the situation we're in. He's all that I have at this point and dominates my thoughts. It's like I'm consumed by him."

"Just don't change your behavior toward him right now. *Please.* You guys want to continue through this mess that you're in with everything staying the same between you. You understand what I'm saying?"

"I don't know."

"Yes, you do. You're smart enough to realize what the potential consequences could be if you all of sudden tell Land you've fallen for him and he doesn't know how to react, or just…doesn't react. Things can really get dicey. Just suck it up right now until you know you guys are in the clear."

"What if we'll never be in the *clear*, Tal?"

"Stay positive. If anyone can get this thing behind you and get you back to where you feel safe and secure, it's Land. You know that. So, have faith in him."

"What about you, Tal?"

"What?"

"Do you still have faith in him? You haven't seen him that much since we all graduated, have you?"

"No. No, I haven't seen him that much. But, he still—"

I see Land coming back to the table and quickly shut up. Gen picks up the map again.

"You kids finished?" Land asks.

"Yup," I say.

"Well, then it's time to go!" Land slaps his hands together. "I already took care of the check up front."

"Thanks, Land. I appreciate it." I say.

"No worries, bra. Just happy that you're here."

Gen and I get up and follow Land to the car. I play it all off, trying not to look at how Gen is dealing with the fact that she has confided in me. Land tells us that he needs some gas and pulls up to a gas station around the corner from the restaurant. I volunteer to run out and buy some goodies for the remaining hour we have left until the border. As I walk toward the mini-mart, I have to admit that I feel validated like crazy thinking about how right I was when I told Gen about my thoughts on men and women having "platonic" relationships. What a crock! And now check this out, here's Gen telling me that she's *beginning to think* she's falling in love with Land. Bullshit. She was into him from the get go. She's just now accepting it because probably like other well-to-do birds she had everything mapped out at first, including the perfect guy that would come along and sweep her off her feet at the smiling approval of her parents of course. Law school was really a diversion for her. She was never going to be an attorney who actually practiced law. The degree was more for decorative value. It would increase her market value and her parents could say things like, "Dr. So-and-so, I'd like you to meet my daughter…and she's a lawyer."

So, then Land comes along. This wild cat with eyes ablaze, talking about wanting to live like a Faulknerian saga—capturing life between one massive subject and a lofty predicate. She was his from that moment on, but she didn't want to believe that this Mexican-Zuni-Rumanian orthodox motherfucker was her destined lot in life. It had to be this kind of hang-up which held her back. Her class-conscious parents would never go for this cat that she would have to one day bring back home to them. She played the role of friend to Land and now she finally owns up to her true feelings when her whole world is on the verge of collapsing. He's all she has got.

And what about Land? Hah. I have a gut feeling that he doesn't reciprocate Gen's feelings. He can't feel the same way about her. He's too much of an opportunist when it came to women, and if he wanted her, he would have had her long ago, and then moved on. He's definitely using her for whatever ends he needs now. So, if shit falls apart over this crazy little thing called love, then the whole shithouse can come down on them. I have got to watch out for myself. I dig Land. He's an old best friend, but I don't want to be what is called an "accessory after the fact." He's not who I am worried about anyway—Gen is the problem. I can't trust her to bottle up her feelings and pretend nothing has changed in the way she feels for Land. It's gonna come out and I don't want to be standing in the middle of them when it does because I'm a firm believer in what Dylan said when he sang: *But, she breaks just like a little girl.*

There's only one choice. I have to cut out on Land and Gen now. There is just no way that I can chance going all the way to Monterrey with them. Things are complicated emotionally, which is the worst kind of complication. I'll go as far as Laredo and then I guess I'll take a Greyhound up to San Antonio or someplace where I can find a flight to L.A. I'll have to break the news to them en route to Laredo. Gotta make up an excuse that Land won't be able to see through. I rack my brain.

There are about four people ahead of me in line. I've already grabbed a couple of Snickers bars and regular-flavored Trident chewing gum—no sugar added—for Gen. I just need to get a pack of Camel lights. Outside, I see Land pumping gas and Gen is in the driver side of the car reading a newspaper she must have found laying around the gas station. The line is slow and the person at the head of the line is holding things up because he can't get his act together. I start getting uneasy as do the other two people ahead of me.

"Come on asshole get a move on," I try to say this low under my breath, but instead I blurt it out loud enough for the guy at the head of the line to hear. He turns around and glares at me. An older gentleman—vaguely Mexican—seems he can't make up his mind as to how much gas he wants in his tank. I feel bad for chewing out this helpless old cat, but I was so preoccupied with making up excuses to get out of this trip that I lost control of myself for a second.

In all honesty, however, I have lost the ability to remain patient with adults anyway. Kids, I can hang with. But, adults, especially those who should know better, I have no patience for. Living in L.A. has also made me experience road rage first hand. Land got a laugh out of me trying to navigate through the streets of L.A. with one hand on the wheel and the other constantly signaling obscenities to those who I thought were intentionally slowing me down or blocking traffic. I even told Land about my rule of thumb: "Always stay in the left lane when you're on surface streets in L.A." When Land asked me why, I told him that it was because those fuckin' Metro buses hogged the right lane and when you got behind one of them you were dead. Buses were the antichrist and could always be found clunkering in front of me when I desperately needed to be somewhere important on time. My habit of constantly checking the time is another symptom of the road rage phenomenon. Because when you're stuck in traffic, you're always checking the clock to see how much time has passed since you last moved one car length. Even when I'm not behind the wheel I find myself looking at my left wrist for an update on the time because I'm always in a rush and someone or something is always holding me up. And even when there's no watch on my wrist, I still look for the time on my empty wrist. Pathetic.

Land never owned a watch, so he claims. He refused to buy into the notion of what he called an "arbitrary" sense of temporal and spatial cognition the Western work ethic had forced us to adopt. This one is rough, but I have to relay it. You see, it goes to the choreographed existence Land thinks people in America lead. We have three meals a day. Breakfast in the morning, lunch at noon and dinner in the evening. We work by keeping hours of nine to five, so called "banker's hours". We have two days that someone decided were to be set aside for us that we call the "weekend". Land's whole trip is that this was not something he had agreed to. It was set up relatively recently with the dawn of industrialization and the arrival of the combustible engine, assembly line, and etcetera. It's completely out of whack with our cicadic rhythm. Cicadas—those giant mechanical flies which inter themselves underground for seventeen years and then come out like clockwork in the summer to molt, mate, and perish. If something all of a sudden forced these bugs to come out, let's say, after only seven years instead of seventeen, then their whole species might be in jeopardy of becoming extinct because the accelerated pace would not jive with their internal rhythm of how to regulate their lives.

Americans, Land once told me, have within the last century created an accelerated way of life that is now so routine and everyone has adapted it to such an extreme extent that we actually look forward to our two weeks of vacation every year like it's an exceptional gift. The whole concept of time as twenty-four/seven was screwing us in the head and gravitating the next generation toward doing time and lines because respect couldn't be taught in sound bites. A generation of sleep deprived, disrespectful, quick to pull the trigger Americans were now molting.

The other thing that Land would say really upset him was that the concept of spatiality had been warped in America. The average American's comprehension of the space surrounding him or her was limited to the town or city they lived in. The simple appreciation of how expansive and multidimensional this world we lived in was non-existent. Thinking about this now, I can see how it ties into Land's belief that the myth having been lost in the Western world eradicated any wonder and humility that man originally had for the world he lived in. I know so many people who think L.A. is the whole world! Not even that expansive—some think Beverly Hills is the whole world!! I understand Land's sentiments on this. There is no question in my mind that the Great American Experiment has had a lot of success, but it has also created a citizenry with no understanding of how insignificant America is in the larger, global picture of mankind. It's not their fault, Land defended them, the images they see on the tube, on film, in print or wherever show American hegemony all over the world. It's all just really a big America. A huge United States of the World.

But, unlike Land, who I know tries to educate others and lead them to question the truth behind our accelerated existence, I have chosen to be part of this same temporally and spatially challenged citizenry because that is where the action is. The action that leads to cash and nice homes and cars and beautiful women. I could care less that I am part of the same decline. Most people realize fast that you gotta get paid in order to *enjoy* life. And that also the finer things in life—birds included—come with *bigger* price tags. That's just reality. Those like Land, who question the very machinery that defines the rest of us are fooling themselves and assign themselves to the fringes. Besides, the eschatological decline he sees in the rest of us started way before I ever got on the scene, so my plan is to ride it out like everyone else and the whole group would go down together if Land ends up being right. That's my reasoning anyway.

I finally get to the cash register, ask for a pack of Camel lights, and then slide over the necessary cash. Land has finished pumping gas and has driven up to the store entrance. Gen opens the door for me and I get in. I hand the cigs to Land, the Trident to Gen and move to put the Snickers in the glove compartment. While I try to place the Snickers inside, I see a black steely object under some papers. When I move the papers away from the object, I discover that the object is a gun and my blood runs cold for a split second. I close the glove compartment and try not to let on that I've seen it, but Land reads my body language all too well. "Don't worry, Tal, it doesn't bite."
I hold back my revulsion. I've never dug guns. I just have never have bought into that whole second amendment mentality for the right to bear arms.
"Why don't you just get rid of that like I asked you to?" Gen asks Land.

"Insurance, babe. I gotta hang onto it like a crucifix while we push through this situation of ours. O.K.?"
"Is it loaded?" I ask.
"No, man."
I exhale out in relief, but I'm still rattled. Seeing the gun convincingly illustrates the situation Land and Gen are in.
"So, is this the glock that made it all possible?" I ask.
"Ahhh! I thought we weren't allowed to fill you in on the details, Tal!" Land answers.
"Yeah, yeah. Whatever, man. Just keep it away from me," I'm annoyed by Land's teasing.
"Not a problem. Just don't snoop around the glove compartment anymore!"
"I wasn't snooping, bra. It was just sticking out when I opened the fuckin' thing."
"Tal, relax, he's just playing around with you," Gen tries to calm me.
"Yeah, it's always just fun and games. I know, I know."
I get quiet and start thinking about when it will be a good time for me to tell Land and Gen that I'm bailing.

We get back on 59 for the last leg of our journey. Land and Gen discuss having Gen make a call from Laredo to her friend in New Orleans to see if anyone has come around her apartment. After half an hour, I see a sign that says "Laredo 10 miles" and I decide it's time to tell Land and Gen about my plans.
"Hey, Land, I think I better call it quits at Laredo."
"What are you talking about?" Land asks.
"I got to be honest. It really is time for me to get back to L.A. It's been nearly a week since I've

been gone and I have a couple of job…er—offers
that I must get back to and follow up on." I know
this is flimsy, but it was the best excuse I could
come up with.

"Tal, this isn't about the gun, is it?" Land asks.

"No, no, man. Has nothing to do with it. I never
planned on being gone so long, you know? It's
been great to see you both, but I really must get
back. I have to pay rent. You know what I mean?
I really need to find work soon, otherwise, I may
have to move back east and stay with my parents for
a while. That's how serious my situation is Land."

"I see." Land says as he looks straight out the
windshield. Gen doesn't say a word.

"Yeah, I'm sorry about this guys. But, I have to go
back."

"No need to apologize, man. If you have to go
back, you have to go back. Thanks for coming as
far as you have," Land answers.

"That's thanks to you guys. Seeing you both, really
brought back memories of the good old days," I say.

"Yeah, it did, didn't it? Huh, Gen?" Land says.

"It was good seeing you, Tal." Gen flatly replies.

"Same here," I answer.

"Well, Gen, it's just the two of us again." Land
says.

"Yup." Gen says and she looks at me from the
corners of her eyes—as if she realizes now that she
should have never told me about her feelings for
Land.

"When we get to Laredo just drop me off at a bus
station. I can take it from there."

"Easy, bra. Sure, I'll do that, but you don't have to
start getting too distant with us."

"Sorry, man."

"It's O.K. But, I have to remind you that you will be missing out on the adventure of a lifetime. Monterrey is beautiful this time of year. And, listen, if it's a money problem, Tal, you know I can take care of that! Heehee!!"

"No, man. It's time for me to get back to Lala land. That's it. Thanks again for bringing me along. It's already been an adventure, Land."

Gen, I think, is really distraught by my sudden decision to bail out on them. I do feel like I am abandoning her after she has confided in me, but I don't want to stick around when things are so emotionally clouded. I take a look at her. She seems so fragile, like a fawn inadvertently left behind by her mother. It's just her and Land again.

We get to Laredo at around 1:10 in the afternoon. There's a dry heat with the temperature in the mid-eighties and it reminds me of the Old West. We take a drive through the center of town and by accident come across a Greyhound bus station. Land finds some parking and I grab my bags and Land and Gen follow me inside the station to the ticket booth. It's a Friday afternoon and there's a shitload of vaqueros, caballeros and cowboy-boot wearing white folk with bus tickets in hand. I ask the lady behind the booth when the next bus to San Antonio leaves. She says 2:30 p.m., so that gives me an hour. I shell out $25 for the one way ticket to San Antonio. I walk back to where Gen and Land are sitting and a kind of sullenness blankets us. It's the end of the road for me.

"You guys don't have to wait until I leave," I say trying my best to be diplomatic about my out-of-the-blue about-face.

"No, it's cool, bra. I wanna see you off. It will bring closure." Land replies.

We kick back for a while, each of us in our own private Idahos. No words are exchanged just occasional glances at one another which bring acknowledgement of what the last couple of days have meant in our lives. Near the ticket counter, I notice two older men start yelling at each other and then one pushes the other. I keep watching them having no idea what has set them off. They end up in a locked embrace. It seems both of them have run out of gas and are now left to stare at each other with gnashing gums. A couple of people move in between them and break them apart.

"I think the guy in the hat just walked ahead of the other guy in line." Gen says.

"Yeah?" I ask.

"Yeah, I was watching the whole thing. The guy in the hat completely ignored the other guy and just stepped in front of him. The other guy then tapped him on the shoulder and probably balled him out. That's when the pushing started." Gen explains.

"How charming," Land says. "And that's why we should reinstate the duel. Let these cats go at it. Count fifteen paces, turn and shoot at one another. Maybe that will deter their eagerness to fight before talking about it."

"You gotta admit it was kinda funny to see these two old timers square off like that," I say.

"I don't go for rubber-necking, bra."

"Oh, yeah. Right. But, if one these guys slapped the other in the face with a glove and then challenged him to a duel outside you'd be the first one there!" I answer.

"Right you are. You're quite perceptive, Tal, old boy. When you drop the gauntlet, I'll be there."

I am slightly puzzled by Land's remark here, which I take as almost threatening. I shrug it off though. Land's words by their very nature usually come off as having double meanings.

It's time for me to board the bus to San Antonio. I get up to say goodbye to Land and Gen and tell them to drop me an email whenever they have time. But, it is a disingenuous goodbye. It's obvious. Gen feels like dead wood when I hug her, and Land hugs me with such fervor that it feels more like an assault.

"Take care of yourself, Land." I say.

"Yeah, thanks. You too." He replies.

"Gen, make sure Land doesn't engage in any off-the-wall behavior when you guys cross over the Rio Grande and through INS border control."

"Well, Tal, if you were coming you could help keep Land in control," Gen says and she looks at me like I've wounded her.

"I know you can handle him, Gen," I smile at her.

"Bye," I say as I climb into the bus.

I walk down the bus and take a seat next to the window where I can see Land and Gen for some final moments before leaving Laredo. They put on tired smiles and I know they are deeply disappointed—each for their own reasons—in seeing me leave. The bus is full of drifters and grifters and this bald, white cat with gray-tinted glasses sits next to me. The bus driver gets in and starts the low growl of the engine. We sit there for a while and Land and Gen still wait outside. Then, the bus starts moving and I wave adios to them for the last time. Land yells out some shit to me that I can't make out because of the engine noise. I press the right side of my face on the glass and see Land

and Gen walk away. A momentary despondency washes over me and I feel that I've passed on the adventure of my life as Land had said. Maybe this was supposed to be *it*? Going to Monterrey with Land and Gen. Maybe something or someone was waiting for me there and I pulled out because of what?? I didn't want to be caught between a complicated emotional situation or caught by the police? I guess those were both the reasons and they seem ridiculous now from my vantage point aboard a Greyhound bus, alone, and returning back to the routine.

I fucked up and this bums me out. I can't pry my face off the cool window and as we head onto interstate 35 north and armadillo carcasses and tumbleweeds whiz by, I am gripped by terror at the thought of what I've done. Cheating my destiny? Who did I think I was? Why did I rush into my decision to leave at the first cracks I saw in this fantastically spontaneous jaunt?

"Where ya headed, mate?" The cat next to me asks with what I think is an Australian accent.

At first, I contemplate blowing this guy off and not answering. But, I realize that it's a long bus ride, so I better make it as easy as possible. I manage to unstick my face from the glass.

"I'm headed to San Antonio and from there back to L.A."

"Oh, L.A. I've had layovers there. City of Angels, isn't that right?"

"Yeah."

I'd like to end the conversation with that, but I have to engage in some conversation in order to get my mind off the doubts that are circling in my head.

"Where are you from?" I ask.

"I'm a Kiwi, mate."

"New Zealand then?"

He nods. "From South Auckland."

"Far from home, huh?"

"That's how I like it. I take off four to six weeks off every year to travel."

"Four to six weeks!" I ask in disbelief.

"Sure. It's mandatory in Australia and New Zealand. You know the term *walkabout* is not just something America cinema introduced."

"Ohhh," I say not making the connection he is insinuating. "Where have you gone?"

"Been all over. Egypt. Most of eastern and southern Africa. Brazil, Chile, Peru and Argentina. All through Europe, the U.S. and I've just come up from Mexico City."

"How did you come up from Mexico City to Laredo?"

"I have a couple of friends who know the country and we drove up the Atlantic coast. Went to these great coastal towns like Tuxpan, Tampico and then turned west and drove through Victoria City and Monterrey—where my friends had businesses to attend to and I hopped on a bus that took me to Nuevo Laredo. Just came across the border this morning. It's been quite a month I can tell you, mate."

"I can imagine. How's your Spanish?"

"Don't speak a word! All I know is *cerveza* and *tequila*!"

"That's probably enough, man."

"Cheers, mate."

"Where you headed from San Antonio?"

"I'm going on to Dallas and will to fly from there to L.A. to catch a Qantas flight to Sydney. From

there, I'm going to Perth for a quick wine tour
before going back to Auckland."

"Perth has vineyards?"

"Sure. Some of the finest wines in the world come
from there."

"You ever been to Napa valley in California?"

"No, and don't intend to. I don't like California
wines. They can grow a decent red, but their whites
are absolutely dreadful."

"Oh, yeah." I don't know much about wines, but
feign interest. This leads to a long conversation
where the Kiwi goes on and on about grapes,
climate, soil and noses. I can't really follow him. I
try to get him to get back on the topic of his other
travels which I find interesting.

"So, you say you've been in Africa?"

"Many times. Beautiful place. You learn a lot
about yourself while there."

"How do you mean?"

"Well, when you go on safari let's say through the
Serengeti or other parts in northern Tanzania, all
your senses become heightened in an amazing way.
You smell different things when you are in the
bush, and then the absence of sound becomes
interesting."

"Absence of sound?"

"Yes, mate. You see, when you are deep in the
bush, there is nothing but nature and silence. There
are no cars besides your Land Rover and when you
kill its engine you are left with nothing but the
sound of the wind and the animals around you. It
really is amazing. At the same time you, as a man,
feel vulnerable in the face of the untamed nature
around you."

"What about the people you must see in the towns
and villages?"

"East Africans in general are incredibly warm and giving people. The traditional peoples, like the Maasai, are also friendly and have learned to be part of the tourist trade as well."

"Yeah?"

"Oh, yes. They put on these performances and dances for tourists and charge $50 a head to do so."

"You see a lot of other tourists then in Africa?"

"Well, sure, it's a big industry. But, the types of tourists are interesting in and of themselves."

"What?"

"I've been all around the world and can tell you that Asians are everywhere. They go all over."

"Mmmhhmm."

"But, in all my trips through sub-Saharan Africa, I've only seen one Asian tourist and that was in Kilimanjaro airport. And I think he was probably a professional mountain climber. I couldn't believe my eyes, mate. By the way you're not Asian, are you?"

"No."

"Just checking. You sorta have a look—"

"I'm *not*, man. Why are you so keen on the lack of Asian tourists in Africa anyway?"

"I have a theory about the whole thing."

"Well, let's hear it."

"Asians only visit first world countries."

"Come on. That's just silly."

"Look, I live in New Zealand. I see a huge, bloody number of Asians visiting New Zealand and Australia each year. I know they flock to America and love Europe too. But, I have never seen them in South America, and while I was in Mexico again I don't recall seeing any Asian tourists."

"Isn't there a big Japanese influence in Peru?"

"There may be, but that's different, mate. What I'm talking about is Asians from Japan, South Korea, or China who come in large groups and are bussed around countries they go to visit purely as tourists. They take pictures, buy souvenirs and in some places, I've seen them do fascinating things—especially in art museums in Italy. I've seen packs of them busy themselves penciling the works of the masters into perfect reproductions on small pieces of paper."

"That can't be."

"Oh, yes it can. For example, they can copy some Da Vinci painting perfectly within minutes. It's incredible—like machines they stand around with their little notebooks and sketch away while others like me simply stand back and look at the painting."

"They must be art students," I respond.

"Don't take me the wrong way, mate. My only point is that they love Western civilization. They are not drawn to South American or African civilization at all."

"Interesting theory," I say, but I think it is apparent this Kiwi just has some kind of problem with Asians in general.

"I must tell you, however, that in all my travels into some of the last jungles and rainforests on earth, the real jungle is right here in the States."

"Excuse me?" I say not certain that I heard him correctly.

"I was saying that the real jungle is in the U.S., mate."

"What are you talking about?"

"Well, no offence, but it's absolutely out of control here. There's imminent lawlessness."

"What? New Zealand doesn't have its share of problems?"

"Certainly. But, I just crossed over into the U.S. today after a month in Mexico and there's a lot of corruption and bribery there, but the first thing I see in the newspapers in Laredo is how this daytrader tells his co-workers, *I'm about to ruin your day* and he opens fire on them!! I mean, it's bloody insane here! And it appears that kind of violence is a normal occurrence nowadays."

"I guess you're entitled to that perception."

"That's just my take on it, mate."

"That's how we really come off, huh?"

"Yes."

I'm surprised by my remarks. I wholeheartedly agree with this guy, yet I only begrudgingly admit to what he's saying. I remember reading an article where John Lennon talked about Mick Jagger bagging on the Beatles for having a conservative "good boy" image and the Stones being responsible for pushing the envelope with their reckless "bad boy" image which supposedly reflected what rock 'n roll was all about. Lennon said something like, "Hey, it's my band and I can go around knocking it, but some other guy knocking my band—*where does he get off?*"

That's what I feel now. Where does this Kiwi get off pointing out shit about shit he can't really understand. It's my country right or wrong. But, I can't go that far. Land's disapproval looms over me and I can see him barraging me with flurries of historical and social examples of American fuck-ups that I have no answer to.

"I didn't mean any offence, mate." The Kiwi again tells me.

"None taken," I say.

"You know though, the same mindset is everywhere now. I was hit by a taxi in Zanzibar and these taxis are not like those in the States. These Zanzibari taxis are minivan Daihatsus which speed around little narrow streets. All of a sudden, this taxi plows through a bunch of tourists of which I was among and clips the right side of my hip and sends me flying into a small area where I break my fall with my wrists. A miracle that nothing broke, mate."

"Did you get the guy that hit you?"

"That's the point of my story. The guy *never* stopped. He kept on going! This was in Zanzibar—which is a very devout Moslem country. That didn't matter for this bloke though. He hit someone with his taxi and kept right on going. I guess his fare was more important than me life."

"Lucky you're alive."

"Take a look at this," the Kiwi says as he rolls up the sleeves on his right wrist. I see an ugly, purple scar.

"Looks like it hurt," I say.

"My souvenir from Zanzibar, mate."

      Fifteen minutes later, the bus pulls into the San Antonio bus station. I tell the Kiwi that it was nice chatting with him and wish him a fruitful wine tour in Perth. I then go outside and hail a cab to the airport. I get dropped off at the American Airlines ticketing booth, show my wasted return ticket from New Orleans, and ask if there is any way to get on a standby for the next flight to L.A. The representative tells me no, but there's a possibility they can rebook me with America West airlines which does have a flight to L.A. tomorrow at 8:10 in the morning with a stop in Phoenix, but I will have to pay a fee. I tell them that I can live with that, so they take my American Express card and rebook me. I get a ticket for the America West flight with the words "Stand-By" printed on it. "Make sure you arrive at the flight's departure gate early and check-in with the America West representatives there, so they can put you first in line as a stand-by if there are any cancellations or the plane is underbooked," the American Airlines representative tells me. "O.K.," I say. "Thanks." I put my American Express card back into my wallet and then bring it back out again thirty minutes later in order to charge it for a room at the Super-8 motel located just around the corner from the airport. I unwind in the room and it's now a little past 7:30 in the evening. I am too worn out to go out and explore San Antonio. I've heard about this renovated riverwalk area in the city, but just can't motivate myself to check it out tonight.

I stay in for the night, order Domino's and watch CNN until I can't take it anymore, so I switch to HBO which is airing a boxing match. Two white commentators who have never thrown a punch in their lives call the fight which is between two black heavyweights. George Foreman is thrown into the play-by-play commentary for comic relief. Perfect.

V

Back in L.A. by 10:16 the next morning.
Plane travel is counter-intuitive. My flight left at
around 8:15 a.m. It took four and a half hours to get
to L.A. (including the stopover in Phoenix) and
fifteen hundred miles later it's just 10:16 a.m.? No
wonder we still hear about Kitty Hawk—it made
time zones credible. Otherwise, like Land says,
time zones are just arbitrary notions someone long
ago convinced us to accept. Now, I have to
remember where I parked my car one week earlier.
I left my parking ticket on my dashboard, so I know
I am screwed. I take a shuttle from the airport to
Lot C and get off at the E-5 section thinking I had
parked near there. I make a quick survey of the
area, but don't spot my car. I start walking from E-
5 towards F-5 and can feel panic start pumping
slowly through my body. Visions of the hassle and
the annoyance I will have to go through if I cannot
locate my car make me dizzy. But, everything is
cool when I suddenly see the familiar bruised
passenger side of my car. Whew. It's like reuniting
with a family member you haven't seen for awhile.
I pop open the trunk and throw my bag in. It's
laden with dirty clothes, beads and doubloons. I
unlock the driver side door, get in and turn the
ignition allowing my car to warm up. Back in the
saddle again, I drive toward the exit gate and give
my ticket to the attendant who puts it through a
device and the amount due digitally appears in a
screen in front of me. It cleans my wallet out, but
I'm happy to be back and head towards the freeway.
But, as soon as the 405 north on-ramp comes into
sight, I look in my rearview mirror and see a police

car with lights flashing and I know that means I have to pull over at the first convenient area. I curse hard and turn my car to the right side of the street and away from the rush of cars getting on the on-ramp.

I hate cops. And if you don't think you can ever get to the point of really hating cops, L.A. is the place that'll do it. I promise you. This cop taps on my window and I bring it down.
"What's going on, officer?" I ask meekly.
"Seatbelt," he says and he tugs on mine which hangs lifelessly next to my shoulder. Here we go again. I play stupid.
"My flight just got in, uh, sir. I was about to go that Mobil up the street to get some gas. That's all."
No answer. He doesn't even acknowledge my lame excuse. He takes my license and gives me a citation and then says, "Drive safe."

I take a quick look at the citation and I see that one of the boxes checked by the cop is for a category designated: *Descent.* I notice the cop marked in the letter "O". Ostensibly this means "Other". Other than what? White? Black?? The forced categorization and labeling of everything in this country is such an arbitrary, ludicrous drag. It tires me out that everyday I have to fit into such nice, tidy cubby-holes of identification and when they can't fit a circle in a square peg, I suddenly become the "Other."
"Touché, mate," I can hear that Kiwi say.

Being on the fringe of society as the designated "Other" is akin to Ralph Ellison's allegory of the invisibility of the black man's existence in America. This cat managed to write an epic and had nothing left afterwards. It exhausted all his powers to expose this existence to mainstream America and he never wrote anything after it. I know Ellison did put together an essay some time later called *Going into the Territory* and even a posthumous *Juneteeth* was published, but these are fragmentary, incomplete memoirs. (I later—through chance—stumble upon the significance of the title, *Juneteenth*, which is June 19, 1865, when Blacks in Texas learned that they had been set free.) To get to my point though, Ellison's *Invisible Man* is the greatest, fleshed out piece of literature in Americana. Yet, it still fails to find a place in public schools, while *Huckleberry Finn* continues to be passed on as if it is the Bible of the American literary tradition.

So, Ellison's writing about the invisibility of Black America ties directly into me being marginalized by this cop as the *Other*. It's an existence forced upon me and it's trying to break me down into a convenient boxed life. But, the fact is, and I'm reminded of James Baldwin's words here, that those who designate me as the Other cannot *know* themselves without me. That is, without the Other, there is no White or Black. There is no "Us" without "Them."

I'm really pissed about being cited and then adding insult to injury I have to be reminded that I am perceived as not being *Us*. How's that for a welcome home.

I get back to my apartment in Hollywood. It's quiet and the same and the red light on my answering machine flashes repetitively. I throw my bag on the bed and listen to my messages. Nothing of consequence. My stuntwoman girlfriend is back from Montana and wants to talk. I unpack my shit

and put *Filles de Kilimanjaro* on my stereo as I
unwind back into life in L.A.

The next day, a Sunday, I touch base with
friends and family and chat about Mardi Gras and
New Orleans. I don't mention anything to them
about running into old friends who are on the lam. I
then go to Kinko's to make some copies of my
resume, but other than this, I spend most of the day
in a funk unsure of how I should proceed with the
coming week. Possibly contact my temp agency
and see if I can be placed somewhere or undertake
my own search for a more long term gig. I can't
make up my mind and when my girlfriend comes
after we have our obligatory fifteen minute sexual
romp, I tell her that through coincidence I ran into
two old friends from college, Land and Gen. She
asks a few questions, probably trying to figure out
who this Gen girl is who hangs out with two guys.
But, other than that, she is uninterested in friends
from my past. Of course, I reveal nothing to her
about the mess that both of them are in and that I
drove with them all the way to Laredo. I just say
that we all partied in New Orleans and caught up
since I had seen neither of them for over three and a
half years. I tell her that I think I sense a post-
Mardi Gras malaise creeping over me. She then
tells me I should go with her to attend a seminar on
how to become a successful working actor and that
it might help me fend off the malaise. I tell her
she's the actor and I'm not interested, but she insists
that the seminar really applies to succeeding in life
in general and that succeeding in acting is the hook
they use to attract people in L.A. I ask her who,
what and how much is involved in this seminar.

"It's gonna be held at Celebrity Centre. It will cost around $11. You can just pay at the door," she explains to me.

Immediately, a red light goes on in my head. Celebrity Centre! That's a big Scientology compound where a lot of their higher profile events take place.

"What do you get for the $11?? A guarantee of succeeding in life in general?" I ask in my unique asshole manner.

"There's gonna be three speakers. Plus it includes a *Components of Understanding* booklet that sorta sums up what Scientology is really about."

She sounds like she has already bought this shit. I gotta get out of this one. I have had various run-ins with Scientologists over the past three years. It all started when I received a mailing from the Church of Scientology when I had just moved to Hollywood. This "invitation" to join had a brief passage from L. Ron Hubbard's *Science of Survival*. The last lines were: *"The goal of Dianetics is sanity. It would be stopped only by the insane."* I was beguiled by the audacity of this statement and kept tabs on the Church by reading what I could find on it and talking to others in the entertainment business that had adopted the teachings in their own lives. But, it was always a very guarded sharing of what the religion was about. I always tried to get an explanation of why people especially in the entertainment industry were drawn to the Church. I can only theorize that it has to do with the founder's own background as a science and pulp fiction writer who also put together some screenplays on the side. The religion itself has a cosmology that is really far out and involves some inter-galactic warlord named

Xenu. I've forgotten all the rest, but what a gas it all seems to be nonetheless! Anyway, because Hubbard was already part of the entertainment business, he probably expounded on his ideas with those in the same circle and it grew from there.

In terms of doctrinal teaching, what I've been able to piece together is the Scientology belief that each individual has two minds: the analytical and the reactive. The analytical mind is the key to succeeding in life because it's like a computer that perfectly records and recalls information needed in making everyday decisions in life. The reactive mind is what holds us back because it involves the moments of physical and emotional pain we experience in life and allows those moments to control our actions, which fucks up the decisions we then make. The whole goal is to get rid of the reactive mind or at least minimize it so you can act rationally and succeed. I have committed the next part to heart because I find it so ludicrous. When you finally restrain the reactive mind, you enter: the "*State of Clear.*"

Now, this sounded oddly familiar. Scientology had added its own mumbo-jumbo sheen to it, but the concept of overcoming the obstacle of the reactive mind and entering the "*State of Clear*" was definitely not new. Then, one day, while I was stuck in traffic I made the connection. These Scientologists had lifted their idea of the "*State of Clear*" from the old British moralists' idea that man was a slave to his passions. It was the same bag! In fact, I remembered that these moralists who wrote nearly four hundred years ago used as a touchstone for their philosophies, the notion of the "*State of Nature*" which described human society as full of war, violence and injustice.

Man was riddled with such destructive characteristics because he was controlled by his own selfishness and immorality, and he could only exit from this "*State of Nature*" by restraining his self-interested passions and taking stock in a common society that would allow for the limited satisfaction of those passions. So, what had Hubbard done? He had come up with a new terminology for man being a slave to his passions. In his philosophy, man had to restrain the destructive impulses of the reactive mind and enter into the "*State of Clear*" which was the *yang* to the "*State of Nature's*" yin. The "*State of Clear*" was the anti-"*State of Nature.*" There was a clear link here. Scientology wasn't saying anything new.

Where Scientology leaves the British moralists and me scratching our heads is the *methodology* they employ to gauge one's progress along the spiritual ladder to the "*State of Clear.*" One way is by actually hooking up the faithful into a machine called an "E-meter" that purports to be some kind of electric scanner. I actually got plugged into this machine a couple of years ago when I went to a Scientology orientation after watching a film that showed the Scientology cruise ship and photographic stills of their opulent headquarters in Clearwater, Florida. The Scientology representative asked me to try out the E-meter. I had to hold on to two silvery, cylindrical objects. One in each hand. They looked like the Seventies incarnation of soda cans. I think another wire was taped in my forehead, but I'm not completely sure. It was all so way out there for me—especially how my guide took it all so seriously as he looked on piously while I was hooked into the machine. He pointed to the little scanning grid which had an arrow that slowly rose up to a certain number or degree. He told me to relax and then pinched my right arm. I clutched the cans in my hands again and this time the arrow swung higher on the scanner. The guide then told me that this increase was due to the "*upset*" present in me, which the E-meter had measured. He explained that the goal of Scientology was to minimize the upset in peoples' lives, so they could then accomplish what they set their minds on accomplishing. I let go of the cans and waited for about thirty seconds as my guide watched me. He asked me to again clutch the cans and told me to think back to the moment when he had first pinched me. I followed his instruction and the arrow then inched up farther on the scanner.

"You see," the guide so gleefully told me. "The upset is still present in you. Even though the physical contact has passed, its impact is still felt in your mind."

I wasn't sure what he meant by this, but I smiled and nodded at his remarks. He then tried to sell me a copy of *Dianetics* which I declined. I think he was stunned at how abruptly I turned and walked away from him as soon as I let go of the E-meter. But, now, my dopey girlfriend is eating all this up.

"Here, look at the flyer I picked up," she says as she hands me a flyer for the seminar. The first words I read are these:

> *Tens of thousands of people are Clears. You can be too.*

I lose it. This jive is just too much.

"What are you laughing at?" She asks.

"Baby, come on. Would you please take the time to think about this. This stuff is ridiculous!"

"You can be so close-minded about things. Why aren't you open to new things? To new ideas?"

"Come on. I have...do you really want to be a *Clear*?" I ask and start laughing again.

"A what?"

I hand her the flyer.

"Read this part," I tell her. I know she's going to get defensive about this.

She takes a second to read the flyer and then angrily flaps it down.

"Why do you have to shoot something down when you never give it a chance? If you don't wanna come, fine, but I still want to attend. It's good to keep an open mind, you know?

"Yeah, I know." I think about sitting her down and telling her about my personal experience with the hazy hocus pocus of Scientology, but decide against it.

"So, are you coming with me to check it out?"

"No."

"Suit yourself. Just don't come around asking questions about the seminar when I get back tomorrow."

"Fair enough."

I then notice that she still has bits of brown paint on both her arms near her elbows.

"You got painted down in Montana?"

"Huh? What?"

I point towards her elbows and she bends them inwards so that she can see what I'm talking about.

"Looks like you missed a couple of spots," I say.

"I can't believe this! I'm really getting sick of this shit!!"

"What a drag."

"Do you have any turpentine?"

"I don't think so. Why don't you try some Clorox?"

She glares at me.

"No thanks."

"O.K. Sorry."

She then gets her stuff together in a huff and heads to her place claiming she has an early audition in the morning for a commercial. I wish her good luck. Man, I need a real life fast.

VI

March comes and goes. I spend days perusing the classifieds in the trades—*The Hollywood Reporter* and *Daily Variety*. I scoff at the listed jobs seeking "qualified" individuals for entry-level positions in agencies. I think about becoming a grip or a gaffer or production assistant just so I can pretend that I'm part of some larger creative entity. But, I stay with temping and bounce around various Century City entertainment law firms and companies which need grunt work done on particular projects. The money is O.K. and it keeps me from moping around Hollywood with the same glassy look I see on countless others. I also get to check my email on the sly when I work in these places because most of them have me working with fast and friendly computers. Otherwise, I would have to go to Kinko's or internet cafes in order to log into a computer because I don't have a PC. Each time I log into my hotmail account, I hope I will get a message from Land, but in the last four weeks I have not received one message from him. Now, he's off on some real adventure and I'm drawn again to the danger and excitement that surrounds him. I'm sure he knows this. That's probably why he has left me dangling for answers as to what has happened to him and Gen.

The only exciting thing that happens to me during this period of renewed temping is that I take a weekend trip up to Frisco to see an old friend from high school, who finally got out of a drug rehab clinic in Sausalito and needed some help moving into his new life in the Mission district. He had come out West early on immediately after high school where he enrolled at SFSU to study dendrology—the study of trees. He was on an environmental kick that lasted only until his spring semester of his first year where at that point he had become a fixture in the underground rave culture that subsisted in the Bay Area during the mid-Nineties. He never passed his first year, and instead, his parents and friends (myself excluded for some reason) did one of those big interventions you read about where they ambushed him as one big group one day, confronted him about his drug use, and then forced him into a three year stint in a rehab center so that he could kick his coke/speed/X habit. But, drugs weren't his real problem. He just had an addictive personality. Drugs were just one of the manifestations of his addictive nature. Problem was that unlike the other things to which he was addicted, the drugs he did unfortunately resulted in irreversible damage to his ability to understand emotions such as getting angry or justifiably pissed off about something.

As I drove up the Pacific Coast Highway, I thought of how he was in the pure *State of Clear*. He had done so much X, and later GHB, a drug which I had never even heard of, that he had lost the capacity to genuinely feel anger, which is an essential part of being human. It fuels our successes and failures. But, the whole trick is that simply wanting to take the world in a love embrace (which is what X does), fucks everything up, because as liberating as that is, the next day always comes around and goddamn you better know how to deal with the losses and setbacks because those are the more important chunks of the journey. Being able to come back after a debacle and appreciating the highs that much more, that's what had been completely erased from his mental database. I'm not sure what happens to your brain exactly, since the word is still out on what prolonged MDMA use does to your mind's control over your feelings, but I'm convinced my buddy was now reprogrammed neurologically because of his own abuse of the drug.

The drive from L.A. to San Fran via PCH takes about nine hours when done non-stop and you drive reasonably fast. But, I broke it up into two days. The first day I drove three hundred and fifty miles from L.A. to Big Sur where I stayed at a $100 a night cottage in Pfeiffer woods. I got there in the early afternoon on a Thursday. There were no televisions, phones, radios or anything else remotely Twentieth Century at this place. What really amazed me was that there were no locks on the doors. "We're on the honor system here," the lady in the lobby told me. I couldn't get over it, and I didn't, as I refused to leave my bag in the cottage when I was not inside the room. I just kept my bag in my car, and after I checked-in, I drove along PCH listening to Sarah Vaughn's *Key Largo* on repeat as I sank effortlessly into the natural beauty of the area. Artists and writers and bohemians and hippies have been drawn to Big Sur for decades and yet it still retains a quiet magneticism that has not been overused and abused.

Driving breezily through Big Sur with my arm slung out the window, I realized that I was an outsider here as evident by my lack of faith in the honor system at the cottage and my quick-in, quick-out plans. But, hey, the fact that I was conscious of my own superficial connection to this place made me feel better than the slew of others who zipped through these parts with no concept of the deeper significance of this place—to literature, art and spirituality. I soon passed by the Esalen Institute which I remembered reading was a Buddhist sanctuary of sorts complete with sessions of communal nude bathing supported by Ginsberg and others connected to the Beat legacy. I continued driving and stopped at the Henry Miller Home and Museum where his books and paintings are for sale. It had a good vibe—a friendly place. I bought a copy of *Tropic of Cancer* telling myself it was time that I read some Miller so I could understand why he was decried by some as nothing more than a pornographer. I got back in my car and then continued up to the grand Nepenthe restaurant where I parked, but could not afford to dine. So, I walked down the steps of the restaurant to a little offshoot food shack called Café Kevah made with people like me in mind. I ordered a chicken quesadilla and took a seat on this granite deck which overlooked the Pacific from a massive bluff.

I couldn't actually see the whiteness of the waves crashing against the mangled rocks below, but I could definitely imagine this spectacle and every once in a while when the wind relaxed, I imagined that I *heard* it. A gigantic crash of land and sea, then a pause, and crash again. I would have to hike down to Pfeiffer beach tomorrow before leaving for Frisco, so I could in fact bear witness to this crash. I sat and ate, and found myself, not surprisingly, easily at peace. I was content to stare out at the sea which stretched like deep blue perfection into the horizon until it met the sky and became one. I tried to sit and read a few pages of *Tropic of Cancer*, but it was not going to happen. My eyes were transfixed on the clearness of the ocean and the sky and I thought to myself this must be what *the end* is like. The end of everything that I *was* was underneath me—the land, gravity and everything physically connected to my existence. Out there…where the ocean met sky and fused into one infinite, unknowable space. That's what we reached for—what we sought to understand, whether consciously or unconsciously. But, it was so distant, so unmoving, and so impossible to fully absorb. I had to grab hold of my chair at this thought.

I snapped myself out it. The view was overwhelming and I had endured enough. I got back in my car and drove north to Bixby Bridge— an artfully constructed span over a mighty gorge. On the way to the bridge, I passed majestic redwoods that were chiseled and preened into neat spires by the onslaught of ocean winds. These trees are so tall that they actually get moisture from the fog that straddles them in the early morning. They've learned to survive by growing tall enough in order to milk the fog. When I reached Bixby Bridge, I drove straight across and parked in a clay, muddy area off to the right side. There is actually a road that leads into the gorge, but you need a four-wheeled drive vehicle and there was no way my car could handle the soft clay. I got out of my car and prepared to walk along the road and towards the tiny wooden cabins dotted amongst the hills falling into the gorge.

I don't know where I was going. I was following some kind of mental trail. It was more to experience remnants—scenes I read in Kerouac years ago, when I could only dream of being able to thumb my way across America to see every nook and cranny along the way. That was before I realized that it could no longer be done. I wouldn't be welcomed and would never have the time or money or resourcefulness to pull such a thing off. I gave up those aspirations, and instead, now was chasing Kerouac's ghost hoping that in finding something of his here in Big Sur, I could connect it somehow to myself.

So, I walked into the gorge with my nose to the wind trying to pick up the scent of his ghost and looking for a certain cabin that I instinctively would be drawn to and know. I went in deep and my feet ached. I thought back to how Kerouac described the place. He had taken a train to Monterrey and then, believe it or not, *took a cab* into the Big Sur area. Yeah, the cat of all cats. The "King of the Beats." Taking a cab! But, you gotta realize he was now coming back out West *after* he had already established himself. After all his wanderings had resulted in his opus cross-country howl of life *on the road*. After the money and the acclaim. After the hot, hot lights of the Steve Allen show made him so uncomfortable and irritable that he walked out on his dress rehearsal. This time out West, he didn't hitch-hike. He took a train and had his own roomette, so he could hole up and watch America unfurl before him no longer being able to enjoy the anonymity of a writer with knapsack in tow. The cab dropped him off at this canyon in the dead of night. Suicidal.

With a little lantern he made his way into the gorge and the cat almost slipped off the trail and into the dark chasm below. I think he just crashed in a sandy area by the creek that first night. Then, he said something about passing a cattle crossing and slipping through a barbed wire fence and finding a pleasant meadow where the cabin stood. I had the sun on my side and I could see a flat

parched field ahead of me. This must have been the
meadow of which Kerouac spoke. Next, I saw
wooden stakes at various distances designating
some sort of lost boundary, but the barbed wire was
long gone now. I passed through the field and soon
saw a modest, dark orange wooden cabin which
seemed unused and vacant. I walked closer. I
remember Kerouac's only complaint about it. That
the windows did not have screens to keep the flies
out. It only had wooden panels that did keep the
flies out, but unfortunately also blocked any
sunlight from coming in and prevented any viewing
of the serene scenery. I tried to focus on the
windows to see if—
"Hey, don't you know this is private property!"
I turned around and saw this old man with a
shotgun. I couldn't believe it.
"I'm just looking for…is this where Kerouac
stayed?"
"What are you saying?"
"Ker—Kerouac…isn't this Ferlinghetti's cabin??"
"—I'm a gonna be nice about this. You best be
leaving now. This is private property, son."
"O.K., O.K. I'm leaving."
            I started to leave and walked within ten feet
of the old man. I wanted to ask him again about
Kerouac. About the scenes that took place here—
the ghosts. But, come on, this old dude, what would
he know? He didn't read and probably was a
johnny-come-lately to the area himself and had
compensated for this by anointing himself as
sheriff. I didn't say a word to him as I passed by. I
walked back to the muddy road and got back to my
car. That had to be the right cabin though. I was
sure of it. It spoke to me.

I drove back to the cottage where I spent the night in complete silence flipping through the guest books left in the room. But, these weren't your usual tourist guest books with lines like "This place is great!!—Jack and Mary Johnson from Peoria, IL." Not at all. The guest books, and there must have been six of them, all were hundreds of pages long and each page, front and back, was filled up. They went back five years to 1994 and each entry I read had it's own *My Dinner with Andre* sentimentality. I'm talking about everything from communing with trees to dancing naked on the surf to making the most perfect love imaginable. The commonality between all the entries was staggering. I was able to compare the experience of a 1998 stay here in the very room I was now occupying to a stay in the same room from 1994 in virtually identical language. As if time stood still here and the experience was unchanging, yet transferable. When I checked my watch it was four in the morning and my head hurt, not as if I had a headache, but as if I had just sampled and lived through the past five years of life staged in this room. I crumbled into sleep.

I left Big Sur the next day and completely forgot about hiking down to the beach. I woke up late and had to make time in order to meet my friend in Frisco at a certain place and at a certain time. He had scored a flat in the Mission district with the help of his folks. It was in a great area—in my book. The Mission district is basically one old barrio. Predominantly Mexican with the highest density of murals per square block than any other area in the U.S. Fantastic Aztec and Mayan images are painted in brilliant, larger than life colors along with portraits of Diego Rivera and Frida Kahlo and the words "La Raza" adorning entire walls. Even an ordinary piece of commercial junk like the local McDonald's is transformed into a canvas of social consciousness by the amazing mural painted on its side.

He had two roommates. Both from the same rehab center, which I at first thought was a bad idea. Why try to start a new life where the focus is on getting clean with others who are already as weak as you? But, when I met the two guys, they seemed serious about turning their lives around. They were buying furniture for the place and already had a Sparklett's water cooler set up. One of them jokingly told me that he was now addicted to the need for clean water, but when I first caught sight of the water cooler, I freaked because it shook me back to memories of being with my friend on a drug run one night in L.A. where he scored GHB out of a Sparklett's water cooler. It was insane. I remember that I drove him to some cat's house who my friend told me was one of the major suppliers of GHB in the country. When we got to the place, there were all these Sparklett's water coolers set up and bodies on the floor drinking the GHB which was slightly pinkish in color and was being dispensed out of all these water coolers. But, there was no GHB here as my friend's roommate assured me. Just plain old H2O.

My friend and I walked around Frisco and first sampled one of the many Mexican eateries located in the Mission. Super burritos that were cheap and good hit the spot big time. We then went up to Columbus Ave where I dropped into the City Lights bookstore to pay my respects to Lawrence Ferlinghetti's belief in the power of the written word. Ferlinghetti, a poet in his own write, was a native and it was his cabin in Big Sur that I was sure I had found. He ran with Kerouac and sent Kerouac to the cabin in order to sweat out the city. The bookstore on Columbus was now over forty years old—Ferlinghetti's brainchild. The alley around the corner was called "Jack Kerouac Alley" and was the site where Kerouac had spent many an inebriated night slumbering in the arms of Bacchus. I tried to explain my search for Ferlinghetti's cabin in Big Sur to my friend, but he didn't get it. His mind was somewhere else and he said something to the effect that the old guy pulling a shotgun on me was funny. We then journeyed to the Haight where I was deeply saddened by the yuppification of the legacy there. So, many fuckers buying into this dead scene. These cats with their tye-dyed shirts and dreadlocks and arrogance. I knew their stories. I used to be just like them. Like they're *entitled* to something because they are the ones now keeping the counter-culture flame alive. They think they are so righteous—the appointed guardians of that time. It was sad and when a kid, probably fourteen or fifteen wearing combat boots with natty hair and a frilled leather vest came up to me and whispered, "Mister, I got some killer bud," I was ready to go back to L.A.

One weekend in Frisco was enough with my old friend. He sounded like a public ad against doing drugs and kept repeating "It's all good" and "One Love" to everything and everyone. That was his mantra. But, it made him feel good about himself, so I didn't mind the incessant muttering of these refrains. Inside though, I did at times want to grab him hard and shake him until he came to his senses, so I could then tell him, "It's not all good!

Your life is fucked up and there's no such thing as one love—everyone is out to fuck each other over." I actually was amazed by my restraint and my ability to absorb his deprogrammed, post-rehab state. I wanted to be a friend by being a silent, reaffirming face. That's how I saw it. I left Frisco irked by the passive ethos etched in the social vibe there and puzzled at why the people I had met became so suspicious of me when I told them I lived in L.A.

Apart from my weekend trip to Frisco, I'm stuck in the boring. I make about $18 an hour doing mindless paper pushing in various offices around Century City. And now, I find myself playing the Lotto and eagerly looking forward to Wednesday and Saturday nights because that's when the numbers are drawn. I've become a great case study as to what happens when motivation slowly eeks out of an individual like air from a tiny hole in a life raft. One day, exactly six weeks to the day that I left Land and Gen in Laredo, I secretly check my email while at work and I see that I have an email from Land. It is short and basically just tells me that things are cool. "Mexico has been a blast." Nothing more. A week later, while I'm at work putting together some copyright information for a terrible film called *Bloodstalking Babes from Hell* produced by Bloodstalking Babes Productions, Inc., I take a quick break to check my hotmail account and there are four new messages—two of which are from Land. I check the one Land had sent first and it says that Gen is back in New Orleans and that I wouldn't believe where he's been for the last month. But, the motherfucker leaves me hanging and doesn't say where he is. The next message which he has sent three days later asks me to email him my apartment's address because he wants to send me something. I write back and give him my address and also ask him to tell me where he is. I return back to work, but get nothing accomplished for the remainder of the day as I keep checking my email to see if Land has responded. Nothing.

Ten days later, when I come home from my traffic-drenched commute from Century City, I go to my mailbox and retrieve my mail. More of the usual shit—bills, missing kid flyers asking "Have you seen me?" and a Scientology announcement which invites me to an orientation by posing the question: *"Have happiness and success been lost to you? Find out how to regain them!"* I still don't know how they got my address as I was careful to put down phony addresses during the time I personally dealt with their representatives. Nestled between all this is an envelope from Mexicana Airlines. Funny, but I think nothing of it because living in what is actually Ixtlan means I'll be targeted for airfares to Mexico by airlines. Nevertheless, I take the time to open the envelope while I'm on the can and can't believe my eyes when I see a first-class airline ticket to Cancun with my name on it. The flight itinerary shows that it is a red-eye from LAX which flies to Mexico City and then to Cancun. I must have received this by mistake, but I'll take it. Upon closer inspection, I see that the flight departs in mid-May and is one-way only. I guess I better pack now for my new life in Cancun.

I think back to Land's email. That he said he would be sending me something. This must be it, but what the fuck? He expects me to get my own return ticket from Cancun?? The next day, I email him and tell him I got the airline ticket but was confused about what was going on. It takes another week until Land responds. His email to me says that he did buy the ticket for me and that it is only one-way because round-trip flights from L.A. to *Havana* are hard to come by especially in light of what he calls the "Trading with the Enemy Act" which Jesse Helms enacted and it fines any American $250,000 or ten years in jail for any violations—that includes unauthorized travel to Cuba. Wait! I stop reading the email to digest things. My ticket was to Cancun, but here Land is talking about Havana. The wheels start turning. Could it really be?

Probably banking on my incredulity, Land's email goes on to say, "Relax. No worries. It's all laid out for you. All you have to do is follow my instructions." I read the rest of the email. He tells me that once I land in Cancun International airport, I will have a window of two hours in which to grab my bags and go across the street to the office of Cubana Airlines, where a reservation for a ticket to Havana will be held in my name. I have to bring $112 in cash to purchase the ticket in person because they can't accept American credit cards and so Land couldn't buy this ticket for me. Land even apologizes for this in the email! Then, Land says that I have to go back into the Cancun airport and to the Cubana ticket counter in order to check in. I have to pay another $20 and fill out a tourist landing visa, so that when I land in Cuba, Cuban customs will only stamp this visa and not my American passport.

Shit. I have to go. Yeah, I know that I might fuck up or some fuck up will find me, but I have to go. I don't want that hollow feeling that I've carried with me ever since I left Land and Gen to linger over me any longer. I can picture Land decked out in a red guayabera, swaying to the rhythms of *son* in the streets of Havana with that omnipresent half-grin of his. What is that crazy cat doing in Cuba? He's outdone himself with this one. I'll probably get shitted on by people for wanting to take this risk and my girlfriend will tell me to stop running away from my life, but I think I'm running toward my destiny and if that ends things here in L.A., well, worse things have happened.

I have two weeks to get things in order, make some quick cash and pack for this sojourn. I'll be in contact with Land via email until my arrival in Cuba. I re-read the last lines of his message to me:

> *I've found it at last, man!*
> *Oh, and ain't it sublime! Unstuck and puro.*
> *See you at Jose Marti Internacional.*
> *Chau—land.*

Part Three

I

The big day. I have my shit together. Tickets, passport, and I even manage to finagle a ride to the airport out of a friend since my girlfriend is now on location in Santa Clarita shooting some Western. I am happy that I won't have to worry about losing my car in the airport parking lot when I get back, and who knows when that will be? My flight leaves at midnight and I check in two hours early at the Mexicana ticket counter. I have to fly to Cancun via Mexico City. It's gonna be a mildly long flight and I hope there will be some empty seats, so that I can stretch out and be comfortable—perhaps even sleep.

As I walk to my gate, I notice a stunning woman with closely cropped black hair and untamed, searing blue eyes. She has the same haunting countenance of that young Afghan refugee that National Geographic used a snapshot of to sell a lot of its products in the early Nineties. She approaches me as I walk by, but my flattery soon turns to disappointment when I see what she is carrying in her right hand. I'm a magnet for solicitation. Always have been. I get hit up by everyone and everywhere I go. As if a green light flashes above my head that welcomes all comers.

She has to be the first female Hare Krishna that I have ever met. She offers me a copy of *The Science of Self-Realization* which encapsulates some of the mantras of His Divine Grave A.C. Bhaktivedanata Swami Prabhupada. I take the book and quickly flip through it.

"I already have this one," I tell her as I hand the book back to her.

She is surprised and probably thinks I'm just saying this to avoid forking over $10 to her. I decide that I better clue her in.

"I'm a friend of Brant's."

She seems to recognize the name. I go on to explain to her that I met this guy Brant in college when he had just dropped out of school and joined the Krishnas. I don't quite tell her that he "dropped out" though. I phrase it more as if he took a sabbatical from school whereupon he found his calling with the Krishnas. He really did just drop out of school though. He was one year ahead of me and when he joined the Krishnas he moved to the City where he began working out of their Brooklyn temple. I tell her I'm an old friend of his and that I've even stopped by for their Friday vegetarian dinner at their Venice Beach location on Watseka Blvd. She now knows who I am talking about.

"Oh, yes. Brant. He is now Chandra Bodhikur."

"Really?? When was this??"

"Ahh—last summer. He goes to India. He met his Swami and receives new name."

"Fantastic! I haven't seen him for a while. Is he still working at the U.S. Airways terminal?"

Let me quickly backtrack. After Brant first began life as a Hare Krishna in the Brooklyn temple, he swiftly moved up the Krishna ranks and earned his stripes. He then was sent on assignment to their L.A. branch which is located in Venice Beach. One day when I was returning to L.A. from a trip aboard U.S. Airways, there was Brant, who jumped me from behind dramatically brandishing a Bhagavad Gita. I immediately recognized him, even though my only previous contact with him had occurred three years earlier when he accosted me on campus while I was hitting on some bird. He just forced himself in between us and demanded that I explain what it was that man was searching for in this world. Needless to say, the bird I was with took off as soon as this loon started with his preaching, but I stood there bear-trapped in my disbelief and wanting to beat the living shit out of him. He caught me so off guard that I was actually goaded into a conversation that lasted half an hour and in the end I had bought a book called *Renunciation Through Wisdom*. He even taught me the Krishna mantra and told me that each time I recited it, Krishna—the Godhead—would do a jig on the tip of my tongue.

After that meeting on campus, I next saw him three years later when I was passing through the U.S. Air terminal at LAX. When Brant remembered who I was after I recounted the story of our fateful first meeting, he was so happy that he said this was cosmic providence. He gave me an invite to the Krishna Friday night veggie dinner at their temple in Venice. He told me that his *post* in LAX was the U.S. Airways terminal where he sold Krishna literature to passers-by.

The Krishna airport infrastructure is truly fascinating, and in all seriousness, deserves to be documented. After bumping into Brant at LAX, I have run into Krishnas in airports at Philly, Pittsburgh, and JFK. The intimacy of their network amazes me. I wish I could just travel from airport to airport and take notes and interview each Krishna and the particular terminal they worked. Find out what they thought about their brother Pras in Charlotte who works in the United terminal or what their thoughts were on their brother Hans who does double duty at the Alaska and Northwest terminals in Seattle. How could one swami in far off India create such Krishna consciousness in America? Was there dissension in their ranks after the swami died? It doesn't look like it. They seem so gentle and concerned for one another as well as for souls like me who they zero-in on in between x-ray scanners and departure gates.

I'm convinced they all know each other and keep tabs on each other's book sales. It's like girl-scout cookies. You sell all you can so that you can have that year-end party or club trip. I see Krishnas with crates of books and I marvel at them as just the concept of selling books in America to strangers is an uphill battle. Who the fuck reads anymore anyway? Most people loathe giving away money to door-to-door salesman, and then being asked to do it for a *book* in an airport where you just want to make your flight. And then, check out the book that is being pushed in your face! Man, these Krishnas have balls. Each time, when the Krishnas I saw in airports outside of L.A. tried to solicit me, I mentioned Brant's name and their faces lit up with reverence. I learned that Brant was a legend among other Krishnas because he held the record for individually selling the most Bhagavad Gitas in one year. He was the supreme example of a good Krishna in their eyes and the Krishna in Philly even gave me a book called *The Quest for Enlightenment* for free simply because I knew Brant. He was a celebrity as much as any Krishna could be considered a celebrity within their own ranks.

"No, he no longer works the U.S. Airways terminal," She answers.

"Oh, yeah? He got too big for his britches??" I laugh. She doesn't catch my humor.

"Uh, no…he now teaches at the temple—mostly. Once in a while he will go to the Promenade at Santa Monica. You know where it is?"

"Yeah."

"He goes there in spring and before our big celebration in Venice in June."

"Tell him I say hi. My name is Tal."

"Tal?"

"Right."

She studies me for a moment.

"Where are you from, Tal?"

Pause. I toy with the idea of getting into my own story, but think better of it. It's long and mixed and I gotta catch a flight.

"That's a long story, but tell me, you're the first female Krishna that I've seen. Where are you from?? Your accent sounds Eastern European."

"Well, I am from Bosnia. You know where it is?"

"I have a general idea. How long have you been in the U.S.?"

"Only three years. I was brought over from a temple in Munich. I learned the ways of Krishna there."

"Did the Krishnas come into Bosnia though before or after all the fighting started?"

"No. They have been in Sarajevo for long time. Since the early Seventies. Even in Rijeka, Croatia."

"What about your family? Are they still in Bosnia or did they move to Germany too?"

"Still in Bosnia."

"Are you in contact with them?"

She smiles at me and shyly lowers her eyes which I know means no. That's the part of being a Krishna that always gets me. Many of the faithful lose touch with their friends and family once they become the faithful.

"So, do you want to get new book?" She asks me.

Not really, I think to myself. Plus, I'm trying to get to know her, and the way she pushes me to buy a book is a lot like those pushy, annoying strippers who purr at you to buy a lapdance. You know how they sound, *"So, you wanna get a dance?"* Same exact thing with this bird. Furthermore, I have a whole stack of these things that I already bought from Brant and his boys through the last couple of years. They just sit on my bookshelf lathered in dust. But, I *still* like her and feel sorry for her. I know Brant too has had no significant contact with his family once he dropped out of school and became a Krishna. He thinks he's happy, but his upper-middle class parents probably went into shock and never recovered when he suddenly dropped out, shaved his head and stopped eating meat. And now this unearthly beautiful Bosnian girl with the wonderful Slavic accent has consigned herself to a celibate, green life serving Krishna. How terrible. But, she has a new family now and I don't doubt for one second that Krishnas come through for one another in good times and bad like families are supposed to.

"Hare Krishna, Hare Krishna/ Krishna Krishna, Hare Hare/ Hare Rama, Hare Rama/ Rama Rama, Hare Hare," I recite the mantra for her perfectly. "What do you think of that?" I say—very proud at my ability to remember these lines.

"Very good! Chandra teaches you well."

"Yeah, he did."

"He is very good teacher. Everyone at temple follows his example."

"I'm sure they do. So, what can you give me for $5?"

She hands me a book entitled *Krishna—The Supreme Personality of the Godhead.* I don't have this one. Maybe I'll flip through it on the plane. There are usually lovely pictures of peacocks and blue bejeweled human bodies laced with flowers in these things. Also, flying always makes me nervous. It will be good to hold onto a piece of Krishna while I'm in the air. I gaze deep into her eyes as I say goodbye hoping that maybe she can read my mind and see how much I want her to go home.

II

    The first leg of the flight lasts around three hours. As we near Mexico City, I look out the window and am engrossed in the endless canvas of golden lights below me. This city is gargantuan. Upon landing, I walk to the departure gate for my connection. I have about a fifty-five minute wait until my flight to Cancun. It is dawn and the airport is freezing. Out of a huge floor to ceiling window at the gate, I can see two volcano-shaped mountains painted orange in the early morning light. I am shivering, but warm thoughts about sunny Cancun keep me from getting carried away by the cold. I close my eyes until I board my flight.

    At ten in the morning, I land in the sun-kissed mecca of Cancun. I have a two hour window before my Cubana Airlines flight to Havana, but not wanting to take any chances I move fast. I shake out the grog of sleepiness and grab my bags from the baggage claim. I then cross the street outside of the main entrance to the airport and find the one room concrete office for Cubana Airlines. Two women with computers are in control of ticketing. I give one of them my name and she brings it up on the screen. After showing her my passport, she asks for $112 in cash. I pull out that exact amount and hand it to her. She gives me a ticket that I notice is round-trip and the flight back from Havana to Cancun leaves ten days from today. Interesting. Land has definitely got something up his sleeve. The lady tells me to go back into the airport and to check in my bags at the Cubana ticket counter inside. I thank her and head out.

The Cubana airplane is a real piece of shit.
A Soviet Yaklovev jet—a relic of the Cold War.
When I get inside, the seats are folded down
because they are collapsible and once I locate my
seat I snap it back upright. The overhead bins are
small and rusted. Basically nonexistent. Any carry-
ons are best placed under the seat in front of you.
Once airborne, I drink a complimentary Cristal
cerveza but then can't lock my food tray back into
place after the flight attendant comes by to collect
my trash. The tray bobs and shakes in rhythm with
the rest of the plane. On top of that, a high-pitch
drone coming from somewhere in the plane has me
worried. Try as I might, I can't hold back
catastrophic thoughts that in some hangar the Soviet
engineer responsible for designing this Yaklovev
made a couple of mistakes and now those mistakes
are going to send me plummeting into the
Caribbean. I white-knuckle it for about forty-five
minutes and rub the Krishna book with my thumbs
reciting the mantra until the calm, reassuring voice
of the pilot comes on and welcomes us to Havana.
It's great when having a little faith comes in handy.
　　I exit the plane and follow the other
passengers to customs. A bunch of wealthy
Mexicans and some European types surround me. I
see a couple of soldiers in army green watch us as
we walk through. Customs takes a while and the
agent asks me what I do in the U.S. I answer back
in my best Spanish that I work in construction.
Then, he asks how I learned Spanish. I tell him that
I studied it in school and he cocks his head to the
side, pinches his lips together and contemplates
ruining my trip by stamping my passport. But,
thankfully, he gives me no trouble and only stamps
the box designating "entry" in my landing visa and

hands my passport back to me. A buzzer goes off, a brown door snaps open, and I enter Cuba. Helms is a moron. Look at me, man! I want to break into song and dance. I have this feeling that I'm bravely going where no American has gone before (at least in the last forty years anyway).

My two bags are already out and waiting for me. I pick them up and head for the exit where I see a mass of curious faces craning their necks for a glimpse of who has made it into their country. I scan the faces for Land, but there are just too many faces to make out any specific one. Cab drivers and those pretending to be cab drivers approach me and ask if I need a ride. I politely tell them that I have someone waiting for me. I still don't see Land, so I walk outside of the airport and wait for him on the street. I get a little nervous because I have no clue what to do or who to contact if he doesn't show up. But, then this old blue '57 Chevy Cavalier pulls up and there is Land hanging out the window like some giddy dog. I explode with relief.
"Heyyy!! Sorry we're late—had a little problem with the gasket!" Land hops out when the car stops and hugs me hard. He takes my bags and throws them in the trunk.

I shake hands with the driver who Land tells me is a friend of the guy from whom he is renting a room. A genuinely happy cat—this driver is. With a toothy grin and earnest eagerness to have me ride in his car.
"So, how the hell are you!" I say to Land.
"Unbelievable. Great. We gotta alotta catching up to do. So much shit, man!"
"I can only imagine. We're in Cuba, bra!! How did this happen! Haha!!"
"I know, I know! How was customs??"

"Asked a lot of questions, but other than that they were cool. Didn't stamp my passport or anything bad like that."

"Good, good. I actually had a little problem."

"Really?"

"Yeah. Get in the car. I'll tell you about it."

I jump in the back and Land rides shotgun. He looks back at me as we start driving away from the airport.

"I don't know if the customs agent I had just had a personal gripe against me as an American or what. But, the guy detained me for nearly half an hour!" Land starts.

"Are you serious?"

"Oh, yeah. He took my driver's license, Cubana ticket and passport and left me in the waiting area. Then, he calls me back to his booth and has me sign some bogus documents. All the while he eyes me and compares my signatures to the one on my passport—like he's establishing if it's authentic. Just a charade, man. He finally drops the act and in English says, *You pay me not to stamp passport.*"

"He wanted a bribe?"

"Yup."

"How much did you give him?"

"Tal, Tal. Come on, now. You know me better than that. You think I just rolled over??"

"Ladies and gentlemen, Land Morales has arrived in Havana!!"

"Of course! I launched into this whole trip about being a lowly tourist who's come to see the beauty of Cuba and its people. I then segue into this Jose Marti poem which is like *the* patriotic anthem of the country, man!"

"Come on!!"

"Yeah! I start bustin' out with these lines—*yo soy un hombre sincero de donde crece la palma, y antes de morirme quiero echar mis versos del alma*— which means, *I am a sincere man from the land where the palm tree grows and before I die I want to sing my verses from the heart—*"
"Oh, man!! You jived him good!!"
"Wait, wait—there's more. This is the good part— *con los pobres de la tierra yo mi suerte quiero echar, y el arroyo de la sierra me complace mas que el mar*—and that means, *with the poor of the earth I want to share their fate and the river from the mountain pleases me more than the sea.*"
The driver starts laughing and Land slaps him on the shoulder.
"Hahahaha!" Land cracks up.
"I don't believe it, man. You've done it again! Wow!! The customs guy musta flipped out," I say.
"Oh, he played it off real nice. He kinda just leaned his head to the side and with a smirk told me I could go on through, but told me not to forget about the $20 departure tax."
"Oh, God! That's a classic, man. You got a lot to fill me in on."
"All in good time, my boy. Just take in the sights right now, bra. We're nearing La Habana."

What sights indeed. The stretch from Jose Marti Internacional to Havana is green jungle and patches of people are on the roads, on bikes, scooters, motorcycles and those motorcycles with the side compartment for your sidekick to crouch in. You see baseball fields in the middle of tobacco fields and orange rusted remnants of hulking Soviet ingenuity. And then the glorious cars! With their wild fantastic colors of bright blues, reds, yellows, and greens. Whizzing and chirping by us.

"Yo, Land. Where do they get parts for these things?"

"Who cares?" He says. "They still run, don't they?"

"Well, what did you do about that blown gasket on this Chevy?"

"Gustavo, here, took care of it with a little home grown know-how, bra."

"What do you mean?"

"Let's just say Cubans know how to think out of the box, man. They got to because they are cut off from a lot of the things that we just grab with ease when we're in a pinch."

Land turns around and laughs.

"Tal, take a gander, man. We're in the city limits."

Poor barrios and tents initially greets us. Kids scattering around in the streets and cat-sized dogs scrounging after them. It's a charming dump. Then, as we enter old Havana or vieja Habana as one sign says, 1999 stops. Ends. And back in time we go.

Land looks back at me again. I know he is gauging my reaction as we cruise through this magnificent pastiche of ornate architecture, narrow colonial avenidas, and apocalyptic calamity. The smell of cheese, bread and shit mix perfectly with the *son* blasting from every windowless balcony and passing car. Men playing dominoes on street corners with giant *puros* dangling out of their chapped lips and women of all sizes in bright, tight spandex. Fords, Chevys, Oldsmobiles and Dodges stuck in a relaxed, gas-guzzling time-warp whoosh by oblivious to the plight of their sleek, disposable cousins dying each day on the freeways of L.A. Multi-colored Ionic, Doric and Corinthian columns adorn gutted townhouses and former palatial homes now collapsing and rubbling after years of neglect. Laundry and Cuban flags are draped on balconies. I see no glass windows or doors on most of the residences and there is a bereted soldier on each block keeping watch. It's grander and sadder than I could have ever imagined. Land basks in the sight of watching my bug eyes dig the scene. He tells Gustavo to take us home and we drive onto the Malecon which hugs the ocean and connects old Havana to new Havana. The architecture changes into Cold War modernism once we enter new Havana. Gustavo exits on to a big street which I notice is named Quinta Avenida and we soon pass by embassies. Land tells me that his place is in the Miramar district—an upscale residential area.

Gustavo pulls into a semi-circle driveway, and the house standing in front us reminds me of a miniature antebellum plantation. It is white and has a little veranda on the left side.

"Pretty amazing, huh?"

"Yeah, Land. This place is nice."

"You know what I pay for a room here?"

"No idea."

"$15 a month, bra!"

"What a country! But, there's gotta be a catch."

"No catch, man," Land says as he grabs my bags from the trunk. "The reality is that fifteen American dollars is alotta cash here. A typical Cuban doctor nets about $20 a month, man."

"Whoa."

"Yeah. You see alotta docs working in bars or as bell-boys in the hotels in order to get tips in dollars. It's a trade-off. We'll talk about this shit later. Just come in and enjoy now!"

Inside, the place is sparsely decorated. Not much of a living room or lobby. A couple of brown sofas and no TV in sight. We take the stairs up and walk down a cramped hall where Land opens a door and invites me in. It's a small room with a large mattress, two wooden chairs and a bunch of books fighting for space on the floor. That's about it. Pictures of Che, Castro, and another cat are on the walls.

"Who's this cat, man?" I ask Land and point to the third guy in a picture standing with Che and Castro who wears a thick beard and a sombrero-like hat.

"Camilo Cienfuegos."

"Never heard of him."

"I know. You gotta *know* history. Something you don't really learn in the U.S."

"He fought in the revolution?"

"Yeah. He was part of the triumvirate, man. Along with Castro and Che and seventy-nine other brave motherfuckers who sailed from Tampico, Mexico to the Sierra Maestra in 1956, there was Camilo."

"So, he was one of the original revolutionaries?"

"Oh, yeah. He led one of the squadrons and strategized some of the big battles that led to the sacking of the capital on January 1, 1959. Amazing story. You'll learn it."

"He still alive??"

"No. He died in a plane crash a couple of weeks after the end of the revolution. The people still love him, man. You'll see billboards with his face all over and the words *Tu ejemplo vive—Your example lives.*"

"Good propaganda."

"Hmmm. You could see it that way. But, there's more to it than that."

Land places my bags in the corner of the room. I look at my wrist for the time, but I don't have my watch on because I took it off at Cancun and hid it in one of my bags.

"You got the time, Land?"

"What?"

"What time is it?"

"Forget that shit, man. You ain't going to work today. The sun is still out, isn't that good enough?"

"Don't tell me they don't keep time here. I just want to orient myself since the time here is three hours ahead of L.A."

"Well, it's around one o'clock."

"Thanks. By the way, how long have you been here, man?"

"Over a month and a half, I think. Don't worry, I'll give you the low down. Uh, you hungry at all?"

"No. Not really. The food here good?"

"It's great, but most restaurants suck ass. You either gotta know which ones to go to or go to these paladars."

"What are those?"

"Remember I told you that Cubans think out of the box?"

"Yeah, man."

"The paladar is an example of that. What it is, is a make-shift restaurant, where people have converted their actual homes into places where the public and tourists can come over to eat."

"That sounds inconvenient, man."

"No, it's not. You'll see. The food is amazing because what you are really getting are fresh, home-cooked meals prepared in someone's house. Like you were a guest coming over for dinner."

"Does the government take a cut of their profits? I mean isn't that like free enterprise??"

"Uhh, it's complicated. I haven't really gotten a straight answer. I've been told that Castro a few years ago granted waivers to allow people to start up these things and then in order to continue to operate they must pay some license fee to the government."

"I bet they have to kick in a little extra from time to time to maintain good relations."

"Always so skeptical, eh, Tal?"

"I'm just messing around. You know me."

"Haha. Well, relax a little, man. You are now in the last great bastion of socialism! So, it's worth keeping an open mind about things."

"I will, I will. But, what happens next, man? After Castro?"

"That's not for me to know. But, I put my trust in the Cuban people—as long as it's not Castro's brother, Raul."

"What's wrong with him?"

"They say he's a friend of Dorothy and that just can't happen here. Not after forty years of Fidel—if ya know whadda mean."

Land tells me that seven other people live in the house including the owner himself who runs an upscale prostitution ring utilizing home grown Cubans as well as Dominican imports to feed the lusts of those wealthy Canadians, Germans, Brits and Dutch who know where to find him. I immediately perk up at this and ask Land if any of the girls live in the house. Unfortunately, he tells me that the girls each have their own set up around the Mariano district.

Lazaro Suarez, the "Cuban Gore Vidal" as Land puts it, this is *his* place. The upscale prostitution ring is his operation. Lazaro is an elder gentleman who is bisexual and speaks six different languages and who can regale his audiences with stories about Batistan Cuba and early Castro and the CIA in one breath, and then switch to his private papal audience with Pope Pius XII, getting lost in the Bolivian rainforest and doing time on the Isle of Pines in the next. Apparently, he claims to have once gone to Castro's law office in old Havana to settle a case because Castro was repping one of Lazaro's servants who Lazaro had fired and not paid back wages. He says Castro was a bulldog of a lawyer, but when Lazaro agreed to settling the case, Castro was a perfect gentleman even getting up to hold the door open for Lazaro when Lazaro took his leave.

Lazaro has not lived in Cuba all his life though. At one point, he had set up shop in Paramaribo in Suriname where he became a celebrity because of the seed finches he kept which sang uncannily on-key melodies. His finches won so many birdsong competitions that legend had it that fed up Surinamese competitors pushed the government to deport him! He then hopped from island to island in the West Indies dabbling in one business after the other making money in everything that he could—from renting snorkel gear to sun-starved tourists in Barbados to managing a casino in St. Martin. He got the idea to finally get into the flesh trade when he paid a visit to this mythic establishment outside Port-au-Prince called "El Rancho" where wealthy Haitians paid lots of cash to come and watch white women fuck dogs, goats and ponies. With the sudden realization that nothing would provide such a great return on his investment than the good old sex industry, he finally returned back to Cuba where, through his guile and ability to play possum at the right times, he managed to grease the right people and gradually take a piece of *La Revolucion* for himself.

Through all his incarnations and globetrotting, Land says Lazaro has been able to reconcile a vicious instinct for high-brow niceties with his devotion to Cuba's simplicities. His guiding philosophy can be summed by a quote from Simón Bolivar that Lazaro is fond of citing: *Para nosotros la Patria es la America.*

Land takes me all around the house which looks uniform throughout except for the master area that is locked up and belongs to Lazaro. We go back to Land's room and I rummage though my bags to take out some cash. I also find my watch which I can't wait to adjust three hours ahead and I slip it on to the disappointing chagrin of Land.
"Had to do it, huh?" He asks.
"Sorry."
"O.K., I'll let it go. Ready for a little stroll around old Havana?"
"Yeah! I've really been looking forward to this."

Land and I walk down the stairs and exit the house. As Land locks up, I see a slightly paunchy, bespectacled, black guy with a gold-plated cane limping towards the house. He hobbles closer and closer.
"Is that…" I whisper to Land.
"That's Lazaro."
"Oh."

Land rushes down to help Lazaro up the stairs and unlocks the door. I take a close look at this cat. He's gotta be in his eighties. But, his face has a youthful glow to it, and except for a few tired wrinkles under his eyes, his face is smooth and round. An unlit Cohiba Esplendido hangs from the right corner of his mouth. I can smell the strong tobacco from where I stand. He's the first person that I've ever seen in my life that I can use the word *distinguished* to describe because that's exactly what he gives off. Land introduces me.

"A pleasure," Lazaro says as he extends his hand to me.

He has a strong handshake and I notice that his brown eyes have flecks of blue.

"A beautiful place you have here, Mr. Suarez," I say respectfully.

"Please, please—call me Lazaro."

"Well, I hope Land is not making too much trouble for you!" I motion to Land jokingly as I say this.

"Hah. I hope I am not making too much trouble for Land!" And Lazaro laughs pokes at Land with his cane. "He's been most helpful to me during his stay here."

"Where's your driver, Lazaro? I didn't see your car drive up."

"No car today, *Landito*. I just come from a walk. I need to stretch out the old sea legs as you say."

"I was just about to take Tal out into the city. Do you need anything?"

"No, no. I am fine. But, let us meet for dinner later this evening. What do you say?"

"Sure, sure. Where would you like to meet?" Land asks.

"You will be in the old town?"

"Yeah."

"So, let us meet at the Hanoi Café. You know where it is?"

"I think so. Just off Calle Obispo?"

"Yes. I see you there at eight o'clock, O.K.?"

"See you then."

I nod at Lazaro as Land turns to leave.

"Chau," Lazaro waves us off.

Land and I start walking up to Quinta Avenida where he says we'll be able to flag down a cab.

"So, what's the story?" I ask.

"With Lazaro??" Land replies.

"Yeah, man. How do you know that cat?"

"Well, there's definitely a story there."

"Let's hear it."

"He lived in Mexico at one time. Back in the Seventies. He was already semi-retired at that time, you know. He was in Mexico more to relax and was doing import/export kinda shit. And through his business became friends with my dad's uncle. I actually met Lazaro once when I was a little kid on a visit to Monterrey."

"So, he's just a family friend then."

"Yeah, I guess you could say that. When he returned to Cuba things were cool for him because I know he had some trouble with the government before. Anyway, my grand-uncle's son—my dad's cousin—who I stayed with in Monterrey still kept in touch with him, so here I come with my own predicament and when Lazaro's name came up in conversation one day, I said to myself Cuba would be the best place to go now."

"So what did you do? You just got Lazaro's phone number and called up out of the blue asking if you could come on over."

"Pretty much."

"And have you told Lazaro anything about your, ahem, situation?"

"Of course not, bra. He thinks I just resigned from a job I had in the City and so I needed to go somewhere to detox from the working world."

"That's a good one."

"Yeah, but I've really wanted to tell him about what I did, you know, to get his advice on things. But, I think somehow that will *lower* me in his eyes."

"Get out of here! The guy's a pimp! What's he care?"

"Nah, man. He's honest and has standards. He doesn't steal, which is what I did. That's like the lowest thing a person can do. Steal."

"Alright, man. At least, Lazaro hooked you up nice."

"Yeah. He had offered me a free room to stay, but I'm the one who insisted on paying rent. I didn't want to use him. Then, he introduced me to the owners of this place, the Habana Club, where I do some bartending at. It's a big tourist place so the dollars flow in nicely. It's been a real good time, Tal, man."

"Do you know the story with his leg?"

"What about it?"

"I mean, he has an exaggerated limp and walks with a cane!"

"Yeah, another story there. One of his girls—and this happened years ago—was pissed off at something he had done. And this bird was Haitian, so she sprinkles some potent vodou powder along the doorjamb of Lazaro's room."

"Oh, shit—"

"—and when Lazaro came home that night he walked through the door into his room and about ten minutes later his right leg just became inflamed. He was in excruciating pain and was thrashing around his room. A couple of people had to come in and restrain him until a doctor came and helped."

"What was it?"

"They don't know, man. The doc, I think, tried to

ice the leg, but nothing alleviated the pain. Finally, the doc had to anesthetize Lazaro and cut into the swelling with a scalpel or something to see what was going on."
"Did anything come out of his leg?"
"After the doc made an incision in the leg, supposedly no blood came out. Can you believe that, man?"
"No blood at all??"
"Not a drop—instead, the doc saw dozens of tiny needle-like formations lodged in Lazaro's thigh muscle. He took each one out one-by-one and had no explanation for what they were. But, when Lazaro saw the needles, he knew what had happened."
"What did he do?"
"He knew he had been hexed and only one person would have done this to him and that was his Haitian girl. So, he shipped her ass back to Port-au-Prince that night."
"Damn."
"Since then, Lazaro has a policy on not having any Haitian women working for him, and, of course, his leg was never the same after that."
"I guess we know the moral of that one."

Land sees a cab coming and signals it to stop. We climb into this white and red '56 Dodge Charger and head to old Havana. The cab driver is another happy-go-lucky sort who speaks decent English, so I start to casually ask him something about the political atmosphere in Cuba. To my surprise, he suddenly throws up his hands and says, "I don't know!" We all laugh it off. He then turns on the radio and the music that plays is Christopher Cross's *Sailing*. The next song is Abba's *Waterloo*.

"Man, is the music here stuck in a time warp too!" I tell Land. As soon as I say this, a wacky, funked out song called *Brown Girl in the Ring* comes on which neither Land nor I have ever heard and it throws me for a loop. So, I sit back in silence taking in the new song along with the street action passing before us.

We are dropped off where the Malecon hits an oak-lined pedestrian boulevard called the Paseo del Prado. On both sides of the Prado are fantastic town homes and estates that are now shells of their former grandeur. Stark and beautiful and imposing their architectural wonder on all. Inside the Prado, locals sit on stone benches, hustlers whisper "*pssssssssst*" as they walk by, and used up whores give you the eye and ask you, "*Que buscas—What are you looking for?*" Hotels from another age where American mobsters like Meyer Lanksy, Lucky Luciano, and Santos Traficante used to frequent still stand shoulder to shoulder. We duck our heads in the Hotel Sevilla where 8 x 10 black and white photos of Joe Louis, Spencer Tracy, Ted Williams, Erroll Flynn and other American celebs of a bygone era hang on the walls. A large black and white photo of Al Capone is placed conspicuously on a center wall beam and the caption underneath says Capone and his entourage stayed on the sixth floor of the hotel for two years. Then, right next to Capone's picture is a photo of Cuban revolutionaries tearing out the casinos of the hotel in 1959. Land and I hoot at this juxtaposition.

We walk through a lazy park where the first of many Jose Marti statues greets us. Across the street is the Hotel Inglaterra and next to that is the Cuban Ballet Theatre and next to that is El Capitolio, which is a smaller duplicate of the U.S.

Capitol building. We head to the Capitolio and I run up the stairs in a fit of inspiration eager to look out over old Havana from the top. I can see glorious ruins of the city from the Capitolio. It really is something to behold. As if nuclear winter has come and gone and now its denizens are living amongst the residue. But, it's not that bleak. There is a charm that's indescribable. There is a sustenance that is palatable. You can feel it. Land and I push open the doors of the Capitolio and I am shocked to see nothing but an empty chamber. I look up at the inside of the dark dome and see nothing. It's like something out of *Planet of the Apes*. This once functional seat of government now sits like a barren cave. There are no lights. Land tells me that Castro moved the Parliament out of the Capitolio soon after he took power, so now the Capitolio is like a big multi-purpose room used for different events. Sort of like the old elementary school cafeteria. A place where you could have lunch or perform plays or hold balloting for elections.

Off to the side, I can hear a sultry voice wafting through the emptiness. We walk towards the voice which is coming from the right wing of the building. There we see a diamond black female singer rehearsing with a six-piece band. Squeaky microphones and jigged up lights surround them. Land and I enter the room and sit on the floor in the back of the room to listen. Our eyes immediately gravitate toward an old couple—probably in their late seventies—who are alone on a raised platform dancing. A few red phosphorescent lights illuminate them. When my eyes finally adjust to the lighting around their bodies, I realize that the couple is not really moving. They seem to simply be holding each other closely and swaying magically to the beat of the music. The red lights above them almost pulse in time to their swaying. Every so often, when the music picks up or changes tempo, they make a couple of conscious steps. I think it is beautiful. I even tell Land that this scene is almost enough to make me believe in monogamy.

"Just imagine, Land, being their age." I whisper. "All the shit they've seen and experienced. And here they are, after the fact, holding each other in sync and being moved by rhythms that are part of them now."

"I know what you are saying."

"The music is who they are now. It defines their essence. You know what I mean?"

"Oh, yeah. I understand fully. I can dig it big time." Land purses his lips as if to emphasize his digging of the scene before us. He continues, "You know, I've always felt growing old was a drag. It's probably the one thing I fear."

"Getting old?? What's the big deal about that, Land?"

"Losing control."

"Hey, man, it's just a natural part of the order of things. It's an arc—all things are bound by it. You gotta give up that control at some point."

"That's what I'm afraid of, man. I don't trust giving up the reigns to the natural order of things as you put it."

"Naw, man. Don't misinterpret what I said. What I meant was—growing old is interesting, man. What a drag it would be if we kept on holding on to everything in our lives with the same mindset, in the same capacity forever."

"Can you believe this??" Land shakes his head.

"What??"

"You're kicking me advice! That I can't believe, man."

"Yeah, well, I still got a trick or two in me."

"I'm sure you do, Tal. So, what do you fear, man?"

"What do I fear? Uh…" And I take a second to think seriously about this. "Mediocrity."

"Huh…" Land murmurs.

"What?"

"Doesn't that in essence mean you fear ending up like most people?"

"Mmm…I guess. I never thought about it like that."

In the back of my mind, I've always freaked at the possibility that I am doomed to the ordinary. That is my fear. I've always thought that I had to be destined for more—destined for, dare I say, greatness. If my lot is to be filled with average experience that kills me inside. Hard as I've tried to let go, this fear has never left. But, Land's remark adds a new wrinkle to things. Ultimately, what I really fear is being thrown into the same dustbin of life experience that most people find themselves in the end. Maybe, it also has to do with a fear of not being remembered. Being forgotten. Ah, I am getting ahead of myself. I have a touch of snobbery in me. No question. I bring more to the table than the average person, and so, I want my props for this. That's all.

"By the way, Tal, what have you been up to after you hopped on that Greyhound and high-tailed it outta Laredo?" Land's question snaps me out of my thoughts.

"Oh. I, uh, not much really. Worked here and

there. Nothing. Waiting to hear from you and
Gen."

"Yeah?"

"Yeah. What's up with Gen anyway?"

"She's back in New Orleans."

"She did go to Monterrey with you though…right?"
I shouldn't have paused there.

"Yeah. She came with me and stayed for a couple
of weeks. And then she went back to New
Orleans."

"That's it??"

"Is there supposed to be more to it than that?"
I can feel a smidgen of discomfort in Land, so I
don't press on this. I go back to listening to the
music and focusing on the old couple.

"She wanted to get back to her life, Tal. That's all.
I wanted her to lay low a bit longer, but she's
headstrong. She made her decision to go back and
there was no changing it. There's no indecision
with her, you know? She makes shit happen when
she wants to."

"That's for sure."

Land was dead on with that. One thing
about Gen, there was no bullshitting with her. She
didn't play a lot of the mind games like other
women did. She was gutsy. But, I can sense that
Land is not being completely truthful to me about
what happened with Gen. If Gen's feelings for
Land got the better of her, then that was the reason
why she went back to New Orleans. It had nothing
to do with her wanting to get back to her "life" as an
assistant at the New Orleans Vodou Heritage
Museum.

"So, everything's cool between the two of you?" I
ask. How this question stumbles out of my mouth, I

don't know. But, it did, and now I better tread delicately.

"What—what do you mean?"

"I mean—you know, with the money and all."

That's a nice recovery, I think to myself, just develop it a bit more. "Uhhh, you both have split the cash and have agreed on the same story to tell anyone who might come around asking questions?" Very smooth.

"Uhh, yeah—of course. No worries with that."

"That's good, good."

"I think we're in the clear, man. And about the cash—sure it was split. She was free to do whatever she wanted with her half. I've done some *investing* myself."

"I bet you have." I nudge Land playfully. I think the tension has been redirected.

"Sharing the wealth here and there. Helping out some family too."

"They don't ask you where you got all this money from all of the sudden?"

"This is me, man. They know what an enterprising and resourceful lad I am!"

The music suddenly stops. The old couple has stepped off the stage and the band takes a break. Land and I both rise to our feet and start walking out. I take one last twirl through the room and notice the old couple seated in seats on opposite sides of the stage. Both are busy chatting with others in the room. I smile and thank them silently for letting me sit in.

As we walk out the doors, Land turns to me with a serious face.

"But, honestly, the whole thing seems like a dream."

"What? Cuba?"

"No. The robbery, man."

"Oh."

"Everything about it. It's as if that was another Land who pulled that off. There's no way I could muster the same desperation to pull off something like that now."

"You just have some distance between it now."

"No, it's more than that. I sometimes think that that it was a *doppelgänger* who pulled that shit off."

"A what?"

"It's German. Means sort of like an evil twin, you know. Some *other* Land pulled it off. And then I awoke later to inherit that guy's spoils. Same with Gen. Two doppelgangers came together for one purpose—achieved it and then disappeared. So, to me—looking back on what happened—it feels like I wasn't there at all."

"I just think—look where you are now, man. In this place, shit, I've been here for a couple of hours and already I've forgotten that desperate loser existence I have in L.A."

"I know what you mean. Let's just say that I've learned the mind sometimes creates its own memory of things and chooses to believe what it wants to believe."

"Well, that goes without saying, doesn't it?"

"I guess I really never was conscious of that."

We go down the steps of the Capitolio and cross the street where we reach Calle Obispo. This is a tourist friendly avenue that is set apart from the rest of the avenues in the area because it is the only one with working lights. Great big balls of yellow phosphorescence dot the street. Little cubicles house vendors who hawk paintings, drums and jewelry. Kids sell counterfeit Cohiba, Partagas and Montecristo cigars and work in pairs or threes so as to avoid any one of them from being spotted by the vigilant eyes of the soldiers stationed on each block. A couple of pharmacies are also on the street and when I go inside I'm surprised by their upscale décor and mahogany shelves which display antibiotics and pills. We hook a left on San Ignacio and Land shows me La Catedral—an old Catholic church from the Eighteenth Century where it was once thought Columbus's ashes were buried. Around the corner from La Catedral is La Bodeguita del Medio. Intriguing watering hole. Above the bar, I notice a framed piece of paper where Hemingway had scrawled the words, *"Me mojito en La Bodeguita/ Me daquiri en La Floridita."* Brilliant.

Land then takes me back to Calle Obispo where he points out a pink building called the Hotel Ambos Mundos.

"Hemingway finished *For Whom the Bell Tolls* in a room there," Land says.

"Yeah. I bet they have preserved the room or something."

"That's right. I think you can tour the room for a couple of bucks."

"I'll have to check it out before I leave."

We continue down Calle Obispo until it spills into this quaint cobblestone square called Plaza de Armes. The square is filled with booksellers and their wooden book stands which rest on wheels. Each morning, Land tells me, the booksellers roll in their wares into the square and set up shop for tourists to stop and buy their books. Because it is getting late in the day, the booksellers now are starting to close up their stands. I move in fast to check out some of the remaining open bookstands. The first thing that jumps out at me is the plethora of books by Castro and Che. Tons of them. One book, which is like the Bible, is Castro's *Historia Me Absolvera* (History Will Absolve Me). It's being sold for $2 a pop, so I buy a copy. I show it to Land and he tells me it is a word for word reproduction of Castro's eight hour self-defense that he gave before the court at Santiago de Cuba when he was caught for trying to take over a military garrison in 1953. Two Che books are omnipresent. One is Che's *Carta de final de Che a Castro*. This is Che's farewell letter to Castro where he resigns from his position as head of the Cuban treasury in order to go and spark a Vietnam in Bolivia. It's only about four pages long, but is laced with raw emotion and the romantic stuff that makes one legendary. The other book is Che's Bolivian diary written from October 1966 to November 1967. I pick up a copy of this and immediately turn to the last page. Che's words are ominous. He writes that there have been reports of the Bolivian army being assembled at a mere twenty five hundred meters from his camp. That's his last entry because the next day the Bolivian army attacked and Che was shot in both knee caps and he and his band of *twelve* men were captured. He was executed the following morning in a village schoolhouse.

Copies of Mario Puzo's *El Padrino* are side by side works by Karl Marx and Hemingway's *El Viejo y El Mar*. I notice that a few of the booksellers wear Star of Davids and one of them is so grateful when I buy $15 worth of books that he puts his hands together and smacks his lips in deferent supplication. I'm embarrassed. Other booksellers I figure out are Russians left over from the Soviet era who have assimilated well into Cuban culture and speak flawless Spanish.

The irony about the Plaza de Armes and its book intercourse is that right next to it is a modern, air-conditioned government-owned bookstore containing each and every book the booksellers in the Plaza sell. When Land and I wander inside the government-owned bookstore, I also see that the books inside are in English as well! I tell Land that this bookstore is sucking the life out of the Plaza. It's like a giant Barnes & Noble erected along side Jose's Used Books. The booksellers must organize and somehow stop this goliath from wiping them out. But, Land tells me not to worry because most people, and especially tourists, find it more interesting to check out the dog-eared, frayed paperbacks posed on the racks in the Plaza, than to pick up the shrink-wrapped, never-been-read books inside the megastore. That makes sense to me. So, maybe the Plaza booksellers' existence is still secure.

It's getting dark and I glance at my watch. It's close to 7:30. Land says that we better start walking to the Hanoi Café where we're supposed to meet Lazaro for dinner. We turn onto a non-lit avenue parallel to Calle Obispo. Many of the homes on this street are doorless and windowless. As I walk by, I peek into people's living rooms. TVs are being watched in some of them. Others have music and bodies dancing. I see an old man take off his shirt to the delight of his family and he starts to undulate his stomach in sync with the music blaring from a ghettoblaster held by a small boy. It's like being on one of those sound stages used for movies—the buildings are like facades and you don't think anyone can really live inside. As we reach a little intersection, a bunch of kids run past Land and I. The kids are chasing another kid and when they catch him, they pick him up and throw him into a dumpster. In a flash, they disappear. The kid in the dumpster then pokes his head out and after making sure the coast is clear, he creeps out and disappears too. Land and I love it.

"That's what they mean when they say *child-like abandonment*," Land says.

"It can exist anywhere, huh?"

"Anyplace, any situation too."

"Is there anyway to recapture that?" I ask.

"I know what you are getting at. Ignorance is bliss, right?"

"Getting back to that time when as a kid you felt the world was new."

"Yeah. Each day was so, so wondrous. You never knew what you would see or experience the next day."

"Things floated by."

"That was it, man. These kids. You think they know about the *politricks* of life as Bobby Marley called it?"

"Nope."

Then, we come to another dark street where I can see the sinewy shadows of women standing around alone or talking with tourist men.

"*Mira*," I say as I motion towards this lanky girl who's wearing tight white spandex shorts and a dark blue bikini top. Land shakes his head at me.

"Bra, she's only like thirteen," he says.

Sure enough when we walk closer, I see her face up close and it still has baby fat. She wears heavy make-up, but it's obvious she's just a kid. I feel a bit creepy.

"Fuck, man. I couldn't tell from back there," I explain to Land.

"It's cool. They call them *jiniteras*. Literally means *riders*."

"Never heard that one before."

"These kids turning tricks. It's become a paradise for Euro pedophiles, man."

"Oh, yeah? Doesn't the government crack down?"

"Come on, man. They got other problems. Sure once in a while they will arrest some pathetic German chap who gets his hand caught in the cookie jar. And they'll make an example of him and things quiet down for a bit. But, then it starts again."

"I don't get it, man. Castro bans certain books, but doesn't ban this shit?"

"Look, Tal. There are a lot of gray areas. Right now, this country is only surviving on tourist dollars. There's no more Soviet Union propping this place up. So, if you got these men coming in spending dollars for some sun and fun. Then, you gotta look the other way some times. That's all."

"I see," I mutter.

As I pass another group of girls, I try hard not to make eye contact. However, one of the girls makes kiss-kiss sounds at me, which really creeps me out.

"Is that the international call of love?" I tell Land.

"That it is."

"Does he—do Lazaro's girls work like this?" I ask.

"No way, bra. Strictly an upscale operation."

"Yeah?"

"They ain't thirteen either."

Land and I continue up the street and every twenty feet or so another pubescent girl solicits us as she stands in front of a doorless doorway. I stop to stick my head inside one of these doorways and I see broken stairs leading up into a dimly lit second floor. Next to the stairs is an old elevator—the kind where you get in and manually close an accordion-like door. The elevator is trashed and somehow vines have grown around it. I come back outside where Land is waiting for me. This entire street has been spooky and sad and I ask Land if we can cut back to Calle Obispo. He agrees and says that the only reason he took me to this street in the first place was for me to get a feel of what survival breeds.

We get to Hanoi. It's a couple of minutes before eight, but there's no sign of Lazaro yet. We get a table and I scan the menu. Pollo asado, ropa vieja, chicaron. Land tells me I have to order the Cuban staple of pollo asado with *moros y cristianos*.

"It's garliced chicken—melts right off the bone," Land explains.

"What are moros and cristianos?"

"Heehee. That's just black beans and rice. Even the food here reflects how racialized Cuba is. *Moros y cristianos* means Moors and Christians. I love explaining that to people."

"That's really an imaginative of way at looking at your food!"

"It's like ebony and ivory—living together in perfect harmony. Here, you just smother the beans on the rice and chow down."

I look up from the menu and see Lazaro limping his way to our table. I alert Land, and then he and I both stand up to greet Lazaro.

"How are you, how are you?" Lazaro asks us.

We shake hands, and again, I notice what a firm, vise-like grip he has.

"Good. I gave Tal a little tour through old town. I think he got a feel for the place."

"Fascinating place, don't you think?" Lazaro asks me.

"Oh, definitely. It has a certain charm. I really dig it."

"Ahh, spoken like a true American. Such poetic words. I always find Americans so poetic, you know?"

"Really??" I ask thinking that Lazaro is joking around.

"Oh, yes. What else do you expect from the land of such visionary ideals?"

I want to tell Lazaro that most of the Americans I know chiefly grunt and utilize a monosyllabic command of the Queen's English, but I let him hold onto his romantic notion.

"Come, come. Let us sit now." Lazaro instructs us.

Lazaro motions the waitress over and she listens attentively to our orders. Land orders ropa vieja and Lazaro selects a pork dish. I go with the pollo asado.

"A good choice for your first meal in Havana," Lazaro tells me.

"I've heard good things about it from Land."

"Did you order one of the pork dishes," Land asks Lazaro.

"You got me," Lazaro laughs back at Land.

"What??" I ask.

"When I first got here, Tal, Lazaro and I went out for a meal and I ordered a pork dish. Next thing I know, Lazaro is chastising me about eating what he calls a filthy beast!" Land teases.

"Hahaha." Lazaro laughs again.

"Is it against your religion or something?" I ask Lazaro.

"That is a good question," Lazaro says as he nibbles on a piece of garlic bread and wipes the corners of his mouth with a napkin. "I follow what I call the *tresillo* approach to God."

"Let's hear it!" Land says.

"You will enjoy this. I know."

"I'm all ears," I join in Land's eagerness.

"*Tresillo* is like how you say, three-piece. I piece together three different religions into one larger belief which I follow."

"Break it down for us, please," Land implores Lazaro.

"I take a little from Catholicism, and some from Santeria and then sprinkle elements of Islam and there I have my own religion."

"It works??" I ask.

"Oh, yes. I feel connected to all of my ancestors, you know. From my African to my Spanish roots. I take from Catholicism and Islam basic doctrinal guidance and ceremony. From Santeria, I take the mystical and get my spiritual strength. I am named after St. Lazarus who is one of the most important figures in Santeria. So, I choose to follow beliefs drawn from all three religions, and tonight, *Landito*, my spirit craves a little pork!"

"I see how it works!" Land blurts.

We all have a good laugh and I can tell it's going to be a memorable stay in Havana. Lazaro brings out some Cohiba Lancelos out of his jacket and offers them to Land and I. I immediately light mine and start puffing away. Superb *puros*. Tasty and rich. This is great. I recline in my chair puro in hand and take a second to think about how lucky I am to be here at this moment. This cat Lazaro is a piece of work. I've never met anyone like him. Look at him, he's probably in his *eighties* and he still has an undeniable, infectious zest for life. That throaty laugh and mischievous glint in his brown-blue eyes makes it seem as if he has discovered some elixir of youth that is not the apocryphal fountain of Ponce de Leon. He has tapped into something real and I gotta watch him close and see if I can pick up on any of his secrets. If Land really fears growing old, then he must be watching Lazaro closer than I. And then there it is—a realization. Land's probably after Lazaro's secrets too.

A phone suddenly rings. This is surprising. I then see Lazaro pull out a cell phone and in fast, rushed Spanish counsels the person who has called. I turn to Land and remark that I had no idea there would be cell phones in Cuba. He waves me off by saying Castro doesn't ban wireless communication.

More than a half an hour after we ordered, the waitress brings us three Hatuey gran cervezas. I'm almost done with my cigar at this point. "Things always take this long?" I say quietly to Land.

"Come on, it's only been a couple of minutes since we gave our order, Tal." Land answers a bit annoyed by my question.

"Land, it took thirty-seven minutes on my watch to bring out our beers. That's a long time no matter how you cut it."

"Relax. You have your beer now, don't you? So, just adjust to the cadence of things here."

I guess he's right. Big fuckin' deal. I'm just used to prompt service and I get anxious when things are slow. At the table next to ours, two men and two jiniteras have taken their seats. I surreptitiously look over my shoulder to check them out. A couple of Germans or Dutchmen—I can tell by the way they have their sweaters slung over their shoulders and by their accents when they speak broken English to the girls. What a slap in the face! They come all the way to pay for sex with underage girls and they can't even speak a little Spanish with the girls at dinner. I notice that the girls are struggling back to answer in their own broken English. It's a bizarre double date. These two older, balding white males taking out two fourteen or fifteen year old skinny, brown girls for precoital, meaningless dinner conversation.

"I guess those cats aren't locals?" I ask Land.

"No sirree. You don't see many locals eating at these restaurants in the first place."

Lazaro gets off the phone and somehow knows what Land and I are discussing.

"It is disturbing, huh?" he asks me.

"What—what do you mean?" I ask not sure about where Lazaro is leading with his question.

"That—behind you. It's revolting. Cuban school girls selling themselves to tourists. It's bad for the country. The future, you know? Castro needs to do more cracking down on this."

"You know, Lazaro, that the country needs dollars from these tourists," Land replies.

"Yes, yes. So, the dollars come in when they stay in hotels and eat out. They buy things, clothes, cigars, art. They go to Varadero and spend a week getting pampered there at the beach. Not this."

I get a real kick out of this. Again, isn't this cat a pimp himself?? I just look back at Lazaro as he speaks and silently challenge him to read my mind. Mistake number one.

"I know what you are thinking," Lazaro tells me.

"Ye-uh, I'm not—" I trip over my words. If he can read my mind, I hope he does not take what I thought as some kind of insult.

"You are thinking, *Who the hell is this guy to be passing judgment on these people*? Am I right? I take it Land has told you that I am in a similar business?"

"No, not really. People have to survive. To each their own as it goes." I throw out some bullshit.

"There is a difference in what I do." Lazaro takes a big suck on his Cohiba. "I provide necessities— that's all. These businessmen—my clientele—they have wives, families back in their homes. They come to Cuba *para negocios*. Whatever that may be for them. They go out to the theater shows, listen to the music, and need a release. I provide that for them at a cost."

I slurp down my Hatuey as Lazaro goes on.

"I give them women. These women on the whole don't speak their language. They don't need to. They are only objects of fantasy. These men call me and I arrange for a meeting with a woman and if the woman agrees, then what they do next is not of my concern. My role is that of the facilitator. I facilitate access to the fantasy."

"Nice way to put it," I say.

"These men, what do they do? Talk all day. About what? Money. So, at the end of the day, they don't want more talk. So, the woman doesn't need to say anything. They only need to smile, hold the men's hands, eat good food, drink good wine, and take it from there."

"Isn't that what the two girls over there are doing too?" I ask.

"No, they're too young to know anything."

"I bet they know a lot!" I try to joke.

"They are not in control. They are like the apple in Eden, you know? Something these men are not to get, you see? In my business, *pu-ssee* is available anywhere and everyone knows how it works. But, for these little girls, they are being raped even though they are the ones selling themselves. The men who want them are not the clients who come to me who want a release. No. The men over *there* want to penetrate something innocent and pure. That's what they...how do you say?? Get off on?"

"They get off on it." Land adds.

"Yes. And that is why it is like a rape because these girls sell themselves to buy food. But, with these men, they don't realize they are robbed of their....ah...holiness as a child of God."

"I completely agree with that. I like the way you put it. The jiniteras here are forbidden fruit. If these men just wanted pussy, they could find it anywhere in Europe. Amsterdam, Frankfurt—any place like that. But, what they want is to steal that innocence only a child can have. It empowers them." Land says.

Lazaro pontificates on and on about the evils of child prostitution in his country. I finally tune out once Land starts weighing in with similar thoughts about child slavery in Thailand and picture brides in China and a whole slew of other factual examples of the child-flesh trade. My stomach is rumbling. A basic urge has me at its command. Every time I see the waitress waltz by our table, I want to grab her and demand that she bring out our food now! Over *an hour and a half* has passed since we first ordered and I finished smoking the Cohiba twenty minutes ago. I have a bit of buzz. I also have nursed my beer ever so carefully because I think that if I go ahead and polish it off and then order another one, I will have to wait another thirty-seven minutes for it to come. I don't think I've ever waited this long for food in my life. God, it's a drag.

The waitress passes by again, and this time Lazaro who probably senses my hunger, taps her on the arm and gives her terse orders in Spanish. She reacts with what appears to be a genuine apology. Lazaro smiles at me. I appreciate his intervention. Five minutes later, our waitress reappears with our food. She passes out our dishes robotically and says nothing. I ask for a glass of water but she just blows me off. Mistake number two.

"What do you think, Tal? They have pitchers of ice water on stand-by and are just waiting to fill your glass upon your whim?" Land bellows.

"I guess that was too much to ask for," I answer.

"I think, Land, you expect too much of your friend here. His first time to Cuba, no?"

"Yeah," I say and I'm not sure if I should be offended by the first part of what Lazaro has just said.

"In Cuba, the *ospi-tal-ity* industry is rather relaxed. You put yourself in the hands of people who are not there really to serve you."

"Right there, I must be outta my mind! I thought that was the whole point of going out to eat!" I say to Lazaro.

"It is funny! I know. But, please listen to this. These waiters and waitresses they work for the government. Not the customer. So, like any other government program they are slow to serve you. You must give your order and wait and wait and wait. Unless you know someone at the restaurant, there is no getting away from waiting." Lazaro explains.

"Sounds like the goddamn DMV," I remark.

"What is this?" Lazaro asks.

"It means, *Department of Motor Vehicles*," Land quickly answers.

"It's a government agency, Lazaro, set up by each state in America. It issues drivers' licenses to everyone and checks your eyes. Something like that anyway," I say.

"And the problem with it, is that they take forever to do anything!" Land interjects.

"Yeah, they are a nightmare." I say.

"Ah, I see—," Lazaro says.

"—speaking of cars, Lazaro, how do you guys keep all these old cars running after all these years?" I ask.

"It's the music."

"Come on!" I say.

"Really. It is. The Cuban *son*. It's like a folk music. Traditional. It has these *reedmic* patterns which repeat and once *son* went to Puerto Rico it became *salsa*. The music grew and grew as it bounced off the two islands. But, back to what you asked. *Son* is the secret to the cars still working. It has never changed in Cuba and continues to be pumped into the cars where it charges the cars like a battery. As long as the music lasts, the cars will last. That is what I believe."

"It is really amazing to see these cars still running. What a relief not to have any big cars like SUVs here!"

"*S-U-Vees?*" Lazaro asks.

"Tal is from Los Angeles, Lazaro, so he's bogged down with cars. That's what L.A. is today—a big parking lot. In the U.S. right now, they have these *sports utility vehicles* that people call SUVs for

short. These are big cars people like to pick up their groceries in."
"No, we don't have those in Cuba."
"At least not yet, Lazaro. But, they may come. Castro still trades with Japan!" Land responds.
"No, the avenues here, they can't fit such big cars."
"Well, they will make the avenues wider!" I say.
"Hahaha!" Lazaro laughs. "Let us eat now! No more talk about such monsters!"

I get down to business. I was already picking at my food and eating unnoticed during our conversation. Now, I vacuum down pieces of chicken without even chewing. When I get to my vegetables—carrots, green beans and corn—I find that they still have ice on them! They have not even been boiled. It's as if after the waitress told the chef that Lazaro had asked about our food, the chef just hastily pulled the barely thawed veggies out of a bag and threw them on the side of my dish. But, I don't mutter a word about this debacle. I instead concentrate on the pollo asado. Chicken marinated in lemon and garlic and melting off the bone just as Land had foretold. It is cooked well and is delicious. I pour the moros over the cristianos and enjoy. Some papas fritas and fried platanes round out my meal.

I check my watch and see that it's near 11:30. The pollo asado acts like a powerful sedative and a drowsiness drifts over me.
"A long day my friend, eh?" Lazaro probes.
"Uh, yeah. What a contrast." I say.
"How do you mean?"
"This morning I left L.A. and all its commerciality, and then from Cancun, which is designed by

Americans for Americans, I come to Cuba which is completely the reverse of all that."

"Ahhh," Lazaro mumbles as he savors a chunky piece of pork.

"Oh, sure, bra. Cancun—it's only forty-five minutes by air from Havana and you just gotta compare the two airports. Both sit on the Caribbean, but when you leave Cancun and go to Havana you go from the cheesy, neon-lights of *Senior Frog's* frat boyishness to serious, bare-walled socialist no-nonsenseness."

"No-nonsenseness?" I throw back at Land.

"I know, no such word may exist, but you know what I mean, man." Land defends himself.

"It is definitely a marked contrast, and I got over a week to take this place all in." I tell Lazaro.

"So, what does Land have in store for you?"

"I, uh, don't really know. Land?" I look over at him.

"I'll take him to the usual sights. We'll go out to the country one day. He can also come work with me in the bar one night. That should be a gas, man!" Land slaps me on the shoulder.

"I don't know. My bartending skills are not what they used to be back in college, man."

"Bullshit! It's like riding a bike, man. It will all come back to you once you get behind the bar. I'll teach you the drinks they dig here. Uh, what else?"

"Going to Varadero?" Lazaro asks.

"I don't think that Tal wants to waste anytime at the beach. Am I right, bra?"

"Yeah, I guess. I rather see the stuff that I can't see anywhere else, you know? The best features of Cubanness."

"What? Is that a word now?" Land jokes back at me.

"Right alongside no-nonsenseness, you will find that the term Cubanness is commonly used to describe these parts." I play the same game.

"I'll take him to some shows, give him a taste of Havana nightlife as well," Land tells Lazaro.

"Don't forget to go to a paladar as well," Lazaro adds.

"Definitely," Land responds.

"Good. I want to invite you both for a *real* dinner before the two of you leave. I know Landito that you will be leaving soon, yes?"

"Yeah. Unfortunately, we'll be gone next Friday."

"So, how about that Thursday night you two be my guests for a last dinner?"

"Of course." Land says.

"Oh, yes." I say.

"Good, good. Let us set dinner for eight o'clock at El Aljibe. You know where it is, Landito?" Lazaro asks.

"Up on Playa?"

"Yes, it is close to the house."

"We'll be there!" Land shouts.

"We will have much better food, I promise you, Tal. And service!" Lazaro winks at me.

When the waitress brings our check, my hand flies out to it like a bat out of hell. Lazaro puts on a mock protest, but gives in after a brief tug-of-war with me and the bill. I bring out some cash—U.S. dollars only of course—and the waitress takes it. She brings back change in local Cuban currency. Pesos. Worthless. Lazaro and Land thank me for the dinner, and I then thank them profusely for having me as their guest and giving me this extraordinary opportunity to spend some time in La Habana. We walk out of Hanoi with full bellies and step out into the dark streets. I crave another Cohiba Lancelo, but don't want to be greedy by asking Lazaro if he has another one available. Lazaro's driver pulls up and moves quickly to get around the car and open the passenger door for us. Lazaro throws his cane in first and then bows low to get inside the car. Land and I follow behind.

The car rolls onto the Malecon which I am now seeing for the first time at night. It is lined with two rows of yellow phosphorescent light poles. On my left side, stand the vacant ghosts of aristocratic oceanfront homes. And on my right, lies the choppy Atlantic whose swells crash over the Malecon's stony walls and onto the street. No one says a word. No one needs to. When you drive through Havana at night in the Nineties in a car from the Fifties and are being chaperoned by a man in his eighties, there is nothing that can be said. It's unimaginable and unprecedented. But, it takes place and I struggle to find the words to do justice to the scene. It's just not possible. So, I leave it at that.

III

  The house is dead quiet. Lazaro bids us
good night and retires into his master bedroom on
the first floor of the house. Land and I climb the
stairs to his room. Once we enter his room, Land
leaves to go to a storage room and returns with
blankets and pillows.
"Thanks," I tell him.
"No, these are for me. You can crash on my bed."
"Come on, Land. It's cool. I don't mind being on
the floor."
"No—it's alright. I got a bad back anyway and that
mattress has been killing me."
"You sure?"
"Yeah."
  I take the bed, which is really itself only a
mattress lying on the floor. Land tells me the
bathroom is down the hall and to the right. I take
out my toiletry bag and go to the bathroom to brush
my teeth. I like the bathroom. It is clean and
roomy. The water runs just fine. When I get back
to the room, Land has made a nice makeshift bed on
the floor with the blankets and sheets he brought
out. He is immersed in reading a book. I flop on
the mattress and let out a big exhale and massage
my temple. Some old relaxation technique I
learned. It may have even come from one of the
Krishnas. After a few minutes of this, I glance over
at Land and make out the title of the book he is
reading.
"*God is Red*?" I inquire.
"It's a good read, man."
"What is it? Fiction??"

"No, no. But, I guess some people would write it off as fiction. It's by Vine Deloria, Jr."

The name is familiar.

"You should know him," Land says.

"Yeah, yeah...I remember," I jog my brain. "He was that—that Lakota Sioux philosopher slash lawyer, right?"

"Yup. I was reading some of his shit in school. I used to be really into what he had to say and his insights about the world."

"So, is this a new book of his or are you just rereading it?"

"I actually found this book in the Plaza de Armes, believe it or not, a couple of weeks ago."

"That figures."

"I had read it before—years ago—but forgot about it. Now, as I reread it, the guy still blows me away. He turns almost all of human history and New World history on its head, man."

"He must be a good writer if he can have that kind of effect on you, man!"

"It's really persuasive writing. Debunks eurocentric thought like you can't believe. It gives you a complete Native perspective on the ways and shapes of things in human religion and history. You gotta read some of his stuff some time, Tal."

"Mmmhhmm."

"Especially since you want to write yourself, you know?"

"Well, if his stuff is all non-fiction, I don't know what I will learn from it except the history he teaches."

"But, you are missing the point. I told you for some people, actually, most, his stuff is fiction! You understand? He writes about things that are the converse of our socialized understanding of the

world. So, fiction or non-fiction, those are fluid
notions. They depend on your point-of-view. Read
his stuff, it will definitely help you, bra."
"Yeah, you're probably right. I will." I then shake
my head. "You know what…shit!"
"What's up?"
"I think we had this exact conversation like five
years ago and back then I said the same thing—that
I would read his stuff! Remember?"
"Yeah, you did! You just shined me on, didn't you?
Motherfucker!"

Land pushed books on me like a dealer
pushed drugs. Now, I dug books too and had
amassed my own little collection through the years,
but Land would find all kinds of books on a wide
range of shit and constantly refer me to them. He
would give me little snippets of what each book was
about, but that was it. He never went into details, so
after he gave me a taste, it was up to me to follow
through and absorb the book itself. To my credit, I
tried to read a lot of the books that he pushed my
way and some of the reads really opened my eyes to
a new way of looking at the world around us. But,
some of the new age shit I just didn't dig as much as
he did. You know the titles: *Journey to Ixtlan, Way
of the Peaceful Warrior, Zen and the Art of
Motorcycle Maintenance* and *Jonathan Livingston
Seagull*. Also, Kahlil Gibran's *The Prophet*. That
whole genre. It wasn't real to me, but Land dug
them all. My kick against them was that they were
too *nice*. Nice in the sense that they fundamentally
romanticized human nature as being a happy
ending. They all professed to give insight into the
human existence and this insight was about
connecting with one's soul through stilling the

bullshit around oneself and concentrating on the oneness between the individual and love. Funny that in trying to explain my thoughts on this, my own words ring of new ageism! And Land knew this about me. So, he would throw these books my way from time to time in order to gauge my reaction. I would read some of them or fake reading them and then bullshit with Land over their merits. Some of the books were pure rubbish, but others did have their moments. One thing I appreciated back then though was that it was good to have someone in your life like Land who exposed you to these things whether you dug them or not.

I'm fading out. It has been a long day. Changing planes twice. About a total of ten hours traveling and the three hour time change as well. It feels like I have made it to the other side. I remember growing up in the Eighties when communism was painted as this sinister force that Reagan fought heroically hard against. It was this faceless, yet very concrete adversary. I was taught to not like communists because they were the scourge of the "Free World." I was never told what exactly the "Free World" meant or encompassed. I assumed it was only America and maybe a couple of our friends—like England and France. Well, maybe not France. However, it was drilled in my head that I knew that the Soviet Union, Eastern Block and Cuba—these were the bad guys. In my social studies classes, any pro-communist discussion was anathema. Your parents would get reamed by the school administration if you were piping up in class with positives about the communist world. I especially remember the 1984 Summer Olympics in Los Angeles when the Soviets boycotted. The press portrayed the boycott as a personal slap in the face of all Americans. Yes, it became personal and everyone then hoped and prayed that America would amass more gold medals than the Soviets had racked up during the 1980 Summer Games held in Moscow, which *incidentally* America had boycotted. It was that intense—the "Us" versus "Them" mentality that we were fed and fed off. It was "Us" versus "Them"— even when we were not actually squaring off against them!! That's how fucked up a time it was.

And now here I was beyond the wall so to speak. A wall of preconception and misconception. The name of this sliver of an island still conjured up such political venom in the U.S. I can't wait to see what the next week will bring.

"Hey, Tal?? You asleep?"

I faintly hear Land. But, don't respond as I am slipping into the throes of sleep.

"Tal??" Land says louder.

"Yeahhh," I grumble.

"You did pick up a return ticket on Cubana when you were in Cancun, right?"

"Uhhh…" I try to recapture the events of earlier today. "Yeah, I think so…"

"I just want to give you a heads up that when we leave next Friday to Cancun, I also have booked you on a plane to New Orleans with me."

I'm drifting off again.

"Tal??"

"Yah, yeah."

"Did you hear me? We're going to New Orleans from Cancun. Cool??"

"Uhhh…yeah, sure. That's cool."

"All right, but if you have to go back to L.A. You gotta let me know."

"Right. Cool."

"Otherwise, I'll just get you a ticket back to L.A. from New Orleans."

"Oh, thanks." And that's it. Maybe Land goes on talking, I don't know and I don't wake up. I'm catching serious Zs.

For the next four days, Land and I go all over Havana and take a couple of forays out into the countryside. We go to Pinar del Rio one day—the home of the most luscious tobacco crops in the world. Then, to Mariel Bay, where in 1980, the Marielitos jumped into boats and sailed to Miami after Castro kicked them out of prison for being traitors to the Revolution. Now, the bay is empty and quiet, but locals still talk about the Marielitos as if they left the island yesterday. I hang with Land at the Habana Club on a couple of nights and watch him make fantastic mojitos—a delightful libation consisting of Habana Club Rum (preferably eight years old), seltzer water, lime juice, sugar and garnished with mint leaves. Very tasty. A bunch of tourists hang around this place which is decked out like a poor man's Hard Rock Café. Most people order their drinks from Land in English and all pay in U.S. dollars. From the looks of it, Land is making a small fortune in tips! The house bands at the club are amazing and the women on stage gyrate fast to salsa and rhumba. I try my hand at mixing some drinks, but just can't make my mojitos taste as good as Land's. So, instead I spend most of the time kicking back and lounging at the bar, getting free mojitos from Land and swapping stories with sun tan lotion smelling Canadian tourists.

One night, Land takes me to a bar/nightclub called "The Rio Club," but for some reason all the locals still call it by its Batistan-era name of "Johnny's Drink." This confounds me big time. These Cubans—ninety percent of whom were not even around when Batista ruled—still referring to the club with a name from a forgotten time. On the way there, the cab driver tells us that Johnny's Drink has the best live music in the city. We pay $15 to get inside and when we walk inside the dark club we find no band or music whatsoever. Instead, some screen shows Latin MTV-like videos of grainy quality and about twenty-five jiniteras stare at our every move. No other men are in sight. I want to stay and get to know some of these girls, but Land says the worst thing I can do is lead these girls on and then bail without closing the deal. I relent and follow him back outside.

On another day, we tour the Museo de la Revolucion, which is Batista's former palace. In front of the building, a tank and a piece of old colonial Havana form a fascinating gate to the museum. Inside, bulletholes are splattered on the marble foyer. There are four floors and the grandeur of Batista's palace is still evident. The door to the stairwell in which Batista fled and disappeared to Portugal is propped open for visitors to contemplate the literal eviction of imperialism from Cuba. The renaissance-like painting of the ceiling of the grand ballroom oddly contrasts with the helmets, boots, and rifles of the Revolution encased behind glass. The best part of the museum, as Land says, is the section which details CIA operations in Cuba since 1960. Everything from the diseasing of tobacco crops to the sabotaging of Cuban activities in

Angola. Photographs and intercepted intelligence all lend support to the CIA's attempt at undermining Castro and stirring the Cuban people against his rule.

Outside the building, stands something truly remarkable. At first, I think it's another tank and Land laughs. He tells me it is one of the most revered objects in Cuba—up there with Che's mausoleum in Santa Clara. It's the *Granma*. "Remember when I told you about Camilo Cienfuegos, man?" Land asks me.

"Yeah. The cat in the picture in your room."

"Well, he, Castro and Che and seventy-nine others sailed from Mexico to Cuba on this boat." Land points up. "They landed in the eastern tip of Cuba in 1957."

"In the jungles."

"The Sierra Maestra region. Anyway, only two years later, they sacked Havana. It's a fuckin' amazing story. And it all begins with this boat. Look at it! How small and rickety it is! But, the history it carried…"

"Hmmm. So, this is it."

The *Granma* sits arisen and centrally positioned inside a large glass cube. It's white and green paint seems retouched and it blows me away that this little dingy was responsible for a good chunk of the last fifty years of Twentieth Century human history. It has an air of the sacred about it. Castro's regime has capitalized on the boat's mythic nature by naming the leading (and perhaps only) daily Cuban newspaper as the *Granma*. That's definitely one secret to Castro's longevity, his ability to transform the ordinary into iconic canons of Cuban patriotism. U.S. policy and the ridiculous embargo have played right into Castro's hands.

How blatantly obvious that is when you are inside Cuba. Because he's been backed into a corner by a behemoth neighbor, Castro has had to galvanize the people behind him through symbolism and mythologizing La Revolucion as a spiritual reclaiming of the soul of the country. I mean everywhere I turn in Havana, I am bombarded with images of Che's angelic face—his eyes fierce and confidently seizing the future. An image on par with the face of Christ that Raphael painted in his *Ascension* where out of a plume of divine smoke, Christ explodes into the heavens. So, here is the risen *Granma* for all non-believers and believers alike to behold. And it works. Trying to break a country through economic deprivation has instead spawned a patriotic spiritualism that will forever burn Castro and the Revolution into the hearts and minds of the Cuban people. Good luck with that.

Tanks and boats and debris from the ill-fated Bay of Pigs invasion surround the *Granma*. A turbine of an American jet shot over Cuba during sorties from 1961 lies next to an eternal flame for those Cubans killed doing their part to protect la Patria. A sign under the turbine states that the body of the American pilot who flew the plane had to be kept by the Cuban government for twelve years because the American government denied authorizing such sorties over Cuba.

"Fuck, man," I remark to Land. "Can you believe that?"

"What?? About the pilot?"

"Yeah. They had to hold on to it for twelve years? That's insane!"

"Hey, that's politics, I guess. But, you wouldn't have learned this in the U.S."

I think about this.

"There are definitely two sides to each story," I say. "Fill in the blanks, Tal. That's what you gotta do in life. Get all the facts and then make up your mind about things. What's right, what's wrong."

"Hah. Even then, though, with all the facts, I don't think you can know what really is right or wrong. You know what I mean?"

"Yeah, yeah. It's a sliding scale between the two. That's why some people cling to their religion so desperately. They get their answers from there."

"And then push those answers down others' throats!"

"It is a cycle, isn't it?"

"Yup."

"That's why it is good to actually come to other places. Cross over like we are doing here. To at least, first-hand, gather history ourselves. It enhances our perspectives of things big time."

After the Museo, Land takes me through Centro Havana. He tells me there is a great paladar that we have to eat at which is located on Calle Concordia. It is a family's apartment and sits in an Eighteenth Century townhouse where the family prepares the meals, keeps delightful Spanish wines in their cellar and the family members are the ones who actually serve you. As we walk in the streets, I see a line of people—mostly women with their kids—waiting patiently outside a government-owned clothing store. It is close to eight at night and it seems that this store has just opened. Pairs of armed soldiers stand sentry at the entrance and allow only two people at a time inside the store. The exit doors are also blocked and guarded. The window displays of the store have Adidas shoes and other sporting apparel. A kid on a bike wearing a

Michael Jordan T-shirt stares with brown, pop-eyes at the shoes. I feel strangely guilty as Land and I pass the line of people.

Land had made a reservation earlier that day for this particular paladar. We get to the once palatial townhouse and push open the doors. The family's apartment is located on the third floor. You can't miss the staircase that greets you as soon as you get inside. It is now decrepit and in disrepair. In its heyday, it must have been the grand focal point upon entering the house. We gingerly creep up the creaking stairs to the third floor and reach a door. I ring the doorbell—it is after all someone's house and we are dinner guests. I ask Land if maybe we should have brought a gift. He laughs, and then with a serious face tells me that that might not have been a bad idea! The owner opens the door and welcomes us in. He introduces his daughter who seats us at a small table next to a small wine shelf. I take a look around the room. Paintings of Havana street life are on the walls and great faded pink wooden shutters are propped open onto a narrow balcony. I step outside to take in the view. Again, no lights illuminate the streets, so all I see are the lights beaming out of the bulbs and lamps inside the surrounding apartments. I can hear scattered voices coming from the barrio below. It's haunting. I envision how magnificent this townhouse must have been in pre-revolutionary Cuba. Now, it's been divided amongst ten or more families, each with a unit to itself and trying to survive any which way they know how. As I come back inside, I drift into a side door and notice an older gentleman sitting in a recliner and watching television. This really is a fully functioning, lived-in house, I tell Land. Trippy.

"How would you like to have your home turned into a restaurant?" Land asks.

"This is far out! But, it looks like they are doing well."

I scan the menu which is presented just as nicely as you would find in a four-star restaurant. I look on the walls and there are photos of famous Americans posing with the owner and his family. Jack Nicholson is on the wall.

"People learn to do what they can to survive here. Like I told you, man." Land says.

Unlike the slow service and uncooked food I had to endure at the Hanoi Café, here at this paladar, I enjoy attentive, fast service. The food is exquisite. Well-prepared and delicious. I have a fish dish—bass. Land has Cuban style pork chops. We each order some café cubitas to cap it off. Excellent.

Another highlight of my week in Cuba is going to the village of San Francisco de Paulo to see Hemingway's villa, "La Finca Vigia." A nice spread. We pay $5 to enter the compound, but no one is allowed inside the house itself. Instead, all the doors and windows of the house are open so you can see the complete interior of the place. But, if you want to take a picture of what you see inside, you gotta pay another $5 per shot. You better play ball with this because one of the Cubans inside the house watches you closely and has a gun. I dig the place though. Books, books, and more books pepper the house. Even the old cat's bathroom is shelf-lined with three rows of books. Empty wine and alcohol bottles are in the living room and heads of Sable antelope, Topi gazelles and Orynx hang in each room. Detached and to the left of the house, there is a three-floored tower, and on its top floor, you see a typewriter atop an ebony desk with a male lion hide underneath. You can see Havana in the distance framed between verdant jungle and tall, skinny palm trees. A black and white photo of Hemingway at the Nobel Prize ceremony for *Old Man* shows him young and dapper but seemingly *uncomfortable* posing within the formal confines of a tux. Right next to this is a photo of a white-bearded, fat, and bare-chested Papa wearing only shorts and helping Cuban kids haul in a fishing net. But, he's got a big smile on his face. Another photo that is dated from 1959 shows Hemingway shaking hands with Castro as he presents him with a trophy. The inscription reads that Castro had not only toppled the Batistan government that year, but also had won Hemingway's annual fishing tournament. The two men wear large toothy grins and are surrounded by fans and tournament officials. It's a dichotomous meeting between two giants headed towards opposite directions in their lives.

Down a slope from the tower, an empty pool greets the visitor. Next, to the pool, sitting at rest on a platform, is Hemingway's boat, *El Pilar*. Land hates the name.

"Why?" I ask.

"Come on, man. What do you think of when you hear the name *Hemingway*?"

"I dunno. A lot of things, I guess."

"Most people would think of *action*. Epic feats, heroic scenes. Bullfights, fishing, war. All that jazz."

"Yeah, I suppose."

"Now, you come face to face with his boat, right? You have a picture of some mighty, battle-scarred vessel. And it is called, *El Pilar*?"

"Doesn't that mean, *The Pillar*? Not such a bad name?"

"It doesn't jive, man. I don't like it."

"O.K., O.K. Let me draw a parallel here."

"Please do."

"Look at the *Granma*. You think of what? Che, Camilo and Castro. Legendary, right?"

Land nods.

"But, what a shitty name! *The Grandma*?? Can you imagine, Batista laughing his ass off when he heard reports that *The Grandma* had landed in the Sierra Maestra!!"

"I hear you."

"So, you have *El Pilar* and *Granma*, two lousily named boats—innocuously named. But, both were responsible for carrying and witnessing such incredible, heroic things."

"Great, Tal. You always bring such insight to things," Land laughs.

"Hey, and let me add this. Both these boats, they've outlived all those who they carried into history."

"Not quite," Land peeps.

"Who's left, man? I'm talking about the main guys here."

"There's still a couple of cats hanging in there."

"Sure. Castro's still around."

"No, I'm talking about Gregorio Fuentes."

I just saw the name and picture inside the house, but for some reason I blank on its significance.

"Who's that?" I ask.

Land points toward a photo below the *El Pilar* that shows a scrawny and wrinkled short man standing alongside Hemingway.

"Jesus, that guy is old! When was that photo taken?"

"It says 1950. He was the captain of the *El Pilar*, bra."

"Whoa…and he's still alive today?"

"Yup. Over a hundred years old and still smokes one puro every day. Lives out in Cojimar. And Tal, he is *the* old man."

"*El viejo*? He must have some stories."

"Oh, yeah. Especially, since Hemingway didn't actually sail his own boat! Fuentes did all the work. Papa fished. But, Fuentes knew the sea. That cat was the man."

Gregorio Fuentes. Lazaro Suarez. Fidel Castro. As Land and I leave Hemingway's compound, I ponder these three men. What is it about these cats? Their longevity and zest for life. They make it—old age—work for them somehow. Hemingway couldn't handle it, so he blew his brains out in the tranquil environs of his Ketchum, Idaho ranch. I think of Land and his fear. Some people forcefully resist the arthritic parching brought by the relentless passing of years. But, it's clear to me when I hear the stories of Fuentes and Suarez and even Castro, if passion remains strong in the person, then exuberance in living can continue. Passion for the seas in the case of Fuentes, passion for La Revolucion in the case of Castro, and Lazaro, well, he is simply passion *incarnate*. He personifies the concept to the extreme and it colors everything he does. Aye though, here again rears the head of those pesky British moralists that propagated the notion that being a slave to passion is what dooms man not liberates him. In rebuttal, I present these three men—one over hundred years of age, one probably in his eighties and the other in his seventies. Their lives have intersected, whether they know it or not, and each has forged a life that beats on because they have capitalized on their own unique passion. Each has, by virtue of now growing old through riding out their passion in full, *self-actualized* himself. So, then that's my answer to Land. You can never self-actualize yourself if you don't grab hold of your passion and take it into the twilight years. Land should realize this. Yet, it is strange because I just can't conceive of Land as growing old. Some people you can just see as becoming silver-haired, immobile and fixed to an indoor existence, but for others it seems unnatural.

I will concede this point, however, that somewhere in all this destiny may play a part and the wick that allows our flames to burn may be shorter for those flames that burn more brightly. So, then self-actualization for only those rare individuals, may be controlled by contingencies that the rest of us cannot and will never understand. For the rest of us, we must try to self-actualize ourselves by living to the natural end of our lives and maintaining our passion. The rest of us need to shoulder up to those brighter flames and for an instant bask in their heat, otherwise, once the flames vanish we are left with afterglows that fade and fade until all that remains are words and memories that we fight over in an attempt to exert our own petty dominion. The mistake we then make is to take the extinguished flame of those few others as our own passion, and in so doing we can never properly self-actualize ourselves.

One afternoon's visit to the Finca brings these thoughts out. Pardon the digression, I'll get on with it.

IV

Thursday. Our last night in Havana. We have a ten in the morning flight to catch mañana. I'm pretty worn out by all the sight-seeing and whipping around the city. Last night, Land and I went out to the Tropicana which blew me away with all these hot Cuban dolls dancing around with chandeliers and other fifteen-pound headdresses. It was outdoors and the food was American-style meat and potatoes along with red wine or Habana Club rum. It's been putting out shows since 1939, so you know where those American gangsters who did business here got their ideas for staging cabaret shows in Vegas. Anyway, we got in around four in the morning, and today I tell Land that I just want to relax and maybe even catch some rays by laying out on the Malecon's wall. Land says that's cool and that it will be good to take it easy.

Tonight will be la ultima cena. We have plans to meet Lazaro at El Aljibe for dinner. I haven't seen much of that cat since the night at Hanoi. Land says Lazaro is incredibly busy trying to get some new ventures off the ground. The house has been empty all week though. Only on one night did I bump into another tenant who lived down the hall from Land. Freaked me out too. This old crow suddenly appeared out of the darkness (no lights at all in the hallway) and I jumped back because she looked like a monster. She scared the hell out of me. Her face was a patchwork of pink and black. Most of her dark skin seemed to be getting sucked into a pinkness of blinding pasty flesh. Unavoidable—even in the dark hallway. Land told me she had the same disease Michael

Jackson claimed to have—it wreaked havoc on one's melanin. She took offense to my reaction and grabbed my wrist with such force that without thinking I tried to strike her with my free hand. Luckily, Land rushed in between us and separated me before I looked like a complete ass. I apologized to her and told her—after instruction from Land—in Spanish that I was drunk and she startled me, so that was why I had been so disrespectful. She didn't buy it. She knew very well that I had reacted that way due to her appearance, but my lip service was enough to make a peace. I asked Land what this woman's story was and he said she was a relative of Lazaro's. He didn't know anything else about her. She was a bit crazy and hung around Plaza de Armes in the area where paintings were sold begging for money from tourists even though Lazaro took care of everything for her.

After I shower, Land says I can watch some television while he gets ready. I tell him that a television with only one channel does not interest me.

"You got a prob with one channel? C'mon, it beats the sensationalized shit you get in America!" Land lashes back.

"You know...I change my mind. I actually would like to check out the broadcast here. Maybe I can actually learn something from the TV for once."

"Just go downstairs to Lazaro's room."

"Hey is that cool? I don't want to intrude."

"Of course, it's cool. No worries. Here's the key for the door."

Land gives me a large, dark bronze key.

"Are you sure?" I again ask.

Land points at the door.

"O.K. See you down there." I head out of the room.

I get to the doors of Lazaro's room. Two thick, wooden doors with one of those large keyholes you could bend down and peek through and see everything. I insert the key and open the door. I enter a large sitting room with a sofa, library, desk, and in the middle of the back wall a small little television sits. It's an old Zenith probably from the 1980s. I try not to notice anything but the television, so I turn the television on and take a seat on the sofa. The reception is rough, so I walk back to the television and play with the antennae. I manually turn a giant dial to find any other channel, but only one channel comes through. Some news program. I try to follow it, but soon my eyes are working their away across the room. The first thing I notice is a Sony stereo complete with a ten CD playing capacity. Impressive. A few CDs are scattered around on shelves and a couple lie on the floor at the base of the stereo. To the left of the stereo, stands a miniature library. A bunch of books of all sizes in Spanish and English are shelved on both sides of the corner wall. I get up from the sofa and walk there. I scan titles. A medley of subjects and interests. Lazaro must have a flair for picking up new tongues because I see books on languages like *Quechua—La Lingua de Las Incas* and *Italian Made Easy*. There are travel books—one is titled *Brasil: From Rio to Manaus* and another *Dentro de Las Islas Malvinas*. I see art books celebrating Caravaggio and Dürer, and various books on ornithology. Also, alotta political shit. There's something by Simón Bolivar, another by Juan

Peron. A couple of works by Franz Fanon like *Black Skin, White Masks* and *The Wretched of the Earth.*

"He met him once."

I turn around to see Land coming into the room.

"Who? Fanon?"

"Lazaro met him once in Martinique when Fanon still lived there."

"Don't know much about him."

"You gotta read, bra." There he goes again.

"If I lived here, I probably would read like a motherfucker. The TV sucks, man. One channel and it doesn't even come in clear."

"Here, let me fiddle with it." Land goes to the television and plays with the antennae.

I resume going through Lazaro's book collection. One book pops up at me because of its title, *Blues People*. The author is LeRoi Jones. I flip through it trying to get an idea of what the book is about and Land catches me.

"Shoulda known you would go after the Amiri Baraka book," Land says.

At first, I don't make the connection.

"It's written by LeRoi Jones. It does look interesting though—"

"Tal, Tal. Get with it! Old Land has to clue you—the literary maestro—in on this one?"

What is he going on about? I think.

"LeRoi Jones *is* Amiri Baraka. He changed his names in the mid-Sixties. You know that, man," Land tells me.

Yeah, I know this. How the fuck had I forgotten? Embarrassing. Might as well bury my head in the sand. This is bad, man. When you start forgetting things that were just givens for you a couple years ago, you gotta check yourself quick.

"Right," I grit through my teeth.

"Hey, it's O.K. Breathe!" Land teases.

"I read a lot of his stuff back in school."

"His poetry?"

"Yeah, quality lines."

"He was a kindred spirit with the Beats."

"Yeah he was. Lives and writes in Jersey now. I think he's the official state poet laureate or something like that."

Land's gotta love this. He is schooling me on things that were once intrinsic to me as salt to the sea.

"Tal, you ever hear about Papa Legba and Robert Johnson?"

"Robert Johnson?" I say. "The blues musician?"

"Jones probably talks about him in that book."

I place the book back onto the shelf.

"I'm sure he does. He was the first real blues artist, right?" I ask.

"But, do you know his story about how in one year he went from a shitty guitar player and singer to the legend he became?"

"That's in the book?"

"Don't know. Never read it. I know the story though."

"O.K., let's hear it then." I plop down on the sofa and am all ears.

"In the turn of the century South, there were a lot of folktales and myths. One was the idea of a giant—a goliath-like black man, you know, maybe seven to eight feet tall who if you wanted to seek out for a favor you would go out at midnight and meet at an area where two roads crossed."

"Ah, yes, the proverbial crossroads. Oooooo-weeeeee-ooooooo." I ham up the spook noises.

"Don't get smart—get this. So, this Papa Legba was believed…," Land just cuts off.

"What?"

"I can't believe it."

"What, man?"

"I just realized this Papa Legba is actually the same cat that Gen was talking about that day when we were at the Vodou museum."

"Which cat? I don't remember."

"Remember when Gen said that Legba held the keys to the underworld and the whole trip about the religion having Legba summon up the order of the spirits to the faithful?"

"Give me a break, man. You remember that shit?" I really can't believe it.

"How could you forget that kinda shit?"

"Been working, I guess."

Land frowns.

"Here's the connection I just put together. This Papa Legba that I was just talking about is really just the black American interpretation of the Legba stories that had passed from West Africa to Haiti and then on to New Orleans."

"You might be right."

"I am right. Blacks in the South—mostly in the Delta region of the Mississippi—they said Papa Legba had special powers and could give anyone what they wanted if they went to the crossroads on a moonless night."

"And let me guess, you gave up your soul in the process." I chime in my take on things.

"Yeah."

"How Faustian."

"Well, what if Goethe ripped off his story from the story of Legba which came out of West African and Vodou tradition?"

"So, Papa Legba is just another incarnation of the devil. That's all. And what, Robert Johnson sold his soul for rock and roll? Played out, isn't it?"

"Slow down, Tal. I remember Gen saying that Legba was associated with St. Patrick, so that power to *expel* serpents makes Legba a very un-devillike character, doesn't it??"

"Uh, maybe, I guess."

"Yeah. Legba was a summoner of spirits and was identified by his very power to deal with snakes in a positive way."

"Where are you going with this Land?"

"O.K., back to Robert Johnson. The guy couldn't play or sing shit. He tried a couple of times. They laughed him out of a dancehall one time. Exactly a year later, he shows up to the same dancehall, takes a seat, whips out his guitar and plays and sings shit which blows everyone away. I mean no one ever heard such sounds before."

"So, then people said he had to have sold his soul."

"He had taken his guitar and waited at the crossroads somewhere near the Delta. Papa Legba showed up, tuned Johnson's guitar and then gave it back to him."

"That was it, huh?"

"When Johnson started to play, I mean he could *play* now."

"A good myth."

"What the most amazing thing is though, Tal, is just the fact some guy found Johnson in the South and recorded his songs."

"That's true. He was like a nomad."

"You ever heard his recordings?"

"I think so—really scratchy."

"You know, there's a story about his recording as well."

"What? Papa Legba set those up as well!!" I kid.
"Maybe, bra. What I heard about them was this.
When Johnson was brought into the recording
studio to record, the producer first wanted to hear
him play a song to get an idea of what he would be
working with. The guy even brought in some
Spanish guitar players who also heard about
Johnson and wanted to check out his playing.
Johnson took out his guitar and put down a chair to
sit in. The producer and the Spanish guitarists
assembled around him. But, then Johnson stood up,
turned his chair so that it was facing within five feet
of the corner of the room where two big walls came
together and then started to sing and play guitar like
it had never been done before."
"Like Miles, man, performing with his back to the
audience!!"
"Well, that's where the riddle comes in. Miles, he
was like the anti-minstrel, you know. He didn't like
to *perform* for people period. He could care less.
He was just there to drop his art and then go.
Johnson though was a mystery. Why had he turned
his back that day? There are three theories."
"Get outta here."
"Check it out. Johnson himself never explained his
reasons for doing what he did. His playing did the
talking and he was all about chasing pussy which is
what killed him in the end. Some bird poisoned
him and he lingered between death and life for a
couple of weeks. But, let's examine *why* he turned
his chair around and faced the corner of the room.
First, he may have been self-conscious about his
voice and guitar-playing, especially in front of those
Spanish guitarists who could play that fast flamenco
shit. But, you can forget this explanation because
Johnson was brash, cocky—he didn't give a fuck

what those cats thought. Now, the second theory. He was so inventive on the guitar, you gotta realize this. He was years ahead. He may have been hiding the new chords and arpeggios he had put together in his songs. He didn't want anyone copping his licks or riffs. This theory is somewhat plausible because bluesmen had a reputation for stealing shit from one another and then passing it off as their own at a gig. Third theory is this— Johnson was a musician. He realized that in the cavernous recording studio the acoustics were bad, so he instinctively turned toward the corner of the room where his guitar playing and vocals would be naturally amplified and bounced off towards those listening. So, most people think he did it in order to enhance his music and it could be fully appreciated."

"There's nothing sexy about that, man."

"Are you kidding? It's the blues, man. It drips of sexiness!"

"Why do you think he did it?"

"The second theory. He wanted to guard his innovative stylings, man. He only had one recording session! This was it—he wasn't about getting big because, first of all, at that time there were no stars—especially black men from the South! The art was his alone and given his lifestyle of being alone and on the run, he had to jealously guard his art. That's what I think."

"Interesting."

"But, you know, I think this story really serves as a nice parable about art in general."

"How's that??"

"Simple. A person who is compelled to create— whether in music or other arts—can either be selfish about his creation and protect it from criticism or plagiarism. Or, the person can take the creation to the fullest level where it can be really shared and dug. It's a fine line. It really is."

"I think you are right."

"About what?"

"That Johnson didn't want those Spanish fuckers walking away with his new chords and licks. The producer was probably already screwing him over on his recording contract and now he sprung these Spanish guitarists on Johnson to watch him play. That wasn't too cool. So, he gave them a show *without* giving them the true show they wanted."

"He did take the guitar to a new level with his innovative fingerings and chords. And that's another amazing thing about Johnson. When you hear the recording, it's just him playing and singing. There's no one else. But, the sounds that come out appear to come from more than one guitar and voice. He played git in such a percussive and full-bodied way and his haunting vocals on top make it sound like there's a whole lot more going on. I think it was Keith Richards who once said that Johnson must have had three brains to be able to create all that sound at once."

"Blues, jazz—that whole time was amazing, you know, man? Probably the most important American contribution to the Twentieth Century."

"I'm all behind that one, bra. Start from the Harlem renaissance. Outta sight, man! You had all these artists coming together crossing all mediums. James Weldon Johnson, Jean Toomer, Claude McCay, Countee Cullen, Langston Hughes, Nella Larsen, Gwendolyn Brooks and Zora Neale Hurston laying down writings and verses. Paul Robeson doing his thing, and then later, of course, those cats—Dizzy, Bird, and Monk and the Pres—taking jazz into bebop. Unbelievable! All that creative energy being bounced off one another and then changing into new art and so on. Mind-blowing time. Easily the greatest thing ever produced in the last hundred years."

"Put rather nicely, man."

"But, the crazy thing, Tal, is that no one *got it*, man!! All that creative force—all that art—it fell on deaf ears for the most part. Til this day that whole time and creative vibe is glossed over in the U.S. It's a minor blip on the screen of American history. You get what I mean?"

"Yeah, I hear you. You don't really hear about it today, do you?"

"Nope."

"That's funny."

"I think the funny thing is that it was the fuckin' Europeans who first appreciated it—jazz. They knew it was something special. They recognized it as a new artistry."

"Yeah?"

"These cats would go to Paris and Rome to jam, because the French and Italians dug the music and weren't bogged down with skin color. Yeah, man. Miles, Lionel Hampton—all those cats would hang out in these European cities playing to jazz fans that got it and who paid them fairly too. There was a big scene in London as well."

"Why, man? Why were these Euros more receptive??"

"I've asked myself that question a lot—that's enough with the TV. Only so much you can do." So, Land moves over to have a seat on the sofa next to me. "It's not that the French or the British, let's say, are less racist. Fuck that, bra. I think it has to do with distance and identity. Let me put it to ya this way. America is a bastard."

"Haha! First time I've heard it called that, bra!"

"Well, it was born by British and French and Spanish interests that all intersected and ultimately collapsed. Like any bastard, America's lost. Looking for some kind of father-figure. In the process, it's become self-hating."

"Man, what are you saying? You got all that wrapped up in the stars and stripes and patriotism and *stand beside her* mentality in the U.S. It's not self-hating. More like self-promoting, Land."

"Look at those very things which are *inherently* American like blues and jazz. O.K.? Those were seen as the devil's work. And that's where the Robert Johnson-Papa Legba story comes in again. The music of that time became associated with the devil."

"Just superstitions, bra."

"No, I'm serious. It was seen as ugly, evil, low-brow. And the fact that blacks were responsible for it really doomed it! Then you got these Europeans sitting on the other side of the Atlantic with several centuries under their belt and fully confident of who they are and where they come from, so they are able to have the luxury to sit back and recognize something good when it comes along. Jazz must have been like what gold, spices and rum represented to the Sixteenth Century Europeans. It was a remarkable discovery from the New World that had to be imported at all costs. So, they did it."

"Another classic Morales' theory."

"I got facts on my side, man. I don't just come up with things in vacuum. So, what do you think?"

"Yeah, I think that America probably had a hard time dealing with it, but it has ultimately come around, you know? It's not as self-hating and embraces the art—music, literature of that time."

"Only a small segment know what that time was about. They appreciate it. Look, the artists from that time are on par with the artists of the Renaissance, no doubt about it. You think you'll ever see that kind of acknowledgment of those cats in our lifetime?"

"Probably not. But, some day, man. It will come."

"Man, you really have a lot of the faith in America, huh?"

"Nah, man. I don't have any faith. I'm just a bum—now. I just cling to a notion that the really good things in life, maybe what you call artistry, always bubble up to the top. Especially in America."

"You're bullshitting, me!"

"Nah. That's what I think, man."

"Wow, times change."

"They sure do, bra."

There's no sense delving into the past again. It's clear enough Land knows what I'm about now. That I no longer even remember the names of authors I used to worship. I'm not ashamed about it and I'm not afraid to let him know. He's gotta know. I'm not good about keeping up false pretenses or phoning in an appearance to Land as his good old buddy, Tal—that cat who in days of yore ran with him and who gave him a run for his money when it came to exploring every emotion from the euphoric to the sullen.

We both tune into the television. Despite Land's fiddling, the reception is stubbornly grainy and the picture is out of focus. A cartoon is playing. It's straight out of the 1970s and continues for about ten minutes. It's the kind of cartoon where you hear the voice first and then the animation catches up with it. It's a gas and there are no commercials which is a welcomed relief. Afterwards, another news program comes on which breaks up into the usual—sports and weather and world events. No reports of murders or rapes or robberies or other violence on the island. Just more warm weather and a great baseball team while the rest of the world is eating itself alive.

"So, this is Cuban television?" I say.

"Yup. It's pretty much news, music, baseball, news, cartoons and more music. Enjoy."

"Well, I'm gonna check out some more of Lazaro's books."

"Suit yourself, bro."

I get up and go back to the bookcases. I mull through other titles and another book catches my eye. It's titled *Keep the River on Your Right*. Written by Tobias Schneebaum. I read the inside jacket which describes the author as the only gay Jewish ex-cannibal artist New Yorker in history. Apparently, he got lost in the Peruvian Amazon while studying a cannibalistic tribe in the jungle. He came out years later, naked and covered in body paint and then wrote this book. Far out and fucked up, man.

"Hey, Land."

"Yeah?"

"You know anything about this one?" I hold up the book.

Land swivels around to take a look.

"Uhh—yeah. A little." He goes back to watching TV.

"O.K.??? You gonna tell me about it?"

"I've never read it. But, Tal, you may freak on this one, bra—"

"Gimme a break, man. Don't worry about my sensibilities. What's up?"

"It's actually kinda funny albeit in a sick way. Listen…" He turns to face me.

"Yeah, I am."

"O.K. One night, Lazaro and I were boozing and he was completely wasted."

"Doesn't look like a boozer."

"He isn't—on certain occasions, he throws them back. So, we're drinking and talking and then get into some of his old exploits. He ran around Bolivia a long, long time ago. I think in the 1930s, if you can comprehend that. And, he starts telling me these stories about his time there and so on, and then next thing I know he's describing what it felt like when he tasted *human flesh* for the first time!"

"Now, I've heard it all, man. This is the cake-taker." I put the book back into the bookcase and have a seat back on the sofa.

"He wasn't lying to me, man. Why would this cat lie?? He already knows I'm in awe of him. There's nothing for him to do—least of all concoct some story about eating others. You know what I'm saying? The cat is for real. I believe it."

"So…what was it like? Eating human flesh?"

"Honestly, I was blasted myself that night, so the details are foggy. I just remember his eyes got all big and he spit in my eye because he talked so excitedly about it! He lived among indigenous tribes in Bolivia where cannibalism was commonplace."

"Commonplace, huh?"

"Yeah, bra, I mean, you captured your enemies and then depending on who they were, you ate them."

"This is a conversation I never thought I would have, man. This ranks up there."

"Even I was shocked, man. Can you imagine me—speechless?"

"That would be a sight. And you never have asked about it ever again?"

"No! What am I supposed to do? Go up to him and say, *Lazaro can you tell me about what it was like eating another human again??*"

"That's a start."

"Ask Lazaro about the book, Tal. Then, maybe you can get Lazaro to open that box for yourself."

I don't know how to deal with the fact that Lazaro has savored human flesh. It's crazy. But, for some reason I'm not that jarred by this revelation. It all makes sense. Part of that youthful, *Dorian Gray*-like magic that Lazaro wields over people. It's dazzling but at the same time there is the inkling of something dark behind the scenes.

Land starts getting restless after nearly an hour of watching TV, so we decide to go out and enjoy the last afternoon in Havana. We turn off the TV, lock up and go outside. We walk along Quinta Avenida and find a park with massive banyon trees forming natural green canopies over vacant benches. We sit down on one of the benches and watch passer-bys. A lazy day. There's a panicky feeling that comes over me when I have absolutely nothing to do and I can sense that feeling sneaking up on me. But, I will myself away from sabotaging this perfectly idle day and stretch my legs before me and sink into the bench and watch the cars drive by.

"You see what I was saying?" Land begins.

"About what? You say a lot of things, man." I laugh.

"About what I've found here."

"Ah, I've been meaning to ask you about that. Your email—you said *you found it.*"

"Check out these people going by—black, white—it don't matter. They get it."

"What are they getting?"

"Yeah, man, what they are getting. They're doing it. *Getting along.* They're years ahead of us."

"So, you've found it? A community?" I ask.

"Community is just a fiction when talked about in the context of the U.S., Tal. Like I already told you before, I went out in search of it and felt like a fool."

"What is it about Cuba then that doesn't make it a fiction here either?" I cut to the quick.

"They hang from the moment they're born. All the barrios spill into one another and they grow up with white and black friends, teachers and doctors. They're socialized from the get go that they're all the same. There's no difference. White. Black. Mulatta. What the fuck does that all mean? The little dogs in the streets come in different colors too. It's all the same. Community here is not controlled by the insiders who tailor it to their own ideas. There are no insiders and outsiders. That's why there was the Revolution, man—it washed away that delineation."

My eyes turn away from Land as he goes on. "Castro's vision for the country was to bring together the lower class Cubans—the majority of which happened to be illiterate and black and who worked out in the sugar cane or tobacco fields—into the literate, white Cuban districts which had kow-towed unchecked for decades to Western imperialism at the expense of the larger Cuban population. Now, what you have is a functional community where people of all colors start on equal footing and have the same chance to partake in the common good for the society."

"I think some people would say that there is nothing to partake in though because economic and political opportunities are so limited," I respond.

"That may be so—but that's not the Cuban people's or even Castro's fault. That's the fault of the embargo—it was slapped on against Cuba only two years after the Revolution, man. The Cuban people never had a chance to fully implement a socialist agenda that could really have worked on an island of this size. Some things have panned out though— like the existence of a bona fide community experience—but the economic and political restrictions, I agree with you they are here, but only because after the embargo hit Cuba became reactionary and Castro lost sight of things. The only people hurt by the embargo have been the Cuban people—not Castro. He lives like a king with residences up and down the island. Yet, these cats out there—" And Land points at the cars and motorcycles chugging by on diesel and the tireless feet pedaling bicycles. "They have suffered for forty years and have had to survive through holding together as a community. As a result, the color line between them became *nonsense*. A fabrication. How liberating, Tal? To wake up here and go into the streets and not automatically categorize your fellow countryman by the color of skin. And then to come together to form infrastructures necessary to survive."

As fetching a scenario as Land has laid out—and it really is fetching—an almost utopian state of mankind where no preconceived ideas exist linked to epidermal hues—I can't hold back pointing out some interesting observations of my own gathered from the last week.

"I see what you're saying. But, you know, Land, it still seems that mostly the white Cubans are calling the shots or are involved more directly as liaisons with tourists or non-Cuban visitors than the black Cubans. I mean look at the government heads. These guys Castro surrounds himself with—prime minister Alarcon? Is that his name?"

Land sits motionless as if he is tape-recording my words to use against me at a later time.

"And even look at the hotels and restaurants..." I continue. "From what I've seen, it's mostly the white Cubans running around making the decisions, greeting you, etcetera. So, the integrated and fused community you think you are seeing may be misleading. Remember the Tropicana? All the lead dancers were white! Nearly all of the background dancers were black—"

"Easy, Tal. You lost me with your Tropicana remarks. Choosing entertainers in any club is arbitrary anywhere. Dig? Too many intangibles. Trust me on this. I'm sure there's been plenty of black leads there. Maybe we caught a night where the understudies were put on?? I don't know, but you don't either."

"Come on, Land. The same shit goes on here as in the U.S. But, I gotta say it does seem to me that for the most part people here get along in a more connected way than back home. They have to..."

"For the *most part*?!?! The fuck are you being so begrudging? What did the U.S. ever do for you, Tal? For me—some good nights partying??!! What's with this new tune of yours?? I don't get it. I just don't get it. Man, you know that despite your fancy words and polished appearance you still have

eyes on you for the wrong reasons in every store
you go to in America. Over here, no one would
give a fuck."

"You had to make this personal, huh? The last I
remembered, none of this had to do with my own
experience. We were just talking generally about
the people here. You're such an asshole to turn this
into an assay into my own particular situation."

"Look—I meant no offense. It's just that, *When I
analyze the stench, to me it makes alotta sense*, like
Marley sang," Land does his best rendition singing
this verse of *Buffalo Soldier*. I keep a serious face
although I'm laughing inside. The cat just can't
carry a tune. He has no ear at all really.

"But, Tal, your *particular* situation is a bunch of
bull. It's the same as my situation. There's nothing
unique about you. You're part of the so-called
browning of America just like me. It's been
documented, researched. There have been
Moynihanesque congressional reports about it.
Yeah, man, they're pissed off! Don't take it
personal. Did you know that salsa is now the top-
selling condiment in America??"

"What the fuck does that have to do with
anything?"

"Everything, bra, everything."

"It outsells ketchup?"

"Outsells it."

"The Heinz family must be up in arms."

"I wouldn't be surprised if a new, salsatized
ketchup is unveiled on the public soon!"

Laughs. It's always a godsend to tiptoe
around a heated argument with someone by
segueing into joint laughter. It's deliverance. Land
and I laugh and smile and are both glad to just drop

the subject. It's not worth getting into on a day like today. I get up and stretch and tell Land that I'm gonna go find some souvenirs to smuggle back into the U.S. He gives me vague directions as to where I should go and says I should meet him back at the house around 6:30 at the latest. I got one thing on my mind—a box of quality puros. Followed by pics of Che and Castro and any interesting books on the Revolution. I cab into the heart of old Habana and start walking through the neighborhoods taking in the marvelous sights, smells and sounds one last time. Though I try to blend in with the locals as best I can, there is still something unavoidably foreign about me and some Cubans approach me and ask me for the time in Spanish just to see if I understand and can reply back in Spanish. One cat though muscles his way up to me and tries to hustle me with cigars and other Cuban delights and speaks English to me the entire time. When I politely shake my head "no" and keep walking, he yells at me, "What, you don't do business with black people here?"

I freeze. This throws me. I mean, really *throws* me. A new one. Can it really be that this cat is actually—pulling—the—race—card—on me?? *On me.* He must be blind or stupid. I just don't want to buy the crap he is peddling. But, the motherfucker has the gall to call me out as anti-black or something. I'm a shade lighter than he is and if I had a chance to catch those rays today by laying out on the Malecon, I'd make him look like the white boy.

I turn around and size up this cat. He's smiling at me know. Like he knows, he got me. "You don't know anything, do you?" I tell him. "Yessss. I do."

I walk closer to him. I am about an inch and a half taller and I puff out my chest to even look bigger when I get within two feet of him.

"I do business with anyone I want, man." And I tug on the skin of my arm. Why? I don't really know. It is some reflexive gesture as if I want him to see who I really am.

"And I don't want to buy fake Cohibas, *entiendes*?"

"How do you know they are fake?"

"Come on. I've been here for couple of weeks. I know the games you guys play."

"Who is *you guys*?"

"You guys that try to sell people like me what you say is really a $20 puro for $10."

"We give you discount. What's problem?"

A smart-ass. But, I'm a sucker for this kind of cat. He's hooked me nicely.

"Alright, man. Let me take a puff on one of your cigars first."

"That cannot be done."

"Why not??"

"If you do not like de cigar, it is no good anymore. I can no longer sell it."

"O.K. How much for one cigar then?"

"I only sell five at a time."

"O.K. How much for five?"

"$30."

"$30!!"

"Yessss. They are Cohibas. Only the best. You will find these for $60 in a store."

"Sorry. I can't do that." And I turn around.

"My friend!"

I look back.

"$25!"

"I just don't have that much in cash with me. I still have to pay a $20 tax at the airport just to leave your country."

"My friend, $20 for five cigars. It is very good deal."

"I can only give $10. That's my limit."

He rubs his face and grunts and fumes.

"I give you only three cigars then."

"Three for $10?"

Fuck it. I give in and he whistles at his compadre who has been standing about twenty feet away during the entire bartering session. He takes out a rectangular tinfoiled box and hands it to the cat who has caught me. He removes three unlabeled cigars out of the tinfoil and asks for the $10. I pull out a $10 bill from my wallet and hand it over. He gives me the three cigars and smiles.

"Thank you, my friend. Gracias."

I flash a phony smile back knowing I've been had. I give a good-bye wave of relief as the cat walks away from me and joins his compadre and goes after his next sucker. I walk a couple of blocks and then stop a Cuban guy on a bike who's smoking a cigarette and ask him for a light. He hands me a *phosphoro* which I strike on the bottom of my shoe and a bright yellow flame appears. I light the puro after biting the tip off. I take full-chest inhales and get the tobacco to burn. I thank the man for the light and start walking towards a government store which Land told me sells Revolution paraphernalia. Within two solid sucks of the cigar, the shittiness of the tobacco comes out. What shit! I wouldn't be surprised if actual manure was rolled up in this thing. All because that motherfucker touched a nerve.

V

I get back to the house right around 6:30. Don't know where the last couple of hours went. I was ducking my head in and out of little souvenir stands and ended up with two bags of Cuban goods which I hope to smuggle back into the U.S. I knock on the door and after a second or two, I can hear someone coming down the stairs. The door opens. "Hey, you made it back. I got a little worried that you had pissed off some locals and bad things had happened."

"Nah...they pissed me off. But, that's another story. I got lost in the neighborhoods though. I sat outside this gem of a barbershop and watched all these cats line up to have their heads shaved."

"Haha! That's the style these days. So, I see you bought some things. You find what you wanted?"

"Yeah, I got some good shit. Check out this statue I bought of St. Lazaro." I take it out and show it Land. "Feel how heavy it is man. That's real ebony wood. Good quality."

"Nice, man." Land studies the statue closer. "You know, it's funny, but the face actually looks like our Lazaro!"

"I know, I know! I was tripping when I saw it. The likeness was surreal. I had to pick one up."

"You gotta show it to Lazaro later tonight."

"Yeah. I just am worried about getting all this back into the U.S. There's that—what had you said?? The Trading with the Enemy Act?"

"No worries about that. Just wear some nice clothes and shave and smell good and you won't get searched. Besides, these little knick-knacks you bought, it's small time stuff."

"Good."

"Well, go on up and start getting ready. We gotta head out by 7:30. Lazaro's meeting us at the restaurant."

A kind of melancholy metastases in me as I wash up and get ready. What a wildly fantastic sad place! I wish I had more time. Land came out here and lived deep, sucking the marrow out of the opportunity Lazaro gave him. Cheap rent in exchange for a couple of months of *sabor*—being able to dig the artistry of Cuban experience which was untouched and isolated from the rest of the world. A glorious side-effect of an otherwise ghastly American foreign policy of suffocating the Cuban people for following leftist ideology. Here, 1959 may live on side-by-side a new generation's yearnings for Nike, but as long as the uniquely Cuban creative impulse remains strong and expressive, Nike-clad son singers and dancers can bridge the old into the new seamlessly. Just give it a chance. Despite my sometimes debunking of Land's take on this place, a week here has given me an understanding of the power of artistry—as Land conceives it. As impoverished much of Havana is and as oppressed the people may be in not being able to express certain opinions, just one stroll through the old town with wide eyes and a clear mind shows how artistry has played a big part in allowing them to keep it together for so long. Yeah, I understand it now. Or, at least I've moved much closer to understanding it as Land does.

I go downstairs where Land is already ready and is in Lazaro's room watching the news.

"All right, ready to jet." I say.

"O.K. What time do you got?"

"Uhh…," I look at my wrist and see no watch. I must have forgot to put it on after my shower.

"What? You don't wear a watch anymore?"

"Just forgot to put it back on."

"Sure." Land says with a wry smile as if he's validated himself in some way.

He gets up and shuts off the TV. I go outside to wait for him. Another balmy night. We stroll up to Quinta Avenida one final time to hail a cab.

"So, this place has good food?" I ask.

"The best Cuban food, man. Lazaro loves it."

"You know I never really saw him much during my stay here."

"Well, he's busy. Wheelin' and dealin'. He's an entrepreneur. Got various projects going on. Plus, it's better that you didn't see him that much. Keeps up some of the mystery around him."

There's a queue outside the restaurant which is set out like a big outdoor dining patio. No windows or doors. A low beamed ceiling with large ceiling fans twirling ferociously above the dinner guests. Land goes right to the front of the line while I hang back. After a few moments of speaking to the maitre'd, Land motions me over. The maitre'd then takes us to a square table where dressed in pearl white linen pants and a white long-sleeved guayabera with the ever present unlit Cohiba Esplendido in his mouth sits Lazaro. He stands to greet us.

"Bon soir," he says as he extends a wrinkled but firm handshake to Land and I.

"Hola, señor," Land replies.

"Please, come sit. I've taken care of the ordering."

Land and I take seats each to one side of Lazaro.

"I can't wait to see what you ordered for us," I say.
"You will enjoy, Tal. Good Cuban food like in that paladar that Land took you to."
"Fantastic!" I'm enthused about the prospect of such good grub.
"But, I will be having something a bit different."
　　Only one thing goes through my mind as you can probably guess. I look at Land to see his face. Nothing. He's all smiles.
"What's that?" Land says.
"I am friends with the owner. He told me that he had my favorite dish available tonight. It's not on the menu either!"
"It's some Cuban delicacy?" I ask.
"Venezuelan."
"Something you can only get in Caracas?" Land probes.
"It's possible. But, it originates from one of Venezuela's islands in the Caribe. From *Isla de Margarita*. It is called *pastel de chucho*."
I can see the wheels in Land's mind turning trying to figure out what this means.
"*Pastel de chucho*? Doesn't that mean like some kind of pie?"
"Good, *Landito*. In English, you can translate it as a dogpie."
"Dogpie?!! They eat dogs in Venezuela? Like the Koreans?" I ask.
"No, no." Lazaro laughs. "Well, maybe in the south—in the jungles there! No, it is a very unique dish. It is like a large empanada, but is made with baked plantanes on the bottom and melted cheese on top. In between, you first have a layer of sweet corn and next, before the plantanes, you have mashed manta ray." Lazaro's eyes glitter blue.

"I've never heard of anything like that!" Land says. "Have you, Tal?"

"It sounds wild. I guess then *chucho* is what the islanders call manta ray, huh? Like fido of the sea?"

"Yes, yes." Lazaro says. "The dish first came from this little town on the north west side of Isla de Margarita called Juangriego. It has a beautiful bay with sleepy, fat pelicans. Beautiful place."

"What does it taste like?" Land asks.

"I will give you a piece to try. But, it's not for everybody, you know! Your mouth gets fooled. It first tastes the cheese and then the sweet corn. These are not such different tastes from one another. But, then you taste the manta ray which is a fish. It is salty and tastes like shark. After that, you taste the baked plantanes, which messes up everything! You really get confused!"

"Eeeewwww!" Land says.

"You must try a little of it!" Lazaro shoots back. "Ahhh, I see our cocktails coming."

The waitress puts down a mojito in front of each of us.

"Gentlemen, these are the finest mojitos in Cuba. Please enjoy."

We raise our glasses and clink glasses and in unison cheer, "Salud." Brilliant. I imbibe repeatedly and salute Lazaro again.

"Delicious, Lazaro." I say.

"Yes. They treat you well here."

"You come here often?"

"Certainly. Just look around you. What I like to call a *buffet* of humanity! I indulge myself in it regularly. There's nothing else like it in Cuba!" Lazaro raises his glass at me and then does a roundhouse salute to the room.

I take a sweeping look around the place and I see some of the most devastatingly sexy, gorgeous women that I've ever seen. I don't know why I didn't get smacked in the face with this as soon as I walked into the place. But, now as I take in the scene there are raven-haired femmes already seated or walking in and being escorted to tables where men alone or in groups await them. Some of these cats get up to greet the women who now join them with the usual awkwardness that all cats fall victim to when face to face with an incredibly beautiful bird. It's there. Obvious. Reduced to pubescent shuffling. Yeah, I see the buffet of humanity Lazaro is talking about. I want to gorge myself on these women, but I also get a funny vision in my head of Lazaro literally *feasting* on the patrons here. Could he still possibly lust after human flesh in a literal sense? I turn back to Lazaro and his eyes are glazed with an undeniable lasciviousness as he absorbs the bevy of bodies talking, eating, drinking, flirting, bullshitting, and scheming. This old crazy coot. Living in Havana out of all places and running an upscale prostitution ring. I find it hilarious. I can't even conceive of myself pulling off all this action at his age. The cat's an inspiration, and I've never been a big fan of homosexuals and bisexuals really confuse me because I definitely think you *know* what you want to chase in this world—tits and ass or just ass. We're driven by our libido and the libidinal instinct dominates everything. So, you know from the start what the chase is. But, a cat like Lazaro. What? He can't make up his mind or something? Or, maybe its just avarice. He's greedy. He wants to feast on it all and not settle for one or the other. In a perverted way, I admire this cat's sexuality. He is liberated in his pursuit as he's transcended the teleology of men and women. He's like the mythical primordial human being who was at once both sexes. Yeah, the motherfucker goes both ways, but how fortunate for him to be an omnivore in the deepest meaning of the word!

"Ah, I love it. Good times with new friends," Lazaro toasts us again.

My thoughts turn toward this amazing piece of ass—a black-trussed leather corset wearing woman with panty-less skin-tight black pants who walk towards our table. My sweet, sweet lord.

"Como estas, linda," I try my best (and only) Spanish line.

She hits me with a big smile, but walks straight to Lazaro and whispers something in his ear. I look at Land and his jaw-dropped face mirrors my own.

I can't hear the conversation, but I have an uncompromised look at this bird's impossibly perfect round breasts pressed up against her corset. Then, she goes. I crane my neck to follow her and see that she walks straight to the bar where she greets some cat and the two are led by a waiter to a table.

"You like?" Lazaro asks.

"Oh, yeah," I say.

"I've seen her before, no?" Land asks Lazaro.

"Probably. One of my girls. She's late." Lazaro drinks his mojito. "Gave me a story."

Lazaro sees that I'm in lala land.

"I know," He addresses me. "She's very beautiful. You ask yourself, how much?"

"She's unbelievable." Her wonderfully perfumed scent still lingers at our table.

"Everything is like you say, *relative*. See the man she's with now?" Land and I look at the table. "He looks like Richard Branson, no?"

I look the guy over. Some limey for sure. Bearded, snaggle-toothed but well-coiffed and wearing a double-breasted dark blue dinner jacket with white pants.

"He's buying some dream like everybody else in this room. Flies in once every four months. Asks for the same girl. Says he wants to leave his wife of the last twenty years and start over with her."

"You think your girl will ever take him up on the offer?" I ask.

"He's not serious. These European or American men nowadays—they are soft. He does not have the guts to go through with it. Another fantasy. Now, if he was Cuban and said he would leave his wife for her, then he would. It would become a matter of pride to go through with it. Because in Cuba *machismo* is very real. It has not become soft or been made, how do you say, *pee cee*??"

"Yeah, p.c.—politically correct. So, you know about that shit?" Land says.

"But, of course! I read, Landito! Let me say this, here in Cuba men are men. They do what men are supposed to do. They yell, smoke, curse, fight, shoot. You know? Women are still women. There is no need for them to take on those characteristics of maleness because machismo—that is energy made by men for men. Understand?"

Land and I shake our heads up and down.

"But, in America, the lines between men and women have been blurred. Women trying to claim male energy. I see American magazines—the women wear pants now!" Lazaro laughs so hard that he starts coughing and Land quickly asks for water from the waitress.

"No, no." Lazaro waves off the waitress who returns with the water. "*Me mojito es todo que necesito.*" The waitress puts down the water and promptly leaves.

"You O.K.?" Land asks.

"Yes, yes." Lazaro finishes off his mojito. "O.K." He pauses for a second to collect his thoughts. "Ah, I don't mean to make fun. What I'm saying is that men and women in America are becoming one and the same. So, you no longer know the woman from the man! Here, just take a look around. You know who is who. Who is calling the shots as you say. The women!"

"That's for certain," I mumble.

"I am nothing without them of course. But, what gives them that control? It is precisely their femininity—not machismo. Their *penchant* for not blowing things up, but instead creating. Aha! You see, here in Cuba men and women occupy distinct positions and each has their own special energy. It is how nature wanted things to be. No blurring of the lines. It goes against nature. It makes a mess!"

"So, what do you think will happen like in America, where the lines between men and women are being blurred?" Land asks.

"Messy. Very messy, Landito. It seems maybe one day in your lives, you will wake up and there's no tension, no more emotional distance between the sexes."

"What's wrong with that?" Land says. "It would be like paradise! No more mind games!"

"Ahhh…but you must understand that the tension, the mistrust between men and women is what has brought us this far in the first place "

"Explain," Land implores Lazaro.

"I explain like this. Look at the story of Adam and Eve—you have tension leading to trust which then becomes mistrust. You take away that natural tension and mistrust, then nobody would *try*. Nobody would want to run faster, to reach out farther, to explore further if it was already there in front of you. The secret to the universe is not out there in the stars. It is right here." Lazaro wags a finger around the room. "Between men and women. The question is, why are there two creatures so different who need one another to survive? I do not know. It is what every person is seeking the answer to, whether they know it or not. I love the humanity of both men and women, so I choose to act on that love. Yet, it has brought me no closer to unraveling the great mystery of why men and women are so different. And I have been around for eighty-five years, believe me, they are *very* different. What I say is, let the differences be, don't try to make them the same. Otherwise, if you take out the natural tension and mistrust between men and women you have chaos. No direction. Nothing to go after. No one would try to understand the other and it would just be taken for granted that everything between men and women was the same."

The mulattas running around here are all high quality. Flat stomached, long-legged with asses that must burn from all the eyes fixed on them. I've been trying to keep an ear on Lazaro's rambling, but all I see are heaving breasts getting up, sitting down and the crossing and uncrossing of tanned, dark copper legs. The food did come fast enough. So, I've been eating and watching and trying to listen to Lazaro. I've been enjoying the never-ending stream of tamales, pollo asado and rice and beans and fries. I'm also on my third mojito at this point and although I'm abuzz in the warm glow of inebriation I nevertheless decline Lazaro's invitation to sample his pastel de chucho. I do wear a permanent grin now because I have lost control of my lips and my mouth has become relaxed and frozen in this position. I gamely try to pull myself back into Lazaro's words and show that I'm actively following by nodding at the emphatic points he makes. Land as usual hangs on each of Lazaro's words as if making mental notes to store each pearl for a later date.

"You agree with that, Tal?" Land asks.

"Uhhh…" Caught off guard with this. "Yeah— what about again?"

Lazaro laughs. I smile back.

"Sorry, I'm a bit distracted. But, I was thinking about something while you were talking Lazaro."

"And what is that?" Lazaro asks.

"It would have been perfect for Land's friend Gen to have chipped in the conversation, huh, Land?"

"Uh. Yeah. That's for sure."

"Why? Ah…let me guess, she has strong American opinions on the subject of how men and women relate to one another?" Lazaro asks.

"Oh, yeah! She got her degree in Women's Studies and was active in lot of seminars and things designed to *demystify feminism*. Right, Land?"

"That's right, Tal. You remembered that conference? I thought you didn't make it."

"I didn't man. You gave me the scoop. But, come on, I've had my run-ins with Gen in the past on the subject."

"Yeah? Like when??"

"Like, uh, back in the days. I don't remember specifics anymore. But, you don't remember either?"

"Nope. I mean she definitely has her views, but for the most part keeps them to herself unless she's in some formal debate or something."

What's the matter with him? Gen *keeps her views to herself*? O.K., Land is trying to do some kind of low-key thing here. I'll play along.

"Well, she and I debated a few times. And for my money, I would have loved to see her get involved in your discussion Lazaro," I say.

"Yes. Me too. This Gen sounds interesting. Why did you not mention anything about her to me, Land?"

"Slipped my mind. She's an old friend."

It's obvious that Land is uncomfortable. Luckily, that old smoothy Land turns the tables back to me.

"You can't keep your eyes off the women?" Lazaro asks me.

"No. I mean, yeah. My God, do all these women work for you?" I ask.

"Ninety percent. Once in a while, like tonight, I bring in other girls who work for my friends or on other islands—the Dominican Republic for example."

"Very nice enterprise you have!" I say.

"Haha. Thank you. But, please let me extend some *ospit-tality*. If you would like I can arrange a lady of your choice to meet you later tonight. It is your last night in Cuba after all!"

"Even the girl with the Branson chap?" I ask and then I feel a kick to my leg under the table. I look at Land whose hard stare tears through me. It's clear that he is telling me with his eyes that I better not take up Lazaro on his offer.

"Except for her! She will be predisposed this evening, I am sorry to say." Lazaro says.

"Well, then, I will have to pass! But, thanks for the offer. I really gotta pack my things up anyway. I bought a bunch of things to take back with me," I say.

"Cigars?" Lazaro asks.

"Yeah," I say. After the disaster with the three fake Cohibas, I decided to play it safe and went to a government tobacco shop where I bought a box of some real puros.

"What kind?" Lazaro follows up.

"I got a box of Romeo & Julietta Churchills."

"Very good cigar. How much?"

"$85."

"$85! They took you for a ride. Where was this?"

"Some government shop across from the park across from Hotel Inglaterra."

"You should have come to me. I would have gotten them for you at a much better price."

"Yeah? But, I have not really seen you over the last week."

"I have been busy."

"Next time," I say.

"Next time. Most definitely," Lazaro smiles.

I never see the bill. After a full night of eating and conversation, we all sort of know that it's time to go. Things have naturally come to a conclusion. The girls are all off with clients. We are one of the last tables remaining and when the maitre'd sees Lazaro attempting to get up, he runs over to help him, steadies him and props him up. He hands Lazaro his cane and Lazaro thanks him. I whisper to Land about the bill, and Land says Lazaro has taken care of everything and not to bring it up. That would be insulting to Lazaro. I go over to Lazaro and thank him for the fine dinner and for letting me stay at his house during the last week. Lazaro winks at me and says it was his pleasure to show us a good time. He will miss the repartee he had with Land. I can only imagine the other discussions they must have had during the time Land stayed.

We walk out of the restaurant and Lazaro's car is waiting for us. His driver comes out and again opens the rear passenger door helping Lazaro get in first. Land and I file in behind him. It's another quiet drive back. Lazaro occasionally points out the former homes of friends he had before the Revolution and says they are all in exile. He speaks with them still—at least those few who are still alive. Most of them are in Miami. One in Caracas and one in Paris. But, they curse Castro and hate what has happened to the Cuba they used to know. They also bombard Lazaro with guilt trips because he returned and survived, while they have become so embittered and entrenched in their position that they will never return until Castro dies. The reality though is they will pass before Castro.

Lazaro's existence here is a testament to how passionately he feels about his country. I think about this and then as if once again reading my mind, Lazaro suddenly says out loud, "But, no matter what happens, I will always belong to Cuba. Good or bad—it is my home. It is who I am and I will be lost without it. I hold no grudge."
I listen to him. He then grabs my right shoulder, pulls me in close and adds, "*Para nosotros la Patria es la America.*"
"I understand," I say in a whispy voice.

Lazaro slowly moves his head up and down twice and then takes his hand off my shoulder and turns away from me. I look to my right where Land sits and he either consciously or unconsciously mimics Lazaro's nodding and then also turns away. I am left to ponder Lazaro's words as I face forward and stare out the windshield. No other words are spoken.

When we arrive back at the house, Lazaro offers us a nightcap. He insists that we must try a special liquor that he has. "It is well-aged and from the old times," he says. "Sublime and perfect for your last night in La Habana." Land and I follow him into his living room and we sit on the sofa. Lazaro disappears into his bedroom and returns with an unmarked label-less brown bottle. It looks ancient and he fill ups three small silver goblets with a dark reddish or black liquid. I can't tell. He hands Land and I each a goblet and I still can't tell what color the liquid is. It appears rich and is strangely odorless. Lazaro says there will be no more toasting. We will all just sip a little of the drink and let the magic begin. Land and I do as instructed and Lazaro watches us closely with wizened steely eyes. It is sublime. I can't parse all the different tastes that my tongue has just experienced.
"This is amazing," I say. Land also wears a look of pleasure on his face.
Satisfied by our reactions, Lazaro drinks from his goblet. He drinks slowly, deliberately. He turns on the stereo and puts in some cassette. Land and I are relaxing on the sofa sipping away trying to figure out what the drink is. It has a salty oak-like taste, but as if blended with sambuca or some other kind

of licorice drink. But, my thoughts on the strange liquid's origins instantly disintegrate as this woman's voice fills up the room.

"*Who* is this?" I ask.

"Ahhh," Lazaro says as he sits down on a chair next to the sofa. "The last great chanteuse, my friend. Nina Simone."

We all three sit there for a few minutes in silence and listen to the words and soft piano tinklings of Nina Simone. Then, Lazaro finishes his drink and gets up.

"Gentlemen, time for me to say goodnight. I will say farewell tomorrow morning. You leave at what time?"

"Ten," Land says.

"Excellent. Please stay up and listen to the music for as long as you would like. Hasta mañana."

Land and I both stand up in respect as Lazaro leaves and goes into his bedroom. The door closes behind him. I then realize that I forgot to show him the St. Lazaro statue that I had bought. No big deal.

"He's definitely a class act," I tell Land.

"I know."

"Eighty-five years old, man! I can't believe that! How he keeps going is amazing."

"Maybe this is part of his secret." Land points to the bottle Lazaro left sitting on the coffee table in front of us. "Some kind of elixir of youth?"

"Has he given you it before?"

"Nah, man. Never had it. Whadda ya think it is?"

"I have no idea. Whatever it is—it's quite the potion."

Land stares out deep in thought.

"What is it?"

"I was just thinking—you know the Maasai in East Africa, they just drink blood raw—right out of their cows."

"Jesus, Land! I didn't need to hear that."

"I'm serious. They just cut open an artery on the cow and the blood spurts out and they catch it in a canteen. Then they pound it down. Simple as that. Apparently, they get all they need from it. Vitamins, minerals, all that jazz. And then you look at them—tall, thin, in good shape, age very well."

"So what are you saying? Lazaro is some kind of vampire!" I crack up.

"Don't get any of those wild ideas of yours, Tal. I'm just saying there's something to be said about sanguine diets. Who knows what's in this?"

Feeling a bit queasy about the subject, I switch gears.

"Nina Simone still alive?"

"Still alive??"

"That's what I said."

"Yeah, she is. She's tired that's all. Another great who's now in self-exile."

"She left America?"

"Yeah, a while ago. Moved around a lot too. I think from Liberia to Brasil to the West Indies and now lives in the south of France."

"Never got into listening to her music."

"You can't categorize it. It's just raw and honest. It's jazz, blues and theater and everything in between."

Land and I sit back and listen to more of her songs. Once Land finishes his drink, he gets up and says he's going to finish his packing. I tell him I'm going to stay a little while longer. I kick back and think about my week in Cuba. So much seen and experienced. Such a rich place in terms of soul and artistry amongst rubble and neglect. That bird that came up and whispered in Lazaro's ear and who made me want to carry her off right then and there. As I close my eyes, I can see her perfect body and still smell her. It gets me worked up, especially, since Lazaro offered me one of his girls for the night. Shake it off. But, then the next song begins and I shrink and feel instead the delicate erection of thousands upon thousands of hairs on my arms. *What* is this song?

I don't know how long it is, but at first it washes over me like a fine mist. Nina's voice rises up and down and conjures up fiery images of passion which are cushioned by the harp-like instrumentation beneath. I fidget nervously not knowing where this song has been for my entire life. I curl up into a ball and hold my breath, while the song escalates and crescendos into a thunderous fever-pitch of calamity. And ends.

I'm left alone. A window in my mind opened where a cluster of truths came out as the song played. Now, all those truths are gone. I try to remember. I'm left with just the mental imprints of those truths. Imprints that suggest my whole life has been aimless. Easy too, because I like it that way. Who am I to come to a place like Cuba with my arrogance and pedantic coddling of things which I am not connected to? And the things in my life that I am connected to are piecemeal. A little family here, some friends there, a job here, a job there. Talk politics here and there. Watch football games on Sundays. Everything so convenient and so fleeting. Just being blown through life like so many others. No purpose, but to self-aggrandize. I want to bawl like a baby, but I'm still reeling from the clarity of my thoughts and cannot do so.

I manage to crawl out of my fetal position and go up to the stereo to see the title of this song. I pull the cassette out. No label. I try to find a cassette cover, but no dice. Fuck. It pisses me off. I turn the stereo off and even contemplate stealing the tape, but get horrified at the thought of doing such a despicable thing to Lazaro. I'll go ask Land. I leave Lazaro's living room, close its doors and then go up the stairs into Land's room. He's passed out. I don't feel like waking him. I quickly throw my things together and pack—taking care to hide the distinctly Cuban goods I'm taking with me. After I finish, I turn off the lights and lie down to go to sleep, but I can't. My eyes won't close and my heart beats loudly—so much so that the mattress shakes. I can hear Nina's song reverberate through the core of my being. It has a powerful hold over me and I can't simply will myself into sleep in order to release myself of its grip. It clings to me deep.

I think about Nina Simone. I don't know what she looks like. I only know a voice which is human and is capable of conveying a full canvas of human emotion. What suffering and mistreatment she must have had to endure that made her break and bid adieu! Prophetic and sad. I find sleep.

Land and I are awake by 7:30 in the morning. We can't take any chances in missing the flight out of Havana because if we do so, then we will miss our connecting flight from Cancun to New Orleans and while there are many daily flights out of Havana to Cancun that are easy for us to book, the flights from Cancun to New Orleans pose a problem. We shower and carry our bags downstairs. I'm surprised that Land has only two bags after staying here so long. It's funny how I forget the situation he's in. He's so carefree. Like he's just finished a semester abroad or something. Now, he's coming home. We have some coffee and bread and cheese with Lazaro in the kitchen. Even in the early morning, there he is with the unlit Cohiba stuck to his mouth. He calls us a cab and I get to observe Lazaro for the last time. This quixotic man. I come to the conclusion it's not that he knows some secret or indulges in a *sanguine diet* as Land alluded to. He does not have some fantastic insight into the nature of being either—as he basically admitted last night. But, it's like he said, *he holds no grudge.* He could very well be a closeted, bitter exile, but instead he knows how to *let go* and allow all things to *pass.* There's a poetry to the way he's lived his life. He has the ability to detach, refocus his energies and come back with open arms. And look at him now—on top of the world. And if he is a mixed bag like the rest of us, he does a helluva job hiding it which in itself is admirable. As the cab pulls out of the driveway and on to Quinta Avenida, I watch with wettish eyes his white house get smaller and smaller and finally disappear.

The airport is clean and virtually empty. Apparently, a slow day for air traffic in and out of Cuba. Land and I have to pay a $20 departure tax and then we walk into the area for customs. Land and I end up in two different lines with Land's line moving faster and I see him get buzzed through to the other side where the departure gates are located. When my turn finally comes, I show my passport and landing visa to the customs official and he examines both and I hear the buzzer go off, but then I hear *two* slams of his stamping device. I get my passport and landing visa back and when I pass through the buzzed open doors, I flip through my passport and sure enough there's a stamp. That idiot customs official not only stamped the "exit" box on my landing visa which I carefully preserved during my ten day stay here, but he also took it upon himself to stamp my U.S. passport! I'm screwed. I run up to Land.

"Yo, I gotta problem, man." I say.

"What is it?"

"Check this out."

I show him my passport and point to the stamp inside.

"Hey, that's great. A nice little memento."

"What are you talking about? I'm fucked! How am I going to explain this to the immigration people in New Orleans? You know we're here illegally."

"Tal, you're gonna have a heart attack, man. Slow down. Let me take a closer look at it."

"O.K. Here you go." I hand him my passport. He scrutinizes it closely.

"Just as I thought."

"What?"

"Did you take a close look at this?"

"Well, uh, no. Not really. Why?"

"You can't make out what it says. Some vague Spanish. Could be from anywhere. Nothing indicates it comes from Cuba."

I grab my passport out of Land's hands. I squint and try hard to see exactly what the stamp says. He's right.

"You're right, bra. You really can't see anything."

"So, if you and I can't see anything and we know what it is that we're looking for, you think some high school educated customs guy is gonna take the time to flip all the way through your passport, find this page, stare at the stamp and then figure out it's from Cuba?"

"No. But, what if they do ask me where it comes from?"

"You're a smart guy, Tal. Improvise." And Land turns and walks toward our gate.

Improvise. O.K. I'll do that. This cat always has the answers doesn't he? And what about his own situation?? I wonder if Land feels any apprehension about returning to the U.S. But, I don't ask him about it. I know his thoughts are on his time in Cuba, his experience with Lazaro. I leave him alone and we both sit by our gate and watch others in the airport waiting for their flights.

We will be back in New Orleans in six hours.

Part Four

I

Back in America with its quagmire of prophylactic rules. As we head towards customs, we are greeted with a huge black and yellow sign that blares: DUMP IT, DECLARE IT, or PAY A FINE. Welcome home. The customs official asks where I am coming from. I tell him Cancun. I start getting nervous as I see him take my passport and scan the page with my photo through some machine. He holds my passport up and I pray he doesn't start flipping through its pages. He then hands it back to me. Thank God! But, you know what, it's not over. He's not finished with me. He has the nerve to ask me how I *paid* for my ticket and *what* I do for a living. I tell him I used my Visa card and that I'm an accountant. He gruffs. He can see that I'm literate and that I am ready to bite his head off if he continues with his tricks. He lets me pass. Land is already at the baggage claim looking for our bags.

"This asshole gave me some shit," I say.

"Who?"

"This customs prick. Asking me questions about where I was, how I paid for my ticket, what I did for a living. What the fuck is that about?"

"Profiling, bra. You match a certain drug courier profile, so they have to check you out."

"Great. Now, I gotta deal with that on top of everything else."

"Hey, welcome back home, man!" Land slaps me on the shoulder. "This place has all sorts of shit in place designed to protect you from yourself. You know the drill. At least, he didn't go through your passport and find the stamp!"

"Yeah, right. That was a prayer answered."

"Come on! It's over now. Grab your bags and let's go."

Thankfully, my bags are not detained and come out quickly. We grab a cab and head for the Quarter. But, returning to New Orleans is different this time. I'm not looking forward to running around and frolicking in the Quarter. It's like a business trip. There's a different agenda and I'm just accompanying Land as he connects with Gen and we'll take it from there. Land tells me he hasn't heard from her for a while, but that he had told her he would be returning around this time. We get to Gen's apartment and Land goes up and knocks on the door. No one answers.

"No worries. I have a spare key," Land says.

Land takes out the spare key to the apartment from his pant pocket and inserts it into the brass knob. I start to walk up the stairs with my bags just as Land opens the door and goes inside.

"Oh, shit." I can hear Land say from inside.

"What?" I then hustle up the stairs.

"Shit."

When I get inside the room myself, I see Land standing in the middle of an empty room.

"What's going on?" I ask. Stupid question.

"I dunno." Land shakes his head in disbelief. "This ain't good at all."

"Maybe she's just moved, man."

"No. She woulda told me if she had done that. Nah—something's up."

Uneasiness spreads in Land. He darts around the kitchen, goes into Gen's bedroom and the bathroom

to find some trace, some hint of what has happened.
Nada. The fridge is unplugged and the door hangs
wide open. It's long since defrosted.

"Let's get outta here, Tal." Land picks up his bags
and heads for the door. I go back down the stairs
while Land locks up. I see Land still standing by
the door with his head down.

"Shit, shit, shit." He says.

"Land??"

He doesn't answer.

"Land, come down, man. Let's try and figure things
out."

He pries himself away and walks down the steps.

We both walk around the corner and stand
there holding our bags. Land contemplates the next
move. Minutes pass. Finally, I drop my bags to the
ground. I don't like the situation at all.

"Can we call someone?" I ask.

"Uh, yeah. I'm gonna call a friend of Gen's."

"O.K. Good. She'll tell us what's up."

"Hopefully. I think I still have her number. It's in
my bag." Land says as he starts to walk ahead
again. Then, he pauses. Still deep in thought, he
adds, "If I can't get a hold of her, I guess we'll just
crash at some motel and I can figure out what to
do."

"O.K."

Land starts walking ahead trying to find a pay
phone. I pick up my bags and tail behind him.

"Land."

"What's up?"

"If Gen is gone, you can always come crash in L.A.
with me. It's not a prob."

Land turns around and nods at me.

We find a pay phone a couple of blocks
from Gen's apartment and Land digs through his

bags until he finds the little contact book that he
keeps. He finds the number of Gen's friend,
Rebecca, and makes a phone call. But, Rebecca is
not home. Rebecca's roommate who does not know
Gen herself answers and says Becky is at a yoga
class and won't be back for another hour.
"These silly birds and their godd-dddamned yoga
classes!" Land stammers as he slams the phone
receiver down. "Tal, I gotta bad feeling."
"What, man?"
"I think something bad's gone down."
"You think Gen cracked or something?"
Land is silent. He tugs at his hair, rubs his face.
"Shit, I shoulda lied."
"About what?"
"When we were in Monterrey. Gen tells me she has
feelings for me. I don't know what the fuck to say.
After all these years? Now she has feelings? I
mean we're no Bonnie and Clyde. We're friends
trying to survive after a situation of our own
making. We don't have to now throw real emotions
into the mix. It's already a seriously charged time.
It coulda waited."
I try to act surprised.
"Ah, man. I had no idea."
"Yeah, man. Could you believe it? The same Gen
who just hung out on our couch like one of the guys
with a brew in hand. I used to talk about *other* birds
that I was into with her."
"I didn't know, man. But, that kind of shit always
comes to the surface. It's unavoidable."
"Yeah?"
"Uh, sure it is."
"But, I told her straight up as is my style—
unfortunately—that I didn't reciprocate. That she

was one of my closest friends and that's where it would stay. I couldn't tell how she took it."

I don't say a word.

"She was so stoic, you know...," Land continues. "Like she expected my reaction. And then, afterwards, I tried to carry on as if nothing had ever been said, but things between us changed. I tried to ignore it away, but that was it, man. Things couldn't go back to how they were between us. She knew that. So did I. She went back to New Orleans five days later."

"Sorry."

"Maybe I shoulda just lied about my feelings and pretended. Given the circumstances, that woulda been the best move. But, I had to be my usual upfront self thinking Gen would just bounce back and we could go on. Boy, did I fuck this one up."

"Hey, bra, you were right to be honest with her. By leading her on, believe me, things woulda got even more complicated and tougher to untangle. You did the right thing."

Land looks me squarely in the eyes.

"Tal, sometimes honesty fucks things up. You should say whatever needs to be said when you have something big at stake."

"So, what do you think then? Gen came back, packed her shit and just moved out? Back to New York?"

"Possible. But, we emailed each other on and off while I was in Cuba and she said nothing about moving out of New Orleans."

"But, didn't you mention to me that you hadn't heard from her over the last couple of weeks?"

"Yeah. I emailed her at least three times and have not gotten a response for close to two weeks now. It's just not like her to blow me off. But, who knows? Maybe she told her friends about my reaction and they told her to shut me out for a while? Fuckin' mind games, you know? Even if she was playing games now, I don't know why she would completely disappear without throwing me a bone."

The sky darkens above us and we better get a move on now. Land says he knows a good place for us to crash for the night. We walk down to Dumaine and make a left on Royal. We brush by the many antique stores and art galleries until we pass Esplanade and near Kerlerec.
"1431 Royal Street. This is it." Land says.
"Looks like some kitschy bar, man."
"It is. It's a bed and beverage."
"You sure they have vacancies? It looks kinda small."
"They do. They always do because nobody knows you can get a room inside. They just come for the bar."
We go inside and all types of wild shit hangs from the ceiling. The bar doubles as a lobby and check-in area for the rooms upstairs. Land tells me that there are only five rooms—all of which have special names like the *Deco Delite*, *Bukowski*, *Kiss and Tell*, *Storyville* and *Ghost in the Attic*. Each room has its own unique theme and interior. Land asks the bartender to put us up in the *Ghost in the Attic* because it has two beds. The rate is $130.00 which Land pays up front in cash. Land gets a key and we walk up three floors of stairs to the top. Ours is the only room on the floor. When I go inside the room I see a perfectly tailored copy of a Nineteenth Century bordello suite complete with kitchenette. It is large with one queen-size sleigh

bed in the middle of the room and one daybed in the corner. Portraits of regal faces in rococo frames are tacked on the walls. I've gone from 1959 to 1859.

I throw my bags on the daybed giving Land the queen-size sleigh bed thinking that since he's paying for the room it is only appropriate that he get the larger bed. Land has just dropped his bags in the middle of the room and gone to the bathroom. I sit on the edge of my bed waiting for him.

"O.K., man. I'm gonna go downstairs and try calling Rebecca again."

"I'll come with you."

So, we both go back downstairs to the bar which I now learn is called the R Bar & Inn. A couple of people have saddled up and are busy drinking and chatting with the bartender while Land goes to the back of the room and finds a pay phone. I sit near the bar and order an Abita and watch him. I can see him talking to somebody. Hopefully, Rebecca has returned from her yoga class refreshed and centered. The conversation lasts about ten minutes. Just based on Land's body language I know what has happened. I hear Land say goodbye and he puts the receiver down. He takes heavy steps in my direction.

"What's up?" I ask.

"Uh, uh—"

"Is Gen in trouble?"

"Yeah."

"What happened?"

"I don't really know—fuckin' Rebecca, she was so hyper about it. Like in a happy way."

"What did she tell you?"

"A couple of undercover—," Land breathes out hard and runs his hand over his chin violently and softly says, "Gen was arrested at her work about ten

days ago. They had a warrant and everything—".
Land stops.

I'm stopped.

"Her apartment was searched. I think she just had the money sitting there, man..."

"Shit, man."

"Gen's parents sent movers down last week to round up the rest of her things and bring them back to New York..." Land blanks out. His eyes black and fixed on the floor.

"How did they...how was she found out?"

"I don't know, man."

"Did you get any other info?"

"She's, uh, she awaiting arraignment in Philly. They got her sitting in some federal pen there. Oh man, oh man..." Land blubbers.

"Land, you gotta keep it together—" I then look around the bar and a couple of people are looking towards Land who has his face buried in his hands.

"Let's...let's go back upstairs, man." I push Land back towards the stairs and we climb back up to the room.

We get back inside our room and Land flops on his bed with his eyes facing the ceiling. I take a seat on a small chair at the far wall of the room. This is New Orleans fucking with us, I think. You can't keep taking advantage of this place and swooping in and out of the city like it was some little seaside destination. It gave you a lot, so it demanded that you focus your intentions on *it*. But, Land and I had just flown in with vague plans of using the city as a means to an end. To just hook up with Gen as if it were to be that easy. Well, we are wrong. So, now what? Land is not talking. I put myself in his place. What would I do? Easy. I would go back to Cuba, back to Lazaro. I don't

know if the cops are on to Land or not, or whether
Gen has told them about Land, but the bottom-line
is I would get out of New Orleans and out of the
U.S.—again. Hah! Lucky for me to be able to sit
here and muse about the fate of another. I feel
guilty for being in the clear, for not being involved
in Land's and Gen's trouble. Then, a sudden
paranoia sweeps over me—I may not be in the
clear. I may be drawn into their mess somehow. I
should probably get back to L.A. pronto. Check
availability of flights on American or Continental
tomorrow. Maybe get on a standby and get out of
here. But, whew, I am getting taken away. I gotta
regroup too.

"Land?" I say, but I receive no response. "Land,
just come back to L.A. with me. You can hang out
there and find out what's happening—what's going
on with Gen from there."

"How?" Land mumbles.

"Uh…you know, by making some calls—going on-
line. You'll be able to find out about her situation.
Trust me. You can keep tabs on what's going on
from a safe distance. You know, if there's gonna be
an arraignment or trial or whatever happens…" I
stop myself because I sound like a dipshit. I have
no idea what I'm saying. I'm just trying to stay
positive. I've never seen Land like this and it's
unsettling.

"Yeah?"

"Uh, sure. Let's look into some flights tomorrow.
O.K.?"

"So, I go back with you to L.A., sit back and
monitor Gen while she goes down, huh?"

"That's not what I meant, man."

"Well, what did you mean then?" Land rocks off
the bed and onto his feet.

"Hey, sorry, I'm just saying, you gotta think about yourself now. There's nothing wrong with that."
"No. I think there's only one thing for me to do."
I don't know what's coming next. But, whatever it is, I brace myself.
"I'm gonna turn myself in, Tal."
I can't believe this. I get up from the bed and walk to where Land is standing.
"Don't talk crazy, man. Think the situation through."
Land moves in closer to me to the point where I can feel his hot breath on my face.
"Tal, it's the only way."
"Bullshit. You can go back to Cuba. Lazaro would love to have you. Go back to Mexico." I can see Land is not listening to me. I get desperate.
"Come on, Land, there's other options. Just don't think about cashing it in now."
"No, no, man. You don't understand. This is not about me. It's about Gen."
"About...*Gen*??"
"Yeah."
"C'mon, bra. Fuck Gen, man!"

Nothing. Land only looks at me in disgust. His silence rips me. I can't believe what I have just yelled out. I didn't even think about what I was saying. It just popped out—unbridled and true to how I see things. But, I'm embarrassed to have said it now at this time in front of Land.
"Land...why—why are you doing this?" I meekly ask.
"Simple, man."
"Why then?"
"It's about friendship."
"Friendship??"

"Friendship."

I stumble backwards and slump on my bed.

"Don't worry. I'll make it, Tal."

I manage to summon one last reserve of what I see as rationality.

"Land—get a grip. Tomorrow, you and I are gonna fly back to L.A. Everything will be all right. Look, if it's about friendship, then Gen won't rat on you. You'll be able to think clearly about things in L.A. But, right now, you are not thinking—you're being impulsive. At least, sleep on it, man."

"No. This is what it comes down to for me. So, I'll probably do time. Big deal. We're all doing time, you dig? Whether on the inside or on the outside."

"Please don't romanticize jail. Please don't, man. When you're taking it up the ass and being someone's bitch, you'll see how romantic doing time is!"

"Haha, that's funny, Tal. You still got a couple of your old lines in you!"

This cat is unglued. He's unglued. Next thing I know, he walks over and takes a seat next to me on the bed.

"Tal, I'll survive whatever they throw at me. I have to go for Gen, bra. I won't let her face this on her own. *It's the business of little minds to shrink.* I remember reading that once somewhere. Do you know who said that?"

"I have no fuckin' idea." I mutter.

"Oh, that's too bad. I thought maybe you'd know. Anyway, that line has stuck with me. This whole world is fucked. It will be interesting to see how shit goes down from the inside. I'm not gonna abandon her."

"You self-important ass. *You're not gonna abandon her?* You already have, man."

"Oh, yeah?"

"Yeah, from the moment you told her you didn't want to love her." I get up from the bed and stand over Land. "You think now you can make things right by standing by her side? You want Gen and her parents and the judge or whoever to think to themselves, *Oh, look what a great cat this Land Morales is—he turned himself in for his friend.* And then they grant you some kind of *intuldo* because of your noble act??"

"A what??"

"Intuldo."

"What the fuck is that?"

"Uh, it's when they spare the life of a bull who fights bravely in the bullring. Some bullshit I stole from Hemingway—but, listen to what I'm saying, Land!"

"Wow—"

"—let me finish. You gotta look at it this way too. If you turn yourself in, you're gonna get the worst of it. Gen's parents are rich. They'll get a big time attorney. A little sob story here, a little sob story there and the jury will buy it, you know, some bullshit like, *Ladies and Gentlemen of the jury the evidence clearly shows that Ms. Klugman was led astray by Mr. Morales who took advantage of her at a time when she was in an extreme fragile state.* You'll get screwed. Think about that, man. Think about how your friendship will fare when the law pieces it up for itself."

"Wow, man."

"That's all you can say?"

"I mean, *wow*. I didn't want to believe it, you know." Land gets up and heads towards the middle of the room. He stops and looks back at me.

"What happened, man? Or, were you always like this and the time we shared back in the days was just one big put-on? If so, you're good, bra. You sure had me fooled."

"Land—"

"—you let me finish now. Get off the fence, Tal. You gotta look at yourself in the mirror and make real choices in life. Choices you're gonna have to live with. Consequences that may even dog you for the rest of your life, but at least you controlled the actions that led to them."

I look dumbly at Land.

"I know you don't get it. That's cool, but I do, and so I knew what I was getting into when all this started and I'm gonna deal. That's it. I'm going to Philly tomorrow and will turn myself in and who knows? Maybe something good can come out of it."

"Yeah? Which is?"

"You'll realize what a fuckin' zombi you've become."

In one fluid motion, Land picks up his bags and glides out the door and out of my life. I'm stupefied. Mouth agape—gaping for air, belief and understanding. I stand there, unmoving and staring at the door that has now closed on itself. It's difficult to describe what I'm left with. I'm surrounded by orderly period pieces and elegance, but a tempest brews threatening to wipe out everything. I try to hold the dark clouds back and reason. I thought I was the one being a friend trying to help Land out of a situation of his own doing. Instead, not even a thanks. I'm the bad guy. That melodramatic motherfucker. He's right. *I don't get it*. But, my chest is heavy and hard. I exhale deeply a couple of times to ease some of the pressure. You think you know someone with whom you have a past and been through some shit. And then in a flurry of angry words *everything* changes. Everything is changed like an out of the blue can of paint someone throws on a painting and you no longer recognize what it was that had been there in the first place.

It all seems so scripted, so planned—Land's actions. He can't be for real, can he? To put it all on me? He used me. Yeah, that's it. My eyes balloon up as I think about this. That motherfucker used me to dangle in front of Gen...while he what??? Kept it all together? But, I must have really surprised him when I bailed at Laredo and left him and Gen to go to Mexico together. He must have not counted on that because he knew Gen was falling for him. I know he knew. He needed me as a third body to keep Gen at bay because he was sure Gen would never open up to him as long as I was there. And then when I do leave and Gen finally opens up to him, he can't reciprocate her feelings and then she bails. Land is left alone, so he plots and everything starts over again. He invites me to Havana and then back to New Orleans under the premise of meeting back up with Gen, but this time I would be used to help him smooth things over with her. Somehow...

I'm reeling. I have no real answers to anything. O.K., if now is the time to talk honestly, I will. The truth is I used Land. I know it and he definitely knows it now. I had zero to lose, and instead hung out, ran around Havana and now came back to New Orleans all at Land's expense. I had seen him only once since our graduation close to four years ago, and now over the last six months, I was quick to join him anywhere, anytime. All because I needed an escape. But, I still don't know why I'm the bad guy. I was there for him and Gen. I could have easily made the choice to *not* get involved in their mess. I could have caught that American flight that next day after I missed my scheduled return flight to L.A. But, what did I do? I stayed. Why? I stayed for their sakes—and my own. For *our* friendship. Don't fucking blame me for that.

II

The rest of the night is silence. There is no
television in the room and I have zero desire to
enjoy the Quarter. I never *ever* thought that I would
say that. But, I have, and instead have no choice
but to try and force myself into sleep. I toss and
turn and turn and toss. Thoughts of misgiving
continue to slam my brain, but somehow after an
hour or so of wrestling with myself, I find the
perfect sleep position and I am sufficiently worn out
to give in. Then, something strange happens. At
first, I think I'm hearing things. Noises of what
seem like dozens of pots and pans being clanged
together grow louder and louder. Howling,
whistling, whooping and bells ringing. I hear
voices yelling out gibberish. I sit up in bed to see if
I can understand what is being said, but I can't
make out any words and just hear something
ungodly clamorous that sounds like:

Zwwizkzkzk Hoooouhuhhu Jyuckkkkkkkkk

And it repeats over and over again.

I dive back down in my bed and try to
muffle the noises by suffocating myself with a
pillow, but that doesn't cut it. I then try to simply
ignore the sounds, but that effort is fruitless.
There's *no way* for me to ignore the racket. It will
not pass, and after about ten more minutes of the
onslaught, I can't take it anymore and pounce to the
window. I open it up and get ready to scream
sticking my head outside, but there is nothing. The
noises have suddenly just dissipated. I think I can

still hear something faintly in the distance but the incongruous cacophony that was killing me has gone. I slink back into bed, but now I can't reclaim the perfect sleep position I had earlier. I'm wired and disturbed. My mind kicks into overdrive as it starts making connections between the parade of noise that just came and went and the name of the room, *Ghost in the Attic*. A haunting is the last thing I need. I try to block out these thoughts and pretend I never heard the sounds and imagine myself somewhere else in some other state of mind where I haven't made any mistakes, but instead have proceeded through calm and collected with everything and everyone under control. I try hard to envision this place.

The next morning, I wake up and feel I've inherited someone else's life. I am withdrawn and anguished. I didn't dream—I couldn't dream last night. It feels as if I slept with my eyes open for the entire night and so I saw nothing but blackness for four or more hours until the sun announced itself through my window and the black was replaced by light. Everything was so emotionally simple for me six months ago. How did all this shit get laid on me? Did I consciously put myself in this situation? I take a long shower standing motionless underneath the showerhead and not bothering to soap myself. When the fact that check out is probably 10:30 finally pops into my head, I manage to turn off the shower and towel off and change. I pack my things, go down to the bar and prepare to check out. I look around the bar hoping to see Land sitting at a table waiting for me. What if he changed his mind and came back? That would erase everything and everything would be cool.

Nothing though. He has gone. As I'm handing in the room key, the bartender/clerk asks me whether I didn't mind all the noise last night.

"So, there *was* something going on?" I ask.

"Oh, yes." he says.

"What happened? Just a bunch of drunkards getting their rocks off?"

He laughs with his head down as he puts away my room key.

"That's part of sleeping in the Quarter I guess," I continue.

"I must tell you that last night wasn't just the typical Quarter rowdiness. It was a *charivari*," he says.

"A what? What is that??"

"Yeah, I guess most folks don't see these things anymore. It is a nearly extinct custom or ceremony, if you know what I mean."

"I've never heard of it. What is it?"

"Oh, it's sort of like a ritual down in these parts. More so in the bayous than in N'Awlins itself. Part of an old Creole and Acadian tradition down here."

"A helluva loud ritual, man."

"It has to be—and the louder the better! See, when a couple gets married, on the night of their honeymoon all the couples' relatives—both sides of their families—gather below the honeymoon suite and serenade the couple. Only it's not the usual serenade! They bring pots, pans, trash cans, kettles, shovels, tongs and bottles—anything that you can hit and make a loud noise with."

"Sounds fun."

"It is—if you're the one making the noise! The families make a parade out of it. Some even wear masks. They take turns walking by the room. First, just the couples' parents will walk by—banging away. Then, the grandparents—if there are any.

Then, uncles and aunts. Then, brothers, cousins and younger kin—that's when the most damage is usually done. Things degenerate into horseplay at that point if you can imagine!"

"So, where was the newlywed couple staying last night?"

"Right around the corner from us—just up here on Kerlerec. There's a cottage there popular with honeymooners. The couples' families got together outside here around midnight and then ambushed the couple around 12:30."

"I've never heard about this kind of parade. It was so noisy. It drove me nuts, but then it just finished in a flash. I was beginning to think it was the room that I was staying in!"

"Oh, we've had reports about that room as well—mostly around the holidays though. No, last night there were no ghosts—just an old fashioned charivari! Count yourself as one of the lucky few to have experienced one second-hand. Believe me, it's better than experiencing one first-hand!! Hahaha!"

"So, what's the point of it all? I mean, is it just to disrupt the honeymoon? Big deal."

"You know…I'm not sure what the point of it all is. It's a *mock* serenade. It's to poke fun—to make the honeymooners take notice."

"I don't understand."

"There's nothing to it. Look, people here love parades—so here's an excuse for another one. But, I do know there are usually two reasons for having a charivari."

"Let's hear them."

"The first is that it serves a superstitious purpose in that all the noise scares away evil spirits who may bring bad luck to the new couple. But, this was really for the charivaris that occurred centuries ago and the families back then believed that the newlyweds were vulnerable to the bad spirits on the night of their honeymoon. So, they had to throw a charivari in order to protect the bride and groom."

"And the second reason?" I ask.

"These days, charivaris usually occur when for whatever reason the newlyweds have neglected a certain societal convention or haven't followed the proprieties expected of them as members of the community."

"Huh."

"So, there you have it."

"The families last night get gold stars from me, man. They made a raucous. I was about to scream my head off, but they vanished."

"Yeah, typically the charivari doesn't last too long. Maybe twenty minutes at the most. It all depends on whether the newlyweds know the rules."

"Rules?"

"They better know that if they get angry and yell or curse at those below, the charivari will just get rowdier and longer. So, hopefully, the newlyweds will realize that in order to end things, they must appear before the crowd and together submit to it."

"What do you mean?"

"They just gotta show both their faces and the groom must say to the crowd, *What do you want, gentlemen?* Or something to that effect."

"Is the groom gonna know to say that?"

"Those are the rules. I don't make them. The groom has got to figure it out—if he doesn't already know."

"I hate rules."

"It's not that bad. I think when you're in that position, you realize it's best to throw yourself at the mercy of the crowd in order to get peace."

"Well, what do they want then?"

"In the old days, the crowd would simply ask the bride to kiss the groom. Now, I hear that all sorts of demands are made! The crowd asks for wine, beer, cake, money or anything else that will buy their silence!"

"No wonder this thing is dying out! I mean who wants to get married and then afterwards you have to pay your family to shut up!"

"That's a funny way to look at it. We had two people staying in another room below yours and they also complained to me when they checked out. So, you weren't alone in being upset by the noise."

"There's not a whole lot you could do anyway. Like you said, it's another parade in a city which loves parades."

"That's right. What can we do? Arrest them? That's a laugh. Especially, since some of the family members had drinks right inside here before they went out and started the thing!"

"Did you go out and see it yourself?"

"No. I started my shift right when it started and I had to tend the bar—we had a full place last night."

"Well, hey, thanks for the education. I learned something new."

"Come back again."

I say goodbye and walk onto the street. Now, what? I will have to make some calls to airlines and see if I can find a cheap flight back to L.A. This will be a pain in the ass. What irony though, huh? Here, I am with time on my hands in the apple of my eye and I am miserable. I have no wish to go play in the Quarter. I just wanna get back to L.A. Wasn't I just in this same position? Very disconcerting.

III

Nowadays, when was the last time anyone was on a long-distance train in America? This is not Europe where a web of high-speed rails and uniform timetables make train travel efficient, reliable and the travel mode of choice. Just ask punk American kids abroad who gladly shell out a few hundred bucks to ride second class coaches throughout every city in Europe with ease and precision. For the first time in my life, I end up hopping on an Amtrak. I catch it in New Orleans and it drops me off—out of all places—in Chatsworth deep in the San Fernando valley where my girlfriend is from. It is a two and a half day train ride away from New Orleans. I'm sorry to say I don't remember much of it. I spent practically the entire time holed up in my couchette still trying to put two and two together. All I absorbed from the ride was my window view of swamp land giving way to pastures giving way to desert and more desert. The only city name I can recall passing though is Las Cruces somewhere in New Mexico and which for some reason I connect in my mind to the town of Roswell where urban legend held that a UFO was shot down in the Forties or Fifties. Other than that, I spent time on the train in a catatonic state where I spoke to no one and awoke only to drink from my large two-liter bottle of Naya mineral water and snack from a pack of trail mix.

Returning to Los Angeles at a point deep in the Valley exposes you to two realities. First, you are surrounded by a great mountain range in the middle of suburbia which you know maintains a healthy population of disaffected middle class white males obsessed with Holden Caulfield. Second, this same suburbia is the global host of porn. It is the second reality which is the more fascinating as I think every suburban outpost in America breeds pro-Holden Caulfield sentiment amongst its white male youth. In one of the law firms I temped at for an extended period, I met a younger attorney, probably in his early thirties, who loved bouncing off his dream to me. He wanted to unionize the porn industry. This was no pipe dream either. He was serious, so serious that he had actually begun drafting a prototype collective bargaining agreement that would mandate the basic minimums for wages and conditions of employment for adult performers.

Oh, this cat was gung-ho! He thought that it was an idea whose time had come. The male performers were getting ripped off big time and were paid at egregiously lower prices than the female performers. He wanted to set up scale salaries for performers and bring more parity to the industry. He also wanted to have performers get royalties or residuals for the DVD/video and pay-per-view sales of their pictures. Though I didn't know anything about unionizing or labor organizing, his ideas seemed well grounded. He wasn't just another pathetic Angeleno with dollar signs in his eyes. All he needed to do he told me was to network with the bigger porn stars. If he could get a few of them to get on board with the program, then a chain reaction could start whereby the other performers would side with them and make the studios consider their demands. And that's what he called the porn companies—studios. He would say these companies like VCA, Wicked, and Vivid were so big and had so much money that they actually had 401(k) pension and medical plans for their employees now. They were part of a multi-billion dollar industry where pictures never flopped. They could teach the mainstream Hollywood studios a few things about turning a profit on films.

Unfortunately, I lost touch with him after my temp agency pulled the plug on my engagement at this cat's law firm. He did give me his number and wanted to stay in touch because he thought I could be useful in his plans. He mentioned that he wanted me to go to the conventions and signings that most porn stars attended, so that I could get their contact information and even pass out his business card. But, I never called him. I'm not sure why. It could have been a fun gig—strike that—of course it would have been a fun gig and if this thing would have worked then it could have been very, very big. Call it laziness or just being unwilling to help someone else get his dream after you had already let go of yours.

I expect my girlfriend to pull up in her red VW Rabbit convertible any minute now. When I first told her I would be arriving at the Chatsworth train station her response was, "*Why?*" I told her because that was where the Amtrak made its stop, and since she still lived in the area there at her father's house, it made sense for her to pick me up—if she was free. She had never picked up anyone at the train station there and to do so now short-circuited her limited programming. But, she agreed, and after bringing out her trusty Thomas Guide, she figured out where the train station was. I also think she was curious to find out what I had been up to in Cuba as we had not spoken to each other for close to two weeks.

"Hey!!" I wave as I see her car pull up to the loading area.

"Get in, Tal." She tells me.

I immediately throw my bags in the back seat and get in the front. I lean over to kiss her on the cheek.

"How are you?" I ask.

"Not bad. Just got off from an early morning shoot."

"How did it go?"

"Oh, it was a pain in the ass. I got in a big argument with one of the A.D.s. A long story. Anyway, how are you stranger?"

"Good. Not bad. I, uh…" I then notice a fleck of dark brown paint behind her right ear.

"What? Why are you looking at me like that?"

"Uh—nothing. You have a little—spot—right— there." I point to her right ear.

"What? Shit. Where? Behind my ear??" She folds her right ear down and looks into the rearview mirror.

"One of those illegal paint downs again?"

"Damn it!" She licks her fingers and rubs out the brown spot.

"You got it," I say.

"I had to pass for a Puerto Rican today. Make-up took forever as you can imagine."

"Yeah, I bet."

"So, enough about my day. How was Cuba?"

"It was—was, I don't know—a life affirming experience. Beautiful, but sad. A lot of history and good music and art."

"Can you be any more vague?"

"It's tough to nail down, babe. Havana has been cocooned by socialism and the embargo so it has stayed pretty much as it was in 1959. I'll show you pictures, then you can see what I'm talking about it."

"And you went with your friends—Lando and Gen?"

"Not Lando—Land. L—A—N—D. Gen wasn't there."

"Oh, right. Who names their child *the land*? What a stupid name!"

"It's not *the land*. Just Land. He had hippies for parents. You know, into the earth and stuff." I feel a bit testy all of a sudden.

"O.K. Don't get so defensive."

"Sorry, been cramped up in the train."

"So, what happened with Gen? Couldn't hang with the boys this time round?"

"Uh, she's in New York busy studying to re-take the Bar exam there."

"She left New Orleans then?"

"Yup."

　　　She pulls into the subterranean parking of my apartment complex. I pick up my bags and we go to my apartment. I throw my bags on my bed and then stick my head into my fridge. Other than some bottled water—zero inside. I pour myself a glass and ask my girlfriend if she wants a glass as well. She tells me yes and takes a seat in my living/TV room.

"A lot of people told me they thought you were crazy for going to Cuba," she says.

"Now, why would they say that?" I answer as I hand her a glass of water.

"Come on, Tal. Be serious."

"There was no trouble getting in or out of the country. The people there love America."

"Really?"

"Sure. Well, I had a little snag getting out. But, that turned out to be nothing really."

"What happened?"

"The customs guy in Cuba stamped my passport, instead of just stamping my landing visa. No big deal."

"Couldn't you have gotten into trouble in the U.S. for that?"

"Yeah, maybe. But, it wasn't decipherable."

"What?"

Sometimes I forget about holding back the bigger words when talking to her. After not seeing her for two weeks, I just forgot about this.

"You couldn't really read it. It just looked like a square of blank ink with some random Spanish in it. Anyway, nothing happened."

"Well, that's a relief."

"About the country itself though. What's sad is this embargo and all—that's our government fighting against the Cuban people not the country's politics. So, it's sad to see such affection for America by the Cubans I met when unfortunately a lot of the people's misery is because of the embargo."

"Huh."

"What else have you been up to?" I figure that's enough on the topic for right now. Time to have her say her piece.

"Busy working. Unlike you, some of us still work, you know."

I don't say anything and just drink my water coolly.

"I have been making some progress though."

"What? Getting auditions for leads??"

"Not yet. I'm talking about with Scientology—I'm making real strides. It's doing wonders for my confidence and my ability to make better choices about things."

I nod mutely.

"It's been fabulous. I've even managed to get Noelle and Dakota to start attending some of the meetings and reading the materials."

The picture in my head of my girlfriend and the starfuckers she calls friends coalescing at a Scientology compound with books and pens in hand makes me gag. I have to hold back fragments from the trail mix I had been munching on over the last two days from hurling into the room. I need to put a new thought into my head quick. One thing about my girlfriend—she knows how to dress. From her black platform sandals up to her light lip gloss which makes her mouth appear so slightly wet. She looks good and tight as usual. That's her saving grace to me. She exudes sensuality and knows how to enhance it in the right way without going over the top. There's a delicate line between being sexy and slutty and she's definitely mastered it. She wears a long, black skirt slit thinly on her right leg up to the beginning of her thigh and a red silk blouse in which her toned shoulders peek at me. Her hair is a bit messy and wet, but that's understandable since she was in make-up and probably wore a wig during her scenes today. Still very yummy.

"So, you said something about the art there?" She asks.

"Oh, it was beautiful. Many different influences and styles in the paintings and sculptures."

"You must have brought back some things?"

I know she phrases this like a question, but it's no question. It's more like a threat. She loves getting presents. If I have come back empty-handed from my trip, she'll parlay this into collateral to use against me for weeks.

"Of course! You know me. Hold on for a sec."

I go into my bedroom and open my bags frantically searching for something appropriate to give her. Truth is, I did not buy a thing with her in mind. Most of the stuff—books, pictures and cigars—were for me. But, ah, the St. Lazaro statue, that may pass muster. I pull it out of the bag and unwrap the newspaper wrapping around it. I inspect it. It survived the trip to L.A.

"Well, I gotta a little something for you. It has alotta significance." I hold the statue behind me.

"What is it, Tal!!" She stands up and tries to look around my back.

"Take it easy! Sit back down!"

"O.K., O.K.!!"

I thrust the statue in her face like its an Oscar.

"This is a real piece of Cuban craftsmanship. Made from ebony and hand-painted."

"What is it?"

She still has not taken it from my hands.

"It's a statue of St. Lazaro one of the great saints of Santeria."

"The island in Greece?"

"No, no. Santeria is a religion in Cuba. Very, very strongly believed in by some. It's a fusion of African and Catholic and Indian religious beliefs."

"The face looks a little threatening."

"What? Oh, come on. This is a good guy. Here, take it."

I push it out to her and she reaches out to take it. But, whether by accident or design, when I release my hold of the statue thinking it is in her grip, the statue slips through her hands and falls to the hardwood floor with a crash.

"Oh, sorry," She says.

I look down and see the head of the statue has broken off. I can't believe it. I pick up both pieces and run my hands over them. I try to fit them back together again, but the pieces are splintered and will need to be glued. I then tilt over the body of the statue because I notice it is hollow. As I turn the body toward the palm of my hand, a bunch of sand pours out.

"Is that sand?" She asks.

"I guess. What the…"

"Must have been a fake, huh?"

"No. It was so solid and heavy…had to be real."

"Tal, Tal. These third world countries, you know they sell these type of cheap things."

"Not this though. It was a *religious* piece."

"Relax. I appreciate that you thought of me at least when you bought it." She swings by and kisses me on the cheek. "Now, I have to get back and get ready for my meeting at six. Call me later." She walks out to the door.

"Get out." I mutter under my breath.

"Did you say something?" She says right before she opens the door.

"Thanks for the ride."

I unpack the rest of my things and when I finish I let out a big sigh and sit on the edge of my bed. I look at the clock on my dresser and it reads 6:15 p.m. I stare out at the bookcase in front of me and yawn so hard that my eyes water. As I wipe away the water from my eyes, I see an old photo album sticking out of the bottom level of the bookcase. Man, I haven't looked at the photos inside for years. I pull out the album and flip through each page. Most of the pics date from my college years and I notice all the photos that were taken outdoors show dark, gloomy skies. I remember when I first came to campus I was told clouds came to die there. I thought that was an exaggeration until I endured a stretch of Hell from November to April where the sun only reminded us it still existed when it poked through the clouds on a handful of occasions. So, as a student dealing with all the pressures of the rigorous academic curriculum in the midst of doomsday gray skies one had to stave of seasonal depression by either boozing hard or making as many friends as one could. I was lucky in that I never got too down by it all because I met Land my freshman year and he put his own unique shine on things.

I find a picture that brings back all sorts of memories. It shows Land standing on a stool in front of the student union on our campus. He wears a brown leather coat and jeans and black boots. A large, wind blown white scarf is wrapped around his neck and he is trying to hold it in place with one hand. You can only see the tops of heads of people assembled in front of him listening. Behind him a few people stand whose faces I recognize, but I don't remember their names. In the upper right side of the photo, there I am. Spellbound.

I remember that day. It was early November of our sophomore year when all the elm trees on campus had broken because of a freak snowstorm. None of the trees had lost their leaves yet and so the snowstorm dumped all this snow that just sat on still leafy branches which all snapped because they could not withstand the weight of the snow. A rally on the administration's recently unveiled controversial student housing policy was held the very next day and it was eerie to be surrounded by all these white trees that had simply bent over like they were kneeling in prayer. Land was a keynote speaker as he was part of some student rights' organization on campus. He started off his speech with the line, "*Welcome to the premature winter of our discontent.*" I thought it was genius. The crowd ate it up too and then he went off against the school administration and compared their student housing policy to the federal government's annexing of Indian land in the Nineteenth Century.

He described in beautiful poetic detail the Native American concept of land as being an extension of the tribe. There was no "owning" individual parcels of land in the Native mind. Such a concept was alien and contrary to the very existence of the tribe. How could one logically own the earth? It owned us—since we had sprung from its fruits. Some land was more sacred than others because of its role in Native cosmology. This idea of sacred land was devoid in Western civilization. In America, the only land sacred in the country's collective memory were places where man's actions had made them sacred. Like a Gettysburg. However, that was the big difference. From the perspective of the Native American, lands were sacred in and of themselves and their own action *not* because they served as the locale for some memorable action of man. Land expertly wove these notions together in order to illustrate his points against the university's restructuring of student housing on campus. Man, he could have had any bird that was sitting there that day. Charismatic and cool. He was in—easy.

After the rally, he had planned on having everyone there recreate some John and Yoko *bagism.* He actually had this zany idea of marching into the administration building, having each person

hop into a sack and then nailing the sack into the
wall. Everyone would stay inside their sacks and
remain nailed to the wall until the university agreed
to have a face-to-face meeting with the student
representatives regarding the student housing
policy. Land, me and a few cronies scoured
everywhere to get some real bags like potato sacks.
Trash bags and the like would obviously not cut it.
The bags had to be made of hemp or some other
sturdy fabric and large enough for the individual to
get inside and then be nailed to the wall. We
couldn't find anything. It was a great idea, but we
just didn't have the resources. Shit, we would have
had some real publicity if we had pulled that stunt
off. The return of bagism! It would have been
fantastic. Instead, Land led everyone who had
come to the rally into the administration building
where he asked everyone to join him in a sit-in. He
then plopped down right then and there in the main
reception area of the building. I sat right next to him
and soon the whole reception area was clogged with
seated bodies chanting, "*No pasaran.*"

Six hours into the sit-in, nervous school
officials after consulting with the J.A. and
ombudsman agreed to Land's demand for a face-to-
face meeting between the students' representatives
and the Dean of Students and the President of the
university. We were stoked and the meeting
actually resulted in the administration conceding to
a few of our demands. Unfortunately, school
bureaucracy and red tape take longer than the four
years it takes to graduate, so we were all gone way
before any of those conceded demands were
implemented on campus. Land had been
magnificent though.

I return the album back to its spot on the bottom shelf. It finally sets in. Once upon a time, man, I knew Land and he knew me. It was a great friendship—more of a friendship than he could ever have with Gen. And then we went our different ways. I tried to change while he stayed the same. We were both naïve to think we could ignore how our lives changed since we last saw one another and to think we could pick up right where we left off running around town like cats with nothing to lose. I want to pick up the phone and call him, but where? I don't have any numbers for him and the cat is one of the last remaining few who does not own a cell phone. I may still have his parents' number, but what good is that gonna do? He won't be there. It's over and I'm not the bigger man to go out now and search for Land. If he did turn himself in like he said, then there's no way to reach him anyway. What happened between us is not my fault, so I should be able to clear my conscience and get back on track. But, I'm not so sure I can wrap myself up in some all-enveloping pursuit that will allow me to just forget about him this time.

Close to four years have now passed since I first came to L.A. and molded myself to what I thought I wanted and what the city gave me. I worked and was part of business—the exchange of people for money leading to collaborative endeavors that in turn reached mass audiences. I wanted what I worked hard for—recognition, promotion and ascension. Instead, I fell victim to the cheap and chippy chipper—my own pig head lopped off and I've flailed away as a headless body ever since.

Lo and behold, I'm now pushing twenty-six and have zilch to show. Out of nothingness comes

nothingness. That's my part in the movie so far—
nothing but background work, Jack. When I hear
Spike Lee made *Do The Right Thing* at twenty-six
and that athletes are in their prime between the ages
of twenty-one through twenty-five and that Hendrix
died at twenty-seven, what do I think? All is lost?
The writing pen has writ and having done so it
moves on leaving me stewing mad in its wake
because I was written out? Perhaps. But, I think I
have some things to work with now. I only need to
run away from the hoots and hollers, the debunkers
and jeerers and naysayers with all their noisome
nonsense. The spine of *Tropic of Cancer* which I
had just bought a few months ago when I visited the
Henry Miller Home and Museum in Big Sur comes
into focus. I remember Miller didn't leave for Paris
until he was thirty-eight years old and it was when
he was in Paris that he got around to writing *Tropic
of Cancer*. There may be life in the old boy yet!

But, it's not that easy. Miller had Anaïs Nin
and her hubby, Hugo, supporting him, giving him
cash, a place to crash and write. I need my Anaïs
Nin if I'm gonna have any chance getting off the
ground. If I stay in L.A., I will regress back into a
fatalist blitheness that will render me meager and
content to sleep away my life. So, I must run off
once more as I, too, still have a quest. One that I
keep starting and stopping.

Part Five

I

I write from a café—the fabled Les Deux Magots—and about four meters from where I sit stands a sign which says "Place du Sartre-Beavoir" and across St. Germain I can see locals and tourists pretending to be locals walking into Lipp's Brasserie with today's *Le Monde* tucked under their arms. I understand existentialism at last as I see the endless varied strides and gaits of so many people pass by while I sit and write. Instead of Anaïs Nin, I've had to settle for Doug Sanders who is another friend from the college days, but a cat who I was not close to while in school. I don't think we ever shared one class. He majored in economics and took nothing else but finance and accounting courses. I actually tried to take a basic accounting class because of his recommendation one semester, but I dropped it after only three class meetings. It was the only class that I ever dropped during college.

When I next bumped into him, he asked about how the accounting course was coming along, I told him that I had a conflict with one of my required courses for my philosophy major so I had to drop the class. I didn't want him to know that I was all right brain and had zero left brain capacity. I had only met him through other friends one day during a game of Ultimate Frisbee and he was a dull and safe cat. He was so WASPy that he was simply out of style on campus. There was not much he could relate to other than joining a fraternity where he could find his own kind and take part in the rituals of keggers and mixers. Each time I would bump into him, I tried to mirror his conservativeness and plain conversational style. Why? Because he knew I was on the *outside*. It was painted all over my face in the way I dressed, my long hair. He was curious in finding out what being me was like. But, I didn't feel like taking him on as my special project in order to give him the kind of edge that he may have been craving in order to break free of the monotony of his fraternity and preppy upbringing. I down-played any of my wild tendencies and though he knew about Land and my friendship with him, I would down-play Land too. We had boring, clipped, run-of-the-mill discussions and I never partied with him as we inhabited completely different spheres of being.

It was only after graduation that I got to know Sanders (as I called him) better because he took a job with a transnational consulting firm's Phoenix office. When I asked why he chose the Phoenix branch out of all the firm's offices, he said he liked a dry heat and where else could he play golf for three hundred fifty days out of the year? He often would fly into L.A. on business and he got my number from another friend who knew me and called me once out of the blue to say he was in town. I went to pick him up at his hotel and he took me out to one of the best sushi joints in town. I think we downed ten carafes of hot sake. In any event, we both were lit and I realized through the sake-induced fuzziness that this cat was definitely going places now and was someone I would need, so I made a *strong* effort to stay in touch with him. All his close to the chest academic and social gamesmanship that he had so excelled at school, and which also made him a guru of ennui in my eyes, was now serving him incredibly well in the real world and he was succeeding in getting to where he wanted to go, which was to work hard for the next seventeen to nineteen years and then retire around forty. He talked to me about the need to start funding an IRA right now and told me to start trading on-line using AmeriTrade. He had tips on good stocks—he loved gold too. I learned some things from him and in a way I looked up to his example. He always had on nicely pressed suits, shoes that shined and generally behaved like a gentleman, man. Not bad for being only twenty-four at the time.

As luck would have it, the last time we spoke he mentioned that he was transferring to his firm's Paris office for a nine month assignment there. I found an email addy of his and shot him a letter asking if he was still in Paris. When he said that he was, I asked him whether I could stay with him for a few weeks and he said yes. I did a dance that lasted all the way from LAX to Charles De Gaulle. I landed in Paris at nine in the morning on a Wednesday. Sanders was at work, but had told me that from Charles De Gaulle I could get on the RER and take it all the way to the St. Michel Notre-Dame station. I had never been to Paris before and was eager to get my first glimpses of the city. But, the thirty-five minute ride on the RER to St. Michel was all green grass and country and then we disappeared underground as we entered Paris. I saw nothing. At St. Michel, I somehow staved off sleep, and made the walk to the other station, Cluny La Sorbonne, that was connected underground with St. Michel. From Cluny La Sorbonne, I took the Number 10 Metro westbound and exited at the Duroc stop. When I got above ground, the skies were gray and the air humid. I saw nothing that I recognized from my fantasies of Paris. To the south of where I stood, I could see a big, black, modern, monolith-like building towering over everything else. Off in the distance directly ahead of me, I could only make out a gold, gilded dome of a church, but I was too tired to walk closer and check it out. I had two weeks here. There would be plenty of time.

Sanders lived a couple of blocks away from the Duroc Metro stop on a street called Rue Masseran. I walked down Rue de Sèvres and made a right on Rue Masseran. His apartment was located at 310 Rue Masseran. He left the key with the doorman who was expecting me. The doorman gave me the key and in hard to understand English directed me to take the elevator up to the fifth floor where Sanders' apartment was located off to the right. When I got inside Sanders' apartment, I found a letter for me on the breakfast table. Sanders had written that I should make myself comfortable and that he would try to get back home by 4:30 in the afternoon. I took a quick look around the place. A smallish one bedroom, but stylishly furnished. A futon awaited me in the living room area, and I dutifully complied by ripping off my shirt, pants, socks and shoes, and collapsed on it. I didn't wake until Sanders returned.

So, I've spent time exploring the city and now that I've put the touristy stuff behind me, I've really been able to tap into things around here. My French is horrible, but I can still communicate effectively enough. It's all in the eyes and hands anyway. I've found that you learn to simplify things real nice when you don't know the language surrounding you. Sanders is fluent in French, so when we go out together it's easy for me to hang back and let him take care of everything from ordering the food, the drinks and all the other usual societal intercourse that comes along. But, when I'm on my own which is during the daytime when Sanders is at work I can concentrate on getting lost in the tight, crooked neighborhoods of Montmartre and observing Parisian life from the point of view of some expat with nothing but time on his hands. It's liberating. To pass through these rues and boulevards with hands clasped behind your back and digging those who go about their ordinary lives unaware of how fortunate you are to be digging them. I've learned that I *learn* more easily as well when I play the role of the expat looking in from the outside. The detachment I have allows for more facts, history, understanding and art to seep into me and I retain more.

One thing I have learned is that the story about the French building mausoleums above ground in New Orleans because of the problem of bodies floating through town after it rained is not entirely true. The French *always* built above ground tombs it seems. A practice that goes back centuries. So, that whole jive about New Orleans being so below sea level that interred bodies became uninterred after it rained was just a *better story* to tell the outsider than simply admitting that when the French colonized New Orleans they continued to build their patented above ground tombs. And I've had a chance to wander through a bunch of those here, including the cemeteries of Montmartre, Passy, and Montparnasse. All of them meticulously constructed cities of the dead, but none of these compared to what lay in wait for me at Le Cimetière du Père Lachaise.

When I got off the Number 3 Gallieni-bound Metro at the Père Lachaise stop, the first thing I did was find a tabac shop where I could shell out ten francs for a *Plan Illustré du Père Lachaise*. I had never had to buy a map for a cemetery before. But, I knew the map was necessary because the cemetery was so massive and contained so much to see. It was going to be like a treasure hunt—searching out the tombeaus of so many artists—painters, musicians, singers, dancers, actors and writers. I had an idea of *who* this place held and *what* I was looking for as I entered the cemetery through Avenue Principale and unfolded the map and scanned all the names. But, once deep inside among the ville of granite and marble, it felt as if I was the one being held. Like I was embraced by ineluctable beatitudes making me feel too insignificant to understand what lives they represented. However, I never hesitated. I knew I could get some answers here.

Let me start by saying I spent nearly an entire day—eight hours or more—visiting, meditating, and observing and jotting down my observations at Père Lachaise. I saw some crazy shit. At one point, while I was sitting on a bench contemplating the biographies of some of the artists who I had just seen, I noticed a French family plucking snails off tombs in a particularly old area of the cemetery where the granite headstones were all black and the names of who they held were inscrutable. There were three of them. A father and his two red-haired, pig-tail wearing daughters. When they saw me intently watching what they were doing, the father smiled at me and in French said something to the effect that these snails were good eating. Not as good as the escargots of Bourgogne, but tasty nonetheless. Sure, he spoke too rapidly for me to understand and used words that I did not know, but for some reason I had a strong idea of what he was telling me and I thought to myself how delightful it must be to pluck a snail off, let's say, Balzac's tombstone and to then eat it later with a good bottle of good French wine!! Marvelous! As if one were ingesting a part of Balzac himself. A lot like holy communion in a way. I smiled back at the man and answered his comments to me by saying "*Bon appetit.*" His two daughters laughed and waved good-bye swinging their pails of snails gaily as they skipped away.

The other thing that was clear to me was that this place was *alive*. What I mean by this is that at the typical cemetery there is an undeniable morose *finality* that surrounds each plot and tomb. Here, at Père Lachaise, like the snail picking I observed there was a lot of activity going on. I'm not just talking about the omnipresent hippies and loafers rocking back to and fro on Jim Morrison's gravesite while listening to *I'm a Spy* and lighting joints. I mean people sitting around Piaf's tomb holding serious conversations about her voice and music. Others bringing extraordinary floral bouquets to place on Chopin's tomb. All the lesbians and would-be lesbians stopping to place a rock on the shared tomb of Gertrude Stein and her lover, Alice B. Toklas—the first truly out couple of this century. Stein was one whom dubbed those of the lost generation the *Lost Generation* and who wrote *Three Portraits of Painters* (Cezanne, Matisse, Picasso) which I read and reread and re-reread and had an idea that she was clearly expressing something. However, like very many others before me I did not come to know what it was that she was clearly expressing. Thank you though for *The Autobiography of Alice B. Toklas*. A classic.

There was Oscar Wilde. People (men and women) had donned bright, red lipstick and then kissed his magnificent tomb for most of the Twentieth Century. So much so that the cemetery caretakers would have to rinse off all the red lips that clung to the granite tomb whenever the lips began to eclipse the tomb itself. There was a definite buzz around his tomb and groups of people were gathered around it busy talking to one another, taking time out once in a while to place another kiss. I had no lipstick and even if I had, I probably would have passed on continuing this tradition. Instead, I viewed Wilde from every vantage point until I reached the back side of the tomb and found this inscription:

> *And alien tears will fill for him*
> *Pity's long-broken urn,*
> *For his mourners will be outcast men,*
> *And outcasts always mourn.*

These lines were taken from his poem, *The Ballad of Reading Gaol* which he had started while doing time at His Majesty's prison at Reading in Berkshire, England. Wilde had been sentenced for two years of hard labor for sexual deviation or whatever ridiculous trumped up charge they came up with to silence him. But, this particular verse of his poem had taken on a life unto itself as Wilde's tomb glistened in the sun with the red lips of hundreds of those who still mourn and long for him.

Just by looking at the people gathered at his tomb it was clear that these were not just some casual fans who had read *The Importance of Being Earnest* in an English literature class of long ago, but were rather outcasts or social misfits who probably had no real jobs and drifted along in their lives on the promise of following their art whatever that was. Wilde was their patron saint. His tomb was alive for them and served as a beacon that called to task each of their subsequent generations as well. I felt at times that it was actually smiling at me. When I turned my back on the tomb to leave and had walked about twenty meters away, I had the very peculiar sensation that I was being laughed at. I stopped and looked back at Wilde and now the hundreds of red lips appeared as hundreds of red eyes and I felt I was locked in a staring match where it was simply impossible for me to win. I must have been hypnotized for a minute or two, and then finally forced myself to look away. I walked away with long, hard strides, and although I still felt that I was being laughed at, I did not turnaround for fear of what the tomb had become next.

Coming then face-to-face where Proust lay at rest, I knew I was now *officially* concluding the Proustian moment that had resuscitated me when Land re-emerged into my life in New Orleans. No one else was near Proust and that was odd because like I said this place was alive with people running around, roaming back and forth and dreaming with each artist. But, Proust was alone as if waiting for my arrival. I stood above him—above his shiny black marble tomb that was so shiny that I could clearly see my own face looking back at me when I looked down into it. I noticed a lone flower laying atop his tomb with each of its petals torn off and

spread in a semi-circle around the stem. Each petal
was perfectly spaced. Each equidistant from the
other. It was remarkable and I managed to position
my face's reflection upon the tomb in such a way
that the petals formed a crest around it. I stood
there for a few minutes imbued with the image of
my crowned face looking up at me and I was moved
to confess. I had never read Proust. I bullshitted
Land all those times when he would bring up some
reference to him. And although Land knew I was
bullshitting him, he never said a thing about it. I
appreciated that because Proust's seminal
Remembrance of Things Past consisted of six
volumes which *no one* reads anymore. I didn't
want to admit to being lumped in with those
nobodies. Each volume was several hundred pages
long creating a complete opus that was thousands
and thousands of pages long.

Although I hadn't read Proust, I knew of
him and of the famous dueling story that I related
earlier, and I did have an intuitive idea of what
Proust's writing was like. I knew he created
delicious scenes of late Nineteenth Century Parisian
life with deft and descriptive cunning. More
interestingly, I had an idea now by standing at the
foot of his tomb *what* Proust himself was like.
Small in stature, sickly. Probably effeminate, but so
tuned into where he was—the time in which he
lived. He imagined a grandiose life that he may
have also instinctively replicated in his own
everyday life so much so that soon the line between
the real and the imagined blurred. It was all art. All
his real life. And then he died before the last three
volumes of *Remembrance of Things Past* were ever
published.

If I had come to Père Lachaise six or seven years ago, I probably would have just gone to Jim Morrison's tomb, paid my respects and left. But, I was not that cat anymore and was instead looking for something more because as I said I had an idea *who* was here. And who was here were all artists of all types from all walks of life. So, I began first with the fine arts. Those who had brushed oils on canvases or panels or wood to create lasting, timeless images. David, Gericault, Delacroix, Gros, Daumier, Corot, Caillebotte, Seurat, Pissaro, Laurencin, Ingres, Modigliani, Ernst and Bellmer. I sought them all out and connected each with a work of theirs that I had seen at either the Louvre, or the Musées l'Orangerie, d'Orsay and National d'Art Moderne. Next, I went after the musicians and singers who either had composed or sung songs still played over the air and readily downloadable on-line today. Bizet, Rossini, Paulenc, Bellini, Chopin (his body is here, but his heart was taken back to Poland), Piaf, Callas (though her ashes are here, her heart was lofted into the Adriatic) and Morrison. Then, I turned to those who were performers and acted or danced. Yves Montand/Simone Signoret, Sarah Bernhardt and Isadora Duncan. Finally, I went after those who wrote plays, books, epics and kept the pulse of the society of their day. Apollinaire, Balzac, Moliere, Stein, Wilde and Proust.

I used the map expertly to orient myself and go from tomb to tomb from painter to writer to singer and back until I was exhausted and could go on no more. It was beyond words and I admit I failed to locate Richard Wright. That frustrated me. He didn't have a mausoleum and because he was cremated his remains were stacked locker-room style along the walls around the columbarium. I went to the exact area of the wall where my map indicated Wright's remains had been encased behind stone. But, as I scanned the wall reading all the names, there was no Richard Wright. This really bothered me. The author of *Native Son* died and was cremated along with a copy of his *Black Boy* in Paris. A bittersweet ending on so many levels. Too numerous for me to even *attempt* getting into. An American in self-imposed exile, and look at this—he got lumped alongside ordinary Frenchmen for eternity. Who let this screw-up slip by?

Although, I didn't find Wright, I knew his story and it was from his story that I started to make connections with the other artists' stories that were at Père Lachaise. The nexus between their artistry and their self-exile, banishment or their premature, self-wrought deaths. The Americans that were here all share a common thread. Jim Morrison dead at twenty-seven, fat, and found in a tub in a Paris apartment after already having faced charges of indecent exposure in the States and escaping to Paris to record his own *American Prayer*. Isadora Duncan the San Franciscan who danced barefoot and lived large, who left behind the criticism of the States in order to be understood in Europe, but whose shawl got caught in the spokes of her Bugatti and she was choked to death while living in Paris. To add another wrinkle in her tragedy, legend has it that Duncan had exclaimed, *"Adieu, mes amis, je vais à la gloire,"* right when the Bugatti pulled out of her driveway. Stein, of course, was one of the first expats who hosted the likes of Pound, Eliot and Hemingway and Picasso, Matisse and Man Ray at her apartment. She was there to be free and live with Alice B. Toklas away from the puritanical repression and crass public opinion of the States. She even continued to live in Paris during the Nazi occupation and died there shortly after the war. And Wright, a black man who at one time married a white woman and who had homosexual tendencies. Nothing more needs to be said. Died in 1960 while living in Paris since after the end of World War II.

All four of these one-time Americans were here because of self-imposed exile or as a result of some kind of banishment or unacceptance they endured while in the States. Add to the mix, Wilde, a Brit in self-imposed exile/banishment. The turbulent personal tragedy of the American-born Greek Callas and the desperate anguish the Polish Chopin went through with his battle with TB. [Let me add to the story of Chopin one of my own. I may not have known the Schumann piece that Land had so perfectly identified that day in Gen's apartment in New Orleans, but I do know Chopin's Nocturne in E Flat Major because the last time I ever cried in a movie was when I heard this delicate piano piece played in the lachrymal scene. Without the piece, the scene would have probably just been another trite depiction of redemption between two adversaries brought together at the end of a film. With the piece, the scene became transcendental and unforgettable. I bought the soundtrack next day.] The madness of Modigliani who finally succumbed to alcoholism and TB at the age of thirty-five, and the day after his death his very pregnant girlfriend jumped out of their apartment window killing herself and their unborn child.

The only French artist here that I could identify as sharing the same masochistic connection between his humanity and his art was Gros who committed suicide after his work fell into obscurity once he switched to a Neo-Classical style that was no longer well received in post-Napoleonic France. But, it is readily apparent how Gros' story differs. He had at one time had it all as Napoleon's official war painter, but as the times changed, his painting did as well and when it was no longer so lavishly received he did himself in. Thus, his doom arose not because of his status as an outsider in his own country or because of his failure to exorcise personal demons, but rather as the result of not being able to stand the thought that public acclaim had abandoned him after sustaining him for so long.

All the artists that I connected—Morrison, Duncan, Stein, Wright, Wilde, Callas, Chopin, and Modigliani—these were essentially foreigners drawn to the Parisian cityscape where their contributions to the arts met their swan songs. What was it then about the connection between great art and the humanity behind the person that created that art? That was what I was hoping to find when I went into Père Lachaise. The answer disappointed me because it was too obvious. The notion of the *tortured artist* really is a truism. Pure artistry—the kind that is on par with genius—finds its roots embedded in some instability, noncomformity, physical or mental deficiency in the heart or body of the artist. So, I may be a lost cause because I lack these hallmarks. I am very much stable and a conformist because I have grown to realize these attributes greatly enhance the monetary quality of our lives in the long run. I have also been erroneously waiting for some kind of epiphany to hit me on the head when really that epiphany should have come out from inside of me like a sunburst long ago. But, try as I have, I do not have the extremist streak in me to push me to the brink of consciousness where I can bring forth into this world a story for all time. Nor do I have the luxury of self-imposed exile. I've been *pretending* to be some kind of expat here. How pathetic! Of course, I would never be able to really do it. I wouldn't survive. You think I could hang around in the Jardin du Luxembourg strangling pigeons for food à la Hemingway in the 1920s? I'm a farce. But, I write nonetheless.

II

Sitting here at Les Deux Magots, I can at last put in writing a narrative spurred by the episodes of the last six months, but borne out of the coping of nearly twenty-six years of life in America. However, a trio of Algerians on my left are gesticulating so wildly with their hands and shoulders that it throws off my concentration. The seemingly endless stream of braless Parisian women—breasts all over the place as they walk hurriedly along St. Germain doesn't help either. When I haven't been in the mood to play the expat American, I've tried to masquerade around the city as a local speaking as little English as possible. Today is one of those days. So, when I have been approached by *les Americains* who mistake me as one of their own and speak English with me, I snort at them and walk on by. They stand out big time with their agonizing loudness and desire to have everyone within a five meter radius hear all their problems. They remind me of all the frantic, nonsensical chatter of home, so I make it a point to hide any hint of my Americaness in an attempt to pass by undetected by them.

No sooner have I written this than this bird on my left says to me, "Are you actually trying to write here?"
I glance to my left. The way the chairs at the cafés and brasseries in Paris are laid out is worth mentioning. All the typically wicker-like chairs are lined up in horizontal rows. No two seats face each other and instead, they each face outward to the street. It's striking. As if the café thrusts out and makes its seated patrons externalize with the world

passing before them. So, on my left there is a table and on the other side sits this chick. Probably mid to late twenties. With sunny bleached, brown-rooted, shortly cut hair. Big brown eyes and lovely bare legs that are crossed at the ankles.

"Is it that obvious that I speak English?" I ask.

"I can see that you are writing in English, so you must certainly speak it."

All of a sudden I become self-conscious of my notepad which lays open on my table for all onlookers. I flip the pad over and hide my words.

"Oh, don't mind me." She says.

"No, it's not you. I just need a break." I pick up on her clipped British accent.

"Are you British?" I ask.

"Yes and no. My mother is English, but my father is Russian. They live here in Paris."

"So, did you grow up here?"

"Yes, but I went to university in England. You must be American?"

Like I said, today, I was playing the role of the Parisian local, so I want to continue with this and concoct some story about being born in Paris and only being educated in New York. But, I don't have the energy to make this put-on stick.

"Yeah, I'm from L.A."

"*Los Angeleez*, is it?"

"I like the way you said that."

"And what is it that you are writing while you sit alone and drink your coffee?"

"Hahaha! Are you always this straight to the point??"

"Yes and is it that funny?"

"O.K. I see it's your style not to pull any punches."

"Naturally. And yours?"

"My style??"

"Yes."

"Uh, you can say that I am more of a bullshit artist."

"A bullshit artist? That's quite a style. So, what are you writing *Mr. Bullshit Artist?*"

Who does this bird think she is and who does she think she is talking too? I'm put on the defensive here and wish I had not taken her bait in the first place. But, she clearly knows how to manipulate men with her sex appeal and wordplay, and I'm in too deep now to back out.

"Well, if you must know—I am writing what may turn out to be the clichéd Great American Novel," I start.

She smiles.

"Quite ambitious, aren't we?" She answers.

"Uh, right."

"So, what's it about? Clichés, then?"

"Good one," I laugh, again taken aback, but at the same time I am bewitched by her needling. "What's it about…"

"That's what I asked, yeah?"

"That requires some thought."

"You don't know?"

"No, I do. Uh, it's about….about friendship. I guess."

"Really?? You don't seem too sure."

"I've just started. Writing. I'm putting down various sketches that have been running around in my head. I'll flesh out the story later."

"Hmmm." She murmurs into her coffee cup.

"What is it?" I ask.

"Nothing, really. You must know then the significance of where you are sitting and writing."

"Tell me please." I say as I turn my chair to the left and face her.

"No, no, no! You mustn't do that."

"What—oh, the chair. What's wrong?"

"You'll disturb the order of things. Keep your chair facing out and just turn your body toward me if you'd like to get close." She says.

Man, is this bird a coy one! She has to be teasing me. *Don't turn my chair towards her*? O.K. I'll do as she asks. I turn my chair back to its original position and it once again fronts the street.

"Better?" I ask.

"Oh, yes. As I was saying, you have chosen a very apropos place to write. This café was the setting for Brett Ashley's dalliances in *The Sun Also Rises*."

"Oh, this is it?" I ask feigning ignorance. I know this was the place. But, I too am in the mood now for running some game in the hope that it may lead to a dalliance of our own. I then throw out something that may just pique her interest in me. "I heard Hemingway wrote the first draft of that book in a sprint of only six weeks."

"You heard? From whom?"

"Er—read. I read it somewhere."

"Interesting."

"Why's that?"

"That you read too…" She bats her lashes at me so that it's clear that I know she's having fun with me.

"Yeah, well, it's something that I unfortunately picked up along the way," I say but I am annoyed at her snobbery. I'm not used to being played around like this by some stranger—let alone some bleached blonde.

"So, let's see if I have listened to you correctly. You are an American bullshit artist from *Los Angeleez* who both reads and writes?"

"*In toto*."

"And uses Latin too. Impressive."

"I'm glad you approve."

"Naturally."

"So, what's your story?"

"That we don't have time for, I'm afraid."

"Your name, then?"

"Marina."

"Marina, can you at least tell me what you do in Paris?"

"I suppose I can concede that to you as well."

"I'd really appreciate any charity you could throw my way."

"You could say I'm an art bullshitter, so we are very closely related you and I!" She laughs. I follow her lead.

"What? Are you an art critic or something?"

"I teach art history at Ecole National Superieure des Beux Arts—it's just up the street behind us."

"Ecole National, blah-blah-blah??"

"I see you've obviously heard of it then."

"A teacher, huh? That figures."

"And why is that?"

"The way you picked me apart with your questions—I felt like I was in school or something. So, the fact you are a teacher makes sense now."

"I assure you my students are never picked apart."

"Oh, right. You just go after unsuspecting strangers." I laugh again. But, she doesn't laugh and goes on drinking her coffee saying nothing. I'm determined, however, to keep things rolling.

"So, what artistic periods do you teach?"

"Fifteenth Century through early Twentieth Century European art."

"You must thrive here with all the abundance of art museums. It must be fun teaching in Paris. Which museum do you recommend I see?"

"Definitely go to the d'Orsay. One of the world's finest Impressionist collections."

"I've already gone. The space they use—it used to be an old train station, right?"

"That is correct. Did you go all the way to the very top of the museum?"

"Uh, yeah, I went everywhere."

"The reason I ask is that many tourists don't make it all the way to the top floor because the lower floors have so much to see and take up so much time. The top floor, however, has all the classics. The Renoirs, Cezannes, Van Goghs, Manets, and Monets. Did you see *Le Dejeuner sur l'herb* by Manet?? An important painting that represents the bridge into the Impressionist movement."

"Yeah, yeah. I saw it. Great painting. He's not buried at Père Lachaise?"

"No, I don't think so."

"I saw Renoir at Cimetière du Montmartre."

"You like visiting artists' graves, do you?"

"Uh, no—I just happened to have seen a bunch of them while, uh, looking around here and there…"

"Hmmmmm…" She thinks for a second. "I know Manet died in Paris, but don't know where he was buried. Perhaps in some family plot."

"You're probably right. Or in some cathedral."

"Well, what did you think of the painting?"

"*Le Dejeuner?*"

"Yes."

"Ummm…," I gotta make this good if I'm gonna have any chance in getting in her pants. "I liked his liberal use of the green and black colors. The picnic setting in the woods with two men in black and two women—one in the foreground who was nude and one just barely clothed in the back of the painting. A sort of bohemia. It worked very well to draw you in and then you realize the impact of the painting."

"And what's that?"

"For me—it was the woman in the foreground who sets it off—and not because she was nude—but because of the look of *bemusement* on her face. You know as she sits in a crouch with one bare leg bent where her elbow rests and in turn her elbow props up her chin. She looks eye-to-eye with you as if asking in a sarcastic manner, *Are you really enjoying this*? And that's the impact—the viewer becomes aware of his intrusion into this idyllic, private scene."

"Perceptive, aren't you? You retained all that?"

Ah, I got her where I want her. Now, I can take the upper hand and play with her.

"You know, I also remember Manet's *Olympia* in the d'Orsay. The face of that nubile young *fille* who reclines on huge, white square pillows with a pink hyacinth in her hair and some kind of black shoelace collar around her neck—her face is very similar to that woman's face in *Le Dejeuner*. It's almost as if Manet is poking fun of Titian's hallowed *Venus de Urbino*, isn't it?"

"Are you asking me or telling me?"

"Asking."

"You have had training, I suppose. I won't fall for your game."

"What!" I crack up. "I'm just asking you. I know nothing about art—except the art of bullshitting as I mentioned to you!"

"I'm not sure your musings on Manet were bullshit. I have a knack for picking up on those sorts of things. Tell me, sir, have you been to the Musée Picasso?"

"No, should I go?"

"I think you would be interested in seeing Picasso's interpretation of *Le Dejeuner*."

"Picasso *covers* Manet??!! This I have to see."

"You could say it like that if you wish." And she says it with a haughtiness that I relish. "You'll be able to see how Picasso takes Manet's work and interprets it with his own artistry. That's when I say art becomes alive."

"And when is that again?"

"When we, as the viewer, understand how the ideas being reflected between two different artists leads to the creation of something new."

"You must be an amazing teacher."

She doubles over in laughter.

"I'm a bit of a maverick, really. You could say some don't appreciate all I have to say. But, it's all good fun just the same. Here, in Paris, I am spoiled. A pity for you though."

"Why?"

"For someone who appreciates art, you don't have much in America, do you now? Who looks at an American picture, you know?"

"Haven't you see Whistler's *Mother of the Artist* in the d'Orsay?"

"Come, come. That convinces me of nothing. Its artistry pales in comparison with all that hangs around it."

"Cassatt, Sargent?"

"Cassatt is essentially a Frenchwoman—though born in the States—she moved to France, studied with Degas and died in France. Sargent—he was born to American expatriate parents in Florence and settled in London where he painted until his death. So, you see the two were not really American."

"Well, what is American then?"

"Being *reared* in America."

"Being reared in America," I repeat. That's kind of a simplistic way of looking at what it means to be an American. But, I don't challenge her on this.

I'm more interested to see what she knows about other American artists.

"Edward Hopper, Jackson Pollock, Franz Kline, Mark Rothko, Jasper Johns, Warhol, Lichenstein and Basquiat—and what do you think of them?" I ask confident that this barrage of American artists will put her into her place and show her a thing or two about the pitfalls of so recklessly dismissing the art of an entire country.

"There's a mouthful!!"

Aha! I got her now!

"Let's start with Pollock, Kline and Rothko—that's that New York abstract expressionist movement which I absolutely detest. Large canvases of nothingness really. This movement lent itself to being the darling of critics who at that time had their own social axe to grind and so made the nothingness credible as some kind of art. Warhol, Lichenstein, Johns and Basquiat? Gimmicky nonsense. Conveniently called *pop art* when there's nothing popular about it. You think the masses understand them? Hopper—there's promise. I will say his paintings are worth looking at—the ones I've seen anyway. I think they speak volumes about the banality and loneliness of American society."

Ding-dong.

"Cat got your tongue?" She says.

"Ou—ouch." I say.

"It's the truth."

"It's the way you see things."

"Whatever you say."

"Have you been to the Whitney Museum of American Art?"

"In New York?"

"Yes."

"No."

"You should definitely go and be exposed to some things."

"I've never been to the States."

"Really? I find that hard to believe."

"Another truth."

"Do you want to go?"

"No, not really—well, maybe, New York City, I suppose. Greenwich Village and Soho are nice from what I hear."

"It's not what you think it is—the Village and Soho."

"And what do I think it is?"

"Probably, a hotbed of artists milling around. Interfacing, writing and painting. In the Village, there's zero authentic artistic activity outside of the usual university nonsense. Instead, what you have now is a bunch of huddled NYU students and wannabe NYU students selling grass and dressing in beige and off-green camflouage—you know, it's funny, somewhere along the line camouflage jackets and pants with combat boots became the apparel of choice for counterculture American youth and stoners in the 1990s. At least, the hippies of the Sixties were more pleasing visually, you know what I'm saying?"

"Thanks for that aside."

"Sorry—just my own two cents. Soho too is just a fancy address now. Swanky restaurants and lousy galleries. But, you should still go to New York to see the city. It makes a serious first impression."

"Hmmm, I'm sorry to say that I'm just not sold on America."

"Why the reluctance to go?"

"From where I sit here in Europe—be it England, France or Italy—all three of which I have spent a considerable extent of time—America comes across as a colossus made of dollars, noisiness and violence. It's not something high on my list to experience first hand."

"Ummm…"

"What I mean is—it is perceived here as a place where there's incessant traffic of money, guns, people and so on. School kids shooting one another, drive-by shootings and people just generally going *postal*—isn't it called that?"

"Uh, yeah."

"I then hear you have New York City and then you have the rest of America which is utterly dissimilar. My friend visited Oklahoma on business, he said the men there actually wore cowboy hats! He couldn't believe it."

"You just gotta realize it's a big country. Each area has its own peculiarities as well as charm. With New York, it is easy to see why Europeans would like it."

"And why is that?"

"Because it's more European than any other American city with its subway and great museums and cultural events. But, it's unfair to use New York as the yardstick by which to judge the rest of the country. There's a lot out there—Miami, New Orleans, Chicago, St. Louis, L.A., Seattle, San Francisco—I mean there's *a lot* out there. You should go and see it for yourself before you make any judgments."

"O.K., O.K. I didn't mean to upset you. I was just speaking my mind."

"I'm not upset at all. I agree that America gets bogged down with all sorts of craziness which the media feeds off on and bombards the public with and the advertisers then cash in on the craziness and on and on. The dollars and violence have dominated life for the last two decades. That's true. But, maybe things will change."

"I doubt that," She giggles and takes a last drink from her coffee cup. "As long as the money train continues, things will not change. That's for certain."

"I guess you're probably right. I just like to think that I *still* live in the best place on earth, you know?"

"It's pretty to think so."

I flip my notebook open and jot down something that suddenly pops into my mind. I can see her watching me from the corner of my eye.

"Do you like Oscar Wilde?" She asks.

I flip my notebook back down. I don't know where this question suddenly comes from, so I look at her confused.

"Since you fancy yourself a writer and are interested in the final resting places of artists, I thought you might be interested in knowing that Oscar Wilde died around the corner from here."

"Really? I just saw his tomb the other day and that was an experience."

"I'm sure it was. He died at L'Hotel which is located on 13 Rue des Beux Arts. Just walk up Rue Bonaparte which is directly behind the café and it's the third street on your right. You can go inside the piano bar, have a drink, and ask the concierge to show you Wilde's room. It's a very charming hotel. Mick Jagger stays there when he comes to Paris."

"Yeah, I will definitely go. Would you like to join me for a drink there?"

"I'm actually late for an engagement. My husband and I are attending a gallery opening tonight."

"Oh." It was definitely worth the shot.

"It's been delightful chatting with you. You definitely held your own."

"Oh," I say again. Still shocked that such a firecracker could already be tied down by some cat. I bet the guy is loaded. That's the only way. And what a hypocrite she is then for bagging on America for its money-grubbing. "Good talking to you too. Have a good one."

She stands and gathers up her things.

"Enjoy your stay in Paris," She says as she extends her hand to me. I don't stand, and instead, shake her hand while still seated. That's my way of looking like that I did not completely fall for her game. On the other hand, it probably makes me look like a sore loser. Que sera sera.

I get back to my writing and squeeze out some more lines as I try to shake out the memory of the hellcat, art history teacher who was as breathtaking as she was a bitch. I finish up my coffee and check my watch. I am meeting Sanders later today for dinner and I have about two more hours to kill before then. I decide it's time to leave Les Deux Magots and check out L'Hotel. I motion the waiter over and ask for the bill by saying with a horrible American accent, "*le addition s'il vous plait*." The trio of Algerians on my right are still bullshitting loudly, but I notice that now a gaggle of American teenage girls—probably students—have taken seats next to the Algerians. Though I try hard to ignore the inevitable, I can't resist in keeping an eye and an ear on the contact between the two groups. One of the Algerians who has to be close to forty years old starts *hitting* on the girls with lines like "*Are you seleepy? Come lay your head over eeer.*" And he pats his shoulder and motions one of the girls over. The girls all giggle and are embarrassed. Another one of the Algerians then asks the girls where they are from. The girls say they are from Washington D.C. One of the girls then takes the lead and asks this Algerian where *he* is from because his swarthy complexion distinguishes him from the typical Frenchmen in the girls' eyes. He answers that he is from Africa. The girls don't believe it and then one of them says, *"So, are you half black??"* The Algerian is stunned and doesn't say a word. His compatriots laugh. My face flushes read in humiliation as if I as an American am also responsible for the girls' ignorance. I curse the waiter under my breath for taking so long in bringing out the bill. I think to myself that the concept of the *ugly* American is a very real one. But, despite France's jealous guarding of its language and culture, the Americanization of Paris is blatant. McDonald's golden arches dot each boulevard and Metro station. American celebrities are on the covers of every French version of American magazines. There's even a Disneyland here that is raking in the francs. The dumbing-down sensationalism that America so excels at is definitely being exported to Europe. But, I've read that there's actually an extremist group in France dedicated to stopping the influx of Americana into France. It has even bombed a couple of McDonald's in the countryside and has endeared itself as a modern day Robin Hood to the French public. *C'est tres intérresante.*

I finally get my tab and pay it off quickly leaving two francs for the waiter as tip. I head up Rue Bonaparte in search of the hotel where Wilde spent his last night on earth. Marina gave very accurate directions. I find Rue Beux Arts and turn right into it and look for number 13. At first I walk the entire length of the road because I don't see any number 13. I double back and carefully go from building to building looking for number 13. To my disappointment, I find L'Hotel hidden under layers of scaffold and ripped apart drywall and plaster. The only thing intact on the building is the "13" proudly displayed in bronze lettering and underneath it is a circular plaque also in bronze with an engraving of Wilde stating his name and the years of his life, 1854-1900. Construction workers trudge in and out of the entrance and I get on my tiptoes in order to steal a glance through a window. I can see the piano bar area that Marina talked about. However, as I struggle with my toes in order to get a better look, one of the construction workers yells at me in French to get out of his way. I give him a dirty look and then lower myself down and leave deeply bummed at the realization that there's nothing sacred. Not even in Paris. Everything at some point gets torn down and put up again, ostensibly better and improved and more user friendly or wheelchair accessible.

I bring out my Metro map and look for the nearest station. I have no choice but to walk back down Rue Bonaparte and go to the St. Germain des Prés station. I need to get to the ritzy George V area where I'm meeting Sanders, so I ride the Metro from St. Germain for only two stops east to St. Michel where I change trains and take the number 4 Metro to Chatelet. From Chatelet, I have a linear journey on the number 1 Metro to George V. It is about five minutes to six and I am meeting Sanders at 6:30 at a restaurant called Chez André located on 12 Rue Marbeuf. I walk down Avenue George V and pass fancy jewelers and designer stores until I hit Rue Marbeuf where I make a left and walk up until I find the restaurant. To my surprise, Sanders is already seated on an outside table on the street. He waves at me when he sees me approaching in the distance.

"You're here early," I say when I reach the table.

"Slow day. Have some wine. I ordered a 1997 bottle of Chateau Haut-Piquant from Lussac-St. Émilion. Very good." He pours me a glass.

"*A votre santé*," I say as I take a sip. Nice.

"So, what did you do today, Tal?"

"I just walked around some neighborhoods. Ended up chatting with a chick while at a café for a bit."

"Oh, yeah? French?"

"Nah—British and Russian. Married too."

"Going after married women are we now?" Sanders says with a chuckle.

"She actually initiated the conversation by first talking to me. I was busy drinking my coffee and watching the street action."

Sanders has no idea that I am doing some writing here. I have my notepad and pen in a little pack that I also carry my camera in. He wouldn't understand.

"Really? The old Tal presence still makes the girls take notice!"

"I wish." I laugh.

"What do you mean? I always remember seeing you on campus with a couple of chicks hanging off you. You were like a babe magnet. You had that suede fringe jacket that just beamed in the chicks!"

"Sanders—you're crazy! I had my fun, you know. But, I was no babe magnet. All the hot chicks went to the frat parties anyway—that's where you came in."

"Whatever. I know you and your buddy Land had some big shindigs as well. Word got around campus about you two."

"Exaggerations."

"By the way, what's up with Land now? I always like to hear about what happened to guys from school. Especially, some guy like Land, it's interesting to know what he did after graduation."

"I, uh, I don't know what he's doing now. We sort of lost touch—you know how it goes."

"Lost touch? Wasn't he one of your best friends?"

I suck down more wine and try to tiptoe around the question.

"I did see him once when he came out to L.A., but after he left, I didn't hear from him. He did a lot of traveling. I'm sure he'll resurface."

"So, he didn't start working or go on to grad school?"

"Not to my knowledge. I think he told me that he did do some business ventures in Vegas out of all places but that didn't pan out, so he moved back East to stay with his folks for a bit."

"Huh."

"Yeah. I, uh, I've been bad about staying in touch with lots of people."

"Well, maybe you'll see him at our fifth year reunion."

"Yeah, maybe."

Luckily, I know that because Sanders and I had completely different groups of friends and none of my friends knew his friends that there's no way he knows anything about what has happened to Land and Gen. So, I don't feel bad about lying to Sanders. He doesn't need to know anything. We go ahead and order our food. Sanders does all the talking. He gets a couple of appetizers—escargots à la bourguignonne and quiche lorraine—which we share. For my entrée, I get the noisettes d'agneau while Sanders goes with the médaillons de veau.

"So, Tal...." Sanders has a mouthful of food. I wait until he swallows. "I gotta secret to tell you."

"About what?"

"Chicks."

"What about them?"

"I know where to find the most beautiful and horny girls in the world."

"I'm all ears, Sanders. Pray tell!"

"Like I said, buddy, this is between you and me. It goes no further than this table. I don't want word to get out. Next thing you know, you got all these Americans flying in looting the place."

"O.K., O.K. What you tell me will not go further than this table."

"Good." Sanders shovels down more food. I gobble up the lamb I ordered. It's creamy and delicious.

"Iceland." He says.

"What? All these chicks here in Paris and back in America and you gotta go to *Iceland*?" I ask.

"I'm tired of American chicks. They see me and all they see is money. I'm not saying I won't settle down with one, but whoever she is, she better be ready to sign a prenup. I'm out there busting my ass making a living and she'll be at the spa getting a manicure, pedicure, mud wrap—all that."

"Come on, you know there are chicks not like that."

"Not the kind that I want! I want *hot* chicks. A chick with her MBA won't be hot. Trust me. It just doesn't happen. If you want hot chicks in America, you're gonna pay for it—in one way or another—you gotta. That's the drill. I've seen it up close, Tal. I'm not just making all this up."

"So, what makes you so sure Icelandic girls are any different?"

"Ahhh. Thank you. Let me explain..." He takes a big gulp of his glass of Chateau Haut-Piquat. "The whole country has a population of about three hundred fifty thousand. Of that amount, two hundred seventy five thousand live in the capital—Reykjavik. Something like *forty percent* of the population is related to one another! You then have all these women with island fever! And these women are the most gorgeous women on earth! Naturally platinum blonde, blue-eyes, high cheekbones, sleek and smooth bodies. They are sick of seeing the same old Icelandic men, so they *crave* the exotic. Well, the American male is exotic to them!!"

"I'm listening—do they speak English?"

"Yeah, they speak English. They also have their own native tongue—Icelandic—which is actually the closest language to the old Norse language the Vikings used. I've been doing a lot of reading on the place so I know this, there is an Icelandic civic group which is responsible for creating new words into the Icelandic language."

"I don't get it."

"In order to preserve their language and prevent it from being mixed with English or French words, whenever something new comes along, for example, when the computer popped up, they didn't just adapt the English word *computer* into the Icelandic language. Instead, this group met and someone proposed a new Icelandic word to mean computer. The group then voted on adopting the new word, and then this word was introduced to the public. Can you believe that?"

"That is really fascinating. What is the Icelandic word for computer?"

"Who cares, Tal! The chicks there speak English!! Capeche?? That's all I'm concerned with!"

"Hahaha!! I don't know what I was saying!!"

"I also read a couple of other things about it. Like everything in the country from electricity to the pumping of water is based on steam energy. You see, the whole place sits on these big geothermal pools, so they tap into steam as the chief mode of power. As a result, there's almost zero pollution. The Icelandic government is even working with Daimler Benz to create the world's first steam based car engine!"

"Wow, man."

"But, back to the chicks. Incredible, Tal. I've seen pictures of them. You can lounge around at these hot pots as they call them—the public geothermal pools—during the day and then at night you party like animals. Downtown Reykjavik is so small, you can walk from club to club and there's no crime at all. Just the usual drunken stupidity and that's it! The women travel in packs, so there's plenty to go around. You just open your mouth and they can tell you're American and then, my man, you are in like Flynn! Especially someone who looks like you—you could make a killing over there! But, like I said, don't say anything about it to anyone when you go back to L.A."

"You've really done your homework, Sanders."

"I'm planning a trip the weekend from next. It is a stone's throw from Paris—a couple of hours northwest. I'm staying at a place called the Hotel Borg which is smack in the middle of downtown Reykjavik."

"Going by yourself?"

"Oh, yeah. I'm not in the mood of sharing this with anyone until I first have experienced it for myself."

"That's definitely another hot tip you've given me."

"Keep it under your hat for now. I'll let you know how it goes!"

"Well, Sanders," I say as I pick up my wine glass. "Raise a glass and let me toast." Sanders brings up his glass. "Here's to French wine and Icelandic women, myrrh and laughter—sermons and soda-water the day after!" We then bang glasses and drink.

"That was a good one, Tal. You always amaze me with the way you speak."

"The way I speak?"

"Yeah, I mean, you always refer to things and speak in such a way that I have to really *think* to understand what you mean."

"Sanders that's the wine in you talking. Also, I feel the same way when you talk about business and discuss the bull and the bear. I gotta think real hard to follow you."

"Nah, that's different though. Like the toast you just gave, did you just make that up on the spot? I could never ever talk like that."

"You got me, man. That wasn't mine. That's from Byron's *Don Juan*—I think. I just switched a few words to make it apply to our own conversation."

"That's what I mean!! *Byron*?? I don't even think I know who that is and I *should* know. You understand now what I'm saying?"

"Yeah. I think I do."

"I think I'm a bit a jealous of you, Tal."

I want to tell him, "Well, if you didn't just take all financing and accounting courses you coulda branched out and taken a course on English poets or the English literary tradition." But, really I think to myself, "*No, no, no, no, no!*" I don't need to hear this now. I want to be like *you*, Sanders. Please don't get all goofy on me. I want what you have going for you. I don't need you out of all people planting any doubts in my convoluted brain. Get a hold of yourself! So, what if I throw out some esoteric references once in a while that you fancy? I have nothing coming to me, man.

"Sanders, I'm pretty sure that's not the case."

"Well, I don't like not knowing—pardon the double negative there—certain things you just casually say which really I should know. We went to the same college after all."

"O.K. I see what you mean."

"I don't know. Maybe it's just regrets I have."

"Regrets?"

"Yeah, you know, I could have done some different things when still in school, but each year from freshman to senior year was pretty much the same experience for me. Not a whole lot of difference between them. When I graduated, it felt like I had just started school the day before. I didn't feel like I had come a long way."

"That's because you kicked some serious ass in school, man! Phi Beta Kappa! That's the toppermost of the toppermost. You didn't have to struggle like the rest of us. That's when you feel the years drag by."

"You think that's it?"

"Oh, yeah. Definitely." Of course I *don't*. But, I do not want to hear where Sanders is going with this. Sitting at this fine restaurant with good wine and food and generally adoring the sharing in a lifestyle experience that I would like for myself, I do not want Sanders to now start getting touchy feely and opening up to me about his *regrets*. I don't like it. It ruins everything that I have going for me at this moment.

"Hhhhmmm. I suppose that is another way of looking at it," Sanders says.

Please let the old Sanders come back to the table!

"Oh, it is, it is," I coo.

"Yeah, well, anyways, Tal, I *did* like the toast, buddy! Here's to Icelandic women again!" He raises his glass and I quickly grab mine and hit his.

"What about Prague? I hear the women there are incredible too," I ask after putting my glass back down. Let's move the conversation forward.

"If you had gone there about five years ago, the really hot ones were still there. But, now, the chicks have all been plundered. Most of the good ones go off to Vegas where they strip and make some money and then come back—others end up in Amsterdam or some place like that. Same thing with Budapest—I was just there two months ago. Nothing."

"Sanders, you've been on fire!"

"I love women, Tal, that's all. My whole goal in life is to make my money and have my fun too. The two go hand in hand for me. I'm not pushed by anything else."

We finish our meals and run through two bottles of the 1997 Chateau Haut-Piquat, Lussac Saint-Émillion. Scrumptious food. For dessert, we forego the crêpes or soufflés and instead opt for *eaux-de-vie*—distilled fruit brandy. There are numerous choices: Kirsch (black cherry), framboise (wild raspberries), poire William (Swiss cherry), calvados (apple), and marc (stems, pits, and skins of red grapes). However, Sanders bypasses all these choices in favor of the mirabelle eaux-de-vie which he tells me is distilled from yellow plums. The waitress comes out quickly with two short stem glasses. As I am smelling the drink and then bringing it up to my lips, Sanders tells me to wait. He gets the attention of our waitress and asks her to bring us something else. I don't pick up on what he's asked her, and he tells me again not to start drinking yet. The waitress then comes back with a small dish of lily white sugar cubes. Sanders takes one for himself and puts it into his drink. He directs me to do the same thing. Curious.

"What's this for?" I ask as I drop my sugar cube into my glass.

"The one thing that I've learned from the French while I've been here."

"I've never done this before, man."

"It's called a *canard*. Sip it slowly and stir every once a while to make sure the sugar dissolves completely. It's an old men's tradition."

I take a first sip. The drink is harsh, I can see why the sugar cube tradition started. A little sweetening definitely adds something to the experience.

"It's, uh, it's good," I say. "You see, you teach me something new each time, man!"

"Haha! Tal, this is what it's all about. Good food, wine, eaux-de-vie—after a hard day's work—and, of course, contemplating the Icelandic damsel."

"Mmmmmhmmmmm." I mutter.

"So, what are you going to do when you go back to L.A.?"

I put my glass down. I've been avoiding thinking about that.

"To be honest, I just don't know, Sanders."

"You still with that chick of yours?"

"I'm not sure about that either."

"Tal, come on, now. You're almost twenty-six! You're a bright guy. Time to get back into the game. Make a boat load of money! You're in California—look into all those dot com companies that are springing up all over the place! They need someone like you—young, good with words, smart. And now is the time to get in!! Who knows? In a year from now, those companies may all tank, so it's best to get in now, make some real coin and position yourself for your next big move before the dot coms go the way of the adding machine!"

"I don't know. I'm not good with computers."

"Who said anything about computers? All I'm saying is that I.T.—information technology is the way of the future. There's lots of money there and it is the smart, young people out there who are leading the way in making the exchange of ideas, goods, and information faster, cheaper and easier. You'd be a definite asset."

"I studied philosophy, man."

"So, what? You're a quick study and like I said you have a facility with words and could help with the organization and filling in the details of these companies. Just look into it. It's one option to consider."

"Thanks. I will."

"Look at your friend, Land, Tal. You don't want to end up like him, do you? Going backwards instead of moving forward?"

"Uh, yeah, well, I don't really know what he's up to now."

"I thought you said something about him moving back with his parents."

"Nah, what I meant, was that he went back East and was gonna stay with his parents until he, uhhh, until he made his next move…" Stupid. I don't know why I'm trying to clarify things on that matter. Let it go.

"O.K. Whatever. My point is what was the good of all of Land's social activity on campus if he couldn't channel it into something productive for himself? All the organizing he did on campus? I mean, I didn't really know the guy, but a good chunk of the campus saw the things he did. He, uh, took some petition out for that Indian dude in prison. Tried to get him a presidential pardon or something? Remember that?"

"Uh, yeah. That was for Leonard Peltier."

"Yeah, yeah, Peltier. Even though any reasonable person who knows the facts of that case would conclude Peltier did in fact kill those two FBI agents and deserves to be in jail, there was Land going right against that and doing a credible job too. I went to one of those rallies and he gave all these facts as he called them and conspiracy stuff, and though I didn't agree with him and thought he was completely out of line, I marveled at all the people who were hanging on his words and how he had such good leadership qualities."

Not to toot my own horn, but I had helped Land a lot in gathering those "facts" that we thought proved Peltier's innocence and warranted a reversal of the two life sentence terms that he currently is serving at Ft. Leavenworth Federal Penitentiary in Kansas. At the time, there was a President-elect and the old one was on his way out of office, so we knew the old one would now be utilizing his pardon power. So, Land and I and a few others banded together and started a petition drive on campus demanding that Peltier be given a pardon or at least that his case be reopened. I even sent a letter to

Peltier's attorney at the time, Bill Kunstler, setting out some new strategies for getting the public's attention on Peltier's plight and using them to help put pressure on the President. Kunstler sent me a handwritten letter back in which he called my letter to him "powerful" and added this: "*I've faxed it to the Prez.*" When I showed the handwritten note to Land his eyes lit up with real hope that we were making a difference. Nothing of course happened. Peltier is still in jail, and you know, I've never thought about him once in over four years until Sanders just brought him up. And about Sanders himself, it's funny that he says he was there in the crowd that day. He would then have had seen me as I was standing right next to Land during the whole thing. He must have missed me or maybe he saw me and didn't want to bring it up because he wanted to avoid talking *politics*. If so, that was a smart (and prescient) move on his part because if he had come up to me afterwards and challenged the "facts" about Peltier's innocence that Land had spoken of and which I had researched (I read Peter Matthiessen's *In the Spirit of Crazy Horse* among other things), we would surely have argued and that argument would surely have led to bad feelings and those bad feelings would never have cleared up and then he would have not unknowingly become the Anaïs Nin that he is today. Good logic, isn't it?

"Yeah, Land's a born leader," I say.
"But, despite all that talent, it seems he hasn't got involved with anything after leaving those college years behind. You see what I'm saying? There's a lesson to be learned there."
"And what's that?"

"Tal, from talking with you over the last couple of years, I know you think big like me and want the finer things in life. Now is the time to get it! When you go back you gotta really apply yourself and make it happen. America is still the only place where you can make things happen. Trust me. Working in France, man, my American work ethic runs circles around these guys. They probably resent it too, but I'm making money for them so even *they* realize they need me around. They also know they need me a helluva lot more than I need them. That's how it goes, so you need to apply yourself. The key to that though is *discipline*."

I hate *that* word. I tried and tried so hard when I was on my game in L.A. to be *that*—disciplined. That's where I bring up genetics again. Just when I'm being *that* and really moving forward and making something of myself, I manage to screw it up somehow. So, how can I maintain *that* while still being true to my intrinsic anti-centrist self?? That's the Sixty-Four Thousand Dollar question, Sanders. But, I'm not gonna tell *you* this.

"Sanders, you always make things so clear."
"That's my job—I look at the bottom line and figure out how best to get there. So, take my advice, Tal, get back in the game. No more sitting on the sidelines and watching the rest of us hoard slices out of the pie. There's room for you too, so get yourself in here and join us!"
"O.K. You convinced me. You're like Tony Robbins or something, man."
"Robbins has got nothing on me. I still enjoy actually working for my living. He just talks now and that's not a real job. So, here's to your future

success, Tal. Cheers." He raises his glass and I pick up mine and our glasses hit each other for the fourth time tonight. I finish the mirabelle eaux-de-vie and it explodes in my chest like a small fireball.

I find myself torn. I have come to Paris with the adamant desire to write something that I am compelled to write, but now I am once again being coaxed back into reality, to the real work that must be done by all responsible people. Sanders' words echo those that Land threw at me, except that Sanders is pushing me to the completely opposite side of the fence that Land had wanted. I feel paralyzed in making any decision of where to go and what to do. I watch Sanders take out his corporate platinum visa card to pay for our bill. It's beautiful. Shiny and whitish silver. It represents success and blares out "Doug Sanders" for all the world to behold. I thank him for the dinner and when I push my chair away from the table and slowly rise to my feet I find myself languid and in a dreamy state. I pick up my pack and then as we walk out of Chez André, I hear a familiar voice. A song wafts through the restaurant and I become still:

> *I'm the kind of people you can step on for a little while, but when I call it quits, baby, that's it.*
>
> *Yes, I'm the kind of person you can hurt once in a while, but crawling just ain't my style.*

I know this voice and I respond. Sanders walks ahead and does not turn around until he is about ten meters away and realizes that I am not behind him.

I motion him with my hands to wait where he is. When the song finishes, I am about to go inside the restaurant and ask who the singer is but then I know. I know her. Again, she brings to life words that move me as if I was meant to hear them precisely in this moment of my life. Another incredible urge comes over me. This time, it is to drop everything and devote myself to finding out where she lives in France and then to show up unannounced at her door pledging my servitude. I would do it too. That's how deep I dig this woman's artistry. She figured it all out and that took—*discipline*. Yes, that's it. It has to be. I've got something here. Now, if I can just remember this and hold on until I have a free moment where I can really meditate on it.

"Tal, is everything O.K.?"

Remember to remember this. Remember to remember this. I come to.

"Uh, yeah. Hold up." I jog to where Sanders is waiting. "I was just listening to something."

"The song?"

"Yeah, it brought back some memories."

"You sure it's not the eaux-de-vie and the all the wine you had?"

"You might be right on that account too, Sanders. Let's go."

As we walk up Avenue George V to the Metro station, I know now that I *must* finish what I've started. I've spent nearly two weeks in Paris and over the last couple of days I have finally done some real writing. I have to finish this. If I do not, the unresolved specter of those thoughts and moments already captured on paper will hound me forever. I must cast off the onus of my ego by finishing. This is a story that is about me and those people and things connected to my existence. I need to let go from the present and detach myself from those past experiences by breaking down my ego piece by piece and then channeling those thoughts into one corpus. That will be the only way that I can put these events and pulsars in my life behind me, so that I can turn back to the real world, to what must ultimately be done. And all this, will take serious discipline.

III

On one of my final afternoons in Paris, I stroll along the narrow corridors of the Rive Gauche district which is resplendent with all its art and sculpture galleries open and airy in full display. I can waltz in and out of the galleries and alleyways here lighting cigarettes for myself and for others who congregate outside enjoying the sunny weather. I could very easily get lost here and never go back to America. Wouldn't that be fantastic? To just walk towards the Seine with an ever quickening pace and then simply disappear among the throngs of people. I came here for a release and to write and to force myself to search for something as Land had. My thoughts turn to him. He had his own vision-quest and it took him all around America and then finally to a place one would least expect he'd find the answers he wanted. But, he *did*. His search was for something greater than himself.

Why haven't I followed what has happened to Land or Gen? Even if we weren't best friends any more when we met each other this second time around in our lives, we still have a past—a great history—with one another and that should have been able to withstand the nonsense that took place between us that day in the *Ghost in the Attic*. If I could talk to him now, I would ask for *his* pardon. Because as it is, I feel like I'm the one going back to America to start his sentence. Maybe it was about friendship? His attempt to reach out to me one last time by showing me what it really meant to do the *right* thing. Maybe it was. But, don't run off getting ready to cue in the Chopin just yet.

Although I realize in order to finish this story, I must cast off the onus of *my* ego, I still don't think I will be able to "get it" like Land does. This isn't about the redemption of yours truly. Not in this go around anyway.

But, what about Land? I can only say that before I left for Paris, a mutual friend of Land's and mine called to ask whether I had heard the news. I asked him what was going on and he said that the faces of Land Morales and Gen Klugman were splashed in the New York Times' *Nation* section along with a headline that read:

Native American Raskolnikov Turns
Himself in for Star-Spangled Bank Heist.

I snickered at this. Look how they marginalized him! How they slapped such a nice and tidy label on him and made a catchy headline out of it too! That was Land Morales they were talking about. You can't just force his life and times into a handy dandy sentence and then sell it to strangers! But, that's what the New York Times did. Bastards! Our friend was about to read portions of the article to me that he said contained quotes from Land and even a couple from Gen, but I stopped him and said that I didn't want to hear it. I could only imagine what Land had rattled off to the press that inspired the comparison of him to Dostoevsky's alter-ego. And poor, broken Gen. How awful for her and her family. It all washes out in the end, doesn't it? So, that's how it would really end for Land. All that fantastic, juiced-up life consigned to the interior of a box. Yet, a twinge of envy tweaks inside of me. Land will get out one day and what he will go through until he does get out—*that* will make him great. He'll be the one who has that bond with those artists that I wanted for myself. I know it sounds crazy, but I look at it like this. If he does get a lengthy sentence, the way he'll face prison will be like Rodin encountering a slab of bronze for the first time. He'll focus on some image in his mind's eye and then sculpt and labor and leave with something monumental accomplished. He'll pass his time, and then those of us who know him will be left in his wake as he soars to new heights of being when he gets back to the outside. He will proceed to self-actualize himself in a multi-dimensional manner that only a few people will ever be able to comprehend. I know this.

I am content to fill up one last afternoon reflecting and digesting my time here. I came here for a search, but unlike Land, I've never searched for anything outside of myself and it is the same with my search in Paris. All my ambling around Père Lachaise comparing notes between the artists there? That was about *me*. I have been desperately looking for a trace of the artist within. After all this ranting and rambling of being this and not *that*, here's Tal who has already admitted to playing *Let's pretend I'm an expat*, still trying to make sure that perhaps there may still be a little of something in *him*. Some little scrap of light that he could look upon until his eyes and heart and mind moisten to the point where he throbs with the lust to create some kind of *artistry*. And I had consciously already attempted this search once before when I went to Big Sur to chase Kerouac's ghost only to be rudely chased off myself. I have come to the conclusion after all of this that I am kidding myself. There is no shared link in my story and those artists whose lives I pondered from which I can plug into and create out of. I am neither black nor white, homosexual nor asexual, nor criminal or even someone of unparalleled wit and charm. I am *other* than black or white, homosexual or asexual, or criminal or even *other* than someone of unparalleled wit and charm. But, I embrace the fact that *I am* Other, so hear me roar! Blow the shofar for me, and stand back, for here I come.

O.K., I can acknowledge being a self-important ass, a lot like Land before me, but nevertheless, I write my story from Paris although I don't have the *luxury* of self-imposed exile. What I do have now is *that* heretofore word of scorn— discipline. Why? Because it became clear to me that night after dinner at Chez André when I heard the voice of Nina Simone again. I'm tired of being stepped on by America so much so that I find myself crawling around Paris looking for answers that will never *apply* to me in the first place. I live in another time. A different America. A harsher time. A confusing America. That is the underlying fallacy in my search—I am comparing apples and oranges. Like Land had told me, the life experience which I sought and which these artists had had, no longer is accessible to me in the first place. It is long gone. My estimations suggest that perhaps it died soon after the second world war when the America that was left triumphant had changed into the military industrial complex. Moreover, I am the Other. How can I seriously hope to connect myself to those artists I saw when despite their own outsider status the time in which they lived still very much allowed for the moving of the human spirit so that it could be captured with words, paint, song, incantation, and dance? My reality is altogether different. I *will* and *must* go back to L.A. in only two more days. And despite my brave face in front of Sanders, I am in fact very much afraid. That's where discipline must come in. Because when I call it quits, baby, that's it. It will happen on my watch then, and only after I have said my piece.

So, I must prepare my return to a cauldron of smoked dreams that can choke as they remain smoldering on freeways. I will need to put together a care package akin to those sent to me during the midst of college exams in order to prevent my being boiled alive. Maybe, then, the first thing I do when I get back to L.A. is to patch things up with my girlfriend. That will definitely help cushion things for me. Her name is Chiana Chase Bentley (né Janice Waldmüller). I call her Jan which she *hates*. There I've said it. Last we spoke, she called me an "escapist" and told me to "grow up." Well, I can do that. I can definitely do that and in return I get a warm body to wake up to until I am strong enough to look elsewhere. A decent trade off.

I am missing one last step however. Sanders missed something too, or at least forgot to articulate it to me. In order to be thoroughly disciplined, one needs to have some force, some kind of unseen hand working behind the scenes to help one believe that being disciplined will lead to what he or she wants. In a word, I guess what I need is *faith*. I've learned a little about that too. Whether through Vodou, Krishna or Lazaro's tresillo approach. It's all the same thing, but that story about the priest and the ark in Ethiopia? That's a little too much. I don't want to be chained into a life where *all* I have is faith and I can never again venture out to see what type of experience exists outside of that. If I can find some kind of middle-of-the-road faith, then

I will really increase my ability to get back into the game like Sanders advised.

Look, I'm not hoping to roll a seven or eleven here. I just don't want to crap out either. The reality is that I will always be a bit player anyway because of my otherness. I will continue to slip away from the center and to the outside by forces and peoples that don't want me there. I can handle that. I just want to *pass*. That's it. Not such a tall order—wanting to pass. And you know what? Scientology doesn't sound so bad anymore because I think the upset is still very much present in me. I don't know why I hadn't just thought of that earlier. It's *clear*. All I need to do then is make good on a few things and the upset will go away. E-meters be damned!

Man, I think it's starting to come together. Starting to make sense. The fear is starting to subside and I am taking control. I can't wait to get back home! I have a direct 11-hour flight from Charles De Gaulle to LAX coming up in less than 48 hours, which will have me back in L.A. on Saturday evening. I'm going to take a shuttle back to my apartment, and hit the sack by 9 p.m. That way, I'll get over the jet-lag grog, find my center, and rise refreshed. I will be focused and ready. It'll be nice to be out of bed so early on a Sunday. Things will be quiet then. No traffic. No maudlin throngs of people marauding and bringing me down. I will get a jump on *everybody*. But, shit, I hate that feeling of waking up before the rest of the world.

CPSIA information can be obtained
at www.ICGtesting.com
Printed in the USA
LVHW101523240422
717094LV00005B/54